D1785602

Elizabeth's Bondage

NIKKI SEX

ELIZABETH'S BONDAGE

Copyright © 2013 by Nikki Sex

This book is protected under the copyright laws of the United States of America. Any reproduction or other unauthorized use of the material or artwork herein is prohibited. This book is a work of fiction. Names, characters, places, brands, media, and incidents are either the product of the author's imagination or are used fictitiously. All rights reserved.

Book 1

Elizabeth's

Erotic Bondage

Chapter 1

Caught

Elizabeth came awake, utterly confused. Her head felt thick and muzzy as if she had been speaking and suddenly woke up to find that she had dozed off in the middle of a sentence.

What? Where am I?

This confusion soon spun into panic as a spike of adrenaline rushed through her veins. She was bound, and there was something covering her eyes, a dark blindfold. Like an animal caught in a trap she instinctively thrashed, trying to break free. No chance.

Oh my God! This is not happening!

Elizabeth forced herself to take long slow breaths, while she attempted to understand what exactly had transpired, how she had gotten here in this place.

She licked her lips and tried to swallow with a dry throat. Fingers and toes were all she could use, and she stretched out, feeling everything within her reach. From what she could tell she was on a four poster bed, securely bound by soft cloth, her arms and legs spread wide. Elizabeth found she could move, but not much. With her eyes covered, she could see nothing - but there was daylight or perhaps just a strong room light shining from above. She could perceive this as a glow, slightly brighter than absolute dark, through her mask.

The soft feel of cloth rubbed against her bare skin, and she shivered as she became aware of goose bumps rising on her breasts and forearms. Fear and imagination had caused this reaction for it wasn't cold under what seemed to be a delicate bed sheet. The temperature in her prison was comfortable.

My prison, the thought echoed, along with a tendril of dread. As a trial lawyer she was used to dealing with difficult circumstances. But who had kidnapped her and tied her up, naked of all things?

A woman used to stress, and not easily put off her stride by unexpected ambushes in court, Elizabeth maintained rigid control of her fear. *Okay, I'm tied up,* she thought. *Fine. I'll just take this one step at a time.* "Hello?" she said out loud.

No response. Her voice came back to her in a dull, non-echoing manner that made her understand she was in a large room, most likely a bedroom with carpets and curtains. Something nearby was humming, a refrigerator perhaps? And she was certainly tied to a bed. Elizabeth cast her mind back, searching, attempting to understand. What was the last thing she could remember?

She and Mark had ten whole days off, and were celebrating their one year anniversary with a vacation in Vegas. They had originally considered a fun, quick wedding in Las Vegas, something that would amuse them, but that had always been out of the question. Her father, John Coit, Senior Partner in Coit, Boynes and Jones, was very rich. Cassy, his third wife, while not burdened with a high IQ, was of a similar age to herself. Given her father's previous choices, Elizabeth had been prepared to dislike Cassy, but instead had found her rather sweet. They both would have been hurt by the Vegas option. A huge wedding had kept Cassy entertained and her father pacified. Not to mention the valuable publicity it brought to the firm.

Right. They had gone to Las Vegas, that she remembered, and then what? As far as she could recall she and Mark had arrived, gone to their room, changed their clothes and left for dinner. What could possibly have happened? Where was she? And where was Mark? She took another deep, calming breath. God, Mark. She hoped he was alright.

The sound of a heavy door opening and gently closing caused instant tension and her whole body went still.

"Hello, Elizabeth," said a deep, soft voice. The tone was composed and cool, the accent was faintly European, French? Not American, that was certain. He sounded as though he was at the foot of the bed.

"Who are you?" Elizabeth demanded in what she hoped was her normal, confident Lawyer's voice. "Why have you brought me here? And where is my husband Mark?"

A drifting waft of nutmeg, cedar and Brazilian Rosewood scents came to her nostrils. She recognized that cologne – it was one of the most expensive on the market. *My kidnapper is rich... and has good taste,* she thought. The knuckles of the man's hand rubbed down her face and she instinctively pulled away. The deep voice gave a low laugh.

"Who I am is not important. You may call me Sir. I will explain why you are here shortly. And your husband Mark is well. He has found himself in a similar state as you have, that is to say, blindfolded and bound naked to a bed, although I have tied him lying face down on his stomach."

Elizabeth remained silent, and for a few moments her captor said nothing, apparently letting her digest these revelations. Mark was tied face down? Naked? Holy shit! What kind of pervert was this guy? Did he plan to rape them both? "What do you want?" She said. But her throat was so dry her voice came out in almost a whisper.

"A very good question, Elizabeth. In fact that is the exact question you should be asking."

Elizabeth felt the sheet gently brush against her skin as it was pulled off of her body. Slowly it was drawn down, exposing her breasts, moving lower. The sheet stopped moving mid stomach. Elizabeth was almost glad that her eyes remained covered. She didn't want to see this man look at her naked breasts. With a completely unintended and uncontrolled reaction, she trembled.

"Mark tells me you are on the pill, and are clean," the man said. "I too have no STDs, thus we shall not have the need for condoms."

Mark? Mark told him? She wondered how long Mark had been conscious before she woke. Obviously long enough for this man to get that sort of information out of him. She wondered what lever he used against her husband. Mark wouldn't willingly tell him anything, she was sure of it.

Elizabeth heard the man move then, not his steps, maybe the sound of his clothes, or his breathing. Blinded as she was, her hearing seemed much more acute. The man sat down on her right, depressing the bed slightly. A part of him made contact with her waist and although she tried, she could not squirm away. With a pounding heart she endured his physical contact for dignity's sake if nothing else.

"Nice, Elizabeth," he said. "Very nice. Such perfect breasts."

She tensed then, fully expecting her kidnapper to touch her, but he didn't, nor did he appear to notice her reaction. He just continued talking in an almost soothing, utterly male voice. "You are a beautiful woman. I can see the physical allure that must have drawn your husband to you. As for any other attractions, such as your personality, courage and character, well, these I have yet to reveal."

Elizabeth pressed her lips together and screwed up her nerve. It wasn't that difficult, because despite the circumstances and her fear, she was furious. "I see," she snapped. "So you are someone who likes to *force* a woman for sex, are you? What did you use, a date rape drug or something? I suppose this is the only way you can feel like a big man, right? Well go ahead then. Rape me and get it over with so we can all go home, will you?"

Her captor laughed, it was a warm, genuine sound that rolled through her and made nothing of her anger. "I do not plan to rape you Elizabeth, nothing so *déclassé*, you understand? In fact, I will not fuck you unless you beg me to." He paused for a long moment. "I think I will enjoy the sound of you begging, *ma chèrie.*"

She mentally and physically recoiled at this totally arrogant and confident pronouncement, but the back of her mind clicked in acknowledgment of what she had originally suspected: *"Ma chèrie" is "My Dear" in French,* she thought. *Okay. The man is French. How can I use that knowledge?*

He placed his warm hand, firm and large on her shoulder, and she involuntarily stilled. "Listen carefully Elizabeth and know this: I will get what I want. I will get *everything* I want. Your wishes, Mark's wishes – they are as nothing to me. But I also make this pledge, you will want to please me, *ma chèrie*, and after six days I will release you both."

"Six days!" Elizabeth couldn't help herself – the words just flew out of her mouth in protest. Almost a week as some sort of sexual slave? How would she survive it? How could she endure and live with herself afterwards? A long future of hours spent with sexual assault counselors swept through her thoughts. Her throat tightened and her eyes burned under her blindfold. *I will not let this monster see me cry.*

As if aware of her emotional overload, her captor patted her shoulder and sat back, removing his hand. "I release you in six days - as long as you and Mark both behave and do exactly as I command. I swear this."

Tense with the need to hold back a flood of useless tears, Elizabeth strove to prevent her nostrils from flaring, and fought to slow her panicked, rapid breaths.

The man remained silent beside her, no doubt watching her reaction, knowing she was distraught. This knowledge made her angry. He moved once more, bending toward her. Something in the shift of the bed, an alteration – a sudden darkening or shadow in the light made her aware or him and where he was.

Elizabeth held perfectly still, preparing herself. When the man brushed his firm, warm knuckles across her cheek this time, she moved. Fast. Flinging her head toward those fingers, mouth open, Elizabeth felt his flesh between her teeth and bit down *hard.* The man gave a grunt of pain or surprise or both, but with astonishing control he made no attempt to pull his fingers away. Instead as she continued biting him, viciously grinding her teeth into his flesh, he put his other hand across her neck and squeezed.

Her captor's hand was warm and big and he pushed down across her throat with inflexible strength, stopping all oxygen and blood flow to her brain, cutting the life right out of her. Elizabeth opened her mouth and let his fingers go – but the man continued to hold her neck down, strangling her. The blood drummed loudly in her head and she felt herself to be in danger of passing out. Terrified, she bucked and thrashed, and he lessened the pressure, but only slightly, just enough to allow her circulation to return and permit her to breathe. Heart pounding, she gasped in a large intake of air.

The hand remained around her neck, a threatening presence. After a minute, or what felt like an eternity to Elizabeth, she came to her senses. This man could kill her! What had she been thinking? *Oh God. I don't want to die!* The pleasure of getting even with him just wasn't worth it. She whispered with her bruised throat, "I'm sorry. I'm so sorry. I didn't mean… I don't know what I was thinking."

The hand left her throat completely and the man stood up.

"I forgive this impertinence, Elizabeth. You are a fighter, a winner, and you like to be in control. This situation must be challenging for you, I know. Further, I have not yet explained the rules. Please excuse me, I will not leave your side for long," he said, and she heard his retreat, and the sound of the thick door opening. But this time the door was left open, she could hear it click against the wall, into some sort of wall latch.

She heard an indistinct mumbling from outside her room. Two or more men were talking. But after that she heard a noise she had never heard before, except perhaps in a violent movie. It was the sound of something hard, hitting flesh. A yell of anger and pain overrode every other sound then. The male scream seemed familiar. Her heart pounded. Mark? Was that terrible sound from her husband, Mark? The angry protest came, once, twice – and then finally whoever it was became quiet.

Oh God, she thought. *Please don't let it be Mark.*

Chapter 2

Five Rules

Many long, long minutes passed. Then came another soft cry, but this sound was different. It was not a cry of pain - it was more like an extended moan of uncontrolled ecstasy. *What the hell? What was going on in there?*

At least a half an hour went by before her captor returned. She heard him walk through the door and shut it, then move quietly back to his place on the bed beside her. Elizabeth was too shocked to do anything other than accept his presence. As his luxurious shirt brushed against her waist, she felt his warmth radiating against her naked skin, through the soft cloth.

Probably Egyptian cotton, she thought, automatically assessing his clothes. *Form fitted and personally tailored. But who cares!* She shouted to herself, in mental argument. *Oh my, God. I'm losing my mind. There are too many disadvantages; the opposition holds all the cards and I just can't seem to think clearly.*

"Elizabeth," the man said, "I have punished your husband Mark for your infraction. From now on this is how it will be. You will do as I ask instantly or he will suffer. Do you understand?"

Elizabeth was still in shock, still in disbelief. Had he beaten Mark, whipped him with a belt? Or what? Almost as an answer to her question she became aware of the flexible leather of a riding crop against her skin. At least that's what she thought it may be - a riding crop. It moved across her cheek, down her neck, and across her shoulder, stopping just under one nervous breast. It felt and smelled like leather and it was still warm - from use. On her husband. Had the man beaten Mark and then masturbated or something?

Oh God. She thought wildly. *Had he butt fucked her husband? Was he some sort of sexual sadist?* The moan of pleasure after screams of pain mystified her. But after being strangled she didn't have the nerve to question him, much less have the desire to know the truth. *Mark and I are in the hands of a psychopath. One should always humor crazy people.*

"Elizabeth," the soft calm voice said, "I asked you if you understand. Answer me. Now."

"I understand."

"You call me Sir." The man's tone was implacable and uncompromising. "You must always address me properly, Elizabeth."

"Oh, I'm sorry. I understand, Sir."

"Good girl." The man ran his knuckles over her cheek again, then a warm finger over her orbital bones, her eyes, her lips. He lingered around her lips, opening them and running his fingers along her teeth, tempting her to bite him again. Elizabeth remained utterly motionless and submissive throughout. The meaning of his actions was clear without words; did she want to bite him? She most certainly did not. When he was apparently confident that he had tamed her impulse to bite, he took his hand away.

"I have brought you orange juice mixed with champagne," he said. "It will relax you, perhaps. Open your mouth, Elizabeth." He placed the straw against her lips. "You will drink, because I wish it." She opened and drank. It was a strange way to ask, but then again, he wasn't really *asking* was he? She had no choice - she had to do what he said.

When she drank until there was no more, one finger stroked her cheek approvingly, "Good girl. You are doing very well, *ma chèrie*. I am pleased with you." His hand came back to rest upon her throat and she tensed from this menacing physical message. This man could kill her, could hurt or kill Mark. It was absolutely in her best interests to keep him happy.

"Listen now, Elizabeth. I have all the power in our relationship. You are not in control, I am. You have no will of your own, no decisions can be undertaken by you, when you eat, sleep, – every bodily function of yours is mine to command. Your body belongs to me for the next six days. I am going to do whatever I choose to you, and I am going to make you do things that you will not want to do. But you will obey me instantly, at all times Elizabeth or both you and Mark will suffer the consequences."

His hand moved from her throat, down to the underside of her breasts. His fingers circled, caressing in slow steady strokes until they reached a nipple. She felt her nipples tighten, and knew an unexpected spike of arousal which surprised the hell out of her. How could she be turned on? By this sadistic rapist? But he smelled good, and his hands were firm and warm and his voice was deep and sexy. And she was entirely under his control. She swallowed.

The man gave another low sexy chuckle. "So sensitive, *ma chèrie*. I assure you, you will want to please me, Elizabeth. Please me, and I may even allow you pleasure."

Elizabeth cleared her throat, reacting to the way he had said pleasure. The last part of the word, the "s" was drawn out in the subtle, sexy accent that spoke to some sensual need inside her. There was something about him that did not put her off, which astonished and shocked her. In fact, she found that she was attracted to him. Stockholm syndrome already? Really? Probably she was simply instinctively trying to give him what he wanted so that he wouldn't hurt her and would let her go. She didn't want to antagonize him in any way. That had to be it.

Unless…never one to shy away from hard truth she examined her circumstances.

Elizabeth had fought to get where she was in life. Blonde, blue eyes, five foot three and beautiful. It all sounded so perfect, "You are so lucky," she had always been told, gifted with such physical perfection. But beauty was a tyranny that carried its own problems. Did her partners really want her or were they merely drawn to her body? Were her friends, true friends? Who could she trust? Ongoing battles with self esteem colored her world, and she hid such irrational internal flaws by being the toughest pit bull in a dangerous litigation yard of dog eat dog. Any woman would have had to be tough to succeed. And as a trial lawyer, her size and outward appearance seemed like only a drawback to her, an additional handicap that could easily keep her below par in a man's world.

Control. That was the key from the moment she could reason as a child. Everything in her life was under her full and absolute control: work, her marriage, any associations, and every interaction with her family…everything. Well, she was powerless in this situation. Could that be what had turned her on? She was spread-eagle and bound, with all control wrested from her. Had this predicament, this forced abduction - somehow liberated her from all convention?

Sir said, "I have five laws for you to remember, Elizabeth. One, you call me, Sir. Two, you will speak only when spoken to. If you have a question you may ask me if you are allowed to speak. Three, when I give you an order, you must do exactly as I say. Four, you will never lie to me, Elizabeth, for I assure you, I will know if you are lying. Five, if you want or need something you must ask me. You will only eat, drink, sleep, wash, use the toilet – in fact, you cannot do anything without my consent. And you are not allowed to orgasm without my permission, and Elizabeth," he added with a tinge of dark humor, "I fully expect you will want to come, in fact you will *beg* me to come, oh so many times." He paused for a moment, letting her think about that, then added, "If you are a good girl, I may even let you."

Her frown came without thinking, because Elizabeth doubted that she'd be capable of coming at a rapist's hands. How could she? She had been having trouble for the past few months getting off with Mark. Why was that? Oh, she could always masturbate, she enjoyed that well enough, and she let Mark use her body, but whatever spark they had had together after a year's marriage had already paled.

Abruptly she noticed that Sir had stopped speaking. There was a heavy silence in the room. Oh, God! Had she upset him? By not paying attention or something? Shit! Was he going to punish her? Or Mark for some unintentional imagined disrespect?

Chapter 3

Elizabeth's Confession

"Elizabeth," he said in a soft, coaxing tone, "when I spoke to you of coming, you thought of something. What was it?"

Oh shit! She thought. The man missed nothing. She was going to have to be so careful around him. She cleared her throat, just as Sir put his hand upon it, around it. It was a warm, living collar; a reminder that he held her life in his hands. "I thought of coming," she blurted out.

"Very good, Elizabeth," the soothing voice said. "You have told me the truth. Now, tell me exactly what else you were thinking, and remember, I will know if you are lying, and then both you and Mark will suffer for your deceit."

"I..I..have been having trouble having an orgasm," she said, "I have kind of lost interest in sex. That is what I was thinking. I was worried that you would be angry if I couldn't climax and I couldn't see how I could be turned on by...this situation." She had been about to say by a rapist, but had filtered those words if no others.

Oh God, what was this man doing to her? She had just told him something she had not even told Mark, the man she loved. What happened to her vaunted courtroom mastery of thought and emotion? Was she going crazy already? A terrible looming fear swelled inside her, as if in answer to her question, and almost made her lose it altogether. She wanted to thrash and scream; to cry hysterically like a mad woman. Savagely subduing these impulses, she wondered, *how can I survive six days of this?*

The hand moved, and the knuckles grazed gently down her cheek and jaw line. Elizabeth had an impression of Sir bending over her, saw the light darken through her blindfold as he cast a shadow, and smelled his cologne. His mouth touched hers in a soft, chaste kiss. This was not passion, this was approval and comfort and reassurance. His lips were warm and gentle and this unexpected kindness he showed her was something she found herself unable to fight. A few hot tears moistened her blindfold and trailed down her cheeks.

"Shhh, shush, you are a treasure, Elizabeth, and Mark is a lucky man," Sir said, and wiped her teardrops with one warm finger. "Thank you for telling me this truth of yours. I am honored. You have not spoken of this to your husband, no?" He began to stroke and gently massage her neck, her hair and shoulders, a course of action that was as soothing as his voice.

"I..no, I haven't, Sir."

"Because you did not wish to hurt him, to make him question his manhood perhaps?"

"Sir, I…I didn't want to hurt him." His hands never stilled, they were a warm relaxing touch that continued to comfort her.

"Because you love your husband Mark, very much, this is so?"

Her captor was so acute! How did he know everything as he did? It was as if he could read her mind. "Yes sir," she said. She and Mark had known each other all their lives. A fling in senior high together was when they both had lost their virginity, but they had separated and gone to different places for higher education. Life intervened, each pursuing individual careers, other interests, other lovers. Intermittent contact was always amicable. Elizabeth had always considered him one of her most trusted childhood friends. Twelve years later, when Mark had moved back to New York, they ran into each other at a mutual friend's wedding. Wow. The sparks flew and the sex was amazing. They had married six months later.

Elizabeth still thought Mark was her one true love. But where had her sexual interest gone?

"Again, I thank you for telling me, *ma chèrie*," he said. "You see? These little truths between us will not harm you."

Elizabeth gave a little hitch in her breath, and while her head was still spinning, she felt more in control. She could do this. It was only six days. Sir was a twisted son of a bitch, but he was not as bad as he could be. It could be worse.

As if aware of her resolve Sir sat back and said with a tone of command, "Elizabeth I am going to make you do things you don't want to do, and I am going to do things to you that you don't want. But remember this: you have no choice but to comply. If you wish to survive over the next six days, your sole interest will be to please me." He stood up abruptly. "Any questions, Elizabeth?"

She swallowed, "No...Sir."

"*Eh bien*. Then I think I will start by examining my prize, this beautiful body that is mine to do with as I please." The sheet began to move once more. As it was pulled fully away from her body, leaving her stark naked, Elizabeth forced herself to remain still, to act unconcerned.

Sir chuckled, a low, sexy laugh that seemed as soft and seductive as a caress. Sir laughed a lot, and she found it disturbing, but not so much in a bad way. Not so much at all. *Oh my, God. I'm so losing my mind,* she thought.

"Where to begin?" he said, apparently to himself. And it was clear to Elizabeth that very shortly she was going to find out.

A thrill of fear, alarm, uncertainty, anxiety, astonishment and shock rolled through her. But at the bottom of all of those overwhelming emotions was something else, something unmistakable: her own lust.

Chapter 4

Sweet Seduction

Elizabeth heard him move to another area, and take something metal as it made a little metallic click. But then she felt a... feather! It did not tickle as it moved over her sensitive skin, starting at her palm and wrist, down to the underside of her upper arm and elbow across her collar bone, rib cage, then down her side, her hips, thighs, calves and feet. Sir avoided any erotic areas. The feather caress was...interesting. Kind of tantalizing.

Her captor kept up a running dialogue as he caressed and stimulated her skin, commenting on how certain touches raised goose bumps here, or caused her flesh to dance and flinch there. He was sharp-eyed and attentive and spoke in a low, seductive whisper. He gave the odd muttered curse as he saw evidence of her arousal glistening between her legs, or examined a mole or dimple. He let her understand in explicit detail how much he wanted her, and how he intended to have her. His frank comments and observations combined with the erotic stimulus of a simple feather began to create a slow burn within her, a sizzling fission of sexual desire.

To her surprise she found herself responding, pulling at her bonds, undulating and raising her hips, making low mews and sounds of need. They were instinctive and unconscious, these responses, and she suppressed them as much as possible, but could not prevent them no matter how she tried. He continued to torment her with erotic words and sensations until she stopped trying to control herself, until she simply gave in and let her body react as it would. Arching and thrashing she had lost all her precious control, and again, with that awareness she felt both fear and excitement.

Recent lack of interest in sex notwithstanding, she wanted sex now.

Right now.

She heard the soft sound of a zipper then. Was he taking his clothes off? For the love of Christ let him be getting naked. Again, as if reading her mind he said, "Yes, I remove my garments but my eyes remain on your breasts. Such rosy pink nipples, so hard, so taut with desire. You are truly beautiful, *ma chèrie*, bound and spread before me as you are. My cock is hard and aching, I have to stroke myself just to ease my need."

Everything this man had done, everything he was doing was the most incredible seduction. Elizabeth licked her lips and took a deep breath, imagining his cock. She was hot, wet and ready and with her legs spread she was unable to hide it. She was a well educated woman, a woman of the world and at this point, what was going on here sure wasn't rape. Oh she could tell herself there was no choice, and indeed, she had no choice, but she wanted his hard body against her, with him inside.

True, if Sir uncuffed her she would find Mark and leave. But she'd regret what might have been, because right now it was consensual. Never had she felt such hunger. His deep sexy voice, his accent, the smell of his cologne, his hands and the way he spoke to her, the things he said! Elizabeth felt like a starving person offered more than food – being offered a tantalizing banquet in scandalous, overwhelming and excessive variety. How could anyone turn that down?

Elizabeth knew the Truth. Body, mind and soul - she longed for Sir to push his cock deep inside her and screw her silly.

Once more he circled the feather caress around her throat, her neck, collar bone and sternum area but always avoiding her breasts. *Why the hell doesn't he stroke my tits with his damn feather?* She

17

wanted to feel it on her nipples. They began to ache with the absence of touch. The feather stopped and he sat beside her, and oh God! Thankfully he began to caress her breasts. His heated mouth came down on one and she gave a moan of pleasure. She had wanted this, needed this.

What was wrong with her? This man had stripped and bound her, taking all choices away - from her! When she was a celebrated trial lawyer, someone who was always in control. Was there an aphrodisiac in that drink? Or was she just this horny?

Again he seemed to be able to read her mind when he said, "Ah, *ma chèrie*. Enjoy my caresses, my mouth and hands and tongue. Take your pleasure now, Elizabeth, by my command. I suspect that underneath that formidable mask of control you maintain in the courtroom, you are in fact a total slut." He continued to stroke and twist her nipples, biting and sucking and squeezing and caressing her breasts and she felt every touch to her nipples down lower as her pussy spasmed with need. She knew she was dripping with arousal but somehow she could not be embarrassed.

"Are you a slut Elizabeth? Do you want my tongue, my hands, my cock? Answer me. Now."

"Yes… Sir," she said and she knew that it was completely, shamefully true.

"Good girl, *ma chèrie*. And so, we progress, do we not?" His wet lips kissed and licked both nipples once more, and then he pulled away. "Now Elizabeth, I am going to put these nipple clamps on you. It will hurt a little, at first, but will please us both. Take a deep breath. Now."

She obeyed and a fierce metallic bite squeezed down on one nipple and she gave a little cry of anguish and surprise at the pain. While still dealing with the initial pinching ache, her other nipple was clamped and she stiffened but bit back her cry. A tiny chain, apparently joining both clamps, rested lightly on her sternum.

"Like so." Sir stroked and kneaded her breasts, soothing them, and licking her throbbing nipples for some minutes while as she began to get used to the pain. The throb hurt, yet it also didn't. If anything it added to her desperate sexual need, creating a peculiar tingling arousal, as if there was a direct line from her clamped nipples to her empty, aching pussy and swollen pulsing clit.

Sir began to kiss down her stomach, and she felt his smile against her skin as he said, "The pain in your nipples, it gives you pleasure, does it not? Answer me. The truth. Now."

"Yes, Sir."

"*Eh bien*, it is as I thought. I read your body like you can read a book, you see? You are a unique narrative, yes. So complex, delicate, yet savage and strong. There are many surprises to be found within you Elizabeth. But I... I am a master of a woman's body and I see though all disguises. It is a talent, you understand?"

He was flicking and pulling her clamped nipples with his clever fingers, and her pussy spasmed with each touch. His words were muffled as he licked and nibbled, caressing her into a roiling state of combustion. She was in a mindless fog, a delirium of pleasure, and he was moving down her body, toward her pounding clit.

What? Elizabeth thought. *What had her captor been talking about?* But with her focus on his lips, his mouth and hands, she realized she hadn't really heard a word he said.

Chapter 5

Please! Please! Please!

Elizabeth was unable to follow what Sir had been saying because he had been nibbling and kissing, moving down her body, and all her focus was *there*. Right *there* at that point that he had not yet reached. It was a particular spot on her body that was burning, pulsing and dripping with need. Was he a generous kidnapper, please God? If so perhaps his mouth and tongue could sooth that incredible ache.

Sir stood up and she heard him move to the end of the bed, felt the heat of his body shift between her legs. He put his hands on her knees.

Oh thank you Lord!

Those warm fingers moved slowly then, trailing up along the sensitive inside of her legs to her inner thighs. His big hands stopped on her thighs, holding her legs down and even further apart. Usually she worried about how her pussy looked, about its smell, about her embarrassing arousal. But Sir had taken all those thoughts away with his genuine pleasure.

"You have a beautiful pussy, *n'est-ce pas?*" he said, "And see how it weeps for me? It craves a man's touch. Later I will shave it to see and feel it more clearly. It should not hide its beauty behind this hair. But for now, I want to taste your sweet honey."

With that Sir licked just her slit, no further. His warm tongue ran just outside her hole, a velvet abrasive stroke along the sensitive edges, never inside. He licked her again and again and again. All the while he made deep male growls of satisfaction and arousal, with an occasional, "Such a perfect taste," or "So wet, see how you drip for me?" His tongue never stopped stroking, but only at the same place each time. It set her on fire, what he was doing to her, but his actions, as wonderful as they felt, would never take her over the edge.

Elizabeth began to moan and squirm, whimpering as if in real pain. And why the hell not? This was agony. Exquisite agony, but torment just the same. Her breasts were throbbing with desire from the clamps on her nipples, and all the while her pussy felt empty. She wanted to be stretched by his mouth, his fingers and his cock. Her distended clit pulsed with every beat of her heart from an ever increasing blood flow.

"I could eat you out all day, Elizabeth, you taste so good," he said. All her awareness was focused on the feel of his hands on her thighs, holding her down and the feel of him, still stroking with his firm wet tongue. "No matter how much I drink, *voila!* There is always more. This gorgeous, so delightful cunt of yours is an endless source of honey." His tongue mesmerized her, never altering its position, teasing the sensitive rim, causing her pussy to tighten and convulse as it tried to clamp down on something, anything.

This was so erotic! His words, his hands, his tongue. It felt so good, him licking her there, him enjoying her dripping pussy. It was slick and she felt it getting slicker all the time. Sir loved it, clearly he did or he wouldn't be doing this. Oh God! It was maddening! Why didn't he touch her clit or spread her lips with his hands and fingers? Why didn't he penetrate her? She could climax so easily. She moaned and squirmed and attempted to arch and push toward him, but his strong firm hands held her exactly where he wanted. Futilely she pulled at her tied wrists and ankles. Elizabeth knew she couldn't move, that he had total control and somehow that turned her on even more. She hardly recognized the noises coming from her own throat.

It felt so good, but being on this knife edge of orgasm was torture.

"Please! Please! Please!" she began to cravenly sob and beg, fighting the exquisite agony of his tormenting tongue. The sensual licking stopped and his hands on her thighs tightened. Elizabeth came back to herself, suddenly aware that she had been moaning words without his express consent.

"Elizabeth, I will need to discipline you for your forgetfulness," Sir said with stern reproof. "To break my laws is not permissible."

"Oh Sir, I'm sorry. May I speak?" Panting with the desperation of sexual need, anxious, wanting to please him and kicking herself for her unthinking stupidity, Elizabeth expelled a large breath while she waited for his permission.

Sir made her wait a full minute, then his hands loosened from where they were tight upon her thighs. He began lightly rubbing her thighs in a circular, soothing manner. "Very well, *ma chérie*," he said. "I excuse you this time." His voice held a trace of humor. "You do not, perhaps, have the control and mastery over yourself that you imagined." He chuckled. "You may speak."

"Oh please Sir, please. Fuck me, oh God please!"

Sir's warm hands solidly pressed against her once more. He moved her thighs apart further, and she loved the feel of them. He had spread her, and held her absolutely still, so his clever tongue could work. His big strong hands held her down, exposed and vulnerable, ready for his pleasure. *I'm completely in his power,* she thought. And that knowledge no longer disturbed her. Instead it caused her pulse to race. But then his hands released her, and her legs trembled with the loss of him. Sir stood and moved toward her, she knew he was coming closer by slight sounds and the now familiar scent of nutmeg and cedar. But there was another smell now, the scent of male musk and arousal.

"Elizabeth," he asked in a soft voice. "Do you want my cock?"

"Yes, oh God yes, Sir please." An electric thrill of joy ran through her, for she felt certain that Sir was going to give her *exactly* what she wanted. But as experienced as she was, Elizabeth lacked not only imagination, but the unique sexual vision and wicked genius of her captor.

Elizabeth could never have expected what Sir actually had planned for her.

Chapter 6

Deeper, harder

Blindfolded, Elizabeth imagined his erection there in front of her. She could almost feel the heat of it and desperately wanted to see it. The bed depressed as he got on it, on his knees this time? He grabbed her hair, twisted it round his fingers and held it tight, pulling her face toward him. Bound as she was, her head remained resting against the bed, but the feel of his hands in her hair, controlling her movements spiked her desire.

"I am going to put my cock in your mouth," he said in a firm, masterful voice.

"Yes, Sir." She was so desperate she'd take it however she could get it. She licked her lips and opened her mouth for him.

"*Non ma chèrie*," he said, giving her hair a little tug. "Keep your lips closed. This is my cock, and because you have begged for it, and because you are trying very hard to be good, I will let you taste it, but only as I instruct."

Elizabeth closed her lips.

"Good girl," he said. "Now lick them, I want your lips as wet as your sweet cunt." She did as he ordered, slathering moisture over them. "And be still. I want to control what I do with my cock in your mouth."

"Yes Sir," Elisabeth whispered, feeling almost like she was undergoing a religious experience in the "Church of Sexual Fulfillment." She had never felt so horny in her life, never so needy. There was nothing she would deny her hot French captor. The man was some sort of a sex God.

Sir pressed his cock against her wet lips and rubbed it back and forth. He was hot and hard yet his skin was soft as velvet. He was marking her lips with pre-cum, she could smell it. She stilled a frantic primal hunger to open her mouth and take him inside. She wanted to taste him, but he had ordered her to remain motionless.

"*Bonne fille,*" he said and his voice was husky with lust. "Good girl. Now open, just a little and remain completely still. I want to put my cock inside you. I want to be the one to stretch that mouth of yours."

Elizabeth froze motionless at this erotic command, desperate to please him. She opened her mouth very slightly.

"*Oui,* just like that," he said. She felt the heat of his shaft near her face; musky and seductive, male and primal. She had to concentrate, ruthlessly subduing an overwhelming impulse to lick it as he moved his hot pulsing cock between her lips. Her hair was tight in his grasp as he moved inside, toying with her tongue. She bit back a moan as he pulled out for a moment. He put his fingers deep inside her, feeling the roof of her mouth, the back and the sides. He paused for a moment. "You can take me all the way in I think."

"Yes, Sir."

"Remember," he gave her hair another little tug. "Be still while I fuck you," he said, his voice a growl. He stretched her mouth slowly, pushing in and out a bit at a time until her nose was right up against his coarse pubic hair. "Yes, good," he said with approval when she had swallowed him down, almost gagging and choking in her desire to give him what he asked for. He did not hold that position long, perhaps aware of how difficult it was for her, but he seemed satisfied that he had achieved his goal.

In total control, he fucked her mouth for many long minutes, pulling her back and forth, faster, slower, moving her head with both of his hands tangled in her hair. Often he held her against him as he thrust right into the back of her throat, but never choking her for long and all the while he made erotic male sounds of sexual pleasure, which joined in concert with her own needy whimpers and moans.

"And so," he said finally, "It is very good. Now I allow you to lick and suck me while I fuck your mouth. Show me what you can do with your tongue and those oh so wet lips."

Elizabeth was inspired. She hardly breathed as she began to vacuum him, her tongue flicking, eager to please him as he had pleased her. He had both of his hands curled tightly in her hair as he pulled her back and forth, up and down his shaft, rhythmically moving his cock in and out of her mouth at his demand. She experienced a kind of delirious buzz at sucking and milking him, teasing his broad head, rolling her tongue around the tip, his slit, and on every ridge and vein. She wanted him to come to completion, she wanted to revel in it, drinking him down.

"Do you want my hot seed to shoot down your throat?" he rasped. With her lips and mouth tight around him she gave a nod, profoundly thrilled by his obvious appreciation of her actions. "Then suck me deeper. *Oui*. Harder," he gave the peremptory demand in a low hoarse voice, his hands convulsing in her hair as he groaned with pleasure.

Good Lord! The things he does, Elizabeth thought. *The erotic words he says and that accent. How does he do it? How has he made me into such a craven slut?*

His thrusts became shorter, and she concentrated on milking and squeezing the head of his cock. He was close, so close to orgasm and she wanted to taste him, to swallow every drop. She began to humm then, and had an internal laugh as her vibrations teased his cock. *This really is a hummer.* She thought. *This must be how they came about, so much pleasure. I just want to hum while I experience such amazing oral bliss.*

In his urgency he pushed in deeper more often, in short fast strokes. Elizabeth had to ruthlessly hold back her gag reflex, but his pleasure was what stirred her. Her eyes teared, there was drool across her chin, and she heard herself making strange whimpering noises in additions to her mmmm's and hums of encouragement.

"Yes, there you go," he said as he thrust right to the back of her throat, burying her nose right into his thick thatch of pubic hair. "Fuck, that feels good...*tres bon...*"

Elizabeth reveled in gratifying him. More than anything, even more than her own pleasure, she wanted to please him. Breaking one of his direct laws was not in her mind. She hadn't planned on screwing up at all.

But she did.

Chapter 7

Displeasure

In a blissful, submissive headspace, Elizabeth sucked and licked. This was all about him, giving him exactly what he wanted. With that odd thought her pussy contracted *hard.* The rest of her body tightened and she almost came. Sir pulled out instantly, ripping her back from his cock with a sharp tugging pain in her hair. Her orgasm stuttered and then stopped. She cried out with the loss of him, wanting him to penetrate her - wanting his hot, thick cum.

"You do not have permission to climax, Elizabeth. Not yet," he said, his voice implacable even though he was breathing hard. He let go of her hair then, releasing her back against the mattress. After a moment he expelled a deep breath and said in unsettling tone of disapproval, "You interrupt me."

Experiencing a moment of panic Elizabeth said, "I'm sorry, Sir." She listened to the sound of his heavy breathing while waiting for his reply.

"*Bon,*" he said. "Then lick my cock and balls. I want to watch as you put your mouth and lips and tongue on them." With one hand idly cupping and toying with her breast he held his cock out for her, directing her to put her tongue in his slit, where she greedily licked him, coaxing out every musky drop, moaning at the taste. She swirled her ravenous tongue around the firm ridge that surrounded the rounded crown of his penis. At his command Elizabeth concentrated on the fleshy part under the head of his cock, and she shivered delightedly at his tightening reaction, instinctive thrust, and subsequent growl.

Licking his length, she reverently sucked, traced and nibbled, putting her mouth around his heavy testicles, taking them in at his exact direction and sucking them lightly inside her warm mouth, one at a time. At his command she licked long strokes down the underside of his scrotum and perineum, stroking, caressing, tasting and worshiping him. Elizabeth, genuinely repentant, wanted to make up for her failing and did everything he asked, following his express orders - exactly as he demanded.

"Enough," he said.

Attentive, she waited for whatever he wanted. Holding her shoulder with one hand, and gripping a nipple with the other he said, "Open for me now and try again. And remember," he admonished with a painful pull of her nipple clamp, "you do not have my permission to come."

Then he slid his hot cock back inside her mouth. "Now, *ma chérie*, do as you feel will best please me. I do not control you in this. Move your head, your mouth. Show me how sorry you are that you interrupted my pleasure. Prove to me that you want my cum."

Elizabeth knew what he liked, she had felt his cock react and heard the sounds he made. As Sir grounded himself by holding on to her breast and shoulder, she enthusiastically hummed, sucking him in. As he didn't move her head for her, she did so, bobbing on him up and down as much as she was able, tied as she was. Elizabeth took him deep, happy for his thick cock to choke her, willing to accept any discomfort, as long as she could suck him to completion. She eagerly worked him, straining to move slow at first, then fast, sucking him hard while the flat of her tongue also stimulated him. As she did so he encouraged her with murmured comments and sounds of pleasure.

In a state of lightheaded bliss Elizabeth was humming once more. They began working in sync, him thrusting, her bobbing down his shaft, each wanting to take each other. His cock plunged into her, huge and pulsing, his testicles slapping against her chin and throat. Sir was breathing heavily when he eventually muttered an intelligible French curse and pulled back from her.

"*Bon, ma chèrie*," he said. "It is well enough I think, for now." His knuckles grazed her cheek in that warm, familiar manner that somehow both calmed and excited her. "Good girl."

Sir approved. She had been forgiven.

Chapter 8

You Have To Beg

Sir he sat down beside her and took her nipple clamps off.

The pain was immediate and Elizabeth cried out as the blood flowed back into her tender flesh. Sir put his warm mouth on each nipple, gently licking, stroking and soothing. He took his time, unhurriedly laving and sucking with his warm velvet tongue. Squeezing and caressing her breasts with his hands, his skilled fingers gently rolled and softly tugged her sensitive nipples. Elizabeth's entire body hummed with sexual desire, and her pussy ached and clenched around the emptiness of nothing. She felt desperately horny and simply had to have release.

"Sir? May I speak?" she finally said.

"You have my permission," he replied, his words were distorted as he was sucking and licking one nipple with his mouth. His fingers caressed her other breast, running under the curves of it, teasing and lightly playing. His other hand had moved lower, between her legs, but his fingers carefully avoided her tender clit despite how she arched and moaned. His mouth and hands continued without stopping, keeping alight the ever increasing bonfire of lust within her.

"Sir, will you put your cock inside me? Will you please let me come?" She felt his smile against the tender skin of her breast, and then he sat up. His hands, his mouth left her skin and she almost cried out loud in protest.

"I had considered leaving you like this, *ma chèrie*," he said, "in a heightened state of arousal with no release. Cruel, no? Perhaps I would fuck your tits to reach my own climax, and then leave you to suffer. A little punishment, you understand? This would make you even more desperate, frantic to serve and obey me later. But if you beg, I may decide to fuck you, and let your cunt milk me as you come. In this you must beg me properly." He chuckled, and his sexy laugh was a strange combination of amusement and threat. "I want to know why you need to orgasm," he said. "I want details. Tell me. Now."

Elizabeth's mind reeled with shock. *Had he planned leave me like this? This horny? No way. I swear to God I will die if I can't climax. I need to come!*

"Sir, I need you inside me," she said, the words pouring out of her without thought. "I need to feel your hard cock jet its thick, hot cum in me. My pussy is aching for you. Fuck me, fuck me oh fuck me please!"

Elizabeth waited for a long moment in utter silence.

"I like this argument very much," Sir finally said, "but I think you can do better Elizabeth. I warned you that I would only fuck you if you begged me, do you remember, *ma chèrie?*"

"Yes, Sir."

"I wish to hear more pleading from your sweet lips. Your body already displays your desire, the pulse, the breathing, and your flushed and sensitive skin. *Mon Dieu,* You have such erect nipples and heavy breasts and your swollen sex drips with honey. I want your tongue to tell me of your desire. You are the trial lawyer. Argue your case in a hot way, a way that will make me hunger to have you. Make me want to give you the gift of my cum inside the heated flesh of your body, and not spend it on your tits. If you want me to fuck you, *ma chèrie*, you must beg for this privilege. Right now."

"Oh God, Sir I want it so bad," Elizabeth heard the earnest pleading in her tone, her urgent beseeching need. "Fuck me anywhere, take me anyway you want. Come on my face, my breasts or down my throat. I swear I will do anything. I promise to be good. You have all the power, all the control. Will you please at least allow me to come? Let me satisfy you and feel you climax? Sir, I didn't understand. I had no idea. You were right. I'm begging you! I'm yours. Your slut, your whore, your sexual slave. Take me any way you want me. But if you don't mind, if you would only consider...." She took a deep breath and said, "I swear I have never wanted anything so much in my life as I want you to fuck me right now."

Sir gave his familiar deep, low chuckle that seemed to resonate throughout her body. He leaned forward and took her in an open mouthed kiss, in an affirmative physical answer. His tongue plundered her mouth and when Elizabeth's tongue found his, she moaned with the pure rapture of it. While he ravished her with teeth and tongue and lips he squeezed both of her breasts, and twisted her nipples, a gentle bite of pain that enhanced the pleasure of that kiss. So many sensations! The heat of his body encompassed her, his clean shaven face, the erotic scent of his cologne, the taste of him.

When he drew back he came off the bed and trailed his fingers down to possessively grasp one buttock. "*Ma chèrie*," he said in a soft, sensual caress, "with such words, from a mouth such as yours, you win. I shall give you what you ask for."

Elizabeth whimpered with relief as he spoke. Burning with sexual anticipation, empty and aching inside, she could hardly wait.

Chapter 9

Elizabeth's Climax

Sir came off the bed, and within moments he was between her quivering legs, running his hands up her thighs, gripping her hips. Then one hand trailed toward her sex, brushing against her pussy and purposefully spreading her lips open for him. Elizabeth bucked and whimpered and writhed with lust within the limits of her binding constraints. Her blood drummed in her ears and her entire body felt heated and sensitized both skin and core. The soft sounds of Sir shifting delighted her, as he moved to position himself with his hips and thighs hard against her hypersensitive skin.

"Be very still now," he commanded in that sexy, demanding voice.

Instantly she went motionless, waiting. She gasped and whimpered when she felt the heated head of his cock searing against her opening. *Don't move! Don't move!* she told herself. Her internal struggle was frantic as she fought an overwhelming need to move toward him, to arch and thrash, bite and scream. Behind her blindfold sweat trailed down her temple. Remaining still was a close run internal battle, focusing all of her attention.

"*Mon Dieu*, you are dripping for me," he said. "Your hot empty cunt will suck me right in. Can you wait? Or will you lose all control and climax the moment I thrust inside?"

"Sir," she gasped at the feel of his heated flesh and the images his words portrayed. "I...I think I might come the instant you push inside of me."

"Very well, *ma chèrie*. You have done well, and me, I have tormented you enough. Try to hold it, just a little, to make it last if you can. But if you cannot, you have my permission to climax - but only once I am fully inside, you understand? I want to feel you come."

"Yes! Oh God, yes. Thank you, Sir," she said. Her entire body shook involuntarily with the exertion of holding completely motionless. As she trembled she imagined his eyes upon her, completely aware of that tremor. Redoubling her efforts made no difference. The man missed nothing, so surely he knew? He must be aware that she was trying to obey him.

There was a long moment of charged silence, where her breathing and pounding heart sounded loud in her ears.

"Elizabeth," Sir said, in a silky, knowing murmur, "You have my permission to move, but again, only once I am deep inside you. Until then, you will continue to remain completely still or there will be consequences."

Thank you Lord! He knows. Of course he knows. I'm trying so hard to do exactly as he says. "Yes Sir," she said in a rasping whisper. Behind her dark blindfold her eyes were shut as she concentrated, striving not to move, not to come.

One of Sir's hands wound roughly around her hair, pulling it tight. "*Ma chèrie*, prepare yourself for I shall not be gentle," he warned and Elizabeth's entire body quivered in a thunderous internal cannonade of excitement, fear and overwhelming desire.

Then his mouth plunged into hers in a devouring, tongue thrusting kiss. His other hand grabbed her right nipple and twisted hard. With that he pushed his cock inside her, filling and stretching her needy channel wide. Elizabeth brutally curbed her desperate need to come, yet she let her body react as it willed.

Sir had given her permission once he thrust inside and he was in her to the hilt right now.

Oh my, God! So good! Giving in to the urge to move was almost a release of its own.

Elizabeth's entire body trembled with exultation and joy and bliss. Moaning, arching and writhing, she moved as much as possible within the boundaries of her cuffed arms and legs.

Fast and deep, Sir's powerful thrusts impaled her with the force of a sledgehammer, the coarse hair on his pubic bone grazed her distended, hypersensitive clit, and her entire body jerked with each savage thrust. His firm male flesh rubbed against her needy skin, his chest hair scraping her aching, tender nipples. Sir gripped her breast and hair, pulling them both hard, using them as leverage to increase the tempo and impact of each thrust. As he rammed himself into her with bruising strength, his balls slapped hard against her spread buttocks. She was sweating and panting and her heart thundered loudly, wild and unrestrained as a tropical storm. The sensations were too much for Elizabeth, far too overpowering to register them all.

As Sir rhythmically slammed into her, again and again, picking up speed, Elizabeth arched and screamed out loud. Mercilessly he continued to pound her, shifting slightly and hitting a particular spot deep inside. Her whole body stiffened and her pussy went tight. It felt as is she had been hit with a hard blast of sensual bliss. All the ecstasy to be had in the entire world was right *THERE*.

Elizabeth's pussy spasmed and began to pulse and milk his cock with explosive force. Her scream turned into a wail as she came apart, experiencing one of the most powerful orgasms of her life. Elizabeth felt it all. Each convulsion was like a pulsing seizure, a tiny climax of its own: contraction, contraction, contraction – they went on and on. She couldn't recall ever having such a fierce physical response during sex - it was like the muscles in her pussy were on steroids. Talk about multiple orgasm. *My God. Sir's cock must be being squeezed like a python with each contraction. Did it feel as good for him as it did for her?*

With a few more fast, short strokes, Sir gave a loud groan of pleasure. His fingers convulsed, pulling her hair so hard that she felt it right down to her tightly curled toes. Squeezing her breast and nipple, his hips strained violently forward, bucking as if he had been electrocuted, and slamming deeply into her one last time. As she felt his taut body relax he muttered softly in a tone of awe, *"Mon dieu cette petite femme obstinée est une bonne baise."*

Elizabeth whimpered with pleasure at his shudder, and was amazed to feel hot tears escaping through her blindfold and coursing down her cheeks - a physical display of her overwhelming emotions. Sir's warm breath swirled against her. She had no idea what he had said, but she reveled in his release and the feel of the weight of him, heavy and relaxed upon her. Sir had done as he promised. He had fucked her. Slowly, with languid pleasure, she smiled. My God had he ever fucked her, giving her amazing orgasms and filling her with the "gift" of his cum. And somehow she had kept up with him and had not climaxed too soon. She felt fairly confident that it was her forceful contractions that had brought him to such rapid completion.

The potent erotic smell of sex and lust and expensive cologne surrounded her, thick as London fog. Sir lay upon her twitching body, the sound of his heartbeat a slow, heavy thud in her ears. God he felt amazing, the weight of him, his slow, deep breaths, his obvious state of almost unconscious bliss. Meanwhile she continued to experience a cascading wave of tremors, contractions and aftershocks. It was so good to lie there beneath him, utterly satisfied, completely spent. She felt unable to even lift a finger.

Chapter 10

Sir's Plans

After some time, Sir nuzzled her neck, nibbled and kissed it, then raised himself off of her. He untied the cuff of one leg, and then both arms. She felt too languid to do anything except to obey him, to submit to whatever he wanted to do next. He sat her up, and she offered no objection as she felt a cool metal handcuff on one wrist, then on the other wrist, as both were cuffed behind her back. The final leg was untied, and he helped her pull her legs together. They trembled as he pulled her sitting up, to the side of the bed. He kissed her cheek, and touched her tears, wiping the salty drops away with one warm finger.

"You are a very good girl, *ma chèrie*," he said in a caressing velvet voice. He moved away, and she heard him open the refrigerator, and return. "This is orange juice only, you do not need the champagne." He chuckled. "Although after such amazing sex perhaps we should be toasting with champagne."

Elizabeth drank all of the liquid. "May I speak?" she asked, still resonating with a blissful sense of well-being. All her cares, for the moment, were gone.

"*Ma chèrie*, you have pleased me. For now you may speak as you wish, until I tell you that you must once more remain silent."

She cleared her throat. "Well, I wanted to say, thank you, for…your gift."

His deep, genuine laugh delighted her. Her thanks had pleased and surprised him and that had been her intention. Part of it was a lawyer's talent, to manipulate, to keep a connection, and to stay in his good graces. But mostly, she had been overwhelmed. Sir had told her that he planned to deny her orgasm, intended to come on her tits, leaving her in the most heightened state of unsatisfied arousal she had ever known. He had said that to receive his cum in her pussy was a gift. Well. That had certainly been true. She didn't know how she would feel about it after she was released from this sensual prison, but right now she felt as if she'd been given something priceless.

A hand cupped her cheek. "We shared the gift, *ma chèrie.*"

She found herself smiling. "Can you tell me what you said in French?" she asked. "When you, um, bestowed your generous tribute within me?"

Again he laughed out loud and once more she reveled in the sound. "I said, *Mon dieu cette petite femme obstinée est une bonne baise.*" It means, My God this small stubborn woman is such a good fuck."

Elizabeth laughed this time, and for some reason she found she couldn't stop. For a moment she worried that it was some sort of hysteria, but she dismissed this idea. Arms cuffed behind her back, naked, with semen from her kidnapper dripping from her pussy – she somehow saw everything with a different perspective and simply had to laugh and keep laughing until tears once more pooled in her eyes.

Sir sat down beside her, his warm thigh against hers, one hand possessively holding her cuffed wrists against the bed, but he was laughing, too.

Her laughter turned to intermittent giggles and as she began to settle, his hand left her wrists, and his arm curled around her waist. Together they sat companionably in silence for some minutes. Sir said nothing, he seemed to be waiting for her to speak, to explain, and so she did.

"I really am stubborn," she said.

"Yes," he acknowledged.

When it was clear that she had nothing further to say he stood up. "And so, we continue as there is much yet to do. Now you must not speak once more, as this is my law. You will stand up." With his hand under her elbow for support she rose to her feet, surprised to find she could stand. "Come, I will take you to the bathroom." They walked only a few steps away, into another room and Sir sat her down on the toilet.

"I wait here until you are finished," he informed her.

Elizabeth nodded, still in a blissful daze. Why not pee in front of this man? But she could never wipe herself with her hands cuffed behind her back. She sighed. At this point, what difference did it make? Besides, she had no choice. After she urinated he asked, "You are finished?"

"Yes, Sir."

She heard the sound of running water. "Spread your legs for me, Elizabeth," he said and she did so without thinking. A warm wet washcloth stroked between her legs, wiping her with smooth proficiency from front to back. He moved away then and she heard the sound of him turning taps and then water running, most probably into a bath. Mindful that she was not supposed to talk, she waited to see what happened next. Her body was still in a dreamy state.

Sir had fucked her almost into a mindless, blissful unconsciousness. Only once before she recalled having as mind blowing sex as she had today. Only one time previously, with her husband Mark. That would take some thinking about.

He took her elbow again, and raised her to her feet. "*Ma chérie*, I will tell you what I have planned next. I will feed you by my own hands soon, and you will eat what I give you. I told you I will take care of you, no? I own you completely for six days, and in all things I shall cherish, control and protect what is mine. But right now we shall have a bath together, where I will shave your pussy. Perhaps I will have you on your knees then, and make you suck me to completion. Or I might choose to bend you over the tub and take you in the ass."

Elizabeth stiffened. *The ass! No! I have never allowed anyone to touch me there.* She had heard stories, and it frightened and disgusted her and she had also heard that it hurt. She blurted out, "But I've never..."

His hand tightened on her arm. Elizabeth cleared her throat. "Please excuse me, Sir. Er... may I speak?"

There was a long silence, then he said with a stern hint of disapproval, "You may speak."

It was his voice that frightened her. She had displeased him, and she felt guilty and anxious about it. "Forgive me, Sir. I spoke without thinking. You know what I was going to say now anyway."

The familiar warm knuckles of his hand ran down her face in a soothing manner, and her anxiety lessened. "You are new to this Elizabeth. I will punish you later for your infraction, and it will hurt very much, but it will also make you hot and then you will beg me to allow you another orgasm. Of this I assure." He stepped into her then, putting his naked flesh against hers, with his arms around her he gave her gentle kiss on the forehead. Already she could feel his cock, hard against her hip and stomach. Good Lord. The man was inexhaustible.

"*Ma chèrie*, I am glad you are an anal virgin. It will please me to break you in, and make you an anal slut, for you will like my cock in your ass. I will teach you everything Elizabeth, just as I plan to teach your husband. And in six days, when I am finished, you will both thank me."

Teach her husband? Poor Mark. Was he having similar lessons? Really? This sex God was bi? Again, she was too frightened of the answer, so she didn't ask. She had enough to cope with. *Six more days,* She thought. *Who will I be at the end of it all? Still myself? Or someone else all together?*

Sir took Elizabeth's unresisting arm and directed her into the tub.

Book 2

Elizabeth's

Anal Submission

# Chapter 1

The Story so Far

Blindfolded and naked, with her hands cuffed behind her back, Elizabeth stood in the bathroom listening to the sound of running water.

A tub was being filled, water rushing out of the taps at high speed. The sound echoed, indicating that this bathroom was very large, and no doubt opulent. Her captor, who she had been compelled to call "Sir," was firmly holding her left arm. Sir, with his deep masculine voice and sexy French accent, was clearly a confident and educated man. Everything about him screamed wealth, too. Like his nutmeg, cedar and Brazilian Rosewood scented cologne – one of the most expensive of its kind.

Elizabeth, who had spent her life around rich, intelligent people, knew the signs even with her eyes shut - or in this instance - blindfolded.

Sir played in the big leagues. But at what, was anyone's guess.

Steadying her with one hand on her arm and the other on her lower back, grazing the top of her buttocks, her captor capably guided her toward the bath. There, Sir had blithely informed her, he planned to remove her pubic hair.

"I will shave your pussy to see and feel it more clearly," he had said. *"It should not hide its beauty behind hair."*

Elizabeth felt her skin flush. *That man,* she thought with the shock of building arousal. *How is it that I have become so shameless?*

In a few short hours he made me beg. Her captor had such a warm, clever tongue and strong, firm hands. *I begged him to fuck me. What was I thinking?* Except that under similar circumstances she could easily imagine begging him again.

Those hands. At one point her captor had scared her to death by strangling the blood and air right out of her. Of course that was after she had aggravated him by biting him, grinding his flesh between her teeth, refusing to release his fingers – which she supposed was provocation enough. Being strangled had been her first lesson, and it was a convincing one. Don't piss off her captor: after all, the man could kill her. After that Elizabeth resolved to simply do whatever he asked, unless some opportunity of escape presented itself.

Tomorrow - at least she thought it was tomorrow - was her anniversary. One year ago she and Mark had been married. They had taken ten days vacation, flying to Las Vegas to celebrate. The last thing she remembered was changing her clothes, and then she and Mark had gone off to dinner together. After that was a blank – until she woke up here.

In the last twenty-four hours Elizabeth had been drugged, kidnapped, blindfolded, and tied up naked, spread-eagled on a bed. She had suffered agonizing and mesmerizing sexual torment and eventual release by her captor, while tied to that bed. Even the momentary recollection of those events caused her pussy to tighten and her clit to pulse. Mindless with lust, Elizabeth had been willingly seduced.

The entire episode had blown her mind. How did it happen? How could she have become sexually craven so quickly? Except that her French captor was a Sex God. Deep and hard, Elizabeth had sucked Sir's cock like a vacuum, wanting to please him. Right at the outset Sir had informed her that he would never commit rape. In his confident, arrogant manner he told her that he would not fuck her unless she asked for it. He had also threatened to deny her sexual release until she begged. And Elizabeth had begged for both. She swallowed with a dry throat as she recalled how she had pleaded in a desperate, frantic manner.

Elizabeth vividly recalled her words to him: *"Sir, I want it so bad,"* she had said in an earnest pleading tone. *"Fuck me anywhere, take me anyway you want. Come on my face, my breasts or down my throat. I swear I will do anything. I promise to be good. You have all the power, all the control. I'm begging you! I'm yours. Your slut - your whore - your sexual slave. Take me any way you want me. I swear I have never wanted anything so much in my life as I want you to fuck me right now."*

She felt her face redden again, but this time with embarrassment. *I'm so bad,* she thought. But Sir (bless him) had given in to her beseeching pleas and fucked her. *Hard.* And consequently she had experienced the most mind-blowing multiple orgasms of her life.

When Elizabeth had been drugged and kidnapped, her husband, Mark, had also been taken. According to her captor, her husband was receiving similar sexual education. Sir had promised to "teach" them equally telling her, *"When I am finished, you will both thank me."* He had sworn to set them free after six days.

Six days! She still couldn't imagine that. And this was only day one. No one would look for them during that time, for she and Mark were on vacation, celebrating their one year anniversary. *Some vacation. Some anniversary!*

Poor Mark. She hoped her husband was alright. Mark certainly didn't have any interest in men. Where her seduction and abject sexual submission to her captor had been frightening, yet erotic and exciting, she couldn't imagine Mark enjoying any sexual experience under a man's hands.

Elizabeth had never felt so helpless. Always blindfolded, she had yet to see the face of the man who was currently directing and supervising her every action. She assumed that if she did see him he would have to kill her or something, so she made no attempt to take off the blindfold. Not that she could have in any case. The man had not once left her alone.

"Come, *ma chèrie*," her captor said, and then, "*Un moment s'il vous plait.*"

He stopped her, positioning her where he wished and began to braid her hair. He continued to touch her, his hands making warm contact against her skin, lightly smoothing over her shoulder, her neck, her back and the curve of her buttocks. They were possessive little caresses, as he physically moved and controlled her. Finally he put her shoulder length braid up on top of her head with what she presumed was a hairclip.

"*Bon*," he said softly near her ear, his warm breath teasing the skin on the back of her exposed neck, raising goose bumps. "Now you are ready for our bath. There, I promise you, I intend to personally soap, lather and scrub every single part of your body."

Oh Shit, she thought. Elizabeth's mouth was dry and she cleared her throat. What exactly did her captor have planned next?

# Chapter 2

The Bath

Being blindfolded was a serious handicap, yet Sir seemed more than happy to guide and direct her every movement. "Here are two steps, one, yes, two. Very good. Now lift the right leg, just so. Into the bath we go."

Elizabeth stepped into the warm water. It rose just above her calves, and felt wonderful. She wanted to ask if she should sit, but she had learned to just wait, and let Sir tell her what to do. She didn't have permission to speak, and she didn't care. Somehow it was so much easier to give in, to let him have all the control. Not that she could fight him in any case. The way he commanded her with that deceptive mildness was a peculiar turn on. What was that about? Men attempting to boss her around had always irritated her - until now.

"*Ma chèrie*," he said, unlocking her cuffs and bringing her hands together in front of her and relocking them, "you must raise your arms now."

She did so, and felt him attach her cuff chain to something above her head. He had the full BDSD bathroom, she supposed. Metal hooks, eyebolts – all one needed. Placidly, still buzzed by her recent multiple orgasms, she stood naked before him, arms raised - but not uncomfortably high, over her head.

"*Bon*," he said and grabbed a tuft of her pubic hair and pulled it gently, a reminder that he planned to shave it. "So pretty these soft blond curls, and yet I prefer to clearly see the most feminine parts of your lips and cunt and clit. And now I begin." She heard a squirting sound and the delicious smell of shea butter came to her nostrils. As she stood facing him he began to rub this soap upon her skin, starting with her neck and shoulders, the delicate pocket between her collarbone, and down her arms.

She frowned for his actions were disturbingly like what he had done with the feather, when he had tormented her, never actually touching her breasts, but then he did. Touch her breasts. Mmmm, God!

Her captor, Elizabeth had discovered, was a thorough man, and washed her body in a slow and sensual pace. Intimate and unhurried, he stroked her bare skin, lathering her aching breasts as if he had all the time in the world. He circled his fingertips around her areola, and molded her into his palms and all the while he spoke in a low, deep voice filled with masculine appreciation. Under his hands her breasts grew heavy, swelling with unquenched sexual heat. Elizabeth's senses reeled.

Sir blew warm puffs of air on her nipples, and gave a short sharp bark of delight. As she was blindfolded, he fondly depicted every aspect of how her breasts quivered and responded to him. Sir described all of her body in detail, telling her how attractive she was. Expressing his joy and commenting on everything from her earlobes, to the exhaustive ways that each feminine curve enticed him. Elizabeth couldn't understand it. These sensual descriptions put her in a strange emotional space where she became both aroused, and soothed by his touch. Rubbing softly, he stroked, kneaded and circled, lathering all of her, twisting and almost roughly tugging her nipples and using both hands to bounce her breasts up and down, feeling the weight of them.

"Such large breasts," he said in a tone of awe and avid approval. "It is not uncommon for a small woman, no? I might fuck them later, while I sit on the side of this tub. I could make them bounce for me with your nipples tight and hard as I spend my cum on them. Or I may sit on top of you, thoroughly wet them with my tongue, push them close together, and then fuck them. I would rub my cock over the soft skin of your breasts on the way to your mouth, squeezing and pinching your hard nipples while you take me deep inside to lick and suck." He paused and she imagined him with a tilted head, studying her. "You would like that, I think."

Oh my, God, yes I surely would, Elizabeth thought. Her breasts were swollen and aching. The man already knew what she wanted, what turned her on. After so many orgasms it was difficult to believe that she was already in heightened state of arousal, ready for more.

Sir continued to ply the soap generously, rubbing and caressing her everywhere, heightening the sensitivity of her skin, worshiping each of her fingers, her wrists and palms, elbows, neck, and throat, rib cage, flank and sides, apparently oblivious to the reaction he was causing within her – but Elizabeth knew better. The man was well aware of exactly what he was doing.

"Blond and beautiful. Fragile and fierce. Petite and pitiless. I read some of your court transcripts as a trial lawyer, did you know?"

"No, Sir," she said. Elizabeth's mind lurched with this information. Had he targeted her and Mark intentionally, had he been stalking them, learning all about them beforehand? Obviously he had.

Sir continued speaking, "You were merciless, yes. You go, how do they say? Ah, for the throat. Yet I did not expect for you to bite me, Elizabeth, but I should have. I was such an *imbécile*. A woman holding her own in a man's world, a woman that looks like you? Of course you are a fighter and trust does not come easily."

Elizabeth could only marvel. How did he know? Blonde, five foot three with blue eyes. Beautiful and rich. "You are so lucky," she had always been told. But beauty and wealth were both tyrannies that created their own evils. Did her partners merely want her money, or her body as a trophy? Who could she trust?

Any woman would have had to be tough to succeed. And as a trial lawyer, her size and outward appearance was a serious handicap.

As he moved lower Sir cupped and soaped her flat stomach, hips and finally her pussy. "*Mon Dieu,*" he said, "Your mound, your clit and lips are still so flushed and swollen." He gave her sex a little squeeze. "Plump and juicy, like ripened fruit. So ripe. Can you doubt that I will eat it?" He gave a dark erotic chuckle, and stroked her outer lips, just touching the tip of her clit. "You are still sexually stimulated and will arouse quickly to climax if I wish it. Such a responsive woman. This pleases me. But you do not feel faint, do you? With so much blood down here, your brain may not be receiving all it needs. Do you feel faint, *ma chèrie?*"

"No, I don't think so, Sir," she said uncertainly.

"*Bon.* Tell me if you do. Those cuffs are not meant to be worn for long, I prefer a padded cuff, but with the water, you understand, it is not practical. And now, I will take the hair off your pussy, so that I can see, smell and taste you all the better."

A rolling wave of emotions cascaded through Elizabeth, and she tried to identify which came foremost in her mind. She settled on nervous anxiety – and lust. *His hands will once more touch me in that sweet place.* And her other thought was: *I'm going to look like a Barbie doll without any pubic hair. Okay, not the doll measurements so much, but certainly the look will be the same.*

But then what would her captor do?

Chapter 3

The Shave

The water swished as he obviously moved to his knees. A warm caress of his hot breath caused her pussy to clinch and she inhaled suddenly. *Shit.* Everything about him made her think of sex: his voice, his words, and even his breath. Sir touched her functionally then, placing a palm against her outer lips and holding them out straight. The slick careful glide of a razor moved over her sensitive skin and she held perfectly still, with all her concentration *there.*

He worked carefully for some time, adjusting her as he wished, pressing a hip one way, raising a leg to spread her a bit for a clearer view, over and to one side with an arm. Shaving her with a thumb here, fingers there, pulling her swollen flesh straight and tight as needed. Every so often he would "accidentally" flick her clit, and the distended nub was beginning to pulse and throb. And all the while she felt his breath, slow and steady, warm against her, teasing her. Elizabeth cleared her throat, and continuously licked dry lips, biting off her whimpers. Primitive sensations flooded back to her as she recalled what he had done with his mouth *there.* And restlessly, wanting to touch him, she shifted and pulled at her cuffs.

He gave a low laugh, well aware of how he was tormenting her, but he said nothing.

Damn this blindfold. If only I could see, she thought, but she kept her eyes shut, concentrating on the unique sensation of having a man shave such a personal part of her body. She imagined his face, intent and focused on his work, his mouth and tongue so close to her pussy. His breath teased her, warm and steady against her sex. What did he look like? Dark hair or light? Dark skinned, tan or white? She had no way of knowing but her imagination was happy to fill in the gap.

Sir began to hum a little song while he worked. He rubbed and applied more soap then gave that deep chuckle as his fingers stroked near her slick, dripping sheath. "You are soaking wet, my little slut, aren't you?"

Elizabeth shivered, but could only nod. Sir used the term "slut" as an endearment, the word trailing fondly from his lips with an affectionate undertone.

He added, "Do you want me again already?"

"I...yes, Sir," she sighed. There was no point in lying to him, he was too aware.

"Ah, Elizabeth," he said. He rinsed his razor – he must have had a bowl of water nearby, as the swish sounded close to her ears. "I enjoy the battle, but I also like that you do not always fight me. This honesty is so much better." He worked the alternate side then and her pussy pulsed. As he turned his hand to hold the outer lips of the unshaven side out, his thumb shifted down, teasing outside her slit. With a moan she instinctively thrust toward him, but he held his thumb back from her.

He paused for a moment, as if considering a response to her sexual need. Then, to her delight, he circled her slick channel with two slick soapy fingers, fingering and stroking around and near her slit. Heartlessly teasing, he made no attempt to palm her, providing friction to her clit, or to push his fingers within her empty sheath.

"Um, ah, ah, ah, oh!" she said and moaned and arched, thrusting her hips. This movement caused her aching pussy to suck his fingers right inside, although that had clearly not been his intent.

Sir gave a murmured sexual expletive of surprise and stood up, holding those magical fingers deep within her. With his hard cock on her well soaped stomach, and his broad chest pressed against her, Sir nuzzled and licked behind her ear and her throat.

"Elizabeth, do you want my cock?"

"Yes, Sir," Elizabeth murmured. His skin felt delicious and warm as he nibbled and kissed. But then Sir bit her *hard* between her shoulder and neck, and she cried out with pain and surprise. In the back of her mind, the practical side of her shouted, *He bit me! And he's still biting! Man, that's so going to leave a mark.* Yet the primitive part of her reveled in it.

Sir held that tender roll of flesh between his teeth, and Elizabeth shuddered. This small biting pain gave an inexplicable jolt of pleasure. Her tight channel flooded, drenching him as he calmly continued to finger her. Sir ran his tongue back and forth against her captured flesh, holding her with his teeth, licking, teasing and sucking her sensitive skin. Whimpering and mewling with pleasure, her knees trembled as he sucked. She just knew she was going to have a hickey, a big one, and she didn't even care. Sir was sucking and licking, exactly like she wanted him to lick and suck her *there*. Unintentionally, and with no ability to prevent it, Elizabeth shivered and moaned and whimpered under his intense ministrations.

Oh God, my clit, my clit, my clit, she thought in a repetitive mindless stupor. *Oh please let him do that to my clit. Please. Please.*

"*Ma chèrie,*" he said, with that uncanny ability he had to read her mind, "I will wash this soap off you now and see how your naked sex looks. I may enjoy to suck, lick and taste it. Would you like that?"

Well. There was only one answer to that question.

"Please, Sir, yes," she said.

Chapter 4

Warm Shower

He turned on the taps and the soft spray of a hand nozzle ran deliciously warm over her naked flesh, rinsing the soap off, erotically moving across her skin. The pressure alternated as he flicked streams of water against different parts of her body. The nozzle began to pulsate and unexpectedly he put it right between her legs, pulsing into her pussy, making her tremble and gasp.

As the soap washed away, Sir commented on her reactions, teasing her breasts, running water over her curves both above and below. He raised her breasts by holding each nipple and pulling up, then rinsing thoroughly. Pinched and twisted, her nipples hurt, but then again, they didn't. Every time he touched them, her breasts ached with desire, and her clit throbbed. A strong jet of water hit her clit and she cried out with the strength of it. As she shuddered and danced and trembled, with her wrists and arms cuffed above her head, Sir made appreciative observations, gave deeply aroused chuckles and made crude erotic comments.

"Magnifique," he said, and turned the water off. He moved down to his knees once more and again his warm breath caressed her. With both hands holding her thighs he said, *"Mon Dieu,"* he said in a tone of reverence. "Your sex is so beautiful. Spread yourself wide for me, Elizabeth. Let me clearly see such glory."

She obeyed him instantly, moving her legs as far apart as possible, without tugging too hard against her cuffs.

"Good girl," he said in a rough kind of awed whisper. Then he pressed his lips to the inside of one thigh and with an open mouth bit her hard, like he had her neck, rubbing her captured skin between his teeth with his tongue. It hurt for an instant each time, yet it didn't. Elizabeth felt sure he was leaving teeth marks. Biting, teasing, licking and sucking. It felt amazing and Elizabeth whimpered and mewled in exquisite pleasure with each bite.

Hickeys, she thought. *Hickeys for sure.* But she simply didn't care. His strong teeth clamped down on her sensitive skin, again, again, again. Slowly he moved up the inside of her thighs, and then to the soft swollen skin above her pubic bone. When he bit down on her plump, aroused pussy she squealed – it was so close to her clit! He held the sensitive flesh there between his jaws, licking, teasing and sucking hard. Then he moved lower, to her pussy's outer lips, and as he worked she gave a strangled sort of choking moan, gasping and crying out with need. She wanted him to bite her *there.*

All the while when he wasn't nipping and teasing her with his tongue he spoke in a deep erotic whisper, telling her how good she tasted, and how much he wanted to put his cock in her luscious cunt, her mouth, and her ass.

The ass comment sidetracked her pleasure for a moment – she didn't want that. But he soon distracted her as he worshiped her flesh with his hungry mouth and lips, his hot caressing breath, his teeth and tongue. And his words! Dark and erotic, filled with lust and desire.

"Tell me you want me, little slut," and again the word came to her ears like a tender, sensual endearment.

"Yes! Yes I want you, Sir."

"What exactly do you want, *ma chèrie?*"

Her words were mindless. "Your mouth and tongue and teeth on my clit."

"What else?"

"Your cock inside my pussy."

"What if I want to put my cock in your mouth instead?"

"Wherever you want it, Sir."

He laughed. "I want to fuck your ass, Elizabeth."

She stiffened and said nothing. He laughed again, cupping and caressing her sex with warm possessive fingers. "But I do not put my cock in your ass just yet. Right now I want to enjoy your freshly shaved cunt." Sir used the flat of his palms to spread her outer lips, and then breathed warm air upon her. His tongue probed and ran lightly just along her slit, again and again and he growled with approval of her smell and taste while she gasped and moaned and shifted, wanting to touch him, or to touch herself, restless with desire. Elizabeth's entire body felt sensitized, hot and swollen, on the cusp of climax, and she closed her eyes with overwhelming erotic hunger.

Broad and warm, his tongue teased her in each place his breath first touched, while deftly massaging her moist slit. Elizabeth endured this torment, breathlessly panting and making various involuntary noises. Completely unexpectedly he put his whole mouth down upon her swollen clit and sucked it inside. The bite he gave her *there* was a gentle, caressing nip and she sobbed with her need for release. The blood in her clit pulsed under the pressure of his mouth and she bucked, thrusting her hips toward him.

Arms still cuffed and raised above her, Elizabeth's whimpers and cries, and rhythmic thrusts unintentionally turned into words and she began to repeat them like the chanting of a Tibetan Monk, "Please fuck me, please fuck me, oh fuck me, fuck me."

He laughed then, for she had spoken without permission, but he didn't seem to mind. "Be still, *ma chèrie*, or I will stop," he warned, and firmly held her in place with both hands.

She froze then, aware that he always carried out such ominous threats. Her voice was hoarse as she gave him a mumbled, "Yes, Sir," that was more of a rasping whimper of protest. When he seemed satisfied that she would not move, he continued, returning to his work, biting, licking and sucking.

"Oh, oh, Sir..." she whimpered. Mindless, and panting, breathless with desire, Elizabeth concentrated on trying to be still, while completely overwhelmed by his mouth, his teeth, and his tongue. The world was gone for her now – there was only him, and what he was doing. "Please," she whispered with reverence. "Please don't stop, Sir."

He chuckled, "You may take pleasure, Elizabeth, but I have not given you permission to come. Now be quiet. You distract me. I am enjoying eating out your sweet cunt and do not want to be disturbed."

Elizabeth swallowed convulsively as she tried to still her quivering flesh. As he worked her clit, she moaned. Two fingers of his hand slipped inside her once more, directly up inside to her sweet spot right behind her pubic bone. "Oh, Sir!" she sobbed, "I...I can't!" A hard convulsion began to take her, a pooling warmth that started from within her core. As it passed through her she shook violently, and Sir began to pull away. Elizabeth screamed and almost came as her slick sheath clamped down upon his receding fingers. She was close...so close! Almost over that edge!

But she wasn't allowed to climax.

 **Chapter 5**

Cold Shower

Her captor pulled his fingers out of her and moved away instantly.

The sound of the shower nozzle running captured her attention, and then suddenly freezing cold water fell on her pussy, spraying on her clit and up between her legs. She screamed louder then, in disbelief and disapproval, but the icy cold water continued to torment her, flowing over her breasts, her neck, hips, back and her ass. Arms cuffed above her head, she shrieked, twisting and turning helplessly, trying to escape this unexpected arctic torture. Sir was remorseless however, covering every inch of her body with freezing cold water.

The water turned off abruptly and all was silent except for Elizabeth's indignant panting.

"You did not come?" he asked.

"No..." she said. Her voice rasped in disgruntled frustration. "I didn't come. Sir."

He laughed then and with one careless finger flicked a taut erect nipple. "The water was very cold, yes? Forgive me, Elizabeth, it was not nice, no? It was unkind. But I am a little bit cruel, I warn you, and I had decided that you were not yet allowed to climax. And still I wanted to eat and taste you, with your clean shaven flesh, so red and plump - swollen with desire."

The feel of his body pressed warm upon her icy skin as he gathered her to him, against his chest and his erection. He nuzzled up against her ear and said, "I enjoyed thrusting my fingers inside you, *ma chèrie*. I felt you clamp down on me hard - like you did with my cock. You have such amazing cunt muscles, remarkably powerful. They squeeze so tight! I enjoyed that very much, as did you. But you are not allowed to come, Elizabeth. Not without my consent, you understand?"

Angry, she remained silent and he twisted one hard nipple. "Do you understand?"

"Yes Sir," she said sullenly, and he laughed once more. The warm knuckles of his hand ran down her face in his familiar, soothing manner as he backed away from her. "Do not be angry, *ma chèrie*," he said, "for I will make you climax on the bed, where we can be comfortable and I do not worry about you falling in this bath. Come now, there is still much to do. Turn around."

His words puzzled her and she tried to interpret them through her sexual haze. It seemed as if Sir didn't want her to orgasm because he was afraid she might fall. Was he really concerned for her? The idea that he cared made something in her stomach flutter, because it just seemed so damn sweet. But he wanted her to turn her back to him now. Why? All this talk of butt fucking made her hesitate. *What will he do next?* she thought, *and will I be able to deal with it?* Befuddled and emotionally overloaded, she didn't move.

"Turn. Now," Sir's voice cracked like a whip, and all indecision and confusion disappeared. Frightened, she spun her back to him.

"Good girl," he said, placing his warm hand on the small of her back, just below her ribs and above her hips. That gentle possessive touch sent of roll of sensation up her spine, out through her breasts and down into her clit. How did he do it? How had her captor made her so wanton? One subject in Elizabeth's Law degree had covered Stockholm Syndrome, also called 'capture-bonding.' She recalled the definition: "Strong emotional ties that develop between two persons where one person intermittently threatens, abuses, or intimidates the other."

Yep, she thought. *Talk about 'if the shoe fits.' Except in this case it was more like 'if the handcuff fits', and boy did it fit.* Bonded and bound, she felt physically and emotionally attached to her captor.

Elizabeth heard the squirt of Shea butter soap and smelled it once more. He began to massage her shoulders and the nape of her neck, in a soothing sensual manner. As he had done with her front, Sir attentively examined and soaped the back of her body, her arms, hips, legs and thighs. She was cold from the freezing water, but his hands warmed her, and from time to time he pressed his firm, broad chest up against her back, heating her both inside and out. It felt divine.

"You see? I make it up to you and warm you once more. This feels nice?"

"Yes, Sir," she breathed.

His hands returned to her ass, his palms and fingers gripped it and she stiffened as she recalled what he had said, *"Ma chèrie, I am glad you are an anal virgin. It will please me to break you in, and make you an anal slut, for you will like my cock in your ass."*

Ever attentive, Sir felt her tension under his clever hands, and paused then gave a low chuckle. "Elizabeth," he said as he spread her cheeks, "I only wish to see if there is hair here to shave. I do not fuck your ass right now." He seemed to quietly study her for a moment, one finger lightly stroking between her cleft. "*Mais no*, so thin and blond," he said. "We can leave this soft hair here to guard its shrine, the entrance to our citadel of pleasure. For we will both receive pleasure from this tight little hole."

He dropped to his knees then and spread her ass cheeks even further apart. Elizabeth felt his breath hot against her skin. He was silent for some time.

"Fuck, you should see this ass. *Ma chèrie,* this ass and tight little hole should win a prize, they are both so beautiful." He began to rub a finger along the rim of her anus, never probing within, just circling. Elizabeth pulled away but Sir simply held her hips and pulled her back, so he could continue his actions. Then she remained very still while he touched her, trying to decide if it felt good – him touching this forbidden area of her body, this dark place where it was wrong to enter. It wasn't really bad, it was ...interesting.

"Elizabeth," he reminded her, "your body is mine to do with as I please for the next six days." Again she stiffened. "Speak, Elizabeth. Tell me what you are thinking."

"I don't want that, Sir. I told you. I've never done that."

"Never? Not with anyone?" Sir suddenly tensed, his hands gripping hard against her hips.

"No, Sir."

"Mark never asked to fuck you there?"

"No, Sir!"

"He has never placed anything inside your ass, not a finger, not a thumb?" Sir's tone was one of surprise, and barely concealed untamed excitement. Elizabeth swallowed. She was absolutely certain that the thought of her untouched anus had turned her captor full on - not unlike the ignition sequence for a rocket launch. The man was excited and going to fire. Elizabeth licked her lips and considered that she looked forward to Sir exploding and jetting his hot, thick, strings of cum anywhere he liked - but please God not in her ass!

"Elizabeth?" he said, recalling her to the question.

She cleared her throat. "No, Sir, Mark has never touched me there," she said in a small tight voice. "And I really don't want you to either. I can't stop you of course, but can't we do other things? Why does it have to be that?"

Clearly amused, he chuckled, and gave her a spank.

"Ouch!" She screamed out loud because it hurt! It was hard enough that she was sure he had left a handprint. He rose and she felt him press up against her, his front to her back. His rigid erection was hard and ready between her buttocks, but he was so warm, and he drew her against him by cupping her breasts, and teasing her nipples.

His face was alongside her cheek as he nuzzled her and said, "*Ma chèrie*, I think your husband has been very careful with you. It is because he loves you, I think. Love is a wonderful thing, but it can complicate oh, so much."

The feel of his warm hands upon her, softly stroking combined with his compelling words mesmerized her. "I know what a woman wants," he crooned to her in a soft, sultry voice. "Shall I tell you?" His cologne and the erotic male scent of him came to her nostrils and she breathed in deeply, attempting to compose herself.

When she trembled slightly at his words, but didn't reply he gently squeezed her breasts. "Shall I?"

"Yes," she whispered, "Yes, Sir."

Chapter 6

What a Woman Wants

He turned the shower nozzle on, briefly rinsed her body, and presumably his own. Whatever he planned, he didn't mean for soap to be a part of it. When he finished he turned off the tap.

"Elizabeth," Sir whispered in his sensual French accent, "Women want a man to lick and suck and squeeze their breasts." He rubbed his erection up against her buttocks, while the fingers of one hand cleverly manipulated one taut nipple, rolling and pulling on it at first gently, and then a bit harder. Elizabeth moaned. His other hand moved down across her flank, and lower. It trailed enticingly between her legs, flicking her clit with his thumb and putting a finger inside her wet pussy. Her body reacted instantly, an uncontrolled reaction, as her spine arched with need.

"Women have unfilled places where they feel so sad, so empty," Sir said in a deep seductive voice, while moving two fingers inside her - in and out, in and out. A flood of arousal covered his fingers, easing his access, making her even slicker. "A woman's sex is one important place, an aching void. Women need to be filled. They want to be stretched and filled by a man's cock." He sucked on her ear, nibbled and kissed and nuzzled her some more, moving his heated male flesh against her, stroking her clit and the inside of her pussy, squeezing each nipple. "Women hunger, *ma chèrie*, they need a man's cock."

He brought his hand up to her mouth and she smelled the rich scent of her own juices. "Open up, Elizabeth." She opened her mouth and he placed one finger, covered with her essence between her lips. Without thinking she shut her mouth and began to suck on him, her tongue and jaw working as she sucked.

His soft chuckle was deep with lust. Hard and ready, his rigid erection stroked between her butt cheeks, in a measured, hypnotic manner. "Women have strong oral needs, too. A woman's warm wet mouth is another such empty place, *ma chèrie*. You showed me how much you loved sucking my cock this morning, didn't you? You wanted it as much as I did," and then he added, "Do you like it, Elizabeth? I smell your arousal and it makes me so hard that I have been stroking myself against you to ease my need. I find your scent and taste sweet. What does it taste like to you, *ma chèrie*?"

"It tastes like me, Sir," she whispered as if not wanting to be overheard. The words this man spoke, in his deep seductive voice thrilled her. They were profound. It was as if she was in a church library, or perhaps confession. She felt in awe, standing in some sacred place where important secrets were discovered or discussed.

Sir's hands grabbed her butt cheeks and squeezed. She tensed. "The ass is the last place, Elizabeth, the last empty place on a woman's body. You do not believe me now, but you will," His voice lowered further, into a sensual whisper. "You will be an anal slut, *ma chèrie*, because you are a woman, and because your ass will open for me. I will make you so hot you will beg to be allowed to push your buttocks down against me, to impale yourself upon me. I tell you, you will beg for my cock in your ass, *ma chèrie*."

With that, Sir reached up and unhooked her arms from the fastener above her. He was at least a head taller than she was, but at five foot three pretty well everyone was taller than she was. He helped her lower her handcuffs so they rested in front. He had one hand on those cuffs, holding her, controlling her, and with his other hand he drew his knuckles down one cheek in that sexy way of his. His seductive voice, his smell, his actions – everything about him mesmerized her.

"Elizabeth," he said with a dark chuckle. "I swear I will not fuck you in the ass unless you yourself beg for it. And you know that you will." Sir grabbed her chin and gave her a possessive kiss, thrusting his tongue inside and dominating her in a way that made her knees weak and her pussy clench with need. Quivering, Elizabeth was unable to subdue her moan.

"Come, *ma chèrie*," he said. He uncuffed one wrist and put it around her back, fastening her arms behind her once more. Then, holding her captured hands, he bent her over the raised edge of the tub. In a mindless sexual buzz, Elizabeth hadn't been paying attention. Sir moved her with such speed that she was bent over and restrained before she was aware of it. One strong hand held her cuffed wrists hard against her back, a reminder that she was his prisoner.

The other held her lower, with a firm grip just above the crease of her bottom.

Elizabeth lay on her stomach, over the side of the bathtub as adrenaline spiked through her. Sir's words he had said earlier echoed in her mind: *I might choose to bend you over the tub and take you in the ass.* Restrained and unable to escape, she was exactly where her captor wanted her.

With her naked ass exposed and vulnerable, sticking up in the air.

 *Chapter 7*

Anal Play

Not only did she think *No!* It was more like, *HELL NO!*

Mortified and embarrassed, Elizabeth had never let any lover examine her ass as he obviously was. She imagined what people would think if they saw her bent over the tub, openly displayed and burned with shame.

"What? What are you doing?" Elizabeth said in a shrill voice, and then remembering his laws she added, "Sir, may I speak?"

"Not now, Elizabeth, and I mean it. You will remain silent for I am speaking now. I warned you that I am going to make you do things that you will not want to do. This is one of them, but it will not be so very bad."

She struggled against him but he held her down with one knee, and reached for something nearby. Elizabeth felt him stretch, felt his knee press with more pressure against her back. Then something came up against her asshole, it was wet and lubricated, some sort of rubber device. Panicked, she thrashed and struggled even more.

"Obey me," he growled.

"I don't want it. I don't!"

"You are a bad girl, Elizabeth, and I shall have to punish you," he said, his tone filled with disapproval and sinister intent.

Sir brought her up and over his lap then, and slapped her butt hard with one firm hand. She screamed and thrashed and he pinned her down with one of his legs and strong thighs covering her legs, and one hand at the nape of her neck. She tried to buck, but found herself immobilized, shaking with fear, or anger, or anxiety – she wasn't sure exactly, perhaps all three. But whatever it was, it was an overwhelming, fierce emotion.

Her face felt hot as Sir's left hand rested on one exposed butt cheek for a moment. "Prepare yourself, Elizabeth," he said.

Crack!

His shockingly hard palm descended at speed with a resounding smack. Elizabeth shrieked as an intense pulse of pain rolled through her, taking her breath away. Merciless and implacable he continued to spank her, left cheek, then the right, alternating his blows. A number of hard strikes, one after another rained down upon her unprotected flesh, and she squirmed and yelped and cried like a baby. It really, really hurt. But it also, in a weird way, didn't. Her belly clenched and her pussy throbbed and seriously, she didn't actually like him spanking her, did she?

"Please, please stop, Sir," she wailed. It was embarrassing, it was demeaning, her eyes filled with tears and she felt like a child. Sir ran his hand over her trembling butt cheeks, soothing the pain. "I did not intend to spank you, *ma chèrie*, but you must not disobey me. Will you behave?" He squeezed her smarting flesh, "Or shall I give you more?"

She gasped, "I… I'll do as you say, Sir."

"Good girl," he said, once more smoothing his hand over her punished and sore bottom. She felt it flinch and quiver at his touch. He held her hands that had been cuffed behind her, restraining them against her back, making his point: *I am in control of you.*

"Stay here, on my lap," he said. "This is better. Do you remain still now?" he asked.

"Yes, Sir."

"*Bon.*" He took his thigh off her leg, unpinning her, trusting that she would wait submissively on his lap as she had agreed to do. Then he blew on her sore ass cheeks, soothing them with a gentle caress. "Your white skin is very pink, *ma chèrie*," he said, continuing to stroke and fondle her buttocks. "I can see my handprints where I have marked you. *Mon Dieu*, spanking you has made me hard as stone." He blew out a deep, lust filled breath. "Spread your legs, Elizabeth," he ordered, and she did as he asked instantly, without one single thought to disobey him.

"You are so very good, *ma chèrie*," he crooned affectionately in his deep sexy voice, as he trailed his hand up to stroke between her legs. "And wet. I think you did not dislike your spanking so very much." He used his fingers to massage her clit, and placed his thumb deep in her slick channel. Elizabeth gasped. Automatically her pussy tightened around his thumb, and his approving chuckle was dark and erotic. He rubbed his engorged cock up against her hip, and said, "I will need you soon, *ma chèrie*. I will use your body to quench this fire, this lust that you have created."

Elizabeth noticed that his French accent always seemed stronger and he used more French words when his cock was rock hard, so she wasn't surprised when added, "Will you be pleased *à remplir*...to satisfy me, Elizabeth?"

She swallowed. "Yes, Sir. I...want to satisfy you." It was so weird, but she really did. She wanted to please her kidnapper.

He cupped her face. "*Ma chèrie, je vous assure*, the wait is difficult for us both." Using both hands he spread the burning cheeks of her buttock, exposing the tender inner flesh. "Be still now while I take my pleasure, for *j'adore* your virgin hole." He pressed a finger just inside the rim, as if wanting to show her exactly what he liked. Then he firmly held her butt cheeks apart and bit her on the sensitive inner flesh. He began his unique biting progression once more, taking a fold of skin, licking and teasing with soft caresses of his tongue, sucking hard enough to probably leave a bruise and then letting it go. It was exactly as he had done with her inner thighs and pussy, and the thought of that ratcheted her arousal, creating a warm, sensual buzz. Sir bit, teased, licked, and caressed, and each time he circled, moved closer to her anus.

Tense and frightened of anal violation, Sir's actions, so methodical, sensual and predicable put her once more into a submissive headspace. It all felt so good, but why, she couldn't say. He spoke to her, soft erotic words when he wasn't biting, and his voice carried a compelling charisma. Elizabeth couldn't help but curl around his strong male legs, pressing her face up against him, her cheek rubbing against skin and coarse male leg hair. She felt as if she was melting – or perhaps floating. Her captor was strong and domineering - in command of her every movement, and if this moment could last forever she would probably be glad of it. Never had she felt so untroubled, because all of the choices were his.

Finally, when he had left his teeth marks and delicious sensations in different parts of both sides of her inner butt cheeks, he held those cheeks open wide, and breathed hot puffs warm of air against her. She felt her anus automatically pucker and her back passage clench.

He gave a low chuckle. "So responsive, *ma chèrie*. This is not so bad, no? For me, it is very good." His tongue circled her anus, which was incredibly arousing, and then he began to lick her asshole in earnest, firmly stroking, probing and questing. To her shock and astonishment, he penetrated her asshole with his tongue, twisting and curling it inside her.

Oh, God! she thought. She had never felt anything like it. Like an exhausted muscle in spasm, when it finally gives in - she felt herself just let go, trusting that this amazing man, would catch her. She was completely mesmerized. In this moment she did not wish to escape her captor. Held by his will, she was an obedient slave to this undreamed of, indescribable erotic pleasure.

What he was doing felt *so* bad, and *so* good. Her mind stopped fighting and her body went boneless and just *felt*.

Obviously aware of the relaxation of tension, Sir's voice crooned with approval when she had fully given in. "Good girl. It is very well, yes?" he asked, petting her, stroking her flank, her back and bottom. "For me, too, because I think of moistening your ass with my tongue, preparing it, so it is wet and ready for my cock." He pushed one well lubricated finger into her tight hole, stretching and pulling at the taut band of skin.

"*Bon. Mon Dieu*, I think this tight little ring of muscle will squeeze down on me *hard.* I want to feel you come while I fuck your ass. This I will certainly do. And so, here is another finger I put inside you," he said, pressing a second digit in, circling and stretching her anus, moving deeper, attempting to penetrate her back passage.

Elizabeth bit her lower lip, worrying it, while all her attention was *there. Oh my, God, that feels incredible. It is wrong and dirty and something I have always thought was utterly disgusting. So how come this feels good?* she wondered, but it did. It was just him. Sir had captivated her and made her wanton. Everything he did - even that spanking had made her wetter. Elizabeth had heard of men and women both wanting to be spanked, but that desire had never crossed her mind, until now. It hurt. But it also made him hard, and that gave her some sort of primitive satisfaction.

I'm definitely losing my mind, she thought. Sir had kept her off guard and busy and exhausted and confused since the moment she had woken up tied to his bed. Not to mention enduring a constant and unrelenting state of arousal. He had also given her the most amazing multiple orgasms of her life.

"Sexual Stockholm Syndrome," that's what this is, she thought. *Maybe it's a new type of condition, where the prisoner wants to please her*

captor because she will do anything for such great sex. Perhaps I will end up as some PhD case study. A mindless slut, that's what I'm becoming. A slut to HIM.

But there is still no way I will let him fuck me there, she thought.

However Elizabeth had no power to resist him.

Chapter 8

The Toy

When Sir seemed satisfied that he had stretched her enough, he said, "Now. Hold still while I put this into your ass. This is a butt plug, something to prepare you for my cock. It is very small, well lubricated and will not hurt you. I don't want you to feel pain, *ma chérie*," he crooned, in a soft, persuasive tone. "I want you to feel pleasure when I play with your ass." A gentle probing of an innate object pressed against her anus. It felt like a sort of slim rubber shaft, and seemed shaped like a very small penis. Sir began to push the strange, well lubricated object slowly inside. It went in a little way, but then stopped.

"Elizabeth," Sir said sternly, "I want this toy up your ass and you have no choice either way. This is my will."

Elizabeth pressed her lips together in a hard line, fighting herself. Fighting him.

Her captor held the toy there, just inside, but did not use his strength to force it further. "*Ma chérie*," he said, stroking her flank and buttocks with a caressing touch. "I will tell you something that you perhaps do not know, even though it is about your own body."

So, Elizabeth thought, holding very still. *He doesn't want to force it in. Perhaps force would tear something. Ugh. Clearly he intends to charm me into accepting anal sex. Well. He can try.*

"*Ma chérie*," he squeezed one smarting buttock hard, and it hurt, which surprised her into alertness. "Are you listening?"

"Yes, Sir," she said, but she thought she may need to rethink things. Sir could still compel her. Use force, no. But would he use pain to gain compliance? She remembered the spanking and knew the answer. Most definitely.

"When I first touched you this morning, with my little feather, your cunt was shut. It was closed to me, your clitoris small and hidden away from my eyes, even though you were fully exposed, bound with your legs spread apart."

His hand moved across her hip, and then down further. Sir began to stroke between her legs, dipping his fingers into her. It felt strange, with a toy slightly pressed against her ass and his hand working against the slit of her pussy and her clit. She knew she had never stopped being sexually stimulated, even when being spanked. As her pussy pulsed and she dripped over his fingers, her captor chuckled, clearly pleased by her obvious state of arousal.

"But Elizabeth, listen while I tell you - the woman's sex, it is a magical thing! Ah! So absorbing and beguiling! As I teased and touched you, I watched, oh, so intently did I watch! For your tight, closed channel began to unlock its secrets and open slowly of its own accord. Soon the outer lips of your pussy spread wide and your sex became thick and plump. As you became more aroused your clitoris began to swell, and then it revealed itself, stiff and turgid. It is the way of your sex, do you see? During arousal a woman's cunt opens like the most magnificent flower, the slick channel, the empty hole – it begins to gape, to open wide and drip its honey, begging to be filled with cock. The enticing fragrance of this flower then perfumes the air, drawing a man toward the scent to smell, to touch and taste."

His fingers caressed her, mesmerizing her with her hands and his words. "It is the way of nature, *ma chérie*," he said in a low voice, "for a man to caress the flower of your sex in order to open its petals. And when you began to open for me, Elizabeth, this gave me such pleasure." He took a deep breath in, and said intently, "To have this power over you, Elizabeth. For your cunt to willingly open, to submit to me and to my cock, this is what pleases me most of all."

Elizabeth became still from the sincerity in his voice, and she was lost in thought with his story. She had never heard such a thing, but knew that what he had told her was true. The damn man was so attentive and observant, and no doubt he had made love to hundreds of women, blindfolding them all so that they didn't know that he was watching their pussies, probably scrutinizing them under magnifying glasses! Yet she knew he was astute in his observations.

She remembered what he had said: *Women have unfilled places where they want to be filled. A woman's sex is one important place, an aching void. They need to be filled by a man's cock.* Sir was absolutely correct, at least he certainly was right in her case: her empty pussy wanted to be filled, stuffed full with his fantastic erection. But not in her backside!

Sir soothed his pussy moistened fingers up and around where the strange object protruded from her ass. He circled the toy, teasing it and pushing it in and out for a bit, murmuring worshipful erotic comments, admiring how her anus quivered and trembled as it reacted to this violation. He exclaimed with joy and delight when it sucked and pulled at his toy, telling her that it would most assuredly suck and pull at his cock, once he had sunk himself up to the balls, deep inside her ass.

"Elizabeth, your ass is not your cunt – *non* - and it will not open the same way, but it will open." His voice lowered to an arrogant, confident growl. "For I know you wish to please me, Elizabeth." He cupped her face as she lay obediently over his lap, vulnerable and submissive. "Take a deep breath, *ma chèrie*. Then loosen this oh so luscious *derrière*. Relax and open for me," he ordered in a stern uncompromising voice. "Right now."

The sensual touch of his warm hands combined with his sexy erotic command melted all resistance. She wanted to say she had no idea what he was talking about, but she did understand. She took a deep breath and through conscious thought, loosened her tight anal ring. With soothing murmurs, and muttered oaths at the erotic nature of her unintentional twitches and sensual responses, Sir slowly breeched her, pushing the toy inside, moving it in and out, then in and out once more, stretching her. Each time he pushed it into her anal passage he pressed it in just a bit further. It took a few minutes, but soon he had it all the way in - so only the tapered edge stuck out.

"*Voila*," he said, "*Mon Dieu*, it is very well to see my toy in there, deep in your tight little hole." He tapped it and sensation rolled through her, sending a jolt of lust straight to her pussy. "This little toy is a mere nothing, *ma chèrie*, but I train your ass to take my cock, you see? My cock is much bigger, but we make a start." He patted her bottom and added, "Good girl," he cooed, "you have done well." After a few last fond caresses of her round buttocks, and a number of admiring comments he brought her to her feet. "Does it hurt?"

"No," Elizabeth said, and swallowed hard in a choked throat. She still didn't want to be butt fucked, but it appeared it was going to happen anyway. To top it off, she probably would end up begging him to fuck her in the ass. Who could resist his seduction? He was powerful and he had all the control and she had none. To her, just then, it felt like failure and with a little hitch in her breath, she felt like crying.

"*Bon.* It was not supposed to hurt, as I told you."

A storm of emotions continued to pass through Elizabeth at the thought and feel of a toy in her ass: fear, anger, lust, shame and embarrassment most of all. It felt so good, her eager pussy was on fire, but it was all so bad and she was a terrible person, and a whore. She wanted to scream and rage, to bite and kick, and she was too afraid to do any of these things and too ashamed to speak. But she thought she might still cry.

Sir gathered her against him, pressing her against his warmth, cuddling her. "Ah, *ma chérie*," he said in a quiet, sympathetic and oddly understanding tone. He uncuffed one wrist, taking it from behind her back and returned her hands to the front, reattaching the cuff. He held each of her hands in his in a comforting manner.

"*Ma chérie*, hold this." Taking her hands he pressed both of them against the hot velvet skin of his cock. Elizabeth, momentarily lost in both mental and physical darkness, curled her fingers around his enormous erection. Somehow the strength of it grounded her, feeling how large and hard he was, how it radiated heat and warmth.

"I distract you a little, yes?" he laughed and she could imagine him smiling. "You feel shame perhaps at this little rubber toy in your ass?" He reached around behind her, grazing her flank and waist and tapped the tapered end of the toy, once more sending a ripple of sensation through her. Barely able to bite back a whimper, she sighed, and continued to grip his cock like a lifeline. "But it gives you pleasure, *ma chérie*," he said. "With your sweet young flesh, in a body that craves such natural gratification - there should be no shame for you."

He wrapped his fists around her hands, as they held his cock, circling his fingers over hers. "Fuck your small hands feel so good," he said, taking in a deep breath. "When I see this toy within that tight virgin hole of yours you make me even harder. I want to take you so much, my cock aches. It is difficult to restrain myself." Then he pumped himself, moving her hands within his, up and down slowly. "*Ma chérie*, together we give it a little relief, you understand?"

He laughed then, a joyous sound that made the whole world seem silly and unimportant. Elizabeth found she was smiling as she held him, as he continued to move her hands up and down, masturbating him. For the thousandth time she wished she didn't have to wear a blindfold. She yearned to see him, and to see that most male part of him. He felt amazing, and she imagined that it was thick, red and swollen. As he moved her up and down she moved over his broad head and considered that his cock would be attractive, straight and well formed. She licked her lips.

Sir had been speaking again, in that soft erotic way he had, telling her how much she affected him and promising her overwhelming pleasure when he eventually did take her in the ass. His words were like a strange buzz in her head. Whatever brain cells she still possessed, seemed to be currently on vacation. Touching his cock, the bizarre object up her back passage, her over aroused pussy, aching breasts and his erotic words all combined to turn her IQ off and her sexual hungers on full.

Sir stopped her movement, and pulled her hands away, bringing them to rest against the coarse hair on his chest. "Elizabeth, are you listening to me, or do I distract you too much?"

"I'm listening, Sir," she said in a dreamy voice.

He laughed and hugged her once more, pulling her against him, rubbing his hard heat against her clit and kissing her. "Fuck, I want you," he said.

I'm losing my mind, Elizabeth reflected but she said nothing. For her immediate thought was, *Fuck. I want you, too.*

Chapter 9

A Question of Power

He guided her then, to sit down in the bath, her back to his front, and he put his arms around her. The tub was still hot and soothing, his arms wrapped tightly around her, one hand securely holding her cuffs, pulling her back against him, his cock hard against her buttocks.

"Elizabeth," he said, "How does it feel to have a plug in your so charming ass?"

"Okay," she said quietly.

"Good. Now prepare yourself," he said. "For this butt plug, it is also a little vibrator." He removed one hand from around her and she heard a small click. Then the toy began to pulsate inside of her, vibrating at a low intensity. As it moved, her pussy clinched and moved, seeking... something. *It's empty,* she thought. *Sir is so right. Women don't like to feel empty. I want to be filled.*

Sir laughed, no doubt reading her expression of surprise and pleasure. His voice was soft and knowing – a promise of bliss and secrets and sexual hunger and fulfillment. It touched the deepest parts of her.

He whispered, "Do you like it, *ma chérie?*"

"Yes," she whispered back, too stunned to think of anything except how his fingers and tongue felt against her in that secret forbidden place. He had put something up her asshole, and for some strange reason, her captor had been right. It actually felt amazing.

"Sir," he said. "You must always address me properly, Elizabeth."

She giggled. "Yes, Sir," she said, feeling strangely freed by the circumstances. She had been frightened over nothing, had been fighting over nothing. Sir gave her an understanding squeeze, then began to massage her shoulders, idly running his fingers up and down her arms, toying with her nipples and cupping her heavy breasts. They were silent together for some minutes, and Elizabeth, despite her arousal, and the astonishing sensation of her ass vibrating, felt languid and relaxed. Comfortable and strangely safe in Sir's arms.

Something shifted and the vibrations increased, pulsing and rocking her from within. Her clit throbbed to the increasing pound of her heart. When her pussy convulsed, Elizabeth's immediate reaction was to spread her legs. She quivered with longing, wanting penetration, needing sexual release. Her hands lowered automatically, to touch herself and Sir caught them.

She heard a click and the vibrations within her ass stopped. He laughed. "*Voyons!* Did you like it? I can see that you did. This is a higher speed. I can set it to rotate, high, low and pulse. It has ten different settings. Together we will try them all." Elizabeth imagined Sir smiling, for there was mischief and amusement in his voice. "I could make you come again and again I think, just with this vibrator in your ass."

Elizabeth laughed. "I don't think that would be fun for you. Where is the fun in that?"

"The fun for me, Elizabeth is in controlling you," he said in a somber, definite manner. "Controlling you completely. I want you submissive to my desires, powerless, and hungry to let me do whatever I wish - to obey and do whatever I say. If I want to watch you come over and over again for twelve hours straight with the use of this ass vibrator, I will do so. In fact you will want to, because you will want to please me. You cannot stop me, *ma chèrie*, for right now you are mine."

Elizabeth shifted and bit her lip at that, and her anxiety level ratcheted up as she felt his hands possessively holding her handcuffed wrists. It was a reminder, underlining the fact that she was completely in his power. The thought made her pussy pulse. His flesh was hard against her and she wanted to make him climax, too. He was in control. Then what did he want, this compelling captor? What else would he make her do? But why did she want to please him?

Sir changed the subject and said blandly, "I stop for a moment, to ask something important." He chuckled. "The plug vibrating, it is a distraction, yes? So we dispense with it for now. I have been thinking, *ma chèrie*. I told you I studied you before I took you. You do not give yourself easily, Elizabeth," he said. "And in this case, as you have been taken against your will, you have no choice. And yet I know you crave me, *ma chèrie*. You cannot hide your desire. Tell me, why do you think this is?"

She cleared her throat. "Sir, I…don't know," she admitted.

"Yet you want me, my hands, my mouth, my cock, this is so?"

"Yes, Sir."

"But perhaps I am ugly, no? You have not seen what I look like, and there is no love between us, there is only sex between us. So why do you submit to me, why are you so willing? Do you consider this, Elizabeth? I want you to think now."

She was quiet for a bit. "I… like your voice and the way you smell," she smiled, "and you are an amazing lover." His instant laughter rolled through her, thrilling her. She wanted him, and wanted to please him, this kidnapper of hers and unless this was a case of some new rapid and unique form of Stockholm Syndrome it made no sense at all.

"*Merci, ma chèrie*. It is true. I am a good lover, but that is not so difficult. It requires only that I pay attention, and watch and listen to a woman and her body. And yet, why do you want me, Elizabeth? It is a puzzle I think I know the answer to, but I want you to seek your own truth. You say after a year of marriage you have trouble achieving climax with the man you love, and yet you do so easily with me. How can this be?"

He shifted slightly, pulling her more tightly against him. "We will not discuss this further for now. But I leave you with this: consider why a woman who has so much control in all things, how can such a woman enjoy powerlessness as you do? For you have no power here, *ma chèrie*. No will of your own. I have all the power and you must do as I wish. But you enjoy it, Elizabeth. You like it very much, I think. Will you consider this matter, *ma chèrie?* And when you find the answer you will tell me."

"Yes, Sir," she said, because it really was a good question. If she really thought about it, for some strange reason, despite the bizarre circumstances and underlying anxiety she actually felt safe, and content. Even happy when Sir bossed her around and took control, making her do things. Even things she didn't want to do.

Which was just as well, because it turned out that he had already thought of something else she didn't want to do.

And Elizabeth had no choice except to obey him.

Chapter 10

Wifely Secrets

"Good," Sir said, "And speaking of power, and me making you do as I wish, I want to see you masturbate yourself. You thought to do it when the vibrator was on high, I perceive. So show me how you play with yourself. Right now."

Elizabeth stiffened, reeling from this new line of attack. The man had her so on guard all the time, but she could never guess what he would do or want next. *Masturbate in front of him? Well why not? I have done everything else.* She sighed and reached her right hand down between her legs and perforce, cuffed as she was, her left hand came too.

Sir's strong finger grasped hers. "Wait. Tell me, have you ever masturbated in front of anyone?"

"No, Sir," she said.

"Not even your husband, Mark?" His tone was incredulous.

"No, Sir."

"How often do you masturbate? And where do you do it?"

"About once per day, I guess, and in the shower."

"Why do you not do it with your husband? He would enjoy watching, I am sure."

"I don't know. I guess I'm a bit embarrassed and ashamed that I even do it. It is an impulse, a need that I just want to get over and done with. I never thought of telling him, or doing it with him watching. I don't even think I could climax with him watching me - it would distract me. Besides, he might think I'm a slut or something."

"*Mon Dieu!* The truth from your lips is like the song of angels, *ma chèrie.*" Sir gave her a fierce hug, and a chaste kiss on the cheek. "You do not shy around the difficult subjects, explain and make the justifications. I bow to you."

This strong praise made her uncomfortable and she had no idea how to react to it.

"Listen to me, *ma chèrie.* I do not keep you from your husband. If he is good, if you continue to be good and obey me, I will let you see each other, spend time together each day. You will like this?"

"Oh, yes Sir, very much," she said, heartfelt relief in her voice. "I have been worried about Mark. Is he alright? Is he...very angry? I don't imagine that he will be good, so maybe you won't let us see each other."

Sir laughed. "You know this man very well. He is very angry and not at all *convenable*, this large, tough husband of yours. *J'asure*, Mark does not suffer too much. The torment that comes to him he brings on himself." He cupped her face. "*Bon.* Do not fear, *ma chèrie.* As long as you are good, I will let you spend at least an hour each day together. If he does not obey me I shall punish him another way, not by robbing you of time spent with him. This I promise. It may take awhile for your husband to..." she felt him shrug, "begin to understand. To see things my way."

"Thank you, Sir," she said, and she meant it.

"One more truth, then *ma chèrie,*" he said. "You tell me that it is becoming difficult to climax with your husband, Mark? And that you have not told him this as you do not wish to hurt him. You are afraid he will feel less of a man, yes?"

"Yes."

"And you masturbate to ease your need, but this is another secret, no?"

"Yes."

"And you do not have the affair or go with another man?"

"No! Of course not. Never."

"Then how often do you fake the orgasm, when you have sex?"

Elizabeth felt her cheeks heat with embarrassment. Sir had not asked, "Do you fake orgasms?" but, "How often do you fake orgasms?" The man knew everything, and her humiliation was complete. She could not orgasm with the man she loved, yet could easily climax with this stranger. There was something seriously wrong with her. "I..well," she stammered, "most of the time."

"Your husband he is a sensitive and considerate lover?"

"Oh yes, Sir," she said fervently. "Mark is always very caring in bed."

To Elizabeth's surprise, Sir laughed unexpectedly, long and loud. "And so, this is where he goes wrong," he said under his breath. "*Ma chèrie*, sex and love are two very different matters." He gave her torso a sympathetic squeeze. "I begin to think that it is very well that both of you spend your vacation with me."

Before Elizabeth could make sense of this comment, Sir said, "Now. You are right handed, no? Then show me how those small sweet fingers can bring you to climax. And feel your clean shaven pussy. It is so pretty. Much more sensitive to your touch, you will find. But do not come, Elizabeth. I want to see you draw close, but do not climax. Naughty girls who climax without permission could find the riding crop striping their ass."

She nodded. *Right. Masturbate but don't climax or I will get whipped like a thoroughbred, when nose to nose near the finish line in the Kentucky Derby.* Well. That shouldn't be too hard. How could she possibly climax anyway, knowing he was watching her masturbate? It was all too weird. She spread her legs, and lay back against him, concentrating, beginning to run her two fingers over her clit, and down into her pussy, then back to her clit. But it what was in her mind was the important thing. And what she thought of was a memory of her captor. Fucking her. *Hard.*

This morning's activities vividly filled her, smells, sensations as she re-lived the experience. *Fast and deep, Sir's powerful thrusts impaling me with the force of a sledgehammer, the coarse hair of his pubic bone grazing my swollen, hypersensitive clit, and my entire body jerking with each savage thrust. His hard male flesh rubbing against my skin. His chest hair scraping my aching, tender nipples. Sir gripping my breast and hair, pulling them both hard, using them as leverage to increase the impact of each thrust, ramming himself into me with bruising strength. I was sweating and panting and my heart thundered loudly, as wild and unrestrained as a tropical storm. So many sensations! Far too overpowering to register them all.*

Sir slamming into me, again and again and again, picking up speed as he neared his climax. Him continuing to pound me, and then he shifted slightly, hitting that particular spot deep inside. My whole body stiffened and my pussy convulsed as I arched and screamed out loud. Then came the feeling of being hit with a hard blast of sensual bliss. All the ecstasy to be had in the entire world had been centered right THERE.

Elizabeth was panting now, her pussy pulsing. She had thought that she wouldn't be able to orgasm, masturbating in front of someone, but apparently that wasn't the case. It was actually pretty hot, knowing that Sir was watching, imagining the hard set of his jaw, his eyes dark, and his pupils dilated with lust. It wouldn't take much to send her over.

Sir grabbed her hand, pulling it back from her throbbing flesh. "Good girl," he said, his voice rasping from desire. A warm glow of pleasure suffused her, knowing she had pleased him, that she had made him as hot for her as she was for him. "Elizabeth, you have made me hard as stone just watching you, and now I know how you like to be touched, too. You see how clever I am?" He stood up suddenly and sat down on the side of the tub, "Now, on your knees, before me. I want to fuck those large breasts of yours."

Elizabeth trembled and found she was smiling.

Because having her breasts fucked sounded absolutely fantastic.

Chapter 11

Elizabeth's Pleasure

Elizabeth spun around on her knees and he guided her between his legs, one hard thigh on each side of her, capturing her and restraining her against him. He took her chin in one hand, and crushed his lips to hers, kissing her, using tongue and teeth and his whole mouth. They kissed for a long time, enjoying and exploring each other while one of his hands reached between her legs and his fingers began to stroke her, exactly as she had stroked herself.

Wow. Fast learner, she thought. Her hands reached out for him and he took them, holding them tightly by the cuffs.

"*Non ma chèrie,*" he said, "Remember, you must ask. You may not touch me without my permission. But for now, do as I say. Hold your breasts out in front of me, raise them and offer them to me for my pleasure, so that I may do as I wish with them."

The handcuffs should have made it awkward she reasoned, but mental rationales were not part of these sexual games. Cuffed, enslaved, and desperate to please him, Elizabeth fell into the role. She raised her large aching breasts out in front of her.

"These are for you, Sir," she said.

His chuckle was sensual and it rolled through her. "*Bon.* Ah, but first." She heard a click, and once more her butt plug began to vibrate, luckily on low. Elizabeth moaned, and he laughed and pinched both her nipples, hard. She gave a little yelp, but the sensation from the vibrator in her ass, and the pinch of nipples both sent a jolt of pleasure straight to her pussy.

"Push them together for me, yes, now shake them. I want to see them bounce, they are so large, flushed and engorged with your arousal, they move well, do they not?" She did not expect his tongue on her nipples, and gave a soft cry when his heated mouth and tongue sucked one hard nub and then bit it. The pain felt good. Hell anything he did felt good at this point. His hands caressed them, then his tongue licked, moistening one large nipple and areola area thoroughly.

"Do you want me to fuck them, Elizabeth? Thrust my stiff cock into them hard and fast?"

"Hell yes, Sir," she said.

His laugh always thrilled her, and she imagined him smiling down at her with approval. Why was it so damn important to please him? *Stockholm Syndrome*, she thought once more. But you know what? She didn't care.

"That is good, *ma chèrie*, because I am going to fuck them. Keep holding them together, I will fuck this wet one now." The sensation was delicious as his hot cock pressed against her, fucking her nipples, pushing deep against her breast, thrusting and ramming against her, again and again. She began to moan and whimper, making odd, inarticulate sounds, writhing with pleasure. He did not tire of this game, until he had fucked both breasts very well indeed. Elizabeth was panting and sweating and her heart pounded. That damn anal plug was sending her mad with uncontrollable lust. That and *HIM*.

"Elizabeth, do you want my cock?"

Her instant answer was "Yes please," but she didn't say it. Instead she smiled, and feeling more relaxed and even playful with him she quipped, "It's what every woman wants, Sir."

He laughed, and cupped her face for a moment. "*Bon*. Put your hands on me now, your hands and your mouth. I want you to suck me off. I want to stretch and fill those soft lips."

His erotic words caused her pussy to clench. She trembled. "Oh, Sir," she said. "Will you please let me come? I swear I'm going to explode."

"No. Not yet," he said. "Please me first, and perhaps. Now, I will tell you what to do." He guided her cuffed hands toward him. "Place them like so, *oui*, one on the root. Ah yes, such small, delicate fingers. You feel good against me, *ma chèrie*."

The heat radiated from his groin and the heady scent of his male flesh caused her to swallow. His shaft was thick and solid in her hands, and her cuffs clinked against each other, while the vibrator buzzed from where it was seated, deep in her ass.

"Touch my testicles, *oui*, squeeze them, just so. You know this part, the perineum? I like for your wet finger to stroke it. *Oui, oui*. Fuck that feels good." He continued speaking then, directing her in each action with a hoarse voice filled with lust as she sucked and licked him, servicing him with her mouth. She tasted his pre-cum musk and she moaned, her whole body reacting, wanting more.

Breathing heavily he pulled back, taking deep lungfuls of air. "Again," he said huskily. He took her head between his large hands, and advised her to relax her throat because he intended to fuck her mouth deeply. Elizabeth's arms and shoulders felt his thighs tremble as he thrust into her, pushing her head down on him. Quivering with desire, she struggled to accommodate him and his length and size made her gag – but only for an instant. One hand twisted itself around her braid, using her hair as a handle to control her; he grabbed it roughly for better purchase. The erotic pull of her braid tugging every hair on her head simultaneously worked just like the vibrator - the pulse of erotic pleasure went straight to her pussy.

"Fuck, *ma chèrie*, forgive me. I cannot hold it. I see you blindfolded and on your knees before me, with my toy shoved up your ass. I see you frantic, wanting to please me, worshiping my cock - and it is too much. I must fuck you hard *sans finesse*. Right now."

He began thrusting into her mouth in rapid rhythm and he moaned and swore and commanded her to suck him, take him deeper, harder, faster. Her eyes were watering, and there was drool running down her chin. Single focused on his pleasure, she didn't care. He pushed into her right up to his balls, they slapped against her each time he flexed and even that gave her a primal, animal satisfaction. Elizabeth began to hum with pleasure, craving him, craving the song of his release, and the spurt of his cum inside her mouth. Like an animal she wanted him to use her, to rut against her body until he spent his seed.

"Take it," he gasped, ordering her in a husky, hoarse voice. "Take my cum. I want to shoot it down your throat."

Then, as his orgasm arrived, Sir rammed into her mouth so hard, pulling her head down upon him, she accidently scored him with her teeth. His cum flooded her, and she swallowed greedily as his thick shaft pulsed and his hot seed jetted again and again in intermittent spurts inside her. As he came he groaned, and grunted and his erotic sounds of climax rang in her ears like sweet music.

His cum filled her mouth and tongue, choking her and she loved every second because she didn't care – nothing mattered, only pleasing him mattered to her, and oh God she did want to please him. Her mouth continued working, sucking, taking him in, and Sir's fingers convulsed on her skull, pulling her braid. A deep guttural groan tore from his throat as he jetted into her one last time. It was an animal sound of total release and she reveled in it.

Elizabeth gagged and choked and swallowed, and all she could feel was a massive thrill of satisfaction. The pungent smell of sex perfumed the air, while her butt plug vibrator still hummed merrily away, keeping her pussy dripping. Elizabeth was on the knife edge of orgasm, she had not had a climax of her own – yet she still felt utterly released.

Holy shit, she thought. *How great was that?* The overwhelming powerful feel of the man, his desperate sexual need, combined with the heavy tension of his body and thick, pulsing orgasm that seemed to go on and on. *Man, oh man, what a thrill.*

Sir sat back on the edge of the tub and in a dreamy buzzing state, Elizabeth, continued to minister to his cock, licking his rounded head and shaft clean, reveling in it. When it began to twitch with overload, becoming too sensitive, Sir grabbed her chin and pushed her away from him. Then he slid into the water, pulling her across his lap, and placing her head on his shoulder and against his neck.

He leaned back against the tub, still breathing hard.

Fuck that was satisfying, she thought, *working his cock until he shot his load right down my throat.* Elizabeth had been tormented for the last hour or more and still hadn't come, but damn! Sucking him off had gone a long way toward appeasing her own sexual needs.

Elizabeth almost giggled as she thought of what Sir had said, his philosophy about what woman need and want. He had told her: *"Women have strong oral needs, too. A woman's warm wet mouth is another such empty place, ma chèrie. You showed me how much you loved sucking my cock this morning didn't you? You wanted it as much as I did."*

Well. The man was certainly right about that. Without reaching her own orgasm she still felt a buzzing glow of satisfaction at having sucked him off. A strong memory flashed back to her for a moment, the smell of him; the strong musky taste of his hot seed and the feel of him pounding into her. He had used her hard alright. And wow, just wow.

Cuddled into him, sitting quietly, she listened to the thick slow pound of his heart, and wondered what this was between them. *I don't love this man,* she thought. She smiled. *But I've gone way the hell to Kansas and back with lust for him.*

After awhile, he grazed his knuckles down her cheek in that familiar manner. He turned her so her back was to his front. "Close your eyes, *ma chèrie*," he said. The sound of Velcro ripping surprised her, and then her blindfold was gone. A soft, warm, wet washcloth bathed her face, wiping his fluids from her lips and the moisture from her eyes – the salty tears she had shed from strain as a result of his powerful thrusts. She wanted to open them.

Again, as if reading her intention Sir said in his deep, compelling voice, "Keep them shut, *ma chèrie.* Later today I remove this blindfold, but keep them shut for now." He untied her braid and combed through her hair with a brush he must have had ready for just this occasion. He took his time, brushing and stroking her hair, sending her into a zone of bliss. Then he gently put supple dark cotton over her eyes once more. It was a fresh blindfold, soft and clean. He attached the Velcro strap, and then swung her back across his lap, tucking her face against his shoulder, and holding her against him once more.

"One must always be careful of the eyes, *ma chèrie,* and I will not let you be harmed. You are such a treasure, and you are my treasure for these few days only. I always protect what is mine, but I particularly cherish you."

"Thank you, Sir," she said, swelling with strong conflicting emotions. Prominent among them was the delicious feeling of being cared for, of being taken care of. So stupid, as she was perfectly capable of taking care of herself, and yet…She took a deep breath and gave a long slow sigh. Her empty stomach, as yet unfed, growled. It wasn't even noon on the first day she had been taken.

From the time she had woken up in her little captive world, Elizabeth had been kept busy with so many completely new experiences her mind was still reeling. At some point today, Sir promised she'd spend at least an hour with her husband, Mark. That would pass some time. But how would they spend the rest? Was it to be sex 24/7?

The thought of Mark brought more conflicting emotions. Elizabeth wanted to see him, hoped he was alright and loved him deeply. Mark was her very best friend, and knew all of her secrets - well most all of them anyway. She hadn't told him that she masturbated daily, or that she was having trouble climaxing during sex. But how could she talk to him about these things when he would take it so personally?

Elizabeth sighed. But what would he do when he found out that she was such a wanton slut toward their captor? Mark tended toward jealousy as it was.

How could she tell him? And the answer to that was; there was no way she could. Elizabeth swallowed nervously, imagining Mark's reaction. Talk about angry! She sighed. Their first year of marriage, with its long anticipated, ten day vacation in Vegas was probably going to end in divorce.

Book 3

Elizabeth's

Pain & Pleasure

# Chapter 1

A Secret from Mark

"Come, *ma chèrie*," Sir said while sitting with her in the bath. "It is time to eat. And after that I want to tie you up and fuck you once again."

At these words Elizabeth's pulse raced, her skin flushed, her pussy moistened and her breathing quickened – all signs of instant arousal that she knew her captor's acute and knowing eyes would spot immediately. Anticipation rolled through her body in a slow, thick wave of heavy sexual heat.

"I want to tie you up and fuck you once again."

Elizabeth swallowed. Just the suggestion of sex had her in an ephemeral buzz of hyper-alertness. This kind of vast emotional swing was something one might experience from caffeine stimulation - after three double shots in a row, perhaps. Her body was alert and more than willing, her mind was still in a daze. My God the pleasure that this man had wrought!

Her captor stood and took her elbow, raising her to her feet in the bath. Elizabeth, still blindfolded and naked, had her hands cuffed together in front of her. Her inability to see was a handicap, yet her captor - who she had been instructed to call "Sir" – was a bone-deep controlling personality. Thus, he was overjoyed to be in charge of her, guiding and directing her every movement.

This morning Elizabeth had woken in her kidnapper's bed, blindfolded, tied naked and spread-eagle. He had then tormented her sexually with a feather, nipple clamps, his hands, mouth, lips and tongue until she begged for him to fuck her. Sex with him had been the best she had ever had - except for one particular occasion with her husband. Or was she just being loyal, she wondered? But no. Nothing could beat that.

For the last hour or so her captor had taken her to the large bathtub and, with her wrists shackled together and restrained above her head, he had lathered up every part of her body. *Yes,* she thought. *And although he has since rinsed the soap off, I'm still in quite the lather. Over an hour of foreplay and I still haven't had a climax.* Elizabeth frowned. Sir was amazing, but he was also a twisted bastard. *I want to come! Why won't he let me come?*

Elizabeth still had no idea what he looked like. The man could be cross-eyed, with a weak chin and bad acne for all she knew, but his voice, his hands, his mouth and tongue! Not to mention that expensive nutmeg, cedar and Brazilian Rosewood cologne. God he smelled good. How had her captor done it? Kept her in this astonishing sexual haze? She would have chewed off her own arm at one point, just to have his cock inside her, or to have some friction on her clitoris or pussy so that she could climax. Sir's rule was that Elizabeth could only orgasm when he said so – and she wasn't allowed to yet. *Bastard.*

Mind you, Sir had "allowed" her to suck him off. That thought made her smile, and she had to subdue a sudden impulse to giggle. Sir gave her his cock as if it were a unique and special treat, something she had to ask for, even beg for!

Well, she thought. *His cock was worth begging for. Man, oh, man. Sucking him off. Yum.*

To Elizabeth's great surprise she had found sucking Sir to completion just as satisfying as climaxing herself. Strange, but true. Emotionally she had an all consuming desire to please him, and that need had simply taken her over - and it was still there.

Her pussy clenched and clit throbbed at the strong recent memory. Elizabeth shut her eyes behind her blindfold, recalling the smell of him, the heat of his hard cock between her lips, the potent musky taste of his hot seed and the feel of him pounding into the back of her throat. She licked her lips, remembering the inexplicable joy she experienced when listening to his male growls of pleasure and having him thrust, frantic with need into her willing mouth. Her captor had used her body like a large, powerful animal in rut and what a *wow* experience. An enormous glow of satisfaction still buzzed through her from having swallowed every drop of his cum. It had felt like some sort of religious awakening, knowing she had given him pleasure.

What was that about? She wondered. *Why was it so important to please him? Stockholm Syndrome,* she reminded herself. *It's the only explanation.*

"*Bon.* Now lift the right leg," he commanded in that sexy French accent, maneuvering her out of the bath. "Just so, and here are two steps back down. One, yes, two. Good girl."

Sir moved her a few feet and then stopped, positioning her where he wished. Her captor seemed big on that, too: moving her around, placing her exactly as he liked. After experiencing his total domination all morning, Elizabeth had absolutely stopped fighting. *Besides,* she thought. *Why not? He was a rock star sexually.* Never had she had a more satisfying partner or so many orgasms in her life. A twinge of guilt momentarily touched her, but she thrust it away. How could she deal with that now? Mark was her husband and she certainly loved him. She had also had excellent sex with him but the truth was - except for that one memorable time - it had been *nothing* like this.

That fact would crush Mark. Elizabeth wondered what would happen after this was over, when she and Mark were set free. She clenched her teeth, resolved to *never* tell her husband what had occurred between Sir and herself.

Mark must never, ever know.

Chapter 2

Resolved Not to Beg

Elizabeth heard Sir step away from her for a moment and then return with a heated towel, which he wrapped around her upper torso. She sighed, enjoying the warmth.

"You like this?" he said, with a smile in his voice. Elizabeth found herself smiling, too. Sir was over controlling, but he was also good–humored, and even mischievous. He sometimes reminded her of a four year old bouncing around in a playground, as he, like most children of that age, always seemed to be smiling. Not that she could see it with the blindfold on, but she could clearly hear it in his voice.

"*Bon, ma chèrie,*" he said. "Time to dry this oh so luscious body of yours. Stand with your legs spread wide. I want to see all of your plump, swollen cunt." She did so, and to make his point, he tapped the inside ankle of her leg, nudging against her to make her move her legs even further apart. "Good. Now, stand straight with the shoulders back and the breasts forward." He took her cuffed hands, and carefully guided her, placing them on top of her head, ensuring that the connecting chain didn't knock into her.

Elizabeth reflected how quickly she had come under her captor's spell. Despite her own history of being stubborn, bossy and used to getting her own way, for some reason she felt herself to be quite unequal to defying Sir. From the very beginning, when she had first given in to his commands his manner at her capitulation showed neither surprise nor triumph. It was as if it never occurred to him that she would not comply. The man had never doubted that she would obey him completely.

Elizabeth felt herself flush, with shame or embarrassment, she couldn't tell. *Because now I simply do as I'm told.*

"Yes. Like so," Sir said, cheerfully. "Now you are open and ready for me. Because, *ma chèrie*, your body is mine for the next six days. Mine to do anything I can imagine - and I warn you, I have imagined oh so many things."

A number of emotions swirled through her. The man continuously kept her off balance. *How did he do that? Create such a thrill of desire and curl of anxiety at the same time? That, and a powerful urge to please him.*

Elizabeth's pussy pulsed and contracted with unsatisfied lust, something it had been doing without break for the last few hours. Sir had a rich male voice that just dripped sex. Not unlike her pussy was currently doing - and probably would be doing for the rest of the day, unless her tormentor let her come! For some weird reason being kept in handcuffs, and bossed around turned her on.

Using the warm towel, Sir rubbed her skin, starting with her breasts, delicately brushing them, over and underneath, drying them fully while touching them in a functional, yet somehow sensual manner. He moved to each arm, her flat stomach, the round of her hips and then he went to his knees to dry her legs.

Enamored with her newly shaven pussy, Sir spent some time there, playfully drying it, while breathing on her pussy and "accidentally" flicking her throbbing clit again and again. He spread the lips of her sex, carefully and completely drying each part of her. Utterly aroused, she ruthlessly suppressed her gasps and groans of desire, but continued to drip from between her legs. Sir chuckled often, wiping up any moisture and then admonishing her in a mischievous manner when he needed to wipe between her legs again.

Each time he acted astonished to find her dripping wet, with her arousal running down her thighs. Then he acted surprised and dried her again. It was becoming an old joke, yet he didn't seem to tire of it.

Ha bloody ha, she thought, trembling with sexual frustration. The man had achieved his own orgasm. Each time he touched her it was literally a breathtaking experience. Freshly shaven, the skin on her pussy was tender and aching, altogether much more sensitive. Sir was driving her mad.

To add to her torment, Elizabeth currently had an anal plug within her virgin ass. It was shaped like a small penis and was a vibrator, which Sir was currently keeping on low. Sir had cheerfully told her that it had ten different settings, including pulse. She had experienced pulse already and, *oh man,* had that ratcheted up her need. Never having had anything put in her ass, Elizabeth had originally objected, but Sir had inserted it into her back passage anyway - after a vigorous spanking. Elizabeth would never have guessed how hot something like that could be, both the spanking and the vibrator. With the butt plug vibrating merrily away, she just kept dripping, unsatisfied and aroused.

Sir moved around back to dry between the cleft in her buttocks, making her bend over, to ensure he reached every part of her body. He often tapped her butt plug and every time he did, a shock of desire rolled through her. In this position the vibrator in her ass massaged different areas, and once more she felt her arousal running down her legs.

Please let me come, her mind shouted urgently, *Please!* But she didn't ask for permission to speak, nor did she want to beg. *Not this time, buddy,* she decided with stubborn resolution. It was too demeaning, her begging him to let her come. There was no point anyway, because Sir, for some perverse reason of his own, had decided to deny her a climax.

I'll just keep my mouth shut this time, she decided. *I'm a strong person, and I can do whatever I decide to do. And in this case, I absolutely refuse to beg.*

Strong as she was, it turned out in the end that Elizabeth had no choice in the matter.

Because Sir was much stronger.

Chapter 3

Bound for Lunch

As Sir worked he continued to touch her naked flesh, occasionally tapping her anal plug, or her clit, his hands making warm contact against her skin. They were proprietary gestures, lightly smoothing over various parts of her body, shoulder, neck, back, flanks and the round feminine curve of her buttocks. Such possessive little caresses, as he physically directed and controlled her.

"You are still so aroused, *ma chèrie*," he said. "Such a plump, needy cunt. It would take only a moment to give you the orgasm, but it will have to wait as it is time to eat."

She snorted, but said nothing. Sir had told her she had to ask permission to speak, but she never had to say what she was thinking. He always seemed to already know. Her captor enjoyed tormenting her. This was just a cruel little game of his that she would, for now, have to make the best of.

When she was dry to his satisfaction, he opened the bathroom door and guided her through. Instantly the heavenly smell of food cooking assaulted her senses and her stomach growled. His did, too, and he laughed.

"Sir," Elizabeth asked, "May I speak?"

"Yes, for now while we eat you may speak freely, *ma chèrie*. It is a little time off for you, you perceive. The lunch break."

Once inside, he put his hands on her waist and lifted her, picking her up and sitting her in what felt like an early American frontier wooden chair. But it was an odd chair, not padded and high-backed, and while she sat in it her feet didn't touch the floor. It seemed huge, as if it could seat a 300lb man. Elizabeth felt like a little girl in this big chair, and began to worry about daddy scenarios. Man, was she going to get spanked again?

"Put your arms on the armrests and each leg around the outside of the chair, *ma chèrie*," he directed.

This action spread her wide, which no doubt was his plan. There was little actual chair beneath her, so he had easy access to her pussy. Thankfully Sir had switched off the toy in her backside as they left the bathroom. It was not vibrating, yet it could be felt just *there* as she was placed down on the chair. This sensation created a pulsing awareness of her pussy as well. Elizabeth sighed, not wanting to think of sex. Right now she was hungry. Glad to be able to speak, she said, "It smells fantastic, Sir."

Sir moved to the ground and began to bind one of Elizabeth's legs to the outer edge of the chair with what felt like a soft, maybe two inch width of perhaps cotton material. Wrapping it tightly around her ankle, foot and leg, he looped it until her left leg could not move at all. While he worked, he said, "My staff have been in and our lunch is in the warmer. Today we have *Poulet et Épinard, crépe* with chicken and spinach. There are also vegetables, *baguettes* with fresh butter and *creme brulée* for desert." He laughed, and the sound caressed her nerves like a playful sensual treat. "And strawberries with hot liquid chocolate."

"Yum," she said. "Sounds wonderful, Sir." Elizabeth found herself smiling. It was the way Sir said chocolate. Kind of like "chalk –au –lat." It was so sexy, that French accent of his. *So,* she thought, *he had a staff?* Of course he did, he was wealthy. But they must be devoted to him if they ignored the fact that he was kidnapping people. But maybe they just thought he liked sexual bondage, and had no idea that he had drugged and abducted her husband and herself.

Sir chuckled. "I make you a large lunch, Elizabeth, because I intend to keep you working hard to serve my every desire. You will need your energy."

Well. No real comment to make about that, she thought and remained silent.

Sir had started on her right leg, binding it, too. Both legs were soon well constricted up just past her knees, leaving her thighs exposed.

"This is not uncomfortable, *ma chèrie?* Not too tight?" he asked.

She shrugged. "I can't move my legs, but it feels okay."

"*Bon.* You will tell me if anything I do becomes uncomfortable, yes?"

"Count on it, Sir," her voice was bitter.

He laughed and stood up. "Good. Now let me see your hands." He took off her hand cuffs, and tut tutted over the few marks they had left upon her soft skin. He found a cream and gently rubbed it into the skin on her wrists, giving her a sensual hand massage in the process. Everything he did felt divine, this captor of hers with the devil-blessed hands. When he finished, he continued his odd game of tying her to the chair, winding the soft cotton bandage over her fingers, wrists and arms, all the way up to her shoulders. He then moved to her hips, constraining them firmly against the wood. That binding felt firm and odd – kind of like he had immobilized her womb.

"It is well, Elizabeth?" he asked.

"Yes, I'm alright."

"*Bon,"* he replied, but there was the suggestion of warning in his voice and she instinctively found herself tensing. "This pleases me. But to achieve what I must, there may be a little discomfort. Do not concern yourself too much, *ma chèrie.* All will be well, *j'asure."*

Easy to say, but now she was worried.

 # Chapter 4

Trust

Sir continued his odd process of restraining her. Her breasts he treated differently, binding them crisscross like a bra, above and below each one so that they were raised up, with her nipples facing outwards.

"Take a deep breath, Elizabeth," he said.

She did so, and tried to gasp for she found she could not take a full breath – her lungs were constricted. "Sir, I..." she began in a panicked voice.

"Shush, this is fine, *ma chèrie*. Just breathe, slow, shallow and steady, yes. You see? You can take the air in perfectly well."

Elizabeth found she could breathe, but not with large lungfuls. This restraint made her nervous. "I'd feel better if it was a little bit less tight, Sir."

"It makes you anxious, yes?"

"Yes."

"Good. You are forced to trust me a little, because I control your breathing. I control everything *ma chèrie*, but I will not hurt you." He chuckled in a somewhat dark and intimidating manner, "Well, I will not hurt you very much, anyway. And I promise you *ma chèrie*, you will very much like all that I do. This I swear."

She cleared her throat, "Sir, you said for me to tell you if I became uncomfortable. I'm not comfortable right now."

"And I heard you. Yet this little discomfort is necessary."

"Necessary for what?"

He stood then, and brushed his knuckles down her face, gently touching any naked skin in a soft, sympathetic caress. "Beautiful girl," he said in a compelling voice. "You must learn to trust me, trust that I will keep you safe. I cannot tell you yet, but there is a reason for all I do. Do you trust me?"

Taking a deep breath, Elizabeth held it for a few beats and then expelled it. "It would be irrational to trust you, Sir. You drugged and kidnapped my husband and me, you have taken us prisoner. Why should I trust you?"

"Speak now," he said in a commanding voice. "The truth, Elizabeth. Do not use the lawyer logic, for these matters that are affairs of the heart and soul. Do you trust me?"

"Yes," she whispered, compelled to tell him the truth and wondering how her captor had brainwashed her so completely so soon.

"C'est très bon. You are so very honest, *ma chèrie*," he said. One warm finger trailed across an eyebrow, caressing down her cheek, brushing her chin and across to softly stroke both of her lips. Sir leaned over and gave her a kiss then. It started as a gentle touch, mouth to mouth, and bound as she was she couldn't move into him, even though she wanted to. Yet she heard herself make a little sound, and Sir deepened the kiss, moving her from fondness to yearning and then turning quickly to breathless need.

He pulled away from her. "You make me break my own rules, *ma chèrie*."

With her head swimming, slightly less anxious and tense, Elizabeth swallowed and Sir simply continued working, finishing up the last of her bandaging restraints. After awhile Elizabeth felt herself relax. The man didn't want to kill her after all, but he did want to stop any possibility of movement.

Sir muttered and commented to himself as he applied her bondage, totally absorbed in his work. Bemused, Elizabeth considered that to him this was some sort of important labor of art. All well and good, but she was really hungry. Impatient, she tried to shift restlessly, but couldn't as he had constrained her so completely. She began to feel apprehensive again then, wondering what new sexual torture he many have devised.

"Almost done, *ma chèrie*," he said. He put a kind of cushion behind her head, with firm sides that held her face perfectly still. The chair must have had some provision because her forehead was strapped down in a way that when he locked it in place she could turn her head neither left nor right. It seemed weird to be so motionless, to remain so still. She bit a lower lip and tried to slow her breathing. Her mouth was really dry.

Sir moved away, opened what sounded like the refrigerator and poured out two glasses. "Water, I think. We are both dehydrated as we have done much exercise already this morning."

She smiled faintly at the exercise comment. Right. Lots of physical exercise, that was for sure. Sex sure got that heart rate up all right. She drank gratefully through a straw, finishing the glass, but then she cleared her throat and tried to steady her ragged breathing. This inability to move at all in any direction was disconcerting.

Sir stroked her jaw lightly and said, "Frightened, *ma chèrie*?" he asked in a gentle voice.

"Not really frightened. Just a little nervous."

"*Bon*," he said and Elizabeth could almost hear the satisfied smile in his voice. "I think I like you to be a little nervous."

She snorted. What an understatement. He liked her a lot nervous, and he knew it. But she did not expect him to scare her to death.

Except that he did.

Chapter 5

Terror and Dread

As she had been given permission to talk she said, "Alright for you, Sir, but I'm hungry. How am I going to eat with my hands wrapped up and my stomach twisting with apprehension?"

A murmured sound of comfort, and once more his warm knuckles soothed across her face. The movement was so familiar. Her pussy clinched and she felt moisture drip between her thighs and on to the hard wooden chair. For some weird reason she trusted her domineering tormentor as he turned her on. His actions reminded her of how she might gentle an anxious mare. *Probably before leading her to a devious stallion,* came the acerbic thought. She took as deep a calming breath as she was capable of, constricted as she was, and sighed. Somehow she would get through this. After today there were only five more days to go.

"I myself will have the honor to feed you, and you will eat as it is my will, *ma chèrie*. All will be well, as I am taking care of you. You will see."

Elizabeth's jaw tightened as she tried to balance her conflicting emotions: irritation as she could look after herself, and euphoria that he was going to look after her. *Yep. Still going mad,* she thought, but said nothing.

"One more wrap, *ma chèrie*," he said, and she felt the soft cotton bandage wrap firmly, twice around her throat, pinning it down against the chair, making it impossible to move her neck.

Elizabeth felt the blood drain from her face, and her head began to spin. The memory returned. She had unwisely bit Sir upon waking in his bed this morning, when he first touched her. As a result he had firmly pressed down against her windpipe, cutting off her oxygen and blood flow to the brain. This inexorable pressure of the cloth against her neck was unpleasantly familiar and similar to that recent event. Post Traumatic Stress Disorder – PTSD. Right then, at that time, she had honestly felt that she was going to die.

Elizabeth's breath came rapidly with her fear. As she hyperventilated, Sir worked to reassure her.

"Shush, shush, *ma chèrie*," he said. With both hands he touched her then, on both sides of her body simultaneously, stroking her cheeks, eyebrows, face, neck, shoulders and arms in a firm, reassuring caress. "This is not the same, it is not. I do not threaten you - I merely confine you, preventing movement. Shush shush, all is well Elizabeth, you will see. Slow, deep breaths, yes, that is right. Good girl. You are doing very well, *ma chèrie.*"

Elizabeth struggled to maintain her composure. With her head spinning it took many minutes before she settled, and she could hardly hear or recall what Sir was saying. At times he had been speaking in French, and his voice had been low, soft and utterly compelling. Without her vision all she knew was the soothing touch of his fingers, and his calm, restful and reassuring voice, murmurs of comfort and understanding and sympathy. But he didn't remove that firm cloth collar from her neck.

'Can you…," Elizabeth finally choked out in a small whisper, "Sir, will you take it away?"

"*Non.* It does you no harm, *ma chèrie.* In fact it does you good." All the time he talked he had at least one hand upon her, letting her know that he was here. Bound with such limited movement, behind the darkness of her blindfold, Elizabeth experienced the panic of a trapped animal. Sir's touch, just knowing he was there, gave her some sort of primal comfort.

"You associate my hand on your neck with that unfortunate and unpleasant incident. I change this, now. The mental connection will amend itself, and when you think of pressure here," he lightly touched her throat and nuzzled her neck. "You will remember a nice meal, a delightful conversation, and oh, many other pleasant things." He tenderly licked her racing pulse, and blew warm breath on it as a sensual distraction. They waited together for some time, until her heart rate and breathing slowed, and she calmed.

"Good girl," Sir said with an approving voice that sent a thrill of unreasonable delight throughout her body. So incredibly stupid how she responded to this kidnapper of hers, but she wouldn't change it even if she could. Elizabeth considered that she'd probably feel protected and secure with him right up until the point where he killed her. *Stockholm Syndrome*, she reminded herself.

But at least she honestly did feel safe. She didn't think he would hurt her.

But she was wrong.

# Chapter 6

Lunch

"Relax now, *ma chèrie*, as much as you are able. It is time to eat," he said. His steady, calming hand lifted as he moved away, and her heart rate increased.

The sound of objects and implements opening, shutting came to her ears, and she heard him move around the room. Blindfolded, in the dark and unable to move, she wanted him to come back - to put his hands back upon her, because somehow with him there she felt she would be alright.

A plate was set heavily down and she could almost feel him move to between her legs, standing just in front of her. He touched her, one hand resting on her thigh and her increasing tension slowed.

"*Ma chèrie*," he said gently with that uncanny intuition of his. "I am here." He patted her thigh. "I am here and you are safe. I will not leave you alone, do not fear."

"Thank you," she whispered, hardly able to speak and forgetting to use his appellation, Sir. But she noticed that he ignored this and continued to pat her, concentrating on soothing her frayed nerves.

"It is my pleasure, *ma chèrie*," he said.

The smell of something wonderful came to her nose, and a shift in the light or pressure of the air – something made her aware when he leaned toward her. "Open, *ma chèrie*. Time to eat," he said.

Well, she thought. *At least he didn't tie my mouth shut.* She opened her lips and felt his fingers push a morsel of food inside. Crepe. Chicken, and a creamy sauce. It melted in her mouth, and tasted divine. "Ummm," she said.

"It is very good, no? I have an excellent chef. He is French, of course," he said and he laughed. Something about his laughter always calmed and cheered her, and she smiled and found she was able to eat, and able to smile while sitting with him, while he placed food in her mouth, describing each treat he had for her. All the time he fed her he also kept a firm warm hand on her thigh, or her knee, or on her forearm. After awhile all her anxiety lessened and eventually disappeared and they talked and laughed together, eating and making insignificant and amusing conversation.

It was an odd meal, him feeding her by hand, and her completely bound, naked and exposed with her legs tied wide apart for him to view every bit of her female flesh. Sir flirted shamelessly with her, always in a flattering and admiring way, and nothing remotely sleazy. Cherished and treasured, that was how he made her feel, and there was no way he could be pretending such regard. Despite every circumstance shouting otherwise, Elizabeth had this crazy idea that her strange captor respected women, and had a high opinion of them, which of course made no sense at all.

After they had coffee and *creme brulée*, she heard a chair shift and Sir sat down, signaling a change. Alarmed, she breathed in – yet his hand squeezed her leg, acknowledging her uncertainty. The hand remained upon her, trailing light circles over her thigh. Something in his aspect or manner had signified a difference, and Elizabeth's body jumped to hyper-alert, utterly aware of him. Without being able to see she could feel his gaze upon her. It was as if he was a hungry predator, and she was his prey.

She heard him moving, standing. "Elizabeth," he said in a low voice, "Open your mouth and try this." His lips touched hers, no, it was warm melted chocolate upon a strawberry. He kissed her with the strawberry in his teeth, pushing the fruit into her mouth.

"Yum," she said.

"You like it? I, too, like it. Have another." This time as his lips met hers and he pushed the chocolate covered strawberry into her mouth, he moved closer, and the hair on his thighs touched her thighs before the heat of his flesh seared her. She felt his cock, hard and ready also moving up against her pussy, and the combination made her give a soft, unexpected moan.

Sir laughed. Both of his hands cupped her bound breasts, caressing and soothing, then pinching each nipple. "It is delicious, *ma chèrie*," he said, "and so are you."

Elizabeth smiled. "*Merci beaucoup*, Sir. You're not so bad yourself."

It seemed like they had finished with their lunch and Elizabeth wondered if chocolate covered strawberries was all he had planned for desert.

Somehow she doubted it.

# Chapter 7

Burned to the Ground

"*Ma chèrie*," he said. "It is time for work, we have had our break. Yet for now I will allow you to continue to speak freely, for we have important subjects to discuss."

Elizabeth once more felt the weight of her circumstances. What did the man want now? She was stark naked, blindfolded and unable to move: totally in his power. With a twist of apprehension she licked her lips and swallowed.

"First I want you to consider, *ma chèrie*. How do you feel as you are? I have constrained you, no? You cannot move. And you are displayed for me, for my pleasure. I can see the marks I gave you on both inner thighs, they are - so sorry - very blue, and there are teeth marks too, you understand. But to me each bruise on your pale flesh is beautiful and very satisfying. When I see them I remember the pleasure I gave you when making them, and I think of the ones I do not see, on your beautiful *derrière*.

He was standing, and as he spoke he moved closer, moving his warm hips between her legs, and placing a hand on each upper thigh. "Think now, *ma chèrie*. You are bound and open to my will, and to my pleasure. Tied as tightly as you are, you are trapped and helpless, unable to do anything," he chuckled, "Except perhaps spit at me. How do you feel? And do not use your mind to find the answer, do not reason. Just speak to me your thoughts as they come, with your oh so charming lips."

Elizabeth said, "I'm nervous, but I don't really think you would hurt me." *At least I hope you won't,* she thought. But no, everything he did, he did for some reason of his own. Too bad she wasn't on the same page, must less did she know the agenda.

"Yes?" he encouraged. "What else?"

She tried to shrug but couldn't move. "I'm scared. I feel vulnerable," she whispered, chewing a lower lip. "Completely at your mercy." Somehow, with that one thought came a pulse of pleasure in her clit, as well as a huge contraction of her slick channel. She felt a gush of liquid from her sex. She was sexually aroused. "Oh!" she said, "I... oh, I..." Elizabeth didn't finish the sentence because with her physical reaction came a monumental revelation. Did it take constraint or a feeling of vulnerability to get her off? How could that be?

Sir remained silent, although from where he was standing, he couldn't have missed her noticeable sexual response. Her nipples felt hard as rock, her breasts ached to be touched and she was sitting in a pool of her own arousal on this hard wooden chair. Sir said nothing, obviously letting her have time to think these thoughts through.

Finally she said, with growing certainty, "I'm sexually aroused. Being tied up like this, being vulnerable, powerless and exposed. It turns me on."

Sir chuckled and gave her a chaste kiss, on her forehead. "Just so, *ma chèrie.* You are such an intelligent woman, so quick to look and see what has been hidden from you. This knowledge changes things, yes? It is something you never considered."

Elizabeth measured her thoughts and her words, trying to reason things out. "You asked me before, why I'm so turned on by you, a man I don't even know. Now I know why – because you tied me to your bed? Is it really that simple?"

"Yes and no. We have a saying in France: *Les vérités les plus évidentes de la vie sont la plus difficile de voir.* Which is: Life's most obvious truths are the hardest to see. The full quote is: 'Life's most obvious truths are the hardest to see but once you've burned everything to the ground they are the only things left standing." His knuckles grazed her cheek in that familiar manner. "You see, *ma chèrie*, I burn all to the ground by abducting you. I take away everything - the mannerisms and mechanisms that you use to survive. I burn away the makeup, props and masks - then, *voila!* The eyes, they open."

Well. She could see it now. To hell with seeing, she could feel it. It explained how turned on she had gotten as a captive. Where did it come from, this quirky desire to be powerless? Her mind spun in many different directions, recollecting incidents in the past, trying to make sense of this new truth.

"Elizabeth, tell me," he said. "What do you think of?"

She automatically tried to shake her head, but of course couldn't move. "I…I'm not sure."

Sir broke into her train of thought. "This will take more consideration, *ma chèrie*, do not let it disturb you. You have done very well to discover this much, and so soon. Many women never find a key to their sexuality. It is a little God humor I think, sometimes. A mischief that the creator plays between a man and a woman. We will put this away for now, *ma chèrie*. It is a matter for consideration when you are alone, as I will leave you for some time today…"

When she stiffened he added, patting her reassuringly, "But of course, I will not leave you alone and tied like this. I will leave you with only one ankle shackle, *ma chèrie*, and a long chain attached to the oh so comfortable bed." He stroked her lips with one warm finger, and then gave her a light kiss.

"All shall be well, Elizabeth," he assured her. "I promise to take good care of you."

Chapter 8

Her Primitive Needs

"*Ma chèrie*," Sir said, "There is something else I wish to understand. Tell me now, in detail. When you masturbate, what do you think of?"

Elizabeth drew in a breath. "I hadn't seen Mark in years, and I think I told you, we saw each other again at a friend's wedding. It was the strangest thing, our eyes met and then suddenly it was like we had to have sex, *right now*. I was a bridesmaid, in full dress and trimmings, hair done up in an intricate coiffure - and it was thirty minutes before the wedding Bridal March. There was no time for sex, the whole idea was insane."

"I went down to where the wedding gifts were displayed, I can't recall why exactly, but I had to retrieve something. Mark was there, with a massive hard on. I told him no, that I was too rushed, that the room was too public, but he was like a bull at a heifer, there was no stopping him. You know how big he is, right? He was a football linebacker, first string at College. Anyway, Mark had his hand up my dress and his big body pressing me against a wall so fast! I pushed against his chest but couldn't stop him. It was like trying to hold back some powerful natural event with my hands, like trying to stop a tornado, or an avalanche. It was the most intense sexual experience and orgasm I had ever experienced."

"*Naturellement*. I see the restraint necessary for the powerful climax, do you?"

"Oh yes. His entire body was one big restraint." She felt her skin flush as she remembered. "The fact that I didn't want to, not where we could be caught in public – but he overruled me. His immense power totally eclipsed mine. I swear there was no stopping him. I was helpless - trapped by Mark's huge body and his lust. It... he," she tried to put it into words what had happened, but all she could come up with was, "Mark had this compelling primal need and all my resistance disappeared like kindling tossed onto a bonfire. That was so weird, too. I really wanted him to ejaculate. I yearned to fulfill Mark's sexual hunger, to do anything he wanted as long as he climaxed, and gave me his cum. The cum thing was strange, I'd never had that desire before. I yearned to have it inside me – to eat it, drink it, by God I think I would've happily bathed in it! Right then I wanted to meet his desires more than I wanted to even live or breathe. It was just ...amazing."

"*Bon*," Sir's voice lowered, and became kind of husky. Elizabeth became aware that something she had said or done had intensely turned him on. "*Oui*. There is another instinctive need you have, Elizabeth. Something deep, that is a fundamental part of your nature. This sudden unwanted yet wanted sex with Mark fulfilled this primitive desire of yours. It was not only meeting your need for constraint. Do you see it, *ma chèrie*?"

Elizabeth frowned and considered. "No. What is it?"

"It is not important then." He gave a mocking chuckle. "I think I continue burning even more to the ground, yes? Until you, *ma chèrie*, see everything oh so clearly." It was a roundabout threat and emotions warred within: fear, anxiety, desire, and lust.

"Elizabeth," his voice held a warning tone, and he changed the subject. "It pleases me to hurt you, just a little. Do you mind?"

"What?"

"I want to cause you pain," he said. "And remember, you must call me Sir."

She tried to keep the fear out of her voice. "What do you want to do, Sir?"

"I pour a little chocolate on you, and then lick it off. It will taste better upon your soft skin. But the chocolate is warm, hot even. It may burn a little. Shall I try it near your shoulder perhaps? To see how it feels?"

Elizabeth thought this over and her lawyer brain considered a mountain of closing arguments and rebuttals. How to get around her captor? But she had no idea. The man was going to get his own way anyway whether she said yes, or no. If she said no, he would give her a lecture and explain all about his will and how she had to do as he wanted. For some reason Sir found joy in making her agree or to even beg for his little tortures. Ultimately he always got his way regardless. The only strategy she could imagine was to give in with dignity.

She took a deep breath and surrendered. "Knock yourself out, Sir."

He laughed, a joyous sound. "*Bon.*" She heard a click and the vibrator in her ass went on high. The combination of complete restraint with the anal vibrator on pulse was devastating. Futilely pulling against her bondage, Elizabeth gasped, "Oh God, Sir!"

"It is good?" he asked, taking his hand from her knee.

"Yes…yes, Sir," she choked.

"*Ma chèrie*, you want to move, do you not? I see the hips, they try to thrust, but they cannot."

It was true. At this high pulse setting Elizabeth was totally craven, her body on sexual overdrive, she quivered and trembled but couldn't move. Of its own accord her voice started a soft, keening kind of desperate wailing sound. Elizabeth heard it but was powerless to stop it. *Oh God*, she thought, *please let me come!* But as she could hardly speak she said nothing. The vibrator in her ass returned to its lowest setting, and she breathed a deep breath of relief.

Sir gave a low chuckle. "It is a little distraction, you see?"

Breathless, she didn't voice her acerbic thought: *That was a little distraction? Right, just like a hundred car pile-up on the interstate is.*

"Prepare yourself, Elizabeth. I pour the chocolate now."

She thought she was ready, but she wasn't.

Chapter 9

Really Hot Chocolate

A burning pain landed, just above her right breast and Elizabeth expelled her breath. Sir, with hands on her shoulders to steady himself, bent over, pressing his erect cock into her stomach. Then he licked her skin clean. The skin itself felt okay. It was perhaps a little sensitive. She was certainly more aware of the small section that had suffered the insult of burning hot liquid poured on her tender flesh.

"I can see the small part I dripped chocolate on, the skin it has become a little red. It does not hurt?"

"Yes it hurts! I don't want it on...on anything really sensitive," she said unthinkingly. As Sir had not reinstituted his rules, she was still able to speak. But maybe not speaking had its advantages. She shouldn't have articulated her desire. That was like red to a bull, he simply had to override her fears then. What was going on in that devious brain of his?

"*Vraiment?*" he asked, strangely pleased with this information. "*Bon.* I avoid these areas." A number of drops fell then, covering her right breast in the raised pillow part, but not the circular areola that surrounded her nipple, nor her nipple itself. She sucked in her breath at the pain, but said nothing. Sir, with a low growl and odd lustful humming noise, began to ravish her, licking the chocolate off. Again Elizabeth found herself breathing in – but this time not with pain. His additional use of French was a dead giveaway, as was his hard on. Sir was getting seriously turned on with the whole 'lick the chocolate off her' thing.

"It is better, no?" he asked.

"It's alright," Elizabeth replied noncommittally. There was pain, but there was also pleasure from Sir's tongue. The vibrator deep in her back passage did act as a distraction, probably on the same sort of scale as a force ten earthquake on the Richter Scale. Sir's devil blessed tongue was of an even greater magnitude of disturbance. She wanted to sob with joy every time he caressed her with it. His every action seemed calculated to madden her.

Elizabeth tried to move, but couldn't. Still her stupid, sexually demanding body was switched on. It writhed and twitched in minute increments, probably only visible under a microscope – or to Sir's observant eyes. Her pussy contracted and she felt new wetness dripping between her legs. There was so much of it she could smell her own arousal over the chocolate, or was that just her imagination?

Damn the man! How does he do this? He drips hot chocolate on me, and I drip sex on his chair.

Yet there was another smell, too. As Sir moved away he left a trail of pre-cum on her stomach. *Good! Let him be hot and needy too.* Once more her pussy spasmed, just knowing that he was hard and wanting her. *Fuck me, please fuck me,* but she wasn't going to ask. There was no doubt that Sir wanted her to beg, and damn it anyway! She wasn't going to. Not this time.

Sir worked on her – it was the only term that explained his actions - for some time, burning and then stimulating her skin with his teeth, his tongue and mouth. Every part of her breasts, stomach, pussy and thighs – anything not covered by the strange cloth binding had been touched by hot drops of chocolate. Only the areola areas, nipples and clit had been left alone – at her specific request.

A heated pool of lust had been building inside her throughout, smoldering outward from low in her core, climbing up through her belly and traveling with waves throughout her body. She was trembling, quivering with need and he still wasn't going to let her come. She just knew it.

This arousing process continued until Sir had made every exposed part of her flesh red. The chocolate remained hot and burned each time, when she felt it should have cooled at least a little bit by now. When she had asked about it Sir chuckled and said he had the stuff on a warmer, at a set temperature. Elizabeth snorted, feeling she should have known.

"Elizabeth," he said in a low husky voice. "I want to pour chocolate on your nipples. I want to cover your breasts. I think it will hurt very much."

Lust disappeared, to be replaced by fear. Licking her lips, she pressed them together and thought about it. Her answer was no. But he was going to do it anyway. So she said nothing.

The vibrator switched off. "*Ma chèrie?* Speak."

"I can't stop you," she finally said in a sour voice.

He laughed and caressed her breasts and nipples with both hands, pressing his cock against her pussy, but always avoiding her swollen clit. She shuddered with need as he held her breasts up, pulling against their bondage, feeling the weight of them. "These are *tres bella*. I will hurt them, and then I will lick and soothe them and make them better." His hands left her breasts and he backed away, taking the heat of his cock and thighs from her and placing his hand, one on each knee. "Tell me, *ma chèrie*, why do you like to suck my cock? For I know you do like it very much."

Unconsciously, she shrugged, which didn't work at all, restrained as she was. So strange to be unable to move. With as deep a breath as possible while constricted as she was, she said, "I really don't know. Maybe it is the female oral thing, the unfilled places you talk about. All I know is that I just do."

"*Bon*," he said. "*Ma chèrie*, do you want to know what I want?"

Elizabeth shivered, filled with lust and nervous anxiety. My God, did she want to know what he wanted? Probably not. Because the truth was, whatever he wanted, she was pretty sure that she would want to give it to him.

 *Chapter 10*

What Sir Wants

Elizabeth sighed and said, "Tell me what you want, Sir."

"Good girl. I will. Why I like this —who can say? You say, '*All I know is that I just do.*' *Bon.* It is the same for me. When I spanked you, *ma chèrie,* it made me hard. I like to make the buttocks pink, to see you squirm and hear you squeal. Yet I would have enjoyed this more if I did not have to force the spanking. If you were willing to be hurt and wanted it – just to make me hard and to please me. Do you understand?"

"I think so, Sir."

"And if Mark wanted to dress himself in feminine erotic apparel during sex, would this disturb you?"

She laughed, a picture of her large husband donning a lacy pink bra and panties, or even a thong! Sir laughed with her for a bit, as the picture of her rugged husband Mark dressed like that was hard to ignore. But when he became quiet and she understood it was a serious question. "Ah, let me see." She considered for a moment, imagining that life, with a husband who got off on wearing women's underwear. "Well, Sir, it wouldn't bother me, actually."

"Why?"

"Because, Sir, I love him, and if that is what got him hard that is probably what would get me hot, too."

It was Sir's turn to laugh unexpectedly, and when he did it was a joyous sound of pleasure. "*Ma chèrie*, you are such a treasure. I so love women. At their best they make the most generous, unselfish and giving lovers of all. You are such a woman, Elizabeth, I think. Your husband, as I have said before, is a very lucky man."

She felt herself blush, unexpectedly embarrassed by this praise. "Thank you, Sir."

"Elizabeth, I can see you do not enjoy the pain, as some do. This arouses me greatly. But will you take it for me? Because I wish it? Because it makes me hard? I can overrule you, yes, of course. You are mine for six more days. But I am glad that you do not enjoy pain. *J'adore* that you may be willing take it from me because *I* want it. Not only because you chose to submit to me, but because you know how much I need and want this. That you would do something you do not like, to generously bestow pleasure." His voice was deep and intent and he took a deep breath in. "To have this power over you, Elizabeth. For you to willingly submit to my desires, even though you do not want it, and it hurts you, this is what I crave."

While he had been talking in that compelling, charismatic voice of his, Sir had also been idly stroking one thigh. "I want to hurt you, *ma chèrie*. Then I want to be the one to relieve and ease your hurt, as I did with the nipple clamps. Can you understand this desire?"

"I think so." Those nipple clamps. Who would have thought that biting pain could be so damn hot? She was frightened of the feelings Sir aroused in her. Not love, no there was no concern that she may fall in love with him. But lust, hell yes. She reflected on what he had said, *"Women are generous, unselfish and giving lovers."* Elizabeth couldn't argue with that. Was it instinct? Some primal feminine need? Because for some unknown reason she really did want to please Sir, to make him happy, to make him laugh. *And most of all to make him come,* she thought and her whole body flushed with lust.

But Elizabeth also needed and wanted his approval. *I'm so screwed,* she thought. *Stockholm Syndrome.* But there was no getting around it. "You are not talking about real damage, right? No scars or anything?" she asked.

"There will be no permanent marks, my pledge on it."

With a deep breath out, Elizabeth said, "Go ahead, then. Do what you want, Sir. I'm willing."

"Elizabeth, are you sure?" he asked. There will be no turning back if you agree to do this for me," he warned. "But," he said with a lowered voice, "I promise that you will not regret it."

Alright already! Her mind shouted. She was nervous enough as it was, and just wanted to get it over with. "Sir…I'm sure."

"*Bon.*" Sir moved toward her, she felt and heard him and then one hand touched her shoulder. He leaned over and gave her a chaste kiss on the cheek. "Will you tell me why, *ma chèrie?* Why do you choose to serve me in this way?"

A flush of heat came to her face. Sir stroked her neck and jaw, brushing his hand over the sensitive shell of her ear. He bent closer and nibbled her earlobe and then bit it, sending echoes of sensation to every intimate area of her body. "Speak, *ma chèrie,*" he said in a soft seductive whisper. "Tell me this thought that shames you and causes your pale flesh to blush so prettily. Do not lie or try to hide it."

By rights she could say that she was turned on by him, or that she loved his accent…almost any truth would do. It wouldn't really be a lie. But he had messed with her mind enough, and she was too vulnerable to be caught out. Already she wondered if he could read her mind. She expelled a large breath of air and cleared her throat. "For some strange reason I do want to please you. I'm embarrassed, because it is an irrational desire and I can't believe how stupid I am. Do I want to be set free? Yes. Do I want to be safe at home with my husband, Mark? Yes. But the strongest desire I have right now – that I simply cannot comprehend, is that I want to make you happy."

Elizabeth was surprised by his instant, kind of sweet, open mouthed kiss. It would have curled her toes – if she had been able to move them. Yet as far as she was able, she opened herself to that kiss, that acknowledgment and basked in his approval.

"Bonne fille, bella fille," he said. "Elizabeth, you are all that is best in a woman. You will please me, *ma chèrie*, and in doing so you will please yourself very much." His voice changed to a more commanding tone. "And now, the rules return. Do not speak, Elizabeth, unless you ask permission. My plan for today and tomorrow was for you to understand that being powerless leads to orgasm. I thought it would take longer for you to realize this, so already so much of my work is done."

What? She thought. *He had planned to make her understand her sexual desire for restraint? But why?*

Just then the vibrator surged on, sending tendrils of pleasure through her body, and her question was lost, overwhelmed by sensation and desire.

Chapter 11

Pain

The vibrator in her ass started up again, set on low. Sir bent over her and industriously worked on her nipples, licking, biting and sucking. Elizabeth began to keen and moan with bliss.

"*Oui, oui*, this feels good, no?"

"Yes," she said, wallowing in the pleasure of his lips and mouth and tongue.

He took his mouth away from her left breast and the pain was immediate. Hot chocolate poured over one aureola and nipple and she screamed out with surprise and pain. Sir ignored her and bent over to once more hungrily lick and suck, removing all the chocolate from her abused tissues. As he did he also put a hand between her legs, gently sliding one finger inside her slick channel and stroked her with delicate precision. Elizabeth shivered and made an involuntary, inarticulate sound, a cross between a plea and sob.

Sir gave a short bark of laughter and began licking the other nipple, while skillfully fingering her throbbing pussy. When his mouth left her breast this time she tensed, expecting pain, but instead his mouth returned to the other breast, and then lower, giving her clit a number of small, delicate licks. While he licked and her attention was *there* the hot chocolate unexpectedly fell – this time on her other breast and again she cried out.

Sweating, sobbing and moaning, Elizabeth had no choice except to endure as Sir continued the onslaught until suddenly to her surprise, about a half a cup full of hot chocolate poured over her pussy and engorged clit. This time she really did scream. Sir immediately went to work, licking her clean. With both hands he spread her outer lips and spoke French continuously as he nibbled and sucked. Elizabeth thought she understood some words like pretty, and beautiful.

Her poor pussy burned, but Sir was distracting her, taking her entire clit into his mouth, sucking and licking, pulling the hood back with one finger and working over her tender slippery nub. She would have come except for the recent pain, but the pleasure! Her entire body was sensitized and she flooded the chair with her arousal. Sir, psychic as ever, always knew when to stop any skillful manipulation, in order to prevent her achieving orgasm.

This activity went on for some time until Elizabeth was a mindless moaning wreck. The vibrator in her ass continued in a low sensual torment while any pain she experience heightened her sensations. "Please, Sir. Please let me come," she began to chant, totally forgetting that she had decided not to beg.

He laughed. "You did not ask for permission to speak, *ma chèrie*," he said and then went back to licking her slit.

"Please? May I speak," she mumbled unintelligibly.

"Speak," he said.

"Please, Sir…let me come."

He laughed. "You are such a good girl." He stepped away from her then, but kept one hand on her stomach. The odd feel of something moving down across her cheek, along her neck to her breasts surprised her out of her daze. *What? Shit! The riding crop.*

"Ma chèrie, I think you are ready to accept more pain, and me, I am ready to administer it. Elizabeth, my cock is so hard, it drips

– but not as much as you do," he chuckled. "I have been pumping my cock with my fist as it, like you, aches for release. It wants to enter your sweet wet cunt, *ma chèrie*. Your cunt is gaping wide open for me, weeping and perfuming the air, yearning for my cum. When I am finished hurting you I will fuck you so hard you will most certainly be allowed to climax. Does this please you, Elizabeth?"

Muddled as she was, it took a few moments for her to comprehend what Sir had said. Her head was strapped so tight, she was unable to even nod. "Yes, Sir," she eventually rasped.

His voice surprised her, as it suddenly, seductively whispered in her ear from somewhere behind her, "I had planned to not let you come until later this afternoon and only when I had my cock deep in your ass, *ma chèrie*. But now, I change my mind."

Without warning, and no preparation, two hard strikes fell on each of her nipples – one, two and she screamed out loud. Sir's hands immediately soothed and caressed her breasts and then his tongue joined in. Elizabeth breathed through the throbbing sting but found it didn't last long. The pain came and left, leaving a pleasant hot glow, sensitizing her sensitive skin. Sir moved lower, his fingers flicked her clit, and his hand rubbed her pussy, and all the while he spoke seductively, telling her how happy she was making him, how beautiful she looked with red welts across her white breasts, and how hard and red her abused nipples were.

Two more strikes came, again without any warning and again she cried out. They each hit her nipples, yet struck another part of her breasts. She imagined that they crisscrossed and she would look like a checkerboard soon. Yet she didn't care. The pleasure and pain had combined together into an amazing ball of erotic sensation.

"It is good, yes?" he crooned in a deep, lust filled voice. "Shall I give you more?"

 *Chapter 12*

Pussy Whipped

Elizabeth was desperate now, willing to take anything if she was simply allowed to climax. She said, "Sir, I can't think. Just...please, let me come," and even to her own mind she sounded pathetic.

"Soon, *j'assure ma chèrie*," he soothed her in a low hoarse voice. "You are so beautiful. But it does not hurt, does it? Not anymore. They are very close together, both pleasure and pain. When I take you in the ass I will first stripe it well, and it will be so much more ready and willing to take my cock."

Elizabeth gave a sort of strangled moan at his words and her pussy spasmed. Her mind reeled with the vision of him whipping her backside hard enough to leave red welts - then him bending her over the bed and pushing his big cock inside. Swallowing, Elizabeth licked her lips. *Shit*, she thought. *Even butt fucking sounded hot right now. If only he would let me come maybe I could get some sense of balance.* But she was too mindless - lost to pleasure - lost to pain and there was nothing she could do about it except experience and endure.

Sir stepped back from her and she tensed, certain he was going to whip her breasts again, but this time two sharp hits landed directly upon the outer swollen lips of her pussy. Her scream this time reverberated through the room.

"*Bon, bon, ma chèrie*, you take it very well," he encouraged. Then he had his mouth over the painful area, sucking and relieving the sting, licking, tasting, while making erotic comments such as "Ah, *pauvre*, see how it weeps? It cries for my cock," and "This oh so gorgeous cunt tastes like honey." He soothed her throbbing pussy for some time, and when he pushed three fingers up into her slick and dripping channel; it clamped down upon him hard.

"*Oui, oui, ma chèrie*," he groaned with his mouth against her pussy, his voice thick with his own lust. "Such a good girl, my so beautiful slut." He softly stroked her outer lips, where he had struck them with the riding whip. "So red and swollen now, *ma chèrie*. Do you feel how enlarged and distended your needy cunt is now that it has been punished? And so red! *C'est magnifique*, this ripe plump peach," he said using his whole hand to cup and grip her sex. "The way you look to me now, bound and spread before me, swollen scarlet, and aching for my cock. *Mon Dieu*, I want to fuck you. Did it hurt very much?"

"Yes! It hurt like hell, Sir."

He laughed and she heard soft footfalls as he circled her, with one hand still possessively gripping her pussy. Moving near her head, he whispered sensually into her ear, "But it is not pain you feel now, no?

She took a deep breath. "No, Sir."

"*Bon*. It throbs, it is swollen, and it is very sensitive." He stood back from her, withdrawing his hand. "You will feel it all the better when I push inside you, deep into your cunt. Prepare yourself Elizabeth, for I give you three more strikes, now."

"Sir! No!" she protested.

"Yes," he said. "To please me you will take two more strikes on this needy cunt and the last will fall very hard on your oh so swollen clit. But this time you will not tense, *ma chèrie*. This time I want you to remain open, embrace this pain and accept it willingly. It is my gift to you, to add to your pleasure. Can you try for me?"

Elizabeth's breath was coming fast and short and her entire body tingled. She was reluctant and she was scared, but she knew that her resistance and inevitable compliance turned him on.

His compelling voice whispered, "Do you wish to please me *ma chèrie?*"

"Yes, Sir," she whispered and her throbbing pussy pulsed and contracted in a physical expression of affirmation. Because she did want to please him, and she wanted his hot cum more than anything and these crazy feelings were visceral and primal and so basic to her personality that they could not be excised. He had burned her barriers and all that was left was her. Beneath the tough no nonsense trial lawyer was a needy sexual slave. Knowing she was a slut didn't disturb her and being a lawyer no longer seemed as important as she used to imagine.

"Have I not bound you to my will, *ma chèrie?*" he asked, tugging her bindings, underlining her constraint. "Have I not taken away your choices?"

At these erotic words Elizabeth's gut twisted and something lower clenched. Once more her pussy flooded alarmingly. "Yes, yes, Sir," she said, knowing that she had already surrendered.

"I control everything, do I not? Even your breathing?" His palm and fingers rested softly against her neck.

Elizabeth moaned. She would've writhed at these words - if she had been able to move. Once if he had touched her throat she'd have been frightened, but now she only felt pleasure, for she had ceased fighting.

"I reward you with my cock, very soon, *ma chèrie*," he said and Elizabeth whimpered, needy, desperate and no longer off balance. Everything was up to him. Sir no longer had to wrest control from her: she had given it all to him willingly. It was irrational, it was insane, but it was also an essential need – like air, food and water – something she could not deny.

"Take these three last strikes *ma chèrie*," he said, gently cupping her face and giving her a soft, chaste kiss on the lips. Stroking her breasts, he added, "I want to watch you embrace the torment of my riding crop. Do not tense. Trust me, this pain will enhance your orgasm, do you understand? Accept these last strikes for me, for my pleasure and yours. Will you do this? For me?"

Elizabeth took a deep steadying breath. "Yes, Sir," she said and she meant it.

"Good girl," he said and his deep lust-filled voice touched her like a sensual caress. Fire burned instantly then, twice more her pussy was hit, in slightly different spots than before, and then finally, the last strike landed directly upon her swollen clit.

Elizabeth screamed and screamed. The setting to her vibrator changed, turning into pulse and high and she screamed and screamed some more. When the vibrator in her ass returned to low her screaming stopped and she only twitched and whimpered from pleasure or pain or shocks of both. She heard Sir back away from her and she tensed, worried and uncertain about another strike and where it may land.

Or was it over?

Chapter 13

Pleasure

As usual he read her mind. "The pain is over, *ma chèrie*. Now there will be only pleasure."

"Thank God! Yes, yes, fuck me," she said. "Please I need you, Sir." In a sensual daze, Elizabeth had been awakened somewhat by her throbbing and physically abused clit.

He laughed. "*Eh bien*. Not yet. I restrain myself, Elizabeth, I want to touch you, but I will not. Not until you climax. For now, I think I can make you come with nothing but this vibrator on low. Your body is bound, completely restrained, *n'est-ce pas?* Do you think you can do it? Will you come for me? It would please me very much if you did."

What? She thought, *Climax with nothing? Just because he said so?* "How?" she asked. "How Sir? How can I do that?"

His voice was deep and commanding as he said, "*Ma chèrie*, you will do it because I order it, because it is my will."

Elizabeth took a deep breath and every nerve in her body quivered. Instinctively she recognized his power over her and wanted to comply with his wishes. But how could she come? With no physical stimulation other than being tied up and a vibrator in her ass? Yet Sir had said she would, so perhaps she could.

Sir was walking around her when he stopped speaking, his voice deep and low as he told her how hard she made him, and all the while he told her she would come exactly when he told her to, and she would come because he wished it. Her body would obey him, because it was his to command. She had no will in this, he informed her.

"Elizabeth," he said. "Take a deep breath, yes deeper. But you cannot breathe deeply can you?" he reminded her. "Because I control everything, even the air you inhale." He placed his hand against the cloth restraint on her neck, a simple message, recalling the memory. Once again her pussy spasmed and a flood of arousal gushed from within her, dripping onto the chair. Sir restrained her, controlled her breathing, controlled all completely.

Everything was his will.

And the truth was - she liked it that way.

Explosive heat was building inside of her from the erotic words and images he gave her, and she tried to thrash and squirm but the bindings held her still. Forced to be motionless also put her whole body on the boil. She wanted to jump and arch, bite and scratch. To touch him, to touch herself! There was too much energy mounting inside her and nowhere for it to go.

"You must use your mind, Elizabeth. Speak to me of what you imagine every time you masturbate. Tell me in detail of how Mark fucked you. I want to hear it."

She got into the head space she usually was in when she masturbated, and began to talk in detail. It was always the same thing, Mark and her at the wedding. Something about that time just did it for her, the way the man took over, and used her body, rutting upon her like the big animal he was. The way she had pleased him. The magnificent unremitting spurts of his hot, thick cum.

"Touch me, Sir," she begged. "Please touch me and fuck me hard, like Mark did."

"*Non*. Not yet. But I will be inside you as you come I swear it, *ma chèrie*. I want my cock to be squeezed by that oh so strong cunt of yours, and you are very close now, aren't you?"

"Yes!" she screamed. Tears rolled down her cheeks, sweat dripped from her skin and she was panting and breathless, yet bound so tightly she couldn't move. Almost there, right on the edge, but how to go over? For she couldn't imagine how to climax without physical stimulation. "Yes, I'm close, Sir, I want to but I can't. I can't!"

"You can," Sir said with a combination of confidence and deceptive mildness. Elizabeth felt that beneath that calm voice was a ruthless persona, a man that would not accept no. He was someone who would always get what he wanted.

"You can and you will," he assured her, and there was a frightening aspect to his voice. Sir was making a demand of her and she had to obey. A thrill of fear rolled through her, for this man was stronger than her - and he was dangerous. Something crystallized within her mind then, something she knew to be true.

Oh God, she thought. *Sir soooo reminds me of Mark!*

Her captor was between her legs now, she could feel the heat of him radiating near her spread thighs, and she was thrilled with the idea that he would enter her as she climaxed.

"*Ma chèrie.* Your cunt is wet, you flood this chair. Come for me, I want to see it. Come. Do it! Now! For me!"

She was close…so close! Almost over that edge! She felt it then – the heat within her core, pooling and spreading as she began to climax. Her body tried to thrust, her back to arch, her head to thrash back and forth, her toes to curl yet restrained as she was she could do none of these things. She was bound by Sir's will, and that one thought caused another flood of arousal. Unable to move, Elizabeth had to take everything from him – everything - anything - or nothing. The choices were all his.

"Scream for me, *ma chèrie,*" he ordered. "Scream your orgasm."

And as it was an unassailable command from the man who controlled her completely, she did.

Chapter 14

Orgasms by his Command

As she started to go over, Elizabeth's abused cunt and clit throbbed and pulsed violently. At that exact point, with perfect timing, Sir thrust his cock inside her, stretching her heated channel. Relief flooded her as he slammed inside, his heated hips and thighs up hard against her.

The vibrating toy filled her back passage, and Sir filled her pussy. Elizabeth groaned from profound bliss as her needy body comprehensively expanded to accommodate both toy and man. Convulsing with animal delight, her cunt clamped down hard on Sir's thick shaft. Unable to physically move and express such intense explosive pleasure, Elizabeth sobbed and screamed and screamed and screamed until her voice was hoarse.

It was ecstasy – ecstasy!

Multiple, endless orgasms rolled over her in a combination of sensations. Every part of her was hyperaware and totally sensitized. Her hard nipples were aching, her breasts tender from being whipped, her swollen pussy and abused clitoris, her skin red and humming with sensation from being burned by hot chocolate and then being bit and licked by Sir's tongue and teeth. And all the while she experienced this totally motionless bondage. All her choices had been taken away.

Sir thrust inside her, in and out in an even, unvaried rhythm while masturbating her clit with one hand and firmly gripping one hip in another. She had flooded his cock with her essence, and he moved in and out with slick ease.

Elizabeth twitched and convulsed in aftershocks, exhausted, and exhilarated with her mind floating on a sea of pleasure. Nothing was as she had imagined. Sex was never as important to her as she had learned from this one day with her captor. Until the experiences of today she had never really understood the value of such intimacy. This was who she was, this feminine sexual being.

The toy in her ass had stopped vibrating, but Sir had not come. She became aware that Sir was still thrusting in an even pattern, and that he was still manipulating her clit. *No! No!* she thought. *It is too much, my clit is still so tender!*

"Sir, may I speak?"

"You may," he said, never varying his measured thrusts.

"Oh God Sir, that hurts. My clit is so sore."

"I don't care, *ma chèrie*. I have decided that you will come once more. I enjoyed it so much. To watch you display such pleasure, to see you try so hard to move while constrained by full bondage while you climaxed again and again. I loved the sounds you made. For me, it was very exciting."

"I can't!" she said, focused on his fingers abusing her clit. "Sir! It hurts, it is too much. Please stop."

"No," he said with a voice of command, and Elizabeth was distracted from the painful stimulus between her legs. It was as if a whip had cracked. All her attention was focused on him. "You will come for me again, Elizabeth," he told her. "You will come for me. Right now."

The powerful almost frightening force of his command, the sensation of his cock, rubbing in and out of her slick channel and filling her so completely, the toy, deep and heavy in her back passage, the feel of fingers manipulating her clit, masturbating her exactly as she masturbated herself was too much for her. So much stimulation! Her entire body throbbed and unbelievably another orgasm flashed through her, powerfully exploding and shattering every logical thought.

"Oh God!" she cried out and then wailed. "Ah! Ah! Ah!" And she moaned and whimpered and her pussy clenched him *hard*.

"*Bonne fille*," he said, powerfully thrusting inside her, immersing himself ball deep into her pulsing pussy. Reaching across her body he bent with his hands squeezing her breasts and nipples. Then he kissed her possessively, ravishing her with his tongue, taking everything he wanted. "You are a very good girl," he said in a hoarse seductive whisper.

Lightheaded and in a daze, Elizabeth felt him withdraw from her, and became aware that his cock was still hard. Sir had not come, she could not smell him. But she sure had. People living outside this room and down the hall could probably pick up the heavy, sweet scent of her sexual arousal and satisfaction. In her mindless happy daze, Elizabeth heard the refrigerator door open and shut. A straw was placed to her lips.

"Drink, *ma chèrie*," he said. "You need fluids, after all you have lost through perspiration and your oh so dripping sex. But I pleased you, did I not?" He stroked her hair and kissed her cheek. "I release you now and then you will please me."

Sir unwrapped her bindings rapidly while Elizabeth shivered from aftershocks and sprawled against the large chair, boneless and unable to move. With a fireman's lift he put her over his back and carried her over, placing her against a wall, "You will come again now, *ma chèrie*."

"Oh Sir, I couldn't, I really couldn't."

He laughed. "Oh, but you will. By my command, by my will, you will come while I fuck you as your husband Mark did." His firm body pressed against her, pushing her tight against the wall. "You make me so hot *ma chèrie*. Do you want to come for me? Tell me what you want."

"I want to come, Sir."

"Good girl," he chuckled, well aware of her reticence. "Yes, but why? Why do you want to come?"

She gasped, and gave a strange choking giggle that quickly turned into a laugh. "I don't really want to. I have had more orgasms in the last hour than I have in the last six months. I actually just want to curl up and go to sleep! I only wanted to come now to please you."

He nuzzled into her neck, licking it, nibbling and blowing softly on her moistened skin, sending delightful sensations through her. "To please me?" he asked, biting and sucking on one nipple.

"Yes, Sir. I want to do everything, anything you want, anytime you want it. Right now I swear I feel like you own me."

Elizabeth was instantly rewarded with a male sound of pleasure - kind of a growl - as his lips pressed against hers and he forced her mouth open with his tongue. His kiss was an instant response, searing and intense and she fell into it, reaching, needing, wanting. His large body pushed hard against her as he pressed closer, crushing her against the wall, flattening her breasts against his chest. His naked sweating skin felt hot upon hers, his cock was hard and throbbing. Elizabeth was thrilled by his well apparent desire and this close to him she could feel his heart rapidly beating.

"You were made to please a man, *ma chèrie*, this is your most basic desire. Tell me how it was with your husband Mark. We re-live this fantasy you recall so well."

"Ah, humm," she said. "Sir, first he pinned me to the wall, and I tried to push him away."

Sir surged up against her and instinctively she put her hands out against his bare chest, trying to stop him. With a gasp she said, "Yes! Exactly like that."

Grabbing her wrists, Sir held them one in each hand, above and on each side of her head. "The big man, he moved your arms away, perhaps like this?"

Elizabeth was panting and tingling all over. Sir held her firmly against the wall - she couldn't even breath in deeply. That was how it was with Mark, his body had almost crushed hers and she loved it. "Ah, well, no, he took both of my hands with one hand, his left."

Sir immediately transferred both of her wrists into the strong grip of his left hand. "And with the other, he ran it up your legs, yes?" As he spoke his other hand trailed demandingly up her thigh. His voice was deep and low as he said, "Up inside the dress to pull the panties down? To reach in and grasp your sex?" As he spoke he cupped her mound, gripping it possessively.

Elizabeth gasped. "Yes, yes and then Mark somehow lifted me off my feet and I threw my legs around him."

Sir pushed up, taking her off her feet and then he penetrated her to the hilt. Elizabeth shrieked. With his left hand in a bruising grip holding her wrists above her head, and his right firmly gripping her buttocks, he moved, not horizontally – more at a vertical angle. Pushing upwards into her needy cunt, he held her up against the wall with his powerful, demanding cock. In an animal frenzy Elizabeth wantonly threw her legs around him, high up on his waist, pulling her to him as he thrust.

"This is right, *ma chèrie?*" he grunted in a husky voice.

"Oh God yes! Exactly right!"

"It was a very fast fuck, was it not?"

"Hell yes! Ah, ah, ah!" she began to moan. "Yes, yes like that. A hard fast fuck, my God!"

Sir powerfully thrust and thrust, he hammered into her, right to the hilt. Each time his hard male flesh beat solidly against her with a resounding slap, slap, slap. The sound was more like that of a boxing ring than that of making love. Sir's thick cock impaled her harder, faster, with punishing, bruising blows and all the time he never faltered, never stopped. As his straining body pounded himself inside her Elizabeth shrieked, "Yes, yes, yes!"

"You will come for me now, *ma chèrie*," he growled. "Because it is my will. Because it pleases me to see and feel you climax as you did for Mark."

"Oh, oh, oh, oh, Sir..." she whimpered. Mindless, panting and breathless with need she cried out. The man had made his point on both her mind and her body. Sir had mastered her completely and she had no choice but to obey him. A hard convulsion took her, starting from within her core, and she jerked and arched spasmodically as if touched by a high tension wires. As the jolt passed through her she shook violently, and her slick sheath clamped down upon Sir's thrusting cock. Screaming, Elizabeth came and came and came in a wave of multiple orgasms.

The world had narrowed. For Elizabeth, there was only the feel of her ass filled by the large toy, her swollen clit, her breasts and cunt and Sir's hard cock - still powerfully hammering her flesh - his large body binding her to his will. Her heart was pounding loudly in her ears and her clit throbbed and pulsed - synchronized with the rapid beat of her heart. Sir stiffened, shuddered and then gave a deep male groan of pleasure. With one final buck he grunted the last of his release. His thick cock sprayed his seed, jetting it deeply within her. When the warmth of his hot sperm touched her cervix, Elizabeth felt another wave of pleasure roll through her in an even more intense climax.

Sobbing mindlessly with pleasure, as Elizabeth came this time, the deep visceral memory of that one life changing moment with Mark enveloped her.

Blissful, utterly fulfilled, she screamed, "Mark!"

Chapter 15

Bodily Functions

Sanity and conscious awareness returned. Elizabeth woke in the bed, with Sir spooning her, his front to her back, and he was touching her, stroking her back, her head and her hair - petting her really. Her entire body ached in a pleasant way, as it did the day after serious exercise. Not an unpleasant feel, a used feeling. Smiling, she gave a little giggle. *Used,* she thought. *That was for sure.*

"*Ma chèrie,*" he said in a smooth voice, "You have come back to me."

"Yes," she said. She didn't know what else to say because, hey, she had just had what felt like hours of the most intense sex she had ever experienced and it had been wonderful.

Sir jumped out of bed, and Elizabeth heard him walk over to the kitchen area, open the fridge and pour something liquid into a glass. "Drink," he said when he returned. Sitting up, and putting her legs to the floor, even though she was blindfolded she held her hand out for the glass.

"No," he said. "It is my privilege to care for you. Hands behind your back. Lace your fingers together."

Elizabeth's mind reeled as she was still dazed with pleasure. Sir had caused her pain, but not as a punishment. He had hurt her to increase her pleasure, and man oh man, it had really done that! Sir kept her blindfolded and confined, but not as a prisoner, but because he preferred that she be dependent on him. Right now her captor wanted to be the one to do everything for her. It was a weird paradigm shift for her to embrace, but through his actions he was teaching her. In the course of one day she had already become a willing student.

She did as he said, and allowed him to serve her, giving her orange juice from a straw. She felt him place soft, fur-lined cuffs on each wrist, and join them together binding her wrists behind her back. As she had to use the toilet, Sir was more than happy to oblige her, guiding her to the facilities. Still burdened with her butt plug, Elizabeth really needed to go "number two," yet Sir refused to leave her. Reminding her of the rules, he said that she was allowed to eat, drink, sleep, wash, use the toilet only with his consent. Sir placed her over his lap, and told her to take a deep breath.

With a gentle pull, Elizabeth felt the butt plug withdrawing from her. When she had an involuntary clench, Sir paused. "Just breathe, *ma chèrie*," he said. Elizabeth licked her lips, and did so. Sir finished taking the toy out of her backside and put it down somewhere. This was embarrassing enough, but however was she ever going to do a number two in front of him?

In the end her normal bodily functions prevailed. Sir wiped her clean with a warm soapy washcloth, cheerfully assuring her that this was normal and he, also, did this "Oh – often!" She had giggled at that.

Afterwards he laid her across his lap and gave her a thorough enema. *Another first,* she thought bitterly. *This just keeps getting better.* Sir blithely informed her that an enema was not really necessary, with her young firm flesh, but as he intended to take her virgin ass he did not wish there to be any problems. "All must be perfect for the first time, you understand?"

Elizabeth suffered every indignity, because she really had no choice. Yet Sir made every action so functional and commonplace, that she found it more than bearable. Not comforting precisely, but Sir was enjoying himself through moving her around like a doll, controlling her completely while looking after her every need and she felt happy that he was happy. And what really rocked this storm burdened boat of insanity was the fact that with all Sir's lavish attentions – as unusual as they were - Elizabeth really felt cherished and cared for.

Elizabeth frowned, well aware of the man's hard cock pressing against her. Draped across his lap, her cuffed hands were behind her back where Sir confidently held them. It was a potent message, with his hand firmly holding both of hers captive and bound behind her. *I am in control of you. You have no power here. You are mine to do with as I please.* While this powerful physical message had initially disturbed her, it unsettled her for an entirely different reason now. By controlling her so completely, Sir really turned her on.

Sir always started using more French when he was sexually excited, and it was clear that her backside was certainly a trigger. He tugged at her captured hands. "*Ma chèrie*, if I release them do they sit *confortable* here behind your back?"

"Yes, Sir."

"You will tell me if it is disagreeable? I do like to hold them, but just now I wish to use both hands to explore and take pleasure in your oh so amazing ass."

She couldn't help it, she just had to laugh and he laughed with her. The man had a thing about her backside. Whatever he planned, she was beginning to look forward to going along for the ride.

Chapter 16

Elizabeth's Derrière

"*Bon, ma chèrie*," he said, "And so I begin." One finger pushed against her anus and then inside her to the knuckle and her stupid pussy immediately flooded. Sir, whose thigh had received her dripping arousal gave a low chuckle. "It will feel *tres bon, ma chèrie*, to take you here," he crooned lovingly. "You will enjoy it very much."

He nuzzled against her neck, licking and nipping as he continued to push that finger inside, pulling and stretching her taut ring with determined fervor. His other hand moved between her legs to lightly stroke her sopping wet pussy. In a husky voice he said, "I want very much to fuck this tight, untouched ass."

Elizabeth moaned unsure if it was his words or what he was doing that caused this reaction.

"You are my little sex slave aren't you? I am going to speak to your husband Mark about how to give you orgasms. He has clearly been doing it all wrong."

"Oh my God no!" Elizabeth said, tensing and struggling against him. "Don't do that! Mark will know we have been having sex, and he will be so angry! Not only that, he will think I'm a slut."

Sir chuckled. "But Elizabeth, you are a slut," Sir said. His fingers ran down her cheek and he cupped her face gently. "It is in your nature. Do not feel shame for this. It is a wonderful gift for you and for your husband." Sir's clever, calming hands began to caress and fondle her in a comforting manner, touching every part of her with long strokes and alternating with concentric circles. "You called Mark's name, when you climaxed, did you know?"

"Yes," she said, anxious that Sir might be upset that she had been thinking of Mark.

"It is very good, *ma chèrie*," he said, perceptively aware of her concern. "I envy this husband of yours. You and I, together we have sex and respect. But with you and Mark there is love, no?"

"Yes. He really is my best friend. I don't know what I'd do without him."

"You will not lose him, *ma chèrie*. I will manage this unmanageable husband of yours, this I swear. He is very *difficile*, no? But I have days to find the lever that will work on him. It is for me to tell him what we do together, and for me to resolve your concerns."

"Sir," she said in a high anxious voice. "Must you tell him?"

Sir's warm, knowledgeable hands massaged and calmed her, distracting her from her problem. "I will tell him and he will yell and be very angry. But I will make certain that he is not angry with you, *ma chèrie*. You are mine and I will not let you be harmed. I thought you trusted me. Do you still trust me?"

His voice, comfortable and reassuring, helped. *Hypnotized as I am, of course I trust him. If I had no cuffs on I'd probably not attempt to leave unless Sir said it was time to go,* she thought. *Stockholm Syndrome. I'm so screwed,*

"Do you?" Sir repeated.

"Yes, Sir," Elizabeth admitted. "You know that I do."

"It is very well, *ma chèrie*. You make me happy. Tell me, Elizabeth, would you like your husband and me, together to make love to you?"

Elizabeth drew in a deep breath at the unexpected vision this created. The picture was of her cuffed to the bed and Mark thrusting furiously between her legs, while she sucked Sir to completion. The concept made her dizzy with desire. Could anything possibly be better?

Sir's laugh was dark and lustful when he sensed - not to mention felt - her immediate flooding response. "So many ways we could take you, the two of us, fucking your oh so feminine flesh. Both of us, using your body for our pleasure."

Elizabeth's pussy pulsed, reacting to the imagined mental image as well as to his unique French accent. When Sir said "pleasure," with the "s" drawn out it simply gave her chills of desire.

"You do not need to answer," he laughed. "I hear your body screaming yes. *Mon Dieu*, you are the slut *idéal*, Elizabeth. I think I would enjoy to see you come once more, this time while I play with your beautiful *derrière*. You make such wonderful noises when you climax, *ma chérie*. And as you are not fully constrained here upon my lap you will squeal and squirm and thrust delightfully. It is a little reward for us both, you understand?"

"Oh God, Sir," she said. "I'm really tired. I have come so many times already. I honestly don't know if I can."

Sir laughed and laughed at her comment, the sound ringing playfully in her ears. Elizabeth winced. She was so stupid! Of course Sir would see that as a challenge. The man was so confident of his skills, of his control of her that she began to laugh too. If she was dead and buried, Sir would probably still feel that he could make her come.

"And so I begin," he said. Using both hands, he gripped both of her soft buttock cheeks and pulled them open wide, exposing the tender flesh, licking and then breathing hot puffs warm of air against her. As before, Elizabeth felt her anus involuntarily pucker and her back passage clench. Sir gave a deep joyful laugh.

Having been here before, she made no attempt to resist him. Expecting him to insert a finger, she was surprised when he swirled his tongue around the rim of her anus, licking and making erotic male sounds of delight.

Good Lord! That feels good. The man had all of her attention. Even if the room was on fire she probably wouldn't notice. Lightheaded and blissful, she relaxed, only partially listening as he spoke soft erotic words, and licked and worshiped her body. Even with her hands cuffed behind her back, she was not uncomfortable. Once more she curled happily around his strong male legs, pressing her face up against him.

Like a cat lapping cream, Sir simply licked and licked at her hole. Elizabeth moaned and restlessly shifted, trying to press her clit against him. Chuckling darkly, he moved his right hand between her legs, placing his thumb in her dripping pussy. Instinctively she clenched and bucked, and he pulled his hand away just before she found her climax.

"Non, ma chèrie," he said. *"Je suis désolé* you are clearly so *fatigué,* but tired as you are, you do not have permission to come yet."

Chapter 17

Spanking

Elizabeth groaned, wanting to take back her unthinking words. *Not again! Why did I tell him I was too tired to come?*

Sir laughed and went back to work on her. He spoke in French now, long sexy sentences that she couldn't understand. His voice was low and husky and his words charmed her, they were a sensual delight. Meanwhile his lips nibbled, circling her anus, and his left hand pressed a finger inside the tight muscle of her rim, pulling her open and available for his invading tongue.

"Oh God!" she cried out, and he gave a perceptive chuckle and began to lick deep in her asshole, stroking, prodding and curling his tongue inside her.

"Ah, ah, ah, ah," she chanted, moaning and squirming, Elizabeth was on a thin thread now, ready to orgasm. If Sir didn't continuously remove any stimulation when he felt her coming close, she would have climaxed long before.

"Now *ma chèrie*," he finally said, "hold still while I put this larger butt plug into you. *Voyons*, you see? Once more I prepare you for my cock." The larger rubber object pressed against her anus. It was well lubricated, and again it went in a little way, but then stopped. Sir stroked her buttocks. "Do not be anxious, Elizabeth. Pretend this is little toy is me and it will go easier. Because I know you want me to fill that empty place in your body. You want what I want, *ma chèrie*."

This plug was much larger, and it took longer to become situated fully inside. He encouraged her to spread her legs, as it may help, which she did. Laughing he added that he enjoyed seeing her so exposed, and even if it didn't help to insert the plug, it pleased him. "*C'ést très agréable de voir*," he said, by which she gathered that he liked to look at her spread wide - easily accessible and available to him, and to his cock.

Once more using a gentle, soothing voice, Sir slowly breached her, pushing the toy inside, moving it in and out, stretching her. While she sweated and whimpered and panted, he became highly aroused, once more commenting on the sucking action of her taut hole, swearing in French and speaking in a tone of joy and awe. Elizabeth was glad at least someone was having fun. While the damn thing didn't precisely hurt, it felt too full and uncomfortable in her anal passage. Sir was kind and considerate but determined, and Elizabeth tried her best, too. But still, it took single-minded efforts on both their parts before it was fully inside her.

As she laid quivering with effort, draped over his lap, and trying to get used to the uncomfortably full sensation in her back passage, Sir massaged her back, buttocks and shoulders, stroking and easing her tension away. When her breathing was no longer ragged, and she became more accepting of the toy, he asked, "It is better *ma chèrie?*"

She expelled a deep breath. "It's not exactly comfortable, but it's better, Sir."

"*Bon.* You are a small woman, Elizabeth, with a small anal passage. *Mon Dieu*, it is such a tight hole! But this toy is of a full size and my cock is not much larger. You will accustom yourself to this, and later today, when I take your sweet ass, you will be prepared for it, no?"

Elizabeth struggled not to giggle, but gave in with a snort. This entire situation just got crazier and crazier. A virtual stranger was gearing up to butt fuck her and she, to the best of her ability, was helping him to do it.

Sir chuckled and stroked and patted her behind fondly. "All is well. You have endured much from me this day, have you not? But you have enjoyed yourself, too. Yet I am not finished, for I see you here on my lap, with this plug in your ass and I want more."

With these words Elizabeth stiffened. *Uh oh.*

"*Ma chèrie,*" he said in a compelling voice. "I want to spank you now, with my hand. Are you willing to take it? Because I want to hurt you, I want to enjoy your reaction. It will please me very much. But I will only do it if you say you are willing."

She took a deep breath, and reflected that the more she gave this man, the more he wanted. *Good lord. Not again. What was this love hate thing she had going with pain?* Sir had hurt her with that damn chocolate, not to mention the riding crop. Even the thought of that caused a throbbing visceral awareness to her clit. Yet pain increased her pleasure… afterwards. Pain. Elizabeth sure as hell didn't like it…but, Sir did. And because *he* did – *she* did.

Two big realizations of what turned her on pierced her awareness. One: constraint may not always be necessary for orgasm, but when she was bound orgasm came easily and, two: somewhere in her psyche and unable to be expunged was a bone deep need to please. No, not just to please, but to cause pleasure for her sexual partner. Elizabeth had somehow climaxed, just because Sir had wanted it – despite no physical touch of her clit, breasts or pussy. Sir had made her do that on purpose, to prove to her that she could. And how had she been able to do it? She who had been having trouble climaxing with the man she loved?

She had done it to please Sir, and because he commanded it. A thrill of sensual excitement trilled through her just at the thought of that forceful command. *"Yes, ma chèrie. You cunt is wet, you flood this chair. Come for me, I want to see it. Come. Do it! Now. For me."*

She sighed. The man had an agenda of his own, but she knew he was also trying to help her. To make her discover who she really was sexually. Mad abducting kidnapper or not, she owed him. And still it was as if his pleasure was hers. Causing him to experience such bliss was even more satisfying to her than receiving such ecstasy. Sir had said that the desire to please was in her nature. She recalled his quote, *"Life's most obvious truths are the hardest to see but once you've burned everything down to the ground they are the only thing left standing."*

Huh. Well, that was certainly true. Aware that Sir had been stroking and softly massaging her back and buttocks while waiting patiently for her answer, she felt herself smiling a broad smile. "If it will make you happy, Sir, go ahead. I'm willing." She laughed then, finding some strange insouciant release in this decision. "No wait. Here, let me really make your day. Sir, my dear Sir, oh Sir, will you please, please spank me? Will you hurt me? Even though I hate pain I really, really want you to. I want you to spank me because for some reason you love to do it. So I'm begging you, spank me."

He laughed then and kissed, nibbled and stroked her, trailing up her back, to her neck. Right between her neck and shoulder was the place where he had first given her a hickey. He kissed and bit her there once more, but didn't suck. Nuzzling her he said, "You are such a good girl, *ma chèrie*. I am going to make you come very hard. *Inestimable, belle* – if you did not so love this husband of yours I vow I would keep you for myself."

Elizabeth giggled for she knew Sir had no serious intuitions to keep her. His comment was a compliment, a sort of sweet attempt to flirt with her.

Slap!

Sir's palm descended, landing on her buttocks, and it wasn't painful. She realized suddenly that he was left-handed as his right hand had remained between her legs, resting possessively against her pussy. Slapping lightly, Sir covered every part of her bottom, yet there was no real sting. This was not like before, when she had refused to obey him. This was sensual and warming.

From time to time his hand landed on the butt plug and a huge roll of sensation went through her, all of it tantalizing.

"It is not so bad, eh?" he asked. "I warm you up this time, to prepare you. Enjoy what I do, Elizabeth." As he said that he began to massage her clit with two clever fingers, exactly as she did when she masturbated.

He began to strike her harder then, the flat of his hand hitting her rounded buttock, making it wobble and shake. She began to flinch and squirm under each tingling, smarting blow, her body drawn between sensations. Without thinking she raised her bottom up, wanting more attention from that cruel spanking hand, that slapped and heated her buttocks so tantalizingly. Yet she also wanted to push against the fingers that moved between her legs. These two sensations, pleasure and stinging pain warred with each other, combining and becoming a ball of heat and shameless, animal lust.

"Oh God, Sir!" - slap – "May I…" –slap- "…speak?" Elizabeth choked out.

"Yes," he said breathlessly, and his voice was thick with his own desire.

"Please, Sir," – slap – "let me come," – slap- "I need to come!"

"It pleases me, Elizabeth," he said, panting lustfully, and continuing his blows, "to torment you by denying you climax, and by making you accept pain. You may come when you accept more pain. Do you want me to hurt you?"

"Yes, yes, hurt me hurt me - just let me come!"

Sir's hand hit then with a resounding smack, and Elizabeth's pussy flooded his hand, but the pain! *Fucking hell!* She thought. *That really, really hurts.*

"No!" she screamed.

"Yes," he said, delivering another blow that echoed loudly in the bathroom.

Elizabeth shrieked as an intense pulse of sensation rolled through her, taking her breath away. Mercilessly he spanked her, left cheek, right, alternating blows and often hitting her plug. Sweating and panting and crying out unintelligibly, Elizabeth, who no longer had any choice, endured her punishment.

Rhythmically his hand struck her, sending shockwaves through her body, and it felt as if her womb contracted with each one. Her belly clenched and her pussy wept and pulsed and all the while Sir stroked her, tracing her sopping clit and labia, running his fingers around her slit, and never quite going in. Yet his thumb was on her clit now, pulling back the slippery hood and he inserted two fingers within her wet channel.

Elizabeth felt as if her ass and her pussy were both on fire and she screamed – from pain or pleasure, she wasn't sure which, but she just had to put a voice to those overwhelming sensual sensations. A shudder was growing, something huge within her core, and she was trembling uncontrollably. It was huge, it was too much – sensations overwhelmed her.

With her entire body quivering, Sir said, "Now, *ma chèrie*. Come for me." Just then Sir stopped spanking her and did a number of things all at once. He inserted his fingers deep within her aching pussy, pressing against her G spot while his thumb flicked her clit hard, and at the same time he pulled her ass cheeks apart and breached the ring of her anus, tight around the butt plug, with his tongue.

No woman could have stood against such a concerted attack, and Elizabeth was no exception. She screamed and screamed and screamed her orgasm, bucking and shaking and trembling uncontrollably with aftershocks for some time afterwards.

As she lay like a dead thing, Sir washed her between the legs and carefully dried her. Then he removed her handcuffs and pulled her into his arms. "Come, *ma chèrie*," he said softly. "You are tired and it is time for bed." Sir turned her toward him drawing her against his chest. He raised her arms and placed them around him, and then lifted her. Immediately she curled comfortably into his neck and shoulder, yet it was an unconscious response.

For Elizabeth was already asleep.

Chapter 18

Sir's Occupation

Gently, Sir placed her onto the bed. Elizabeth instantly curled on to her side, moving into a loose fetal position, and he chuckled at her trusting body language. The woman did not fear him right now and perhaps never would again. Oh, she might be apprehensive, but she knew his intentions were honorable. He had wanted to help her, and he had. Sir bent over and attached a cuff to her left ankle. The cuff had a long light chain that was attached to the bottom left bed post. Elizabeth, already fast asleep, didn't move.

He sighed, thinking of his aching erection. He should have had her suck him off first, but never mind. He smiled. He had wanted to get at that beautiful *derrière* of hers. Later today his cock would get all it needed, for he planned to come back and take her in the ass later. That was one thing that he would not put off until tomorrow.

Sir reached down and found the sheet and pulled it up over her, tucking her in and then checking the room temperature. Assuring himself that she would not be too cold or too hot, he went to the bathroom and got a warm washcloth. Then he removed her blindfold and washed her tear-stained face, leaving the blindfold off. Elizabeth barely stirred throughout, which again was extremely satisfying to him. One did not sleep so soundly when one felt unsafe. Even when unconscious Elizabeth clearly trusted him, believing that he would take care of her.

He placed the note he had written on the bedside table, for her to find when she woke.

André Chevalier moved to the door, quietly opening it. Smiling fondly as he took one last look at the utterly exhausted woman. He said under his breath, "For now, *ma chèrie* you are mine. Mine for five more days." Then he softly left the room,

He had intentionally pushed her hard all day, keeping her off balance and forcing her to re-examine the fixed patterns of her current lifestyle and to make her look at her own needs and desires. Stripping her down like that had been hard on her, but such a result! Elizabeth was perfect.

In his profession he had found that it was not uncommon for the most strong, intelligent and powerful women of the world to be submissive in bed. This was possibly some sort of natural selection, a way to improve the species. Perhaps in the prehistoric past it was in the genetic best interest for the most promising female to seek the strongest, most dominant partner. Considering the millions of years such a woman was in the making made him smile. Elizabeth was worth every eon of it.

A good outcome for his efforts with her was never really in question, but he had expected it would take far longer to get to this point. She was such a clever girl, and so willing to look at herself when directed. At thirty-six, André was an accomplished master. Women, all women were his forte, he understood them, their bodies and their psyches both in and out. Elizabeth's husband, Mark, however, was going to be much more of a challenge.

As André passed into the adjoining chamber, the man in question began a vicious string of invectives: "Is that you, you lying, cheating fucking rat bastard? I swear to God you are finished. I'm going to sue you for everything you've got, and then I'm going to kill you, you miserable piece of shit."

André drew a deep breath, and moved to the chair near his bed. The male half of this troublesome project lay face dawn, naked and chained spread eagled to the bed, his large body vibrating with explosive tension. Mark Nelson, Elizabeth's husband, was a much tougher case than she was.

"*Mon ami*," he began, "I had hoped that we could talk, that you may be willing to see reason…"

"I'm not your fucking friend! You have been fucking my wife! MY wife! Cheating bastard. This isn't what I signed up for. This isn't what we agreed! I paid you big money. You were highly recommended by Billingsworth. He is another rat bastard that I'll get even with. Bastard!"

"*Imbecile!* This is exactly what you signed up for. You cannot sue me, you cannot touch me for I am not so *maladroit*. You have signed both non-disclosure and forms and agreement for me to deliver a service, in front of witnesses. Sexual counseling and remedy. Me, I am perfectly safe. For I am doing as you have instructed - what I was paid to do."

"You are fucking my wife! And making me watch!"

André struggled to hide his irritation, and took a deep breath. He looked over at the large screen displayed upon the wall. A professionally edited version of the last many hours with Elizabeth showed, and he smiled as he observed himself guiding his cock deep into her throat for the first time. Mark, tied as he was, had to crane his neck to see it. André thought he could easily imagine smoke and fire boiling from the big man's ears he was so enraged.

"It was *malchance* to show you these without the sound track," André said. "Yet I did not know there was a problem with the audio. *C'est la vie*. My staff assures me that the track will be available later today, *mon ami*."

"I'm not your friend!"

"Perhaps not, but I am yours. Your wife and I speak of you often, Mark, and already I have solved the problem you came to me with. You are a lucky man. Elizabeth is *une femme fantastique* and she loves you very much."

"But I notice that she is happily fucking you!" Mark said and raw jealousy rang in his voice.

"This was not her choice, as you well know. I scared her and threatened your life. This was part of the plan. I have learned, oh so much. I wish to share this knowledge, but matters of this import can only be discussed by reasonable men. You are not at all reasonable."

A tray of food had been placed near the bed and André picked up a large glass of orange juice from it. He put in a straw, and held it to Mark's lips. "Drink." The man must have been very thirsty, André reflected, because he drank the entire glass without objection or even one "fuck you." Wordlessly he offered him another tall glass, this time of water. Mark again, drank it down. André had no intention of feeding the big man until the idiot saw reason.

"Uncuff me," Mark said when he finished.

André laughed. "I think not. The result would not be unlike the running of the bulls in Spain - but without the barricades."

"You can't just keep me like this."

"I will keep you exactly like this until you see reason, *mon ami.*"

"Stop calling me that. I'm not your fucking friend and I swear to God I'm going to kill you when I get out of here!"

"With this attitude what makes you think I will let you go?" André asked.

# Chapter 19

Mark's Punishment

André sighed. "I have spent many hours gathering information and researching your wife to comprehend her psyche. Unfortunately I did not spend time investigating you. You *monsieur*, gave every appearance of being a rational, experienced man of the world, in agreement with our stated goals."

He stood and picked up the riding crop. "Forgive me. I am not as accomplished with men, you understand, but I believe the principles are the same." André gave Mark ten lighter licks and then ten hard ones with the riding crop as the man had a large, muscular body that could take such a punishment. Besides, André reasoned, Mark needed to be aware of what it felt like in case he ever wished to crop his wife.

Elizabeth's husband bellowed and cursed throughout, never once begging for André to stop, even with the last five strokes, which André delivered with much increased force. When he was done André picked up the vibrating butt plug and Mark, who was watching, then did protest. "No way, not again!"

"Yes, again. And again and again until you become a sensible man." With professional experience André knelt on the bed and guided the plug inside, directing it to the man's prostate. Then he turned the vibration on low to start. Mark moaned. "Do not resist, *mon ami*," André said, "for as before, I am going to make you come."

"Bastard," Mark mumbled in a hoarse voice.

André put one hand on his captive's lower back and simply upped the vibrating pulse. Mark began to swear and buck and thrust against the friction of the bed. It didn't take long until the man spent himself against the sheets and collapsed, hurling angry abusive words at him throughout. André turned the plug off, but with some effort - working it in and out - he fully inserted it into the huge man's muscular behind. Mark had tried to prevent this, but changed his mind and complied when André threatened to whip his testicles with the riding crop.

"This is set on rotation vibration," André said, sitting on the bed beside his captive. "Every thirty minutes you will have an orgasm, then a thirty minute break. Then we begin again until you come to your senses. It is up to you how many times you fuck this bed." André stood up. "I make you my complements, *mon ami*. Of all the clients I have had over all the years I have been in this profession, you are the most stubborn."

Mark said nothing, but sullen resentment positively radiated from the man.

André laughed. "I leave you now, and go to shower and dress," he said, as he walked away, down the hall toward the lifts. "I will return in an hour or two. If you were not such an obstinate man, you and I could both enjoy your wife - the man she loves and myself. We could give Elizabeth a holiday full of sexual fantasies. Together we could use her body for our pleasure in every imaginable way."

"What?" Mark shouted. "What are you talking about?"

André paused, turned and sighed. "You comprehend perfectly, *mon ami*. You have no one but yourself to blame for this stubborn, prudish and childish stupidity of yours. *Imbecile.* As things stand, I am going to fuck Elizabeth's virgin ass on my own." André's voice echoed through the room.

Mark screamed, "No!" and the despairing sound was pitiful. "Wait!"

But André had already left.

Chapter 20

Andrè Chevalier

Merciless André ignored Elizabeth's husband. He pulled on his embroidered silk dressing gown with the green velvet trim and continued walking until he could no longer hear Mark yelling. The bathrobe had been purchased in the United Kingdom, as the British, unlike everywhere else, really knew gentlemen's dressing gowns. André had a weakness, the love of quality clothes - he only wore the very best.

As he walked, he fumed with irritation. *Américains!* Elizabeth's husband was sexually backward, narrow-minded, and was burdened with a mountain of unshakable fixed ideas. Yet he desired a consummate sexual relationship with the woman he loved. André smiled momentarily, recalling when Mark had first come to him, begging for his help. The poor man had been worried that he would lose his wife because after only a year of marriage as she had become disinterested in sex.

The lift doors opened and André used the security card in his robe to travel straight up to the penthouse. The big man did love his wife, and this love, André assured himself, was the lever that would eventually resolve this case *difficile*.

André thought of the saying: *'Life's most obvious truths are the hardest to see but once you've burned everything to the ground they are the only things left standing.'* By the time André finished with Mark, there would be little left standing. Perhaps only the man himself - and the love he had for his wife.

Alas, André thought, *sometimes one has to be cruel to be kind.*

André nodded to a member of his personal household staff and entered his bedroom imagining how it would be when he succeeded, when he brought the two lovers together sexually, and he smiled. Elizabeth had discovered much about herself already with his help. What her warrior husband would learn would be fascinating. Mark's social veneer had fooled him during the initial interviews, but André saw the primal, jealous caveman underneath now. André wondered how it hard it was going to be to move the man from his primitive attitudes to the present.

Whistling happily, André considered how much he loved his profession. *I am a very lucky man*, he thought. *It must be karma. I am a good person, and as such I deserve my good fortune.* Elizabeth had been naive yet eager and responsive to anal pleasures. As a sexual submissive she would quickly become an anal slut, and he was the lucky man who was going to teach her. *C'ést fantastique!*

The *petite* woman, his captive and willing slave, no longer wore her blindfold, and this fact made him grin. While a blindfold was necessary initially, to underscore vulnerability and helplessness, he preferred to see a woman's eyes. The eyes were the window that he used to view passion, to know a woman's soul.

He had seen a picture of her, of course. Those stunning blue eyes! How he had longed to see them all through this day as he had sexually tormented her. André entered his massive bathroom, switched on some of his favorite classical music and turned on the shower. When he took her innocent ass, Elizabeth's eyes would widen with surprise as he entered her, darken with lust as he fucked her, and glaze with mindless pleasure when she came.

Quelle chance! So much to look forward to!

After braiding her shoulder length hair, he would use that tightly wound braid as reins as he rode her. *Mon Dieu* that *magnifique* filly would be lovely to break in. Such an oh so delicious mount! André intended to cuff Elizabeth bent over the bed and crop her *derrière* - and perhaps even her pussy - making her skin extremely sensitive, hot and needy. There was nothing quite like fucking a well-striped ass. It would radiate heat, burning like fire against his thighs, and it would be so pretty with its red welts showing vividly against her pale, creamy skin.

After checking that the water temperature was perfect, André stepped into the shower and stood underneath the hot waves of heat, thinking of Elizabeth the entire time. *Such a small, graceful filly,* he thought. *With such a tiny tight hole.* His cock twitched, remembering how they had both struggled to get the larger plug inserted into her ass.

It was likely he would fuck the woman doggy style in front of the full length mirror. Perhaps he would also clamp her nipples? The dragging chain would add extra sensation while her large breasts swung and bounced as he thrust into her. Elizabeth would see him take her ass by being commanded to look into the mirror. André longed to watch her, watching him. Then he would be privileged to see Elizabeth' eyes, observe her expressions, and watch her react to everything he did to her.

When the music switched to a Roman Catholic composition with a distinctly spiritual theme, André's grin widened. It seemed extraordinarily appropriate to such heavenly anticipation. *Bonne chance!* He would have the privilege and honor of being Elizabeth's first. For later this very day his cock would be deep inside her tight virgin ass - an ass which he planned to fuck for a very long time.

The woman would squeal and sob; whimper and beg, making all those lovely sounds she made when maddened and sexually desperate. But André planned to prolong the sacred event as long as humanly possible. Then, when he finally allowed her to climax, that tight ass of hers would squeeze him so hard he would lose his oh so considerable control, and come and come and come.

Joyous and carefree, pleased with his imminent future, André - enjoying his shower - laughed out loud.

Book 4

Elizabeth's

Cherry

Chapter 1

Movie Time

Elizabeth woke from a dead sleep refreshed and sore - pretty well all over. Her anal passage had a butt plug in it, a big one. Her pussy, clit and breasts had been cropped with a riding whip and they were still really tender – but she would do it all again. What amazing sex!

Holy shit! she thought. *That man fucked me senseless. Literally. Man, what an unmitigated stud my captor is.* Frowning, Elizabeth realized that her husband Mark had every bit as much staying power as Sir did, but he just didn't seem to know how to get her off like Sir could.

Guilt hit her then, pinching her conscience like a vice. She loved Mark, but here she was enjoying sex with Sir. The morning of constant sex, the pleasure, the pain, all of it rolled into her mind. Pragmatic as always, Elizabeth thrust these conflicting emotions away. She was captive. This was not her choice, and she would be damned if she would allow her emotions to mess with her mind. *Later,* she decided, *I can crack up over all this later.*

She sat up, and then, noticing something missing reached for her blindfold. No blindfold. She searched the bed, it hadn't fallen off – it had been taken off. Like a child searching for presents under the Christmas tree, she gazed around the room, the place where she had been held captive in the dark for at least twelve hours.

The TV on the far wall instantly captured her attention. It was huge, more like a movie screen. She froze and had the dubious pleasure of feeling her face heat, no doubt flushing scarlet, when she became aware of what was playing.

The big screen displayed her, tied spread-eagle on the bed and being fucked by Sir. Elizabeth remembered this well – it had happened only this morning after all. At this point on the screen, she was just about to climax. Spellbound, unable to even breathe, Elizabeth watched her own head thrash, her golden hair spread on the pillow, her hips and back try to arch and her hands clench. Meanwhile Sir thrust his cock into her, pumping vigorously, while his muscles bunched and flexed. His powerful buttocks, hips and thighs, tightened and released, tightened and released. So beautiful! So virile! *And such an amazing fuck.*

A different view of the same thing came on the screen, and she realized that a number of cameras must have been working, taking in every angle. Apparently Sir had already had this morning's activities professionally edited into a cinematic feature. She took a cursory look around the room and lost count of the number of cameras with little red lights flashing upon them. Apparently she was still being recorded.

What the fuck? she thought, as tendrils of dread ran up her spine. *Man oh man. This is incredibly hot to watch, and I do really want to see Sir, as I finally have that damn blindfold off ... but I'm so screwed.*

Elizabeth considered her professional integrity, her position in the law firm, her husband Mark and her *father.* This was serious blackmail material right here. Yet despite her fear she continued to watch until Sir came, his last thrust, his amazing release. The view changed to them sitting on the bed together and then him guiding her into the toilet and she tore her eyes away.

Noticing a note on the bedside table, Elizabeth picked it up. It was written in pen and ink with an elegant hand. It said:

Ma cherie,

Do not be alarmed by the recording of us together. There is a reason, but it is not blackmail or mischief of any kind, j assure. As you trust me, you will know that I write the truth.

Even with her cynical and suspicious lawyer's brain, Elizabeth felt the knot in her stomach loosen. She felt completely reassured. Was it the intimacy they had shared? When blindfolded and cuffed she had been totally at Sir's mercy, utterly dependent upon him. Had that built this instinctive yet irrational trust she had in him? Just like that, Sir had allayed all her fears. She continued reading.

I am pleased to have removed your blindfold for I want very much to look into your eyes when you next climax. This I will do, when I return.

Elizabeth shut her eyes and swallowed. *This I will do when I return.* God, such a promise - such a threat. These few erotic words sent a pulsing flow of blood to her clit and her pussy. *Sex. Sex with Sir. Yum.* She kept reading.

If you wish to hear the sound track while watching, feel free to use the remote on this little table. There is also cheese, water and wine. You are free to feed yourself this once ma cherie, as I am not there to feed you

*by my hand. After you have eaten,
you will dress for me. I have left a
corset, stockings and shoes. Put them
on. I will tighten the laces when I
come to you. For an event such as
this, your first time, we dress up for
each other, you understand.*

Elizabeth smiled, imagining Sir speaking. He even seemed to write with an accent! While the idea of anal sex had always been out of the question, now she simply didn't care. Sex with Sir was great. Anal sex, while scary, would no doubt be great, too. She looked over and saw the remote, the cheese and wine, and the corset. *Wow.* Never had she worn such a thing.

Entranced, Elizabeth set Sir's note down, and picked the corset up. It was red satin, with a black lacy overlay. There were wired molded cups, which, with her big boobs was a good plan. A tiny black G-string and thigh-high sheer stockings – no doubt French, and black high heel shoes completed the ensemble. Elizabeth found herself smiling and then giggling as she ran her hands over the amazing outfit, absolutely certain that it would fit perfectly. How had he gotten her exact size and the outfit so quickly? And why was it she never once managed to dress up in something like this?

Elizabeth lay the outfit down on the bed, and picked up Sir's note, reading once more.

*When you wake the vibrator in your
so luscious derriere will begin to
cycle. So sorry, this is to keep you in
a high state of arousal. YOU ARE
NOT ALLOWED TO CLIMAX. I*

*intend to crop your innocent
buttocks for my pleasure before I
take you in the ass.*

Oh, my, God, Elizabeth thought with a flush or sexual heat. *Why does the idea of him cropping me turn me on?* There was no explanation except anything with Sir seemed incredibly hot. She continued reading.

*However, if you come while I am not
here I will double this punishment.
I always keep my promises, ma
cherie, and I will know if you
climax.*

Could she stop herself from having an orgasm? Not if the damn vibrator cycled to high. But then again perhaps Sir planned to make her climax, so that he could punish her. Elizabeth shook her head. It was all too deep to figure out. Gut clenching with lust and apprehension, Elizabeth took a deep, steadying breath and continued reading.

*I do not keep you waiting long after
you wake. I know you are as anxious
to lose your anal cherry, as I am
honored and excite to take such a
tight virgin offering.*

A bientot, belle fille,

Sir

Elizabeth swallowed. Anxious didn't cover it. The rush of emotions that rolled through her was pretty comprehensive. Apprehension, mental conflict, anger, guilt, shame, resistance, curiosity, the desire to fight - the need to surrender and to top it all off she was overwhelmingly horny. What was this constant physical yearning? Like a trained dog ready to fetch, Sir only had to mention sex and she sat up on her hind legs panting, ready to go.

Man, she reflected, *I'm a mess!* Elizabeth snorted when her father's words echoed in her mind: "Honey, things often get worse before they get better." *Yeah right. How could they get any worse?* She wondered.

Yet she was going to find out.

Chapter 2

Getting Even

Still contemplating Sir's letter, she gazed around her room. It didn't look like a prison. The chamber she was in was obviously underground, but it was done in tasteful male colors, tan, ochre and yellows. The floors were dark hardwood, mostly covered by no doubt genuine Persian carpets. Persian carpets? Really? Man this guy must be loaded to put expensive stuff like that in his underground playroom. The enormous mirrors on the ceiling, and covering the walls on either side of the bed amused her. She had no idea that anyone even made mirrors that large. Of course Sir would have mirrors. It kind of explained why he never seemed to miss a thing.

Two nice dark wooden beams ran across the ceiling, which was probably sixteen feet high. A black wooden cross, complete with handcuffs and big enough to hold a person was in one corner, not far from that was a huge sofa with lots of pillows and a large antique armoire. Her bed had four large posts and was also dark wood, with eyebolts for chains and cuffs, of course.

So, she thought. *This is a dungeon, but a modern one, built and decorated by an artist.*

Elizabeth's mind surged back to her captor, Sir. The man had taught her so much. Once virtually unable to orgasm, now couldn't seem to stop, or at least she easily could at Sir's command. Denial as a mental state was so difficult to perceive.

Honesty had been a large part of her problem. Elizabeth had been lying to her husband Mark. She had learned two very important things about her sexuality: one, while she may be able to climax without constraint, she could always climax when bound or physically overwhelmed. And two, she had a bone-deep need to please her sexual partner. In fact, satisfying her partner gave her as much or even more pleasure than being satisfied herself.

Using the remote, Elizabeth discovered that she could fast forward and rewind, virtually reliving her entire experience at her captor's hands. While captive she had worn a blindfold, so it had been amazing to actually see everything that Sir had done to her. More enthralling, she had been able to see Sir himself, his appearance and what he looked like naked.

She had been worried that he was cross eyed or ugly – but of course he wasn't. Physically he seemed to be in excellent shape, flat stomach, broad shoulders - but one wouldn't pick him out of a crowd for his looks. Dark hair, cut short around his neck and ears, tan skin all over – perhaps relating to a Mediterranean heritage? His face seemed average: brown eyes, clean shaven, with eyebrows thicker than most. There were many pock marks on his chin and cheeks – either from acne as a boy, or perhaps from chickenpox, yet it didn't detract from his healthy good looks.

She admired his cock, tall proud and straight. Elizabeth had known it would be well formed, he was a virile young man of about thirty-five. The best thing about Sir was his smile and the depth of mischief in his eyes. How could anyone not like him? Her mind went to her husband Mark, and her heart sank. Mark would hate Sir, because he was jealous and possessive, not only of her body but of her time. They were madly in love with each other, but why couldn't Mark make her climax like Sir could?

Reliving her experiences through video rewind had been difficult, mainly because it made her seriously horny, and the damn vibrator cycling through and keeping her aroused wasn't helping. Yet she couldn't stop herself. She wanted to see Sir again and again, watch him take her hard and fast, see him throw his head back, and enjoy the look on his face as he came. Resisting the impulse to watch 'just once more' she turned the TV off and put the remote down. Enough.

An article about BDSM had been left on the bedside table, obviously put there for her. It was short and to the point and she read, "Per a study published in the Journal of Psychology and Human Sexuality, there is no evidence that BDSM and psychopathology are connected. It has been well established that BDSM is not proof of mental or physical illness, and practitioners of BDSM are generally, in comparison to other populations, well adjusted. The desire for BDSM does *not* come from emotional damage, from trauma or childhood abuse. People cannot – and should not – be treated to cure it."

So, she thought, *trained mental health professionals don't consider BDSM irrational. They think it is part of a person's basic nature. I guess if someone has a kink, it's their kink…so what?*

The article went on to say, "Interestingly, true Dominance has with it a deeper need to take care of and protect the person dominated." Elizabeth snorted. Well, that was true. Sir wanted to look after her alright, right down to feeding her himself. It went on to say, "Sexual submission has to do with serving and making the individual the submissive cares for happy."

That seemed to resonate with Elizabeth. *I'm a sexual submissive,* she thought. *It explains my desire to please my captor as much or even more than Stockholm Syndrome does. Sexual submission is part of my fundamental personality.*

But only in bed. In the rest of her life she was anything but submissive, from her pit bull courtroom style, to her management of others. Elizabeth giggled. Once, while visiting the Sistine chapel, an old bent over Italian lady, all dressed in black, reached into Elizabeth's pocket to steal a coin. The woman was surprised when Elizabeth had caught the taller woman's hand, and wouldn't let her go. Sure it was only worth twenty cents, but it was the principle of the thing. Why did everyone assume a short person was an easy mark? The woman shrieked loudly - in the chapel! Unintimidated, Elizabeth had stood fast. In the end the old lady gave up, and gave Elizabeth back her coin.

I like to win, she thought, recalling the incident with satisfaction.

The early American high chair was in the tiny but fashionable kitchen area, and Elizabeth's eyes immediately went to it. Stomach fluttering, she had a vivid mental memory of what had been done to her on that chair. Without warning the butt plug began to vibrate on low once more. While she tried to process that, it began to climb in slow increments, and then it began to pulse.

Shit! Elizabeth fell back on her bed, grabbed a pillow and hugged it. *Not again! I must not come, I must not come, but man oh man!*

The temptation to touch herself, to finish off her building orgasm was overpowering, and she thrashed, cried out and rolled, trying to subdue the impulse. Eventually she locked on to a yoga course she had once taken and concentrated upon her breathing. Breathe in with the nostrils, out with the mouth. Nose in, mouth out.

Oh god! She shut her eyes and tried to remain still, imagining stepping on slugs with bare feet or worse – stepping on watery dog poo or fresh throw-up. Anything disgusting that would take her mind off her burning lust. The vibrator suddenly went to low, and then stopped altogether.

Expelling a deep breath, Elizabeth sat up, opened her eyes and looked straight into a mirror. Her hair was disheveled, her skin flushed. She looked like a mad woman, and come to think of it, she kind of felt like one too. Frowning, she saw a glint of something spiteful in her eyes and clenched her teeth. Right then she vowed that come what may she would eventually get even with Sir: sometime, somehow, someway.

Chapter 3

Andrè's Case *Difficile*

Merde! Sitting in front of his computer André Chevalier swore out loud. Furious with himself, he slammed his hand against the desk and stood up.

André had been studying up on Elizabeth's husband, after employing his confidential and very expensive sources. Mark worked at one time for the American Government as a consultant. Whatever the big brute had done, it was locked away in classified files. Espionage? Counter espionage? But the man was a lawyer! How could this be? Yet he had worked for the Judge Advocate General.

Still in his dressing gown after his shower, he began to pace. Well, whatever the man Mark had been or done, André didn't want to know more. Checking his Platinum Cartier wrist watch and well aware of the time he began a string of invectives in French. The big man was due to climax any minute, and André had wanted to be there, to prevent it. By his calculations Mark would have already climaxed three times, which was more than enough for an unfed and probably dehydrated man.

By the time he got down the lift and to the lower floor, André was too late. As he walked in he saw the powerful man's face, his head raised off the bed, where he was tied spread-eagle. Mark was grimacing, furiously fighting his own body and trying not to climax. The angry man had no chance. There was the hint of vulnerability in Mark's eyes, a lost, almost little boy look of surprise, then his body lunged forward, rattling the metal cuffs, pulling on them and threatening to break them with the strain as he came and came and came.

Mon Dieu! Elizabeth's husband was *vraiment magnifique!* With his huge chest heaving and powerful hips and thighs pumping, Mark's strong buttocks clenched and clenched as he climaxed. The smell of him permeated the room, a heavy potent scent of a male animal. André wanted to genuflect, or clap, or at least yell, bravo! Such a man! He recalled Elizabeth's words, when Mark had taken her by pushing her up against a wall, just before the wedding march: *It was like trying to hold back some powerful natural event with my hands, like trying to stop a tornado, or an avalanche.*

And so, he thought. *I see the avalanche in action.*

Like any accomplished Dom, André had experienced submissive training. The best Tops were also experienced Bottoms. While André didn't normally bottom, he would seriously consider bottoming for this man. Provided Mark was a Dom, of course, which remained to be seen.

André shook his head, as he recalled Elizabeth's experience at the wedding. No. this man's preference was dominance. There were so many possible reasons why Mark withheld his natural inclinations - guilt, religion, moralistic concepts of right and wrong, or childhood experiences. Had his father physically abused his mother perhaps? Yet even as an untrained Dom, André felt compelled to risk being under his hand. Such a man! Making love to Elizabeth with him controlling the scene would be a unique experience.

André's gut twisted with premonition. Mark had displayed vulnerability and panic when his body had taken control – every other time he had successfully hidden such weakness with anger. It was *malchance* to see Elizabeth's husband in a moment where he had let his guard down. This was going to complicate things. André had unintentionally observed Mark's moment of helplessness and whatever else the man forgave he would not easily forgive him that.

Maintaining a deliberately bland expression, André took his phone out of his top pocket and speed dialed a number while his captive watched. Any other man would have looked away, laying his exhausted head down facing the other direction - but not Elizabeth's husband. Mark's expression was one of malevolent spite and André's spine tingled. There was no point in pretending he hadn't seen the man vulnerable. It was best to simply move forward.

Yes, André thought with melancholy regret. *If for nothing else, the big man will make me pay for this.*

Chapter 4

Managing Mark

Act normally, André decided as he moved toward the bed.

"*Monsieur,*" he said, "do not abuse me, as I will not tolerate it and I have no wish to gag you." He gestured to a ball gag that lay on a side table nearby. "You are hungry and you are angry, and yet there is work to be done."

Elizabeth's husband, still breathing hard, remained silent. André locked a large black collar around Mark's neck, then put another cuff on his right wrist. He uncuffed the right wrist and immediately Mark attempted to grab him, but André pulled the chain attached to the new cuff and connected it to the man's neck collar. He did the same with the other wrist, until Mark was secured with both hands behind his back, each chained to his neck.

"Now *Monsieur,* I am going to move you to another room that my staff have prepared. You will find food, clothes and a shower waiting for you as well as a key to uncuff yourself. Do you come willingly or will you fight me? I am going to uncuff your ankles now, but I have this taser, do you see?" He showed him the black gun with the yellow stripe. "So sorry, *Monsieur,* but I do not trust you at all. May I have your word that you will submit to this? For I am persuaded you do not wish to stay on this, bed oh so *désagréable.*"

Mark gave one curt nod. André raised his eyebrows and Mark added, "I'll come willingly if you swear you're going to set me free."

"On my honor, it is as I say. Once in this secure room, you may take your cuffs off."

"Alright," Mark said. "My word on it."

"*Bon.*" André uncuffed his ankles, keeping his distance. Then as if gesturing to a valued guest, he directed Mark to walk toward another room. Once inside he said, "Please, sit." Mark sat down on the comfortable couch.

André took a deep breath. "*Je suie desole, Monsieur.* Mistakes have been made, yes, many mistakes have been made. And yet I still believe that all will yet be well and you will be very satisfied with my services."

Mark snorted at that.

"*Non.* It is true. Your desire is to keep the wife you love, yes? I know what she needs, and if you can overcome your natural instincts to perhaps tear me limb from limb, then you will learn, oh, so much. Please excuse me, you will be watched *Monsieur* at all times so do not try to escape. This door is locked. And here you will find everything you need.

"What are you planning you little shit?" Mark said. "Are you going to try to appease me? So that I won't beat the shit out of you?"

André's smile was genuine and he laughed. "I do like you *Monsieur*, indeed I do. This is my hope. I am a professional. Why did Billingsworth guide you to me? He was satisfied with my services, yes? Or does he hate you? You are angry *Monsieur*, but use this time to think things through, *s'il vous plaît*. I do not covet your wife. Elizabeth is yours, completely yours, as you will learn when you listen and watch those tapes."

Mark snorted once more, and he eyed his captor with calculated malevolent intent. "I have seen all I need to see of those tapes."

"Perhaps. But have you heard all you need to hear? For I have told you before. Elizabeth talks of you often, and she has spoken to me of her sexual troubles. You were wise to come to me."

Mark gave a scornful scoff.

"*Non*, it is true. You may keep your anger *Monsieur*, but it would be stupid not to take advantage of this opportunity. I have had my staff compile a list of audio – only those words that are relevant to your concerns. You will find it on the menu when you switch the TV on."

André gestured to a booklet. "I have also left you this small book that concerns BDSM, and the nature of such things. It is necessary, if you please. I will need to know, *Monsieur*, what you like, what your sexual fantasies are and how they will fit together with your wife's.

Mark gave an ugly laugh. "Right," he said in a snide manner. "As if that's going to happen. Forget it. I'm sorry I ever got us into this."

"Do not be stupid *Monsieur*, for you are not *l'homme imbécile*. Think with the mind not the natural jealous inclinations. Pretend you are French, a much more sensible race altogether on the matters of the heart! Now I leave you. The remote is here, and I ask you consider watching the recording of what I have done with your wife – but if not - at least listen to only the audio. You will hear how much we speak of you *Monsieur*. She has oh, much to say. Eat, shower, sleep…do as you will. Remember, do not try to escape as my security staff have been alerted. They watch always, and you will not get far. You do not know it yet, but this is exactly where you need to be."

André put the key to unlock Mark's cuffs on the coffee table. "*Je regrette, Monsieur*. I thought to dominate you as I have done to so many others. So stupid, for I suspect you would rather die than submit. So be it. Now I ask for your willingness to obey my requests. *Mon Dieu*, I beg for you to stop and think." André moved toward the door as Mark turned his back, reaching for the key to his handcuffs.

"All will be well, *Monsieur*," André said. "I do not seek to appease you, I only seek the lever that will help you choose to listen. Do this because you love your wife, and because she loves you. Do this because you need the skills I have to offer, *Monsieur*. I can and I will assist you. Together we will save your marriage."

Intent on uncuffing himself, Mark did not reply.

Without another word, André left.

Chapter 5

Dress up's

Yowza, Elizabeth thought. *How seriously hot do I look?* Dressed in her red satin corset with the black lacey overlay, Elizabeth studied herself in the mirror. The tiny black G-string, thigh high sheer stockings and black seven inch high heel shoes made her look soooo totally sexy.

She smiled broadly, turning sidewise and front on, and even getting a look at her back in the mirror. She also looked tall. Too good for mortal man, she assured herself. Speaking of men, where was her husband Mark? She was supposed to be seeing him sometime today. A part of her wanted him to see her like this – although that would cause nothing but trouble.

The butt plug had stopped vibrating, but she could still feel it, an unpleasantly full sensation heavy in her back passage. She heard the sound of a door opening and spun around quickly, her heart pounding. André, walking with confident grace, came into the room and paused about fifteen feet away. His eyes, dark and expressive went directly to hers and he smiled.

Elizabeth melted. *Oh my, God! That smile!*

"*Salut, ma chèrie,*" he said with a soft, low voice, in that sexy French accent. With his eyes never leaving hers, he strode toward her, and this made her stomach flutter. People often stared at her - she was considered beautiful - even if she was short. But Sir seemed be intensely focused on her eyes, drinking in *her*. It was comforting and refreshing that although Sir considered her physically attractive, he was also interested in the person that she was.

With a perverse, inexcusable double standard, she on the other hand only wanted to see his body.

Elizabeth was captivated. She had seen Sir, by way of watching him sexually torment her on the big TV screen, had observed his face and his reactions, even his orgasm when she had serviced him with her mouth. Using the remote she had spent some time going over and over the scenes where his face was clearly displayed, particularly when he climaxed. Not only was it hot to watch him come, but it seemed only fair after he had watched her reach orgasm so many times. But the full screen view of him was nothing compared to seeing him in the flesh. She found her body immediately reacting to his presence, to that wonderful scent of nutmeg, cedar and Brazilian Rosewood cologne and the deep melodic sound of his voice.

Elizabeth's captor, Sir, was shorter than Mark, perhaps exactly six foot to Mark's six foot four. His figure was slimmer, too; well proportioned in a lithe yet muscular way - he obviously worked out or played sport.

Sir looked fantastic. He wore a perfectly tailored suit, probably from Savile Row, with a well ironed and fitted, crisp white button-down tailored dress shirt with gold cuff links and tie pin, each adorned with what looked like rubies. His necktie made her blush for she knew it exactly matched her outfit, with the precise same red and black running through it. Elizabeth knew that he had dressed up for her and foolishly, she felt unreasonably flattered. His dark shoes were hand-made, distinctive Berluti footwear. Elizabeth, well aware of fashion, knew they were probably close to two thousand dollars a pair.

As he drew closer, Elizabeth instinctively lifted her hands, wanting to touch him. Sir stopped, just out of reach.

"*Ma chèrie*, do you forget yourself already?" he asked in that deceptively mild, yet authoritative voice. "Hands behind your back, lace your fingers. I have not given you permission to touch me, have I?"

Lowering her eyes, and blushing Elizabeth immediately complied. "Sorry, Sir," she said. It was stupid to feel embarrassed and even guilty, but she couldn't help herself. She wanted to obey him, and she had determined to no longer fight that particular crazy desire. She craved his admiration, his acknowledgment, or his approval – whatever. Every particle of her being wanted to please him. Sir dominated her and she wanted him to. Instinct? Madness? Insanity? Or just Stockholm Syndrome. Whatever it was, she had already surrendered.

Sir stepped right up close to her. Nervous, she swallowed.

"Look at me, *ma chèrie*," he said and she did. Like the sun, warm on her skin, the man smiled at her and she smiled back, absurdly happy that he was not mad at her.

"Elizabeth, do you want to touch me?"

"Oh, yes, Sir," she replied.

"*Bon*," he said. "Soon you shall get your wish." He raised both hands and stroked her hair back from her face, putting it behind her ears. The smell of him, freshly showered with that wonderful cologne, caused a flutter of somersaults in her stomach. Cupping one hand on one cheek and one behind her neck, he bent forward and slowly kissed her. It was a warm, lazy kiss and Elizabeth melted into him, answering his lightly probing tongue with her own. Her eyes closed in a breath-robbing spike of desire. As their bodies smoothly came together, Sir's hard form pressed up against her.

Sir pulled away. "You are so sweet, *ma chèrie*," he said and stood back a step. "But right now, show me this outfit you wear for my pleasure. Display yourself."

Elizabeth raised her hands, and did a little spin. It was kind of awkward with the chain on one ankle and with the uncomfortable toy in her backside, but she managed to walk slowly and sensuously, a few paces back and forth. Then she stopped and gave him a sultry pose. She giggled, because dress-ups were fun, and she could see the undisguised admiration in his eyes.

He laughed. *"Fantastique! Mon Dieu,* the big man would eat you if he saw you like this, *n'est-ce pas?"*

Elizabeth's hand went to her mouth as she choked on an involuntary chuckle. Wouldn't Mark's eyes bug out if he saw her dressed as she was, like a high class courtesan? Her husband had never treated her with anything but love and respect both in and out of the bedroom which, she was beginning to realize, was a real pity. "God yes," she said. "Mark would love this outfit, Sir. I can't believe I've never worn anything like it before. When I get out of here, I'll buy us both something special."

"Bonne idée," he said with a nod of agreement.

But Elizabeth wondered what would happen when she and Mark were freed. Would she ever be able to dress like this for him? When she had dressed in a corset for her captor first?

Chapter 6

Corseted and Cuffed

The corset had pushed Elizabeth's breasts up and out, making the tops of her bosoms rounded, kind of like two large pillows. Sir ran a finger lightly over this skin, moving along her breasts, from one side to the other. His actions raised gooseflesh, and a rush of exquisite longing. Elizabeth cleared her throat.

"Such soft, soft skin, *ma chèrie*." Sir lowered his face between her breasts and took a deep breath in. "*Mon Dieu*, you smell good. I did not provide perfume, *belle femme*. There is nothing better than your own seductive female scent." He pulled back from her then and said, "Turn around and I will tie your corset properly." She did, and as he pulled the lacings taut, she took in an anxious breath and chewed a lip. "Yes, *ma chèrie*, I make it shockingly tight. Do you know why?"

"So I feel constrained, Sir?"

"Just so, clever girl. This garment is firm and stiff against you, and every time you inhale you will remember who controls you, who owns your body, and who can do anything he wants to you," he breathed into the back of her neck, his warm breath seductively caressing the hollow behind her ear. "And," he added darkly, "at any time I wish."

Elizabeth's womb contracted at this erotic wording, and her gush of arousal could not be managed with the tiny little G string she had on. It began to drip slowly down her thighs. When Sir finished tightening her corset, he ran a finger over the slick drop, wetting himself with her slippery essence. "Open," he said, putting his finger near her lips, and she did. When he had placed his finger inside she moaned, and sucked it like she would his cock.

"Good girl," he said in a deep soft voice. "*Mon Dieu*, you are so good. I shall reward you by making you climax hard, oh many times. This I promise."

Cuffing her arms behind her, he removed her ankle chain and took her to the bathroom, all the time keeping his hands on her cuffed wrists. He liked that, letting her know that he was in complete control of her, and frankly, she liked it too. This time Elizabeth complacently went along, following his instructions. Then she used the toilet, but when she asked if she could speak, and then requested he remove the toy from her backside, he refused.

"Not yet, *ma chèrie*. Later." Afterwards he washed her well with a warm washcloth.

When they returned to the bedroom, he uncuffed her wrists from behind her and placed the cuffs in front. He got her to lie on the bed, where he attached her cuffed wrists to the headboard. Then he shackled her legs together, attaching them to the end of the bed. The result was that she lay straight along the middle of the mattress with her arms and legs tightly bound, with a strong enough tension that she had little ability to move.

But why had Sir chained her with her arms and legs together? It would be difficult to have sex like this, or would it? *Damn that imaginative man!* she thought. Excited and apprehensive, Elizabeth found she was hyperaware, alert and eagerly waiting to discover what he would do next.

She didn't have to wait long to find out.

Sir sat down beside her and smiled. "This corset makes your breasts look oh so enticing. They thrust themselves out, just begging to be stroked. You are chained to my bed, *ma chèrie.* Tell me, how does this make you feel?"

Elizabeth gave him a tentative smile. "Sexy. Nervous. A little breathless. Turned on."

"Very good," he said. "I like for you to be all those things. First, I wish to watch you come for me. You are right handed, no?"

"Yes, Sir."

He uncuffed only her right hand. "Masturbate for me, *ma chèrie.* Play with yourself until you climax."

Elizabeth licked her lips. There was no way she could talk him out of this, she knew. This would be the second time she had ever masturbated in front of him, in fact in front of anyone, and she still found it embarrassing. Without foreplay and with him watching it would be difficult, but she shut her eyes and got started. She was unable to part her legs because of how she had been bound, so access was difficult. She slid her hand down under the G string moving her fingers into the dampness between her legs to lubricate them, and then came back to manipulate her clit. After a few minutes, she began to feel a bit more confident, particularly as his comments proved that she was arousing her captor.

"*Oui, oui, ma chèrie,*" Sir encouraged. "Do not stop." His voice was deep, lust filled and very French. His accent she noticed always grew stronger when sexually inflamed. "*Regardez. Il est agréable de voir.* Bound, blonde and beautiful, you touch yourself in this oh so sexy corset, with the stockings and heels. *Mon Dieu,* your mound swells between those lovely thighs. But they are too close together, no? Because I have cuffed your ankles and pulled your body tight. You want to open your legs, yes? Spread them wide so that I can fuck you?"

"Yes...Sir,' she said, breathing raggedly. The trousers of his perfectly tailored suit were straining, unable to contain his swelling erection. Sir's blatant desire from watching her masturbate was a serious turn on.

"Stop," he said suddenly, placing his hand upon her hand and fingers, holding them still. Her eyes flew open, and she stared at him, wondering if she had somehow done something wrong.

"*Un moment, ma chèrie,*" he said. She watched him move to the armoire and open a drawer. Her face heated when she saw him pull out nipple clamps. Holding them, he came toward her with a happy grin. "We will both enjoy these, *ma chèrie.*" He sat next to her and bent over each pillowed breast. Slipping her left nipple out of the cup, he pulled and rolled it between his thumb and finger, making it stand up, ready for him.

He paused a moment, apparently entranced with her nipples. Then he bent over her and licked each one, thoroughly laving them, leaving a fiery trail across her breasts with his warm tongue. He sat back up. "Look at me," he ordered her. "I want watch you take this pain for me."

Of course you do, Elizabeth thought, tensely licking her lips. *Sir had a thing about pain.* And of course what was even stranger was - that was okay with her.

# Chapter 7

Clamped and Coming

Elizabeth gazed into Sir's eyes. It was no hardship to do so, for his dominance mesmerized her. When he clamped the first nipple, she flinched and gave a little yelp as the aching throb of it knifed through her right to her core. Sir stroked her breast and said, "Good girl," then he studied her once more as he clamped the other nipple.

"*Je l'aime, ma chèrie.* I love to see you accept pain for me, and yet it does not really hurt now, does it?"

"Not really, Sir," she said in a breathless whisper. *Pain? No,* she reflected. *It ached.* The ache echoed and radiated in sensual waves through her breasts, pussy and clit. It was a dull empty throb, that made her needy and wanting – which no doubt is exactly what Sir intended. But it would help her masturbate and achieve a climax.

"*Bon,*" he said. "Now, before you begin again, tell me, what were you thinking of to help you achieve the orgasm?"

Her frown came automatically, before she thought to hide it. Elizabeth seriously considered lying. But could she get away with it? Sir wanted every secret Elizabeth had, but she wanted to keep at least some things to herself. It was embarrassing.

"Elizabeth," he said. "I will know if you lie to me," he said sternly. His face was implacable, and she felt a thrill of fear. "Do you want to be punished? Right now you are mine. Every thought, your body, your orgasms and the very air you breathe. I own it all. Do not displease me, for *j'assure* you will be very sorry if you do. Now I asked you a question and I want an answer - an honest answer. And I want it right now."

"I'm sorry, Sir. I was thinking of the movie you made of us having sex."

This didn't seem to surprise him. With no discernible change of expression he asked, "What part?"

Elizabeth felt her skin flush with humiliation, "I was replaying you fucking my mouth, that time in the bath. I saw you, the way you thrust and finally climaxed. I...I watched it a number of times - it was very erotic, Sir, and that was what I was masturbating to."

"Very good," he said. "This is acceptable *ma chèrie*, but you must always tell me what you are thinking the moment I ask. I will never be angry with you for honesty, I swear. If your sincere thought is that you hate me then tell me. Not idle thoughts *ma chèrie*, but honest feelings. If I am to achieve my goal, then this is what you must do, no matter how difficult it is, you understand?"

"Yes, Sir, but may I ask, what is your goal?"

"No. You may not ask. Not yet," he said, dismissing the subject. "Now, I want you to play with yourself until you climax. But you will imagine that it is Mark you are pleasing in the bath, that it is your husband who controls you. Mark has bound you and forced you to service him. Can you do this, Elizabeth?"

"Yes, Sir."

"*Bon.* One more thing. I do not want you to shut your eyes. This may be difficult, but it is my will. You will keep your eyes on me while you play with yourself. Nothing will be hidden from me – I want it all. I will watch you come, *ma chèrie, comprenez vous?*"

"Yes, Sir."

"Begin," Sir said in a quiet, unassailable voice.

Elizabeth stiffened and stopped breathing for a moment. Every time he commanded her, she felt it like a heavy wave, flowing through her entire body. Sir's voice caressed her, yet powerfully compelled her obedience.

Sir was sitting right beside her, and it was effortless to look at him, she didn't even need to crane her neck. Yet it wasn't easy to expose herself. It was as if the man wanted to see right down into her soul. Stubborn to a fault, Elizabeth made up her mind that she could do this. Of all the things she had already done, looking into his eyes was nothing.

The ache in her nipples helped, and Elizabeth stroked her clitoris, imagining Mark. Her clit enlarged and responded eagerly as desire surged through her. It was said that woman could imagine more easily than a man, that a woman's mind was geared to fantasy, while a man's mind was visually focused. That certainly explained the number of romance books that sold. Not to mention the very few woman's magazines picturing naked men verses racks and racks of naked women in men's magazines in the newsstands. What was the saying? How did you turn on a man? Just turn up. Preferably naked. But to turn on a woman - well that was something else entirely. For desire began in a woman's mind.

Sir continued muttering soft words of erotic encouragement, mostly in French, and Elizabeth's eyes remained upon him, but she wasn't really seeing him. In her mind she was imagining Mark, physically demanding, powerful and overwhelming, taking exactly what he wanted from her. She began to pant and perspire, while working her clit over, picturing him firmly giving her orders, telling her how to suck him, what he wanted – exactly as Sir had.

Mark stood before her and she could picture him so easily. Not the sweet, considerate Mark that she knew, but that other Mark, the Mark who had taken what he wanted at the wedding, who had fucked her hard and fast. Jaw tight, expression uncompromising, the primitive, primeval warrior - the man who would fight to the death for her. She imagined his huge, tough body demanding things that terrified her, demanding her compliance, charged with dominant male energy. Her breasts throbbed and she gave a ragged moan as she pictured obeying him instantly, submitting to whatever he commanded, giving him anything – giving him everything.

"Yes, yes, Mark," she heard herself murmur. Mark was telling her that he was going to come right down her throat. That she was going to drink it all down, swallow every drop and thank him afterwards for allowing her to suck him off. The idea of Mark dominating her was so amazing that she felt herself begin to go over.

"Come for me, *ma chèrie*. Come now, I want to see it," Sir said in a deep, lust-filled voice.

Sir's forceful male command made her insides quiver, spark then burn. Constrained as she was, Elizabeth could still thrash her head side to side and barely thrust her hips. Her pussy squeezed down on empty space, and her anal passage clenched tight onto the fullness of the plug. Sir pulled her nipple chain hard, and instead of distracting her, the brutal pinching torment added to the power of her orgasm. As she started to go over, Sir thrust two fingers up under her G string, into her pulsing channel. With her legs chained and pulled tightly together the space for him to push inside was constricted, so he had to force his way in. When he did so he slammed right up into her G spot with bruising strength.

"Oh! Oh! Oh!" she gasped. It felt amazing. Writhing and jerking she screamed and screamed, obeying Sir's command to climax.

# Chapter 8

At His Feet

When she came down from her orgasmic high, Sir's manner was utterly approving. "*Ma chèrie,* I am proud of you. It was very exciting for me, to see you climaxing so hard. You called Mark's name, did you know?" He removed her nipple clamps and put them in his pocket. Then Sir's large hands caressed, and fondled each swollen breast.

Elizabeth watched as Sir bent over her upper torso and took one nipple into his mouth. A noise came from somewhere deep inside her, a low sound of raw pleasure. "Ahhhh! Mmmmm." It was so erotic to see him suckle her, to see and feel her engorged nipple pop out of his mouth when he moved to the other breast in a path of electric sensation. Tenderly licking and sucking, he caressed each breast, his mouth and tongue restoring her in a soothing balm of moist heat. Elizabeth stared up at the ceiling, to look away and catch her breath, but the overhead mirror only reflected his dark head working diligently against her pale skin.

"Oh God," she whispered, while his lips and tongue nibbled and circled around her areola. He gently and thoroughly laved her nipples, easing the stinging ache. Within his hands her breasts tingled blissfully. The man took his time, clearly enjoying himself.

Elizabeth blinked back tears, utterly off balance. What was happening to her? If Sir wanted to make her climax all day long, he could easily do it, for she had no ability to withstand him. She was completely in his hands, and somehow she didn't care. This entire situation was so baffling. Confusion, fear and arousal all mingled, warring inside her mind.

Sir caressed her jaw in a compassionate manner, then bent and kissed her forehead. "It is only emotions, *ma chèrie,* nothing to signify. You are very brave to face so many new things all at once. But see how easy it is? To masturbate in front of another? You can do this for Mark now, and he will enjoy it very much. There is nothing to disturb you, *j'assure.*" He began to uncuff her legs, and arms from the bed, taking his time, allowing her to compose herself.

Then he helped her stand up. "It is well?" he asked kindly, with a reassuring smile.

Elizabeth couldn't resist his smile. "Yes, Sir. It is well."

"*Bon,*" he said. "Come sit with me now. We will drink wine, and then I will have you service me well while on your knees. We will both have climaxed then. It will take the edge off so when I take you in the ass I will be able to fuck you for some time before I need to come again."

Elizabeth stood on shaky legs, trying to absorb all that Sir was saying in her dazed post climax haze.

"*Ma chèrie,*" he said, "for now I relax the rules and you may speak as you wish. It is a little break, you perceive."

"Thank you, Sir," she replied.

Sir sat on a dark brown wood kitchen chair, his knees spread wide. After taking a pillow from the bed he had Elizabeth sit on the floor in between his legs, her shoulder leaning up against the inside of one thigh, her cuffed hands resting comfortably in her lap. She was getting used to that damn plug, at least when it wasn't vibrating. It was a bizarre, yet fantastically intimate scene, sitting on the floor between his knees, and even though she was allowed to speak, she didn't feel the desire or the need to do so.

Sir poured himself a glass of red wine and took a drink, and then kissed Elizabeth, filling her mouth with wine. This was new, too, and bizarre but kind of nice. While Sir sat and pet her hair with long sensuous stokes, and continued to feed her wine from his own mouth, Elizabeth reflected that she was like his dog. Sitting up and panting for his treats, absorbed in him completely. It seemed right to sit at his feet because it made him happy. And because he was happy she was happy. This was not something Sir was making her do, she realized. It was something she *was:* Sexually submissive. Elizabeth understood now that she was receiving pleasure by giving pleasure.

"Look at me," he said, tipping her face up toward him with one firm finger. Elizabeth looked up, and saw Sir searching her expression with a speculative glint in his eye. "Tell me *ma chèrie,* what are you feeling right now?"

Three words: safe, comfortable and happy sprang into her mind. *Shit,* she thought. *Why do I feel that? So, so idiotic!* She pressed her lips together.

Sir gripped her chin firmly with one hand. "Tell me," he demanded.

"It's stupid! They were just idle thoughts, and I don't see that it means anything!"

Sir gave her a slow, knowing smile, "*Ma chèrie,* do not be angry with yourself. One does not easily control one's feelings, one controls one's actions." He stroked her hair soothingly. "You are happy, are you not? Content to sit here at my feet? Tell me now what is the answer that you try oh so hard to conceal? What makes you so angry?"

She sighed, and leaned her head against his knee. "I immediately thought that I felt safe, comfortable and happy. There! It's insane! I've been kidnapped, chained up, and I've cheated on my husband, who I love. I'm such a slut."

He laughed. "Yes, you are a slut," he said, which didn't help to pacify her hurt feelings at all. "But that has nothing to do with it," he added. "If you were sitting here, in cuffs at Marks' feet, how would you feel?"

"That is a different matter, Sir," she said primly. "I'm always happy with Mark. I shouldn't be happy here with you."

Smiling knowingly, he said. "Do not fight your nature, *belle fille*. You are *exactement parfait*, the ideal woman to me, and to your husband Mark. Sexually, your preference is to submit. This makes you, and oh so many women, content. It also makes them into shameless whores."

Elizabeth gave an inarticulate choke, too insulted to speak.

"It is true, *ma chèrie*. Such submissive women are bewitching sluts *magnifique*. They adore sex." Sir continued to stroke her, petting her hair and playing with it, running it through his fingers, tucking it behind her ears and generally fondling it. "Nothing could be more desirable, than such a woman, *j'assure*." While clearly attempting to soothe her hurt feelings, Sir still seemed to genuinely enjoy playing with her hair. "Shall I tell you, *ma chèrie*," he said, "Why I so look forward to fucking your virgin ass?"

She was still digesting the slut and whore concept. *What?* she thought. *He is back to talking about my ass. Where did that come from?*

But no doubt she'd soon find out.

# Chapter 9

What Sir Wants

Against her inclination she laughed. "What a thing to say, Sir! Just as I was getting comfortable again, too. Okay, go ahead. What is that about? Some men really get into it."

"I cannot speak for others, *ma chèrie*, I can only speak for myself. Turn now, I will give you *un peu* massage." She shifted so that her back was to him and she rested directly between his knees and thighs. Sir began to rub her shoulders, head and neck, occasionally kissing her in the sensitive areas behind her ears, throat, and collarbone. Elizabeth decided that he was turning her on and relaxing her, both at the same time – somehow creating longing and languor in equal measure. His erection was stiff against her, so she was well aware of his interest.

"You are innocent to anal play," he began, "naturally nervous, and unaware of the pleasure it will bring. I am honored to introduce you to this. But more than that, few women are virgins, but many are anal virgins. Why? They do not trust the man. To bring you to a state, *ma chèrie*, where you are willing…." He paused, cleared his throat and then said, "where you beg me to take your virgin ass, ah, it is very well. For you to trust me, Elizabeth, with such an important part of your body - the forbidden, the unspeakable to many, this is something I crave."

She thought about it for a bit. "What if I say no?"

He laughed and squeezed her shoulders. With a sensual touch, the fingers of both of his hands caressed her neck and collarbone. "I planned to deny you orgasm, to make you so frenzied that you would be willing to have sex, any sex, even in the ass. For I could make you so frantic that you would beg, *ma chèrie*, as you well know. But such a method is unnecessary, for you are such a sweet horny slut."

"Sir!" Elizabeth said. She was going to protest further, but the way Sir said slut always seemed to melt her inside. The word on his lips was so endearing and affectionate, not to mention that accent of his.

He rose up and stood before her. "But you said so yourself! You said, 'I'm such a slut,' no? I only agree with you. Me, I do not wish to contradict such lady *desirable*. *Ma chèrie*, my cock is hard, and I want to use your mouth. You shall suck me to completion and this time I think I shall spend my seed on your face and breasts. Stand up," he pulled her to her feet. "I will let you undress me. Do you still wish to touch me, Elizabeth? To see and feel my body as I have seen and felt yours?"

Elizabeth's mind reeled. He went too fast for her, but she managed to find an answer to his last question. Did she want to touch him? Absolutely. "Yes, Sir," she said.

He uncuffed her, and for the first time, while in his presence, she was free of all restraint. Somehow it made her nervous.

Watching her, Sir undid the top button of his shirt, worked his tie free, and threw it on the table. "It feels wrong to be unrestrained, yes? For me also, it looks wrong. Take my clothes off, I will let you look and touch your fill. You may explore my body as I have explored your oh so feminine flesh, Elizabeth. Then I shall bind you with my necktie afterwards."

With a deep breath, taking in the scent of him and his sexy cologne, Elizabeth moved to his buttons, carefully unfastening them, running her hands up across the fine crisp hair on his chest. The man was warm and solid beneath her. Elizabeth found herself making an unintentional little noise from the back of her throat, an ummm of pleasure.

She examined his face then, touching it. He was smooth shaven, and she noticed a small dimple in the middle of his chin. The jaw was strong and determined – no surprise there. It had been childhood acne that had made the pock marks, she felt certain of that, but it definitely didn't detract. Ordinary, she would say his face wasn't remarkable in any way, except for the implacable determined look in his currently smoldering dark eyes. But when he smiled, man oh man, he was really something then. And when he gave her a direct order she felt it from the top of her head right down to her toes.

Sir remained still while she removed his business suit jacket and hooked it on a chair. Sir's hands, resting at his sides, caught her attention. They were large and warm, and well manicured with his nails trimmed short. She stroked and examined his fingers, aware of how much pleasure they had wrought. She kissed each palm and released them. Sir moved against her then, fast as a leopard. With one large hand at the nape of her neck, the other on her cheek and jaw, he pulled her to him and gave her a penetrating kiss. When he pressed his hard body against her, including his rigid cock, her legs turned to liquid. "Ahhhh," she murmured against his demanding lips.

Pulling away, he smiled down at her. "*Excusez-moi, ma chèrie.* The impulse to kiss you was irresistible."

That was alright by Elizabeth. She had found the impulse to kiss him irresistible, too.

Chapter 10

Undressing Sir

Her laugh was a little breathless. After removing his cuff links, she pulled each sleeve and removed his shirt, trailing her hand over him, moving to his back. His shoulders were broad and she traced his skin, feeling his strength and lean muscle. "Do you play sport?"

"Football. It is named soccer to Americans."

"But why are you so built?" She asked.

He laughed. "Personal trainer. Why is the big man so big? Does your husband Mark train?"

Elizabeth snorted. "He doesn't lift weights if that is what you mean. He plays any sport, every sport, tennis, racket ball, gridiron – everything. He also likes boxing – you may want to keep that in mind. Mark isn't happy unless he is doing something physical. It's all that energy, I guess. If he doesn't use his body hard I think he'd explode." Unbuckling his belt, she drew it out of the belt loops with one long pull, dropping it to the floor. Sir's eyes remained hot upon her, keenly watching her every move.

"Does this include sex?"

Elizabeth frowned. "Not as much anymore."

"Do you think he loses interest?"

She bit her lip. "I don't know. I certainly have lost interest. I think he knows it, and doesn't push me."

André took each of her wrists and twisted them roughly behind her back in one sharp, fast move, stepping in close to her, trapping her with his body. His actions were savage in their intensity, and his indomitable cock pressed hard against her. Elizabeth gasped and her knees almost gave way. Instantly aroused, a burning fire began in her core, spreading outward.

"Mark should be more demanding, yes?" he whispered seductively behind her ear.

"Oh God, yes!"

Sir laughed and let her go. "Fear not, *ma chèrie,* together we shall teach him. I flatter myself that I am making progress with the big brute."

"Sir, can I ask you something? Something I've been afraid to ask?"

"You may ask me anything. I may not tell you…but I will if I can."

"Sir," she looked away from his penetrating gaze, "you haven't been having sex with Mark have you? Something you said, well…I just wondered."

"No, Elizabeth, no *j'assure,*" he said. "I have punished him for not cooperating, but I no longer do this. He is a stubborn man, and yet I cannot compel him. He is more stubborn even than you, Elizabeth."

"Will I see him today?"

"Most certainly. Now finish undressing me. I want to fuck your mouth."

This sudden authoritative demand set every nerve alight. Elizabeth had enjoyed sucking Sir off so much the first time she was looking forward to going down on him again. For fun she moved sensually, swaying and swinging her hips as she walked, intentionally attempting to allure him, enjoying the way she looked in her tight corset and stockings and high heels. His bark of appreciative laughter thrilled her. Elizabeth was teasing him, yet his eyes burned with lust. His heated desire for her was empowering – it gave some sort of primitive, feminine satisfaction.

Bending gracefully onto her knees she pulled off each shoe, including the socks. He had long, narrow feet, slightly sprinkled with hair and she wanted to kiss them, but determinedly withheld that urge. While still on her knees she pulled down his zip, then with firm resolve she met his penetrating gaze. The man always wanted her to look into his eyes. Well, he was holding still for her this time, and she was in control. It took audacity to appear calm as she casually pulled his boxer shorts and pants down at the same time.

Sir remained perfectly motionless, although his jaw tightened almost imperceptibly. Elizabeth's thighs were slick with arousal as she stared at his large jutting cock. She ran her hands up his powerful legs, admiring the shape of him, and then caressed the most male part of him. Sir didn't move, keeping his promise to let her touch him as she wished. She held his warm sac with one hand, fondling each testicle, then softly ran the other hand up the shaft. *So soft yet so hard,* she thought in wonder. *And so beautiful.* Unable to stop herself she gave the head of his cock a delicate lick, and then taking just the tip and head in her mouth, she sucked. He caught his breath and she had the joy of finding both his body and his shaft stiffen under her lips and hands.

"So beautiful," she said. Like Mark, Sir was also so *male.* Being near him made her feel vulnerable, yet somehow powerful, too. He wanted her. Badly. Inexplicably shy, she looked up at him. "Do you mind turning around?" she almost whispered. He gave a low chuckle and did so. "Jesus," she said, running her hands over his hard buttocks ripped abs and flat stomach. "Even your backside is a work of art. You're beautiful, Sir. You're seriously hot, pretty well everywhere, as far as I can tell."

André turned and pulled her up into his arms, tilting her backwards in a crushing embrace, combined with a bruising, open mouthed kiss. The combination made her head spin and her womb tighten with need, and perforce her asshole clenched too, constricting on that large plug. Elizabeth gave a low, husky moan as he thrust his tongue inside and dominated her with his strength, his mouth and teeth. One hand moved down to grip one of her breasts and she made a strange sound, a cross between an 'umm' and an 'ah.'

He pulled away then, raising her back up to stand straight before him. Looking down, he stared at her with a possessive, lustful gaze. Elizabeth wanted to flinch and look away from his fierce, stern expression, but found she was unable to do so.

"Put your arms behind you," he growled.

Elizabeth did and André grabbed his necktie and with savage intensity wound it around her wrists, binding them together behind her back. She took a deep breath, tremendously aroused by his rough, demanding treatment.

With her hands bound behind her back, Elizabeth regained her equilibrium. Sir was fully in control of her once more. *I'm bound and captive,* she thought. *But why the hell does that make me feel more comfortable?*

Chapter 11

Andrè's Trick With Mirrors

A true submissive, this one, André Chevalier thought. *She embraces bondage and desires to give away sexual control.* He studied her expressive eyes, seeing only the desire to please him and the need to serve him within her open regard. *Such a treasure. J'adore cette petite femme. The husband, Mark, is a lucky man.*

Standing in front of his captive, less than a foot apart, he gazed at the lovely expanse of her *décolletage.* Elizabeth's breasts were rising and falling erotically with each short panting breath. Her large tits were thrust forward by the shape and fit of the corset and by having her hands bound tight behind her back with his necktie.

Women had loose tongues after orgasm, due to the release of the hormone oxytocin and Elizabeth was no exception. André recalled her sitting at his feet. It seemed so natural for her to be there. When he asked her how she felt, completely against her will she had innocently spoken the truth as only a submissive would know it, *'I feel safe, comfortable and happy.'*

A wave of intense sexual hunger flowed through him and he felt his cock thicken. *Merde! Such complete submission provokes me.*

"The rules, they return, *ma chèrie,"* he said with a growl. Do not speak without permission. Come with me." He took her by the arm, and guided her over to one of the wall to ceiling mirrors, standing her in front of it. "Stay right here," he said.

Then he searched and found the nipple clamps in the pocket of his trousers, and while he did Elizabeth's gaze never left him. It was as if he was the only thing in her universe. André felt the compliant yet sexually aroused heat of her gaze and was thrilled by it. As a Dom there was nothing more satisfying than having the full attention of an eager submissive. Finally he picked up the pillow, walked over and put it down in front of her. A large ottoman was just behind him, something to sit down on when he finished.

André looked at her image, as they both stood side on in front of the mirror, and smiled. He wanted to watch his cock thrust in and out of her mouth, and now he could. Satisfied all was prepared, he looked down at Elizabeth, *la femme idéale*. The woman was quivering from a combination of apprehension and sexual excitement. His jaw tightened and his lips compressed as his natural instinct to dominate her took over.

With proprietary self-assurance and without speaking one word, he folded down the cups of her lovely red corset. This particular style of garment made it easy to bend over and thus fully expose her to him. The woman's large breasts were flushed and swollen, and as he had expected her nipples were hard. She had such soft, pale, feminine flesh. André gave her a tight smile.

"Look at me and remain still," he said.

He stared down at her, and watched her gasp and her eyes darken further as he clipped the first unforgiving clamp on her nipple. The next nipple clamp caused a flinch, but breathless and aroused she managed to remain motionless as he had ordered. Slipping one hand down under her G string he dipped one finger into her dripping sheath, enjoying the abundant flood of her honey, and the thick, heavy feminine scent of her.

"You are soaking wet, my little slut, aren't you?"

Elizabeth shivered and nodded. "Yes, Sir," she whispered.

He thrust two fingers deep inside her then, hard and demanding and Elizabeth's breath caught and she swayed slightly. Dripping and slick he pulled his wet fingers out and traced her labia and circled her engorged clitoral nub, pulling the hood back and teasing her. Quivering, Elizabeth moaned and moved toward him.

"*Non*. I told you to be still," he reproved.

"Sorry, Sir."

André saw her eyes widen, with a satisfyingly desperate look to them. "*Ma chèrie*," he reminded her. "You are not to come until I say, *comprenez vous*? For the next time I allow you to climax I will be deep in your ass." To André's delight, Elizabeth's face blushed, and the red spread right down across her neckline and down to her pale breasts.

"Yes, Sir," she said.

"On your knees, Elizabeth," he said with a peremptory demand. As she had her arms tied behind her back, he helped her move down to where he had placed a pillow for her comfort. She ended up at the perfect angle to take his engorged, jutting cock. He grazed his knuckles down her cheek in the way that he knew both calmed and excited her. "You are a good girl. I know you will please me."

"Yes, Sir," she said.

André held his balls at the base of his shaft and was stroking his cock. Pre-cum had already gathered in the slit. "Do not move, Elizabeth," he said in a firm voice. "Lick your lips. I want you wet for me."

"Yes, Sir."

"Elizabeth, you masturbated and climaxed, did you not?"

"Yes, Sir," she said.

Elizabeth's eyes were focused on his now massive erection, and André was amused. "Now it is my turn, but it pleases me to use your mouth," he said. The woman's eyes, filled with lust, remained on his thick swollen cock, while he pumped it in front of her face. Smiling, he caressed her cheek with his other hand. "You may suck and lick as you like or as I command, but I will move your head and will fuck you exactly as I wish. It is a little like masturbating, only with the use of your hot wet mouth, no? When you are still, and I move you on to my cock or I thrust it inside you, it pleases me, *ma chèrie*. It is as if your body is an object, only there for my pleasure. I can use you as I wish. You have no choice - no say in the matter. I do not know if you understand, but this makes me very hard."

When she didn't reply, he tapped her chin, taking her by surprise. Elizabeth started, tearing her focus away from his cock and looking up at him, as was his intent. She looked beautiful on her knees in front of him, enthralled by his cock, her ass stuffed wide with a large toy, her breathing ragged, desperate as she was with heated, unfulfilled lust. The clamps that were making her nipples ache and throb, his demands, the sight of his red, engorged shaft, one or all of these things had made her wet and ready for him, André knew.

"I understand Sir," she said. "Oh God, I don't know why, but I get it."

"Bon," he said in an unintentionally stern voice. He wanted to smile, or to acknowledge her further but more than this he wanted to take her, to use her, to savagely rut in her mouth until he came. "Now open. I want to put my cock in your mouth."

"Yes, Sir," she whispered, as though in a place of worship. Elizabeth's moist lips parted, just a crack, exactly as he liked it. André smiled because he liked to stretch her open with his cock. Elizabeth had learned that from when she had been allowed to suck him previously. André slid his cock inside her warm wet mouth and she moaned.

"Oui, oui," he said. "You like this, yes?" and with her mouth filled with his cock she mumbled an affirmative. He withdrew and pressed his rounded head against her moist lips, rubbing it back and forth, marking her with pre-cum. Again she moaned

and her eyes, already heavy-lidded, drifted shut with pleasure. He decided to allow this for now, but he intended to look into those blue orbs as he climaxed.

He took his time, jacking off in her mouth, working his way all the way in, watching her swallow his cock deeper and deeper with the use of the mirror. Once his cock was seated well inside and her nose was pressed up against his coarse pubic hair, he grasped her head in his hands as he moved in and out. "*Oui, ma chèrie*, suck hard and use the tongue, *merde*, it is good. Fuck."

Deep in submission, the woman was his sexual slave right now, and would deny him nothing. He loved the small helpless little sounds she made from deep in her throat. That he had brought her to this point, had mastered her so fully, discovering her sexual needs and desires gave him profound pleasure.

Tears ran down Elizabeth's cheeks from the effort of taking him. She was moaning in earnest now, humming and drooling, utterly transported just to be sucking him off. André chuckled darkly, but deep in sub-space, Elizabeth remained oblivious. Her audible humming joy was enough to distract him, but not in a bad way. André continued pumping her mouth, watching his actions in the mirror – seeing his cock disappear down her throat as she swallowed him. There was no hurry to release. He loved seeing her on her knees in that tight little red and black corset, thigh high stockings and heels, her nipples clamped, her wrists bound together behind her back, the large anal plug rammed up her ass, her hands in tight little fists. With unflagging zeal Elizabeth worked hard to please him.

He pulled the nipple chain up, giving it a slight tug, and it put her off her stride. She gazed up at him with dilated pupils and heavy lidded eyes - alert to whatever he wanted. He pulled out of her and said, "Prepare yourself *ma chèrie*, for I am going to fuck you hard now, and when I say, you will open wide. Then I will shoot my seed on your face, in your mouth and on your breasts. What do you say?"

"Oh, thank you, Sir," she said, in a tone of respectful gratitude.

André barked a delighted, lust-filled laugh in rely. Then he thrust himself back between her swollen, wet lips, and deep into her mouth.

Chapter 12

Face, Mouth, and Breasts

Aching now with urgent desire, André's hands tightened against her and he pulled her back and forth, faster and faster, moving her head with his fingers tangled in her hair. Most women enjoyed having their hair pulled, he knew, which was fortunate for them, as he liked to pull it.

"Elizabeth," he growled, and he knew his voice carried an indomitable threat. "Do not take your eyes from mine. Look at me. I want to watch you take my cum."

She nodded her agreement, making an inarticulate 'uh huh' sound around the thick cock that filled her mouth. Elizabeth looked up at him, and all he could see in her eyes was a kind of bliss-filled rapture.

The mirror was such a turn on, seeing himself slide balls–deep in and out of her mouth. The woman moaned constantly now, worshipping his cock, wanting him to climax. Goaded by the needy sounds she made, André began to grunt and thrust in short fast strokes.

The sensation of her wet lips tight upon him, her tongue flicking, and her mouth sucking him, overcame all his resistance. His buttocks, hips and thighs flexed *hard* - while his testicles tightened. His pulsing shaft convulsed and swelled as blood and semen shot into it.

"Now. Open," he demanded, pulling out of her and continuing to pump himself with his hand.

Elizabeth obediently opened her swollen lips wide. André gave a low primal growl as his cock spurted blinding pulses of release, his hot thick cum jetting over her in long ropy strands. André jacked off onto Elizabeth's face, into her mouth, and across her breasts. He saw her blink when he shot his load on her cheeks and nose and was thrilled when her eyes widened with surprise.

André expelled a deep breath of satisfaction - the woman was covered in his seed. The potent smell of his cum filled the air, mixing with the heavy scent of her unique feminine honey. Emptied of all ejaculate, breathing hard and utterly released, André touched the rounded head of his cock against Elizabeth's cheek, intentionally moving it through his slick cum, enjoying the sensation of rubbing it along her pale, soft skin.

Elizabeth, flushed and aroused, immediately turned her head in order to lick him, taking him into her mouth and suckling his still erect shaft with genuine delight. André softly chuckled while watching her pay homage to his cock, enthusiastically cleaning it with her tongue, listening to the eager sounds of her enjoyment at attending to this service, lapping and swallowing every drop of his male essence. Elizabeth's eyes were shut with pleasure.

André tapped her chin, getting her attention and she opened them, looking up at him with dark, lust-dilated pupils. He smiled down at her approvingly, and with his hand on her forehead, pulled his now clean cock from her mouth. Then he sat down heavily on the ottoman, one hand possessively gripping the nape of Elizabeth's neck.

"Good girl," he said, stroking her hair with sensual affection. André stood up and took a handkerchief from the pocket of his jacket that was draped on the back of his chair, and wiped his cum from her face and breasts. Then he released both of her nipple clamps, licking and sucking each smarting nipple in turn to ease away the sting. Her nipples were huge, extended, swollen and red. Elizabeth made small plaintive sounds as he freed them.

To distract her from this ache he slid his hand down, sliding under her G string, between her legs, cupping her swollen pussy. Her slick channel spasmed instantly with his touch, and he gave a muttered oath against her breast as she filled his hand with hot liquid. Fuck she was close!

Completely charmed, André laughed. "Elizabeth, you are such an insatiable little slut," he said. He had intended to withhold her orgasms, only letting her climax when his cock was deep in her ass. This was to ensure that she was frantic and needy, eager to be butt fucked. Yet this woman was a true submissive, and would be desperate and needy for anything he wanted. If she were his, he would train her to even enjoy being caned. She had served him well, and he didn't want to deny her. Indeed, he wished to reward her eager passion.

"*Ma chèrie*," he said, "Do you want to come for me? Now, before I fuck your ass?"

"Oh God, yes please, Sir!"

"*Bon.* But you will not climax until I say."

"No, Sir."

With his hand cupping her pussy, André pushed two fingers into her soaking wet heat and earned himself a sound from Elizabeth that was a cross between a cry and a groan as her tight cunt pulsed. "Ah, ah, ah," she began to chant as André's thumb stroked her engorged clit in a manner that was expertly calculated to madden her. Elizabeth shivered & trembled as if enduring some sort of an internal earthquake. When André felt her entire body tense and still, ready to explode he said, "Come for me, *ma chèrie*. I want to feel it. Come now."

Elizabeth reacted instantly, screaming as the walls of her pussy contracted tightly around his fingers. "Oh! Oh, ohhhh!"

Wailing crazed shrieks of pleasure, Elizabeth fell against his arm, thrusting against him, thrashing, whimpering and moaning.

André watched it all by looking at them together in the mirror. The woman was ravenous, so hungry for sex. She had been deprived for too long. It awakened a primal ruthless urge to give her exactly what she sought. From the first, he had been guided by the numerous and varied noises she made – such thrilling sounds from her sweet lips! And for the climax it was always the so vastly eloquent and affecting screams. André held her steady with his other arm, wrapped around her waist, while still continuing to finger her through her aftershocks murmuring soft French words of endearment.

There was such power in Elizabeth's orgasms, and such force in her internal muscles. How amazing would it feel when she climaxed with his cock deep in her ass? For the muscles in her asshole would be stronger than those in her sex. They would squeeze down upon him like a vice. And even though he had only just climaxed himself, his cock began to twitch and harden once more with the thought.

Sir arranged a light afternoon snack and sat Elizabeth, still restrained, on his lap. There he hand fed her cheese and crackers, and generous liquid refreshments. After a forty minute rest, he was ready to attend to her *derrière*. He had put it off, savoring the idea, imagining all the possibilities of how he would go about it, but now the time had come. With her arms tied behind her, he took her to the bathroom, one domineering hand on her bound wrists. He sat on the toilet and bent her over him, removing the large anal plug when she lay upon his lap. Then she used the toilet once more and afterwards he again washed her well with a warm washcloth.

André took Elizabeth over to the four poster bed, and removed her corset. He teased her for some time, kissing and biting, fucking her mouth with his tongue, making her whimper and moan while running his hands over her back and buttocks. When he finished, Elizabeth's hair was mussed, her lips were swollen, and she looked ravenous and wild-eyed, desperate to have him, exactly as he had planned.

"*Ma chèrie*, we leave the garters and stockings, you understand. But now we are both naked, yes?"

"Yes, Sir," she said.

André loved how the woman blushed over almost anything. She was not such an innocent, surely? And yet, all that he was doing to her was new. His shaft began to harden further as he thought of what he would teach her and all that he wished to do. "*Un moment.* Turn around, Elizabeth, I wish to braid your hair." He took a brush and hair tie from the bedside table drawer, and brushed her hair out, competently braiding it. "It will be a handle for me, *ma chèrie,* like a horse's reins. Something to hold when I mount you, you understand?"

"Yes, Sir," Elizabeth said dreamily.

Chapter 13

Spanking and Cropping

André laughed, pleased at how responsive she was, how utterly under his control - this woman who had been unable to orgasm. He took the necktie off her wrists and put the soft fur cuffs on them. Then he moved them to her front, attaching them to the bedpost at the foot of the bed at shoulder height. "Hold on to this post, Elizabeth. Do not take your hands from here."

André stroked her back, pushing it down and bending her forward. This way her buttocks stuck out behind her. "*Oui*, like that *ma chèrie*," he said. "Spread the legs." When she did, he tisked disapprovingly and nudged them much further apart. "I want access to both your oh so luscious feminine holes," he explained and laughed when she blushed once more.

André didn't pause to explain. His cock was rock hard, and he was hungry to take Elizabeth's final virginity. With one hand on each of her white butt cheeks, he spread them wide, focusing on her rosebud entry point. His tongue began to lick around the rim, teasing her, and he squeezed her cheeks. Something low in his gut clenched with desire as her tight little hole contracted. Restively shifting, she tried to evade him.

"Don't move," he said and pulled her closer in order to get her ready her for his cock. When André put his firm heated tongue right into her, Elizabeth gave a small cry of surprise and shifted forward.

"Be still and let me touch you," he said. There was nothing he liked better than preparing her for penetration, and he imagined slipping his cock into her taut hole exactly as his tongue was doing. Once more he ignored her, pulling her back into position, tickling and stroking that ring of tense nerves. But she was flinching and restless and wouldn't hold still. Well. He would give her something to think about.

"Elizabeth," he said in a quiet, somber voice. "Lift up on your toes." When she did he stroked her buttocks and said, "Higher," he said. "I want you to feel it in your calves and thighs." He stood back and looked at her, and she turned and regarded him with a wary expression, clearly uneasy.

"*Ma chèrie*," he said. "I am going to spank you, because you are misbehaving." He watched her body tremble. "You will thank me, *ma chèrie*, when I am done. Prepare yourself, and do not try to evade the pain. Accept it and it will go easier."

Without waiting for a reply he struck her with the flat of his hand on the curve of her buttocks, a nice, hard crack to start. Elizabeth gasped and cried out and her feet moved flat to the floor. "*Non*. Back up on your toes," he demanded fiercely. She obeyed, and he hit her again, making her buttocks shake. She tensed and struggled to be brave, and something in his chest clenched hard as he watched her. This small stubborn woman was trying very hard to please him, and he felt privileged and grateful to help her discover her sexuality.

André had a lot of experience spanking women, and he was simply warming her up for now, waking up her nerve endings, bringing the lower half of her body alive. *Merde* she was so sexy in her garter and stockings, her luscious *derrière* and pussy displayed for his use. Even though he had recently climaxed, his cock pulsed to life, excited at the sight of her accepting his punishment. He struck her again and again across both buttocks, a little harder now, and then paused and caressed her abused *derrière* and moved to her waist. Elizabeth was breathing hard.

His palm slid down her back and belly, cupping her mound with his hand, softly stroking her clit.

Mon Dieu! The woman was dripping - she did not dislike this spanking so much after all. Elizabeth made a noise then, a hungry sound of need and André smiled, knowing that he was causing powerful and sensuous stirrings in her swollen, engorged sex. But she had closed her legs slightly and that annoyed him. He told her to put her feet down flat on the floor while he moved off to the armoire. When he came back he had a set of brutal nipple clamps, a crop, a cane and a spreader bar. He cuffed both of her ankles to the bar, and he explained what it was, as it was her first time.

"*Ma chérie*, you annoy me by closing the legs. Now I prevent this. You are helpless to my *désires masculines*. I have been patient, but now I am not. My cock is hard and you are wet and ready. I want you. I will cause you pain, yes, but we have discussed this. Your pain is part of my pleasure, yet you will like it, *ma chérie, j'assure*. First I take your pussy and then your virgin ass."

When she didn't reply he said, "Elizabeth, what do you say to me?"

"Yes, Sir," she said, her eyes wide with alarm.

He bent over her neck, and spoke in a slow, low whisper into her ear. "You have no choice, *ma chérie*. Be brave now and take what I give you. You will scream and cry and beg me to fuck you in the ass before I am done, I swear." He felt a shudder go through her at these words, and he tensed holding back a wave of palpable lust. André cleared his throat. "When I finish *ma chérie*, you will thank me, *j'assure*."

He took his time to run his hands over her body then, admiring her shapely, red buttocks. Then he fingered her moist folds and tapped and stroked her clit, keeping her eager and on the edge of climax. Elizabeth arched and squirmed, making soft, needy sounds. He put nipple clamps on. They were a particularly vicious set and she cried out and complained but he ignored her.

André would not be able to keep them on long, but they would give her something else to think about other than her sore buttocks.

When all was ready he made her stand on her toes once more and began to really lay into her with his hand, striking both round globes, leaving her buttocks red and warm. From time to time he stopped and stroked her sore cheeks, running his hand in circles and fondling her slit, her outer lips and clit. Elizabeth was panting. The pulse in her neck was beating rapidly, her eyes were heavy lidded and lust dazed. She was wetter than ever, and her sweet scent filed the room, while her slick essence coated his fingers. Utterly aroused, Elizabeth now made continuous inarticulate sounds of need.

"Do not dare come, *ma chèrie*. Not without my permission. Do you want to come for me?"

"Yes, Sir! God yes."

He laughed. "I told you that you would like what I do. But I am not finished." He took the riding crop then and began with lighter stokes, building up to something fierce, she cried out in protest but he ignored her, his cock getting harder and harder as he watched her struggle to accept the pain. Her white orbs had red welts now, as well as numerous handprints. He stopped often to finger her, playing with Elizabeth's clit and gaping, needy cunt. With his hands possessively gripping her thighs, from time to time he ate her out, licking her slit and wet folds, bringing her close, so close to climax.

As Elizabeth was too close to coming, he tugged on her nipple clamps to distract her. Elizabeth cried out, and while her attention was on her nipples, he gave her two hard crops on her pussy – just the swollen labia area. She shrieked and wailed and André quickly moved to soothe her, putting two fingers into her glistening moist hole, while licking her slit and engorged clit.

Elizabeth moaned, and he didn't know if she was moaning from pleasure or pain. But he spread her hot butt cheeks and licked and teased her rim and asshole, thrusting his tongue in. When her cunt began to pulse and she made shaky, uncontrolled sobs of desperate need he drew away, pleased that he had brought her back to the edge of climax so quickly.

André adored it all, causing her pain, causing her pleasure, making her mindless, begging and pleading with utterly shameless desire. Elizabeth's legs were too tired now to remain on her tip toes and he allowed her to relax them, yet he knew that in the time that she had been on her toes she now would have the maximum amount of blood flowing through her calves, thighs and pelvic regions. It would all contribute to delicious sensations in her anus and her sex.

But he wasn't finished yet.

Chapter 14

The Cane

"*Ma chèrie*," he said in a warning tone, stroking her hair and her nape. "I want to hurt you now, with this cane." He showed her the object and she stared at it with sex-glazed eyes. "I want to give you three hard strokes." As he spoke he pulled on her nipple clamps, making her whimper. "They will hurt, and they will mark your skin for a week, perhaps more. This will be the last of all punishment this day, I swear. This is what I desire, *ma chèrie*. I will not do it if you refuse me. May I mark you? If I hurt you with this, you must try not to brace and flinch. You must accept this pain for me. For me, *ma chèrie*, to please me and make me happy. Do you agree?"

Panting, sweating and breathless Elizabeth said, "Not...not between the legs?"

"No. The buttocks only."

"Then I can come?"

André laughed. "I do not make the bargain with you, Elizabeth." His palms both ran over her body, in sensual, teasing caresses, moving lower then holding and softly tracing her mound and folds, with a delicate alluring touch. "You will climax for me, yes and it will be an explosion of memorable proportion, but *je suis désolé*. You will not climax until my cock is deep in your ass *ma chèrie*. *Non*. Neither of us will – so together we suffer, you and me. But you must accept this pain because you want to please me, or not at all. Make your choice, *ma chèrie*. Now."

"Go ahead, Sir," was her immediate response. "The more you hurt me it seems the more I want you to. It's too much to figure out right now. I trust you not to *really* hurt me. Do your worst and I'll take it."

André laughed and gave her a chaste kiss on her forehead. "You will not regret it, *ma chèrie*. You make me very happy." The husband Mark, André knew, would not be pleased with her welts, but *c'est la vie*. The man was already angry. In preparation, André spent some time licking her asshole, curling his tongue inside her while stroking her sensitive nub and putting two fingers inside her slit. He knew exactly how much he could do before she came, and when she was shuddering, on the edge of climax, he stood back and hit her hard with the cane.

"Owww!" Elizabeth screamed in surprise and clenched her butt cheeks. André immediately stroked them, circling them softly and blowing on the red heat.

"*Ma chèrie?*" André saw that there were tears running down Elizabeth's face. Her body was flushed and shining with sweat and he thought that he had never seen her look so beautiful. She was taking this pain for him, and his heart swelled as he thought how generous she was, and how much he appreciated her. He murmured soothing French words into her ear, stroking her hair and telling her just how much he cherished her. Then he went back to her feminine folds, her clit and pussy, working them over with his mouth and tongue and fingers, bringing her back to the brink of orgasm.

"*Ma chèrie*, do not flinch. Push your delicious *derrière* out for me, and accept this second stroke now." He was impressed - she had courage this small submissive woman. Elizabeth pushed her ass up and out for him and took a deep breath. Once more he struck her with the cane, this time in a different place. Once more she screamed and once more he went to soothe the ache, blowing on the welt and stroking and soothing and whispering French endearments. Then he brought her back to near climax by lightly stimulating her sopping cunt and engorged clit with soft, clever caresses from his fingers, mouth and tongue.

Elizabeth's eager little sounds of pleasure were sending André mad, and from time to time he stroked himself to ease the ache of his rigid cock.

It took awhile to bring her to the edge of climax once more, but soon enough she was mindless with her hips arching.

Oui, he thought, *Sharp pain, followed by soft, intense pleasure.*

André knew that this stimulating torment would meld into a consuming fire, resulting in one of the most extreme orgasms Elizabeth would ever experience. She was sobbing with need, begging for him to fuck her, fuck her anywhere, in the ass, in her pussy, in her mouth – but please, please, please would he please let her come?"

André soothed her and apologized and vowed that it would all be worthwhile, but she needed to make herself ready for he wanted to give her the last stripe with the cane. As her breathing slowed, he gave her warning. Once more he struck her and she wailed, a delicious musical sound that made his thick shaft twitch. More tears sprung to her eyes and rolled down her cheeks, trailing down like a river of anguish. He soothed and blew on the welt, and then got a wet washcloth and cooled down the heat of her stripes.

"It is over, *ma chèrie,* and I am oh so proud of you," he said, putting as much approval as possible in his tone.

"Thank God," she said.

He removed the spreader bar, and holding her hips, he moved behind her, placing his heated cock up against her wet folds. Elizabeth groaned. "Remember *ma chèrie,* you may not climax. If you do I swear I will cane you as punishment. I will be careful, but you are close, are you not? You must tell me if you cannot control yourself and I will stop, yes?"

Still breathless, and wide-eyed at his threat, she nodded.

"*Bon*," he said, and thrust his cock into her hot, soaking cunt. Elizabeth moaned in an endearing manner, and he chuckled, knowing how pitifully desperate she was. But he was desperate too. He fucked her slowly, and after moistening his thumb with her slick essence, he put it in her ass, thrusting in and out, synchronizing it with his cock as he fucked her.

"Do you like my thumb in your ass, Elizabeth?"

"God yes!"

He laughed. "Tell me what you want, little slut," he said, intentionally caressing her with a low seductive voice.

Elizabeth whimpered and mewled with need. "Oh please, Sir. Just fuck me like this and let me come. You feel so good. Please, please let me come!" she begged.

"Soon, *ma chèrie*," he assured her. "You and I will both climax when my cock is deep in your ass, remember?"

She groaned, and André callously laughed at her frustration.

He didn't touch anywhere near her sex, certain she would release if he did so, but he wanted her to get used to the feel of his thumb and his cock together fucking two of her three holes. After long minutes of slow, measured strokes, Elizabeth was wailing, sobbing and screaming for release.

He made her stand up straight and removed her nipple clamps, sucking, licking and soothing each tortured nipple. The woman was too close. She didn't have control, so André wanted to give her time to catch her breath. He turned her toward the bedpost and had her rest against it, while he massaged her shoulders, her back, thighs, and calves, carefully working out all the tension from the punishment she had taken for him.

When her breathing was deep and regular, and her heart rate had slowed, he said, "*Bon, ma chèrie*. It is time for you to find what it feels like to have a man's cock deep inside your tight little asshole." Elizabeth whimpered at this, and he chuckled at her need. "Do you want me to fuck you in the ass, Elizabeth?"

234

"God yes, Sir!"

"Good girl," he said. He uncuffed her from the bedpost. Her nipples were large and red, just as he had planned.

"On the bed now, on all fours, ass in the air, rest on your forearms," he directed. She complied instantly, and he cuffed her wrists to the side of the bed. He stood behind her then, and nudged her legs apart until his cock was at just the correct height to take her. For some time he studied her, making approving, erotic comments.

"You should see your beautiful sex, buttocks and ass! *Mon Dieu, c'est fantastique!* Your pussy blushes crimson and is oh so swollen, and your cunt hole is gaping wide – it tries to entice my cock. Your *derrière - pauvre -* it also is red from having so willingly accepted its punishment. I could climax right now, simply by looking at it. *Bonne fille, bella fille. Merci* for such a gift. The three red stripes from my little cane are so very pretty."

He reached over her and pulled on her braid, raising her head. Elizabeth looked directly into the floor to ceiling mirror.

Their eyes met and André smiled. *Magnifique!*

Chapter 15

Plucking the Cherry

At the sight of Elizabeth's ass in the air, André's throbbing cock twitched and pulsed. He stroked it once more, pumping it to ease his need.

"*Ma chèrie,* now I see you clearly, I see the eyes, I see the red sore nipples and your breasts. Such large breasts! They hang so well. When I thrust into you, those breasts will swing back and forth and the nipples will rub on this sheet, no? It will feel very well I think."

He bent over her and played with her clit and traced her labia, and she made a number of sweet helpless sounds, needy desperate noises. André laughed. "I know how you feel, *ma chèrie.* I, too, shall soon burst. Keep your head up, and look into the mirror. I will hold your braid to steady myself, when I ride you - you are such a luscious mount. It may be a rough ride, because you are a little worked up, yes? You will thrash and buck, as I fuck you, I think. Yet I have ridden difficult mounts before. It is such a privilege to break you into this pleasure, Elizabeth, to show you the joy of a cock in your small hole. But I want to watch your reactions as I fuck your ass for the first time, so look at me in this mirror."

Elizabeth, who was watching him, nodded wordlessly. Her countenance was heavy with lust and exhaustion yet André could see by the whites of her eyes that she was anxious, too, afraid to have her ass violated. He had been keeping her off balance and preparing her, charging up her entire body for this one moment. And now the moment had come. At first he would go slow, but by the end she would love anal sex. Elizabeth was ultra sensitive as he had planned... and ultra horny.

"Spread your legs, *oui* like that. Now don't move."

André looked around one last time. Elizabeth was still wearing her stockings and garter belt and the sight of her in them with her ass in the air heated him up. Her buttocks were red, with hand prints, whip marks and three large welts from the cane. He felt the heat of her burning buttocks radiating to his hips and thighs and cock. Her eyes were on him, her tits hanging low, her legs spread just right. The woman was highly aroused, flushed and breathing heavily. Perfect. All was ready.

Spreading her butt cheeks, he began to lick deep in her asshole, stroking, prodding and curling his tongue inside her. Elizabeth gave a strangled moan and began making incoherent sounds, "Ah, um, ah, ah, oh!"

André's lips circled her anus and he pressed a finger inside the tight muscle of her rim, pulling her open and available for his invading tongue.

"Oh God!" she cried out.

"*Oui, oui*, it is good, and you are ready. You can take the toy, *ma chèrie*, so you can take me." With his cock hot against her entrance, Elizabeth trembled. Sir leaned over and wet his fingers in her channel. Then, slick with her essence he circled and stroked her engorged clit, exactly as he had learned she did when she was masturbating herself. Elizabeth groaned and thrust against him.

"What do you want, Elizabeth?" he whispered in her ear.

"Sir! Please let me come!"

"Do you remember what I told you? When I would let you climax? What has to happen, Elizabeth?"

"You said I could come when you're in my ass, Sir."

"*Oui*," he said. "Do you want me to fuck your ass, *ma chèrie?*"

"God, yes!"

"Fuck it deep and hard? Do you want me to make you scream?"

"Oh please, Sir! Yes please. I beg you, please just fuck my ass and let me come!"

He laughed. "*Eh bien, bella fille* I like to hear you beg, as you well know. Very well, I shall do as you ask. *Ma chèrie*, this is what I do now," he said, pulling out a jar from the bed side table and taking a large dollop of lube he began generously covering his cock with it. "I put the lubricant on my cock and in your ass. Then I will work my cock inside you. You have a small tight hole, *ma chèrie*, but it has had a large butt plug in it much of this day so you will be ready for my cock. I warn you that it will hurt at first, but not as much as the cane, of this *j'assure*."

André began to put lube on her anus, pressing it inside with a finger - abruptly he remembered the anal syringe. He pulled it out from the side table and inserted it, squeezing the bulb, squirting a large portion of lubricant in. "I will tell you what to do, how to breathe through it. Relax and take my cock, Elizabeth, just as you took the toy. Then all will be well. I told you before that you will be an anal slut, and it is true. You will adore my cock up your ass, *ma chèrie*. Do you have any questions?"

She shook her head and André smiled. The woman was so ripe with unsatisfied lust that she was simply overwhelmed. An abject, servile slave to her submissive nature and sexual hunger, Elizabeth would deny him nothing right now. This was exactly how he wanted her. Knowing that he had brought her to this pinnacle of voracious lust gave him an absorbing sense of triumph.

"Look at me, Elizabeth," he said and she instantly complied, gazing back at him in the mirror. "*Bon*. Now take a deep breath and push that tight rosy asshole against me. Open for me and take my cock. Impale yourself upon me. Take a deep breath, *ma chèrie*. Then loosen this oh so luscious *derrière*. Relax and open," he ordered in a stern uncompromising voice. "Right now."

Elizabeth bit her lip and appeared to concentrate. As she pushed back against him her head began to lower.

With this his hand wrapped in her braid he jerked her head back. Her eyes, heavy lidded, flew open and André met her gaze in the mirror. "I want to see you, *ma chèrie*," he reminded her. "I want to see you as you take my cock into your ass." Elizabeth took a deep breath and André braced himself over her, guiding his cock inside. Her hips slowly pushed against him. As she worked herself down onto him, with careful control he thrust deeper, letting his weight fall forward so the head of his cock breached her.

Instinctively she tried to thrash and struggle but he held her immobile. "Oh God," she yelled. "It's too big!"

"Be still," he reproved. He gripped her firmly, one hand on her hip, pulling her braid with the other, telling her to take this stabbing torment for him. It would not last long, her anal passage would adjust and accommodate him soon. Just like the cane, she must accept him. Accept this small pain, endure it in order to enjoy it, as it would soon be so much better.

"But it burns!"

"Do the cane strikes hurt now?"

"A little," she said in a forlorn voice, in between breathless little pants.

To divert her from her misery, he pinched her clit hard and she yelped. "Your body is adjusting. Concentrate. Let the tension go, *ma chèrie.*" He rubbed her back and shoulders, and stroked her buttocks, leaving just the head of his cock inside as he could go no further. *Fuck she was tight!*

"You are so good," he crooned in a caressing voice. "You make me very happy. It feels amazing, to feel your tight virgin ass, to know you will take my cock, because you want it. It will be wondrous, I swear. Do you want my cock, Elizabeth? Tell me you want my cock in your ass."

She expelled a deep breath and said, "Yes, I want your cock in my ass, Sir."

He knew the moment she relaxed and stopped bracing. Elizabeth made a harsh cry as he immediately took advantage and slid further inside. "Breathe, *ma chèrie*. You are doing very well. It is not so bad, and soon it will be very good." She trembled and whimpered. Intently watching her in the mirror, André could see her focusing, with both her lips pressed firmly together. He slid deeper then, just a bit, stretching her, and Elizabeth's blue eyes flew wide open as her anal passage expanded to accommodate him.

"Oh," she said with surprise and he slid all the way inside her then, in to the hilt. "Oh! God! My God!"

André's smile was tight as he fought for control. Yet intense satisfaction resonated throughout his body.

For he had taken Elizabeth's cherry.

Chapter 16

Accepting Andrè

André felt his balls press firmly against her dripping, heated pussy.

"Good girl," he said in a hoarse voice. "Just hold me. I am deep in your ass, *ma chèrie*, all the way in. Relax now, let your body adjust." He held still, letting her get used to the rigid length of his erection. His palm grazed her flank and cupped her swollen feminine mound, her outer lips and clit, flicking and teasing, transforming her discomfort into voracious sexual need.

"Oh, oh, oh! Ahhhh!" Elizabeth cried out, instinctively bucking and jerking from the concentrated pleasure he was giving her.

André held on tight to her braid and pushed against her, riding her as she bucked. Waves of intense sensation rushed into his testicles, thighs and shaft, along with a pounding pulse of blood, making him feel large as a house. The woman was so hot, so small and unyielding! André was having trouble maintaining control. He wanted to thrust, he wanted to pound inside her taut little hole until he came, but he fiercely subdued these natural impulses. "It does not feel bad now, does it?" he said in a choked whisper.

"No Sir," she breathed. There was awe and wonder in her voice.

André delicately traced and stroked between her legs. Elizabeth's pussy pulsed, and as a result her ass clenched down on him. Striving for control he groaned, and felt Elizabeth quiver beneath him. He pulled out a little, then moved back in, allowing the lubricant to coat her - back and forth, in and out, until she stretched and accepted him more easily. But *merde!* This *petite* woman was the tightest thing he had ever had.

He pressed his body on to hers, driving deep inside, feeling her flesh quiver. "Do you like it?" he asked, speaking near her ear. He intentionally let his breath tickle her, one hand keeping her hair pulled tight. The entire time he watched her in the mirror, and she watched him. It was perfect. "Do you like the feel of my cock deep in your ass?"

Elizabeth moaned and bowed her ass back into him, then her eyes shut while her face screwed up into a grimace. André felt her buttocks contract. He tugged her hair, hard. "Open your eyes, Elizabeth." Her eyes flew open wide, searching his face. "You do not have permission to come, do you understand?"

"Yes, Sir."

"Can you control yourself? For if you can't I will use the cane."

She paled at this threat, then swallowed and bit her lips. "Yes, Sir."

"Good girl. *Ma chèrie,* remember how I used your mouth like an object to masturbate?"

"Yes, Sir."

"*Bon,*" he said. "Now I do the same with your tight ass," he told her and firmly gripping her hips, he slowly pushed his cock inside her until he was in to the hilt. Elizabeth groaned. "*Oui. C'est très bon. Ma chèrie,* be very still. I move you now, off my cock." He pushed her forward, and his shaft drew out of her, slowly, slowly until only his round head remained in her sensitive anal flesh. Then once more, again very slowly, he drew her toward him, until his hips and thighs were flush against her burning hot round globes, and deep inside her. He did this three more times and Elizabeth began to writhe and groan, trying to arch toward him. He stopped and slapped her buttocks.

"Behave, *ma chèrie*. You must be still, and let me use your body. It is here for my pleasure."

She moaned, giving a little cry of protest, or a strangled groan of aching need. "Oh God," she mumbled, probably unaware that she had even spoken. André chuckled, knowing his words had turned her on even more.

"Perhaps later, when Mark joins us I will take your cunt and he will take your ass. Would you like that Elizabeth? Would you like to be fucked in both holes at once?"

Elizabeth's response to this was an inarticulate moan and a rippling pulse that sent a wave of sensation through him. "Fuck!" he said, and pinched her breast, twisting it hard. It surprised her and her building orgasm stopped.

"Do not come, Elizabeth. You are not allowed to come." After that he didn't goad her further with erotic words, yet he continued for some time, moving in and out of her with measured, even strokes. He himself was breathing faster, yet still low and slow. "*Eh bien*, Elizabeth, you are doing very well. It is not *difficile, n'est-ce pas*? I move you as needed."

"Yes, Sir," she choked.

"Now *ma chèrie*," he said. "We add one more thing." He drew her toward him, sinking himself inside her to the hilt then holding her perfectly still against his hips and thighs. "Good girl, Elizabeth. Now, squeeze down on me with that oh so delicious *derrière* of yours. I want to feel those muscles." When she did so he groaned.

"*Oui, oui, merde!*" he said in a ragged voice. If the woman squeezed again he would probably come, for her ass was like a hot pulsing fist. With a deep breath he got control of himself and then laughed. "It is very good, *ma chèrie*. Yet it takes concentration. For the present, we do this many, many times, and each time I pull you down on to my cock you must stop there, and squeeze me hard, *comprenez vous?"*

They got into a slow, inexorable rhythm. He pulled his cock all the way out of her ass, then pushed it all the way back in. Then Elizabeth would squeeze down hard on him like a vice. Then out of her ass once more, and all the way back in, then she would obediently squeeze down hard on him like a vice, and so on.

But what would it feel like if Elizabeth did all the work? he wondered. *If he simply stood still while she fucked him with her ass?*

But never in a million years could André have expected the result of this impulsive decision.

 *Chapter 17*

Tantric Anal Sex

When he was satisfied André said, "You are very good, Elizabeth. You know what to do. I want you to continue these actions, but now you are to fuck me with your ass, you understand? Impale your hot tight ass on my cock and then when it is deep inside, as deep as it can go, you will squeeze hard. Then move off my cock and so on. You go at the pace I have set, you can do this?"

"Yes Sir," she said and she did.

André stood still while Elizabeth fucked him, pushing her beautiful ass up, taking him inside her and each time squeezing his cock hard. Holding her braid in one hand, and carefully fondling her clit and pussy with the other, he made her move in slow, measured strokes. Because of the concentration it took, Elizabeth didn't climax. Instead both of them remained on the cusp of ecstasy.

Long timeless minutes passed.

André reflected that what they were doing was like a Buddhist exercise or mindfulness contemplation. His mind and body confronted contradictory sensations: to take – to give; to resist - yet to yield; to submit - yet to refuse to give in to orgasm. Delirious with pleasure, time stood still for André.

He came to himself suddenly, unaware of how long he had been standing there, absorbing and enduring such pleasure. He couldn't even explain what had suddenly recalled him to his senses. André found his hands gently resting on Elizabeth's hips and could not recall having let her braid go, or having put them there. How much time had passed? Experienced Dom that he was, he had lost all awareness and control during sex. Somehow, for some odd reason this worried him not at all.

This was divine. It was intimate. It was profound, and if he had been told that this was what it was like in heaven, he could well believe it. How had he come to this mystical world? This strange euphoric state? It was a place that he had never heard of, a place only saints and poets might have imagined.

"Elizabeth?' he said, looking into her dreamy, heavy lidded, lust filled eyes in the mirror.

"Yes, Sir?" Her voice was soft, yet euphoric. André knew she was joyously transported to be serving him as she was, awed to be giving him such pleasure, and to be receiving such pleasure. All power exchange was altered, for right now, he was under her control. Again, this did not bother him. Yet it should.

"*Ma chèrie*," André whispered, "tell me how it is with you? What do you feel?"

All the while Elizabeth didn't stop. She continued as she had been bidden, pushing herself, impaling herself upon his cock, then when he was deep inside of her, squeezing him firmly. Then drawing away, letting him pull out of her tight ass, almost to the sensitive rim of her flesh. It was very slow, extremely deliberate and it took complete concentration. André felt that for both of them, sex in this manner was like a form of delicious, sensual meditation.

"Sir," she said in a tone of awe. "It's pure bliss. I'm on the cusp of orgasm, yet I'm in full control. I have never experienced such pleasure. It is beyond anything."

"For me, also," he said. "And yet while our spirits are willing, our flesh cannot continue like this. *Je regrette* we must leave this heavenly plane *ma chèrie*, and return to our base desires."

Suddenly disconcerted, and wanting to regain his customary dominance, André said, "Stop now." Then, holding her hips still, he pulled out of her.

Elizabeth gave a little sound of protest. This was not surprising, he thought, for neither of them had climaxed.

Focusing upon her physical needs, André determinedly set aside the profound experience he had just had. While he didn't understand exactly what had happened, he needed a breathing space in order to get back into control. Attending Elizabeth's after care would manage that. Opening the side table drawer again, he found another anal syringe and inserted it, squeezing the bulb.

"Oh!" she said.

"It is only more lubricant and an herbal..." André broke off and said, *"Je ne sais pas,* how do you say? Oh, I do not know the word but it soothes abused tissue, *ma chèrie.* It feels good?"

"Yes, Sir."

"Bon." He then took an antiseptic cream and rubbed it on her buttocks, mainly to soothe the three angry red welts. Afterwards he lay her down on her stomach by simply picking her up and shifting her to where he wanted her. "Do not move," he ordered. His cock was at half mast when he went into the bathroom and pulled three towels from the warming cupboard, bringing a Shea butter moisturizing cream. When he put the towels over her body she moaned. He straddled her back then, careful not to touch her bruised backside, and began to massage her shoulders and neck with the cream.

"Ma chèrie, what did you think of anal sex?"

"Thank you, Sir," her voice was muffled by a pillow. "You said I'd thank you after you had taken me in the ass. Jesus. Thank you, thank you. I'd no idea. It was everything you said it would be. Better in fact. It was divine."

"Just so, I agree," he said. His skilled hands finished with her shoulders and neck, and moved down to her thighs and calves. As she had been on her tip toes during her spanking these were tight, and Elizabeth purred with pleasure at his thorough after care. "But Elizabeth, did you not find that it was a little too divine, yes? Me, it was very good but while not wrong, it was not precisely right."

What we did together was too intimate, too spiritual, he thought. *This woman, this wife should share such a connection with her husband, Mark. Not me.*

André, having finished with her body, sat beside her and examined her cuffed wrists. "With you *ma chèrie*, I am happy to be the animal, with animal needs, and hungers. Sex is strange – it is not unlike food." He took her hands in his, gently turning them palm side up, discovering a desire to kiss each little palm. He ignored the impulse. There had been too much intimacy already. He began to give her a hand massage, rubbing moisturizer into them, taking his time with each small finger.

"Elizabeth, food is very important if you do not have it - not so important if it is available in endless supply. Yet I firmly believe that without sexual intimacy, without skin to skin contact we are something less than human, *ma chèrie*."

Elizabeth, resting on her forearms, had been giving him all her attention. She tilted her head and studied him with penetrating blue eyes and an intuitive, compassionate expression.

André mentally flinched from her knowing look. There was a long moment of silence and then he laughed. "*Mon Dieu*, listen to me! It is usually the woman that talks nonsense after sex."

Elizabeth giggled and the sound was a delight, honest and pure. André suddenly understood why he stopped the tantric anal experience he had accidentally fallen into: it was too intimate. It brought them too close. She belonged to another, and yet he had begun to know her too well, to connect too fully.

This was always a possibility in his work, one for which he had carefully protected himself.

What did he feel for this woman, this giving, generous wife of the angry man Mark? His heart gave a tug, a little pang of anguish for the one thing missing in his life. He cared for her, yes, he cared for all of his clients - it could only be so. How else would he be able to understand them enough to help them? Yet this *petite* powerhouse had touched him.

It is love I feel for her, André thought with shattering insight. *And this cannot be. Can never be.* Fire began to rise within him, a burning, angry heat. *Imbécile! imbécile!* he mentally chastised himself, succumbing to an instant rage.

It was time for the animal, not the man.

Chapter 18

Animal Anal

The Dom in him came to the fore, saving himself from such foolish, irresponsible and dishonorable imaginings. "Up now, Elizabeth," he said harshly. "On your hands and knees on all fours, ass in the air, rest on your forearms."

"Yes, Sir," Elizabeth said, complying instantly with wide, surprised eyes.

He wrapped his hand in her hair, pulling it tight and she gave a little cry. "Keep your eyes on me in the mirror while I take my pleasure, Elizabeth. Now I fuck your ass as it should be fucked."

"Yes, Sir," she said.

André saw a combination of fear and lust in her eyes at this rapid change of pace, yet she could keep up with him. The woman knew him now, for there *was* a connection. If he beat her silly and only pleased himself she would still be content, because she trusted him. The caring went both ways and it made him angry and wild with unrestrained need. He wanted to keep her, to take her captive forever and make her his. And he wanted to punish her for being so perfect, and for engaging his heart against his will.

"I will ride you rough and fast," he growled. "I won't be gentle. Open for me now, and prepare yourself, Elizabeth, for I am going to thrust into you hard." He squeezed her round buttocks fiercely, wrenching them open wide and she screamed out and whimpered, yet even this had further aroused her. The woman was dripping with the inherent desire to serve him in whatever way he wished. It made his blood boil. With one hand he guided his cock to her entrance.

Taking her braid in his hand, and holding one hip with the other, with very little restraint he drove inside her. Elizabeth screamed, but André wasn't worried, for she had opened her tight ring for him and fuck! Her taut heated passage felt *so good*.

This time the anal sex they shared was unrestrained and primitive - it was not the sex of close communication and love. André did not intend to fall into that trap again – instead his hungry soul intended to dominate her and take, take, *take*. He slapped her butt cheeks hard, and pulled her hair, and fucked her as fast and forcefully as he could, savagely erasing kindness or care, in an effort to please himself alone.

It was an attempt to relieve his loneliness — that terrible aching loneliness he had only just become mindful of after that intense connection with Elizabeth. He wanted to be brutal with her, to drive away his shivering conscious awareness. For despite his lifestyle, despite everything he had achieved, he still faced the world by himself. André, without a companion of the soul, had to confront the unfathomable abyss of life alone.

Enraged with his own stupidity, André was furious with her. With unbridled, ruthless fervor he hammered himself into her, burying himself in sensation.

"*Out! Oui!* Move for me, push that tight little ass up against me. *Oui!* Just like that," he said with another slap to her red buttocks. "Fuck I cropped your ass well, didn't I? I still feel the heat of it. You want my cock to pound into you, don't you? Because you're a slut. A horny little slut who will do anything for my hot cum."

He slapped her again, watching her face in the mirror. "Tell me, Elizabeth. Are you a horny little slut? A slut that would do anything for cum?"

"Yes! Yes, Sir!"

"You want my cum in your tight little ass, *n'est-ce pas?*" He said savagely. "You want to drink it, to eat it, to swim in my seed, don't you?"

"Oh, God, yes! Yes, Sir!" she shrieked.

Elizabeth began to make unceasing noises, keening sobs that could have been pleasure or pain. "Ah, ah, ah, oh!" she wailed and shrieked, bucking and squirming beneath his demanding body. André saw that tears were falling from her now, streaming down her face, and this did not surprise him nor did it disturb him. These were tears of release. Such was frequently the case when violating a woman's ass for the first time - there was often so much emotion bound up in this forbidden area.

"Do you want it now, Elizabeth?" André went on relentlessly. "I am pounding your ass so hard, and fuck it feels good. Shall I empty myself, my thick hot streams of cum, deep inside you?"

A raw moan tore from Elizabeth's throat. Still valiantly attempting to meet his eyes in the mirror, she opened and closed her mouth but seemed quite unable to answer. Her blue orbs, André saw, were heavy lidded and dark with extreme pupil dilation. Other than pulling her hair or slapping her *derrière*, he had no intention of touching even her breast - much less her pussy. The woman would climax instantly, and he wanted this to last.

With primitive satisfaction, André growled. For right now she was his, completely in thrall to his desire. If she was being whipped with a bull whip, with her skin being flayed from her bones, André knew that he could still make her climax, using only his command to do so.

"But it doesn't matter if you want my cock hammering into your ass, does it, Elizabeth?" André thrust on, unyielding and remorseless. The muscles in his jaw flexed as he intentionally pushed her to fever pitch. "You are mine to do with as I will.

You are chained to this bed and have no choice, do you, you little anal slut?"

Elizabeth cried out and stiffened underneath him at these erotic words. André felt her body - a tense ball of need - give a hard shudder. He recognized the unrestrained urgency in her eyes, they fairly blazed with frantic desperation as she heroically tried not to come. Elizabeth thrashed and jerked like a wild animal. André, not unlike riding a bucking bronco, held on tight while waves of sensation moved through him, all culminating in the erotic pleasure that pulsed within his balls, his groin and his engorged cock.

"Beg me, Elizabeth. Beg me to come in your ass," he demanded.

"Please, Sir, please!" she wailed. "Oh God, please, I beg you, Sir, please!" she began to chant over and over in a mindless trance of pleasure.

He wanted to fuck her ass forever, to make her take it all, take everything he wanted to give her. André swore viciously as he realized he was going to climax and could do nothing to prevent it. Watching her breasts shake and rock as he pounded into her, seeing her under him, chained to his will, knowing that for now she was wholly his was more than he could take.

"Come for me, Elizabeth," he choked out in a hoarse voice he could hardly recognize, jerking her head up by her braid. "I want to see you come with my cock up your ass."

Yet despite his vaunted control, André came first.

# Chapter 19

Connection

He stared into Elizabeth's sex-glazed eyes, rejecting all connection, yet looking for... something. Chest heaving, pushed beyond his limits, dismayed at his lack of self-control, André felt the familiar sudden sensation of cramping then release of the internal muscles of his groin, as well as the lower abdominals. Consequently with his next brutal stroke, he climaxed just before Elizabeth did.

His head flew back and his hips thrust forward as he convulsed.

As he released, electric heat exploded within. This pleasurable sensation extended out in a powerful rush, into the tendons of the upper thighs, the lower buttocks, back, shoulders, thighs, waist and abdominals. His orgasm was so extreme that the exquisite pleasure registered almost as pain, yet the torturous agony of it was superb.

Elizabeth, moaning and keening, blinked, and then shrieked. Her scream continued, unbroken, like the anguished wail of inevitability.

Deep inside her, André felt her internal muscles grip him, exerting a fierce powerful pressure that squeezed his cock in contracting waves, milking his seed. Astonished and amazed, he ejaculated violently and repeatedly, with terrific volume and velocity. All control fled, as he thrust and pounded in a primal animal reaction to the frenzied thrill of intense pleasure.

Unable to contain such rapturous torment, André voiced an awe-filled volley of crude French oaths. Impulsively he bent over and bit Elizabeth hard between her neck and shoulder. Together they both came and came and came.

André's deep breaths turned to shudders as he returned to earth. He could not recall a more powerful orgasm - nor one that seemed so endless. At one point, he was certain that he was continuing to ejaculate past the point of having any cum to spray. The fierceness of his climax had made him wonder if he might pass out.

At the finish, while he had worked to take, take, *take,* André could wrest nothing from Elizabeth. For the woman — *une femme ideal* - big hearted and sexually generous to a fault had already openhandedly given him everything. And she did so willingly, without self-consideration, or restraint. One could not force or steal what was freely given. Elizabeth understood this. She was a treasure, this small clever woman. And while innocent of the exact details of his life, she knew him better than anyone else in the world.

I spend my life knowing and helping women, he thought. *Yet this woman alone knows me. Yet she cannot help me.* He sighed. *And she knows this, too.*

For a long time André lay heavily upon Elizabeth's back, well aware that he should get off and uncuff her. Yet instead he kissed and nuzzled her neck and shoulders, softly stroking her skin, petting her again and again and again.

"Good girl," he whispered affectionately over and over. "You are such a good girl, *ma chèrie.*"

Chapter 20

Elizabeth's Realization

Who is this person I have become? Elizabeth thought, unable to recognize herself. Yet this sexual being had always been with her. She had denied that part of her personality, and ignored it, and buried it – but it could not be vanquished, for it was the real her.

Elizabeth lay nestled with her head on Sir's chest. Completely naked, sore and thoroughly used, she was in a warm, happy daze. Never had she experienced such an intense, explosive, mind-blowing orgasm. They just kept getting better and better.

The garters and stockings were gone, she had been washed and cosseted and fed. Once again she was chained to the bed with only one ankle cuff. This captor of hers had vowed to care for her and he certainly was fulfilling that promise. Sir was slimmer than Mark, and he had pulled her into his arms so closely that as they lay together on the bed, she was almost completely draped across him.

"Sir," she said. "May I speak?"

"You may speak freely, *ma chèrie*," he replied, still stoking her hair. The man had undone her braid and never seemed to tire of stroking her hair. It was comforting and relaxing and she certainly wasn't going to make any attempt to stop this wonderful quirk of his. "And my name is André," he said. "André Chevalier."

"Your name is André?" she asked, taken by surprise that he would openly tell her who he was.

When he looked down at her his smile was warm. "Yes. Do you know that I have had an irrepressible desire to hear my name on your sweet lips, Elizabeth? And I like the sound of it. Say it again. Say my name."

"André. André Chevalier," she repeated obligingly. She was going to ask him why he had told her this, but she already knew why, so she said nothing. Both of them knew, but in tacit agreement, they had not spoken about the large, uncomfortable elephant in the room. "André Chevalier," she whispered once more, and he gave her a tight hug.

Elizabeth remembered the saying André had told her, the knowledge that had so opened up her awareness: *'Life's most obvious truths are the hardest to see but once you've burned everything to the ground they are the only things left standing.'*

The saying was accurate for everyone, including *Monsieur* André Chevalier. For Elizabeth knew him now, from this one intense day in his company. Unexpectedly, while André was finding and unlocking the key to her soul, she had accidentally done the same to him.

We have both come through the fire, she thought. *And with the debris cleared away I see my captor clearly now.*

Elizabeth understood something about André that she felt he was only just beginning to understand about himself. Like linking to a computer, data transfer could occur in both directions, and that is what had happened through their coupling. Although she was the one that was chained, André Chevalier was the real captive. Somehow she knew that he had never understood that hard truth until today. Their amazing sexual connection had exposed it to him – and to her.

Thoughtlessly she had looked at him with compassion. Elizabeth shivered as she recalled André's murderous look. He had responded to her sympathy with savage dominance. *"Up now, Elizabeth. On your hands and knees on all fours, ass in the air, rest on your forearms."*

The man had wanted to be cruel, to distance himself and separate from her, and even then she hadn't been frightened of him. *I know him,* she thought. *André Chevalier has no power to hurt me, because I understand him.*

She and Mark did not have a good sex life, but they would now, thanks to André. For, come hell or high water, she would confront Mark, tell him all her secrets and repressed desires and bare her soul. Only denial and cowardice had prevented her from looking at herself and exploring her sensual needs. But what was Mark's reason for giving up sexually on her? Had he been afraid to lose her?

Elizabeth smiled, inexplicably certain that that was his biggest fear. The big tough guy had his own weakness. He was afraid because he valued her too much. Well, together they would work it out. For Elizabeth was not alone. Mark was her own true love and she was his. He was her best friend, a man to cherish and care for, a man who was unconditionally on her side.

And André? While Elizabeth knew nothing about the man, she did know this: he had discovered a real bond with her. But she wasn't his to have, and she would soon leave him and then he would be alone. Her heart twisted at his pain.

After discovering the joy of honest connection, Elizabeth knew that André Chevalier had realized that he needed what she and Mark, for all their problems, already had. André was lonely because he was all alone. He understood this now.

André Chevalier was missing the profound satisfaction of true love.

Book 5

Elizabeth's

Love Ties

Chapter 1

Mark Nelson

Life sucks, Mark mused, burning with resentment. My wife has been fucking André Chevalier. And she loved every minute of it.

Upon being left alone, Mark had listened all the way through the audio of his wife and the counselor. It had shocked him to the foundations of his entire reality, making him re-think everything. Immediately afterwards he had taken a long cold shower, ignoring the enticing smell of food and the rumbling complaints from his stomach.

Elizabeth has been faking orgasms, he thought. But she can come with Chevalier, alright.

Somewhere in the back of his mind, Mark knew that the anger he was directing at his Lizzy was unfair, but he couldn't put any of it aside. She hadn't wanted to hurt him, but it had hurt him, knowing that he couldn't satisfy his own wife. After toweling off he noticed the array of clothes that had been left for him. There was plenty to choose from. He settled on an up market, black tracksuit and black T-shirt. Black. The color of my mood.

He pulled on the T-shirt and scowled. Mark had watched every bit of the video of Chevalier sexually tormenting and fucking his wife. Even wild with fury and burning with jealousy as he was, it had still given him the hard on of all hard ons. Why hadn't he been the one to unlock Elizabeth's sexuality? But Mark didn't need a brain like Einstein to answer that question. The real question was, why hadn't he figured out his own sexual preference?

Dressed, Mark slammed out of the shower area in disgust. So many years in denial as such perverse desires had been too uncomfortable to accept. But right now, even more than he wanted to kill Chevalier, Mark wanted to dominate and fuck Elizabeth silly, exactly as that rat bastard had done.

A smorgasbord of food had been left in heated and cooled compartments on a table near the wall. Ravenous, he piled a plate full of a number of delicacies without thinking, sat on the couch and began to wolf it down. While he did, he read through the little booklet, the training manual concerning BDSM. Mark was a quick study, and while the subject was new to him, it was also bizarrely familiar. It was like finding an old photo of oneself and suddenly remembering completely forgotten moments from one's past. Only BDSM was not anything he had ever experienced. Perhaps it was more like learning another language as a child, moving to another country, and then suddenly finding you have the ability to understand and speak it as an adult. Sexual domination for him was inbuilt and instinctive, like some sort of natural law.

I'm a dominant and Elizabeth is a submissive, he thought, and the truth of these statements seemed as certain and definite as gravity. "Dominant," he said out loud. And his lips curled into a smile of genuine pleasure as he whispered, "Submissive." Even the word made him hard. Mark felt a surging sense of 'rightness' inside. These concepts, instead of being foreign, were as recognizable to him as his own face. For so many years, he had repressed his own desires, forcing himself "to be good." When all along Elizabeth had wanted to relinquish control in bed - she couldn't orgasm unless dominated, and by God he had wanted to dominate her. Both of them had been denying and suppressing their sexual needs. The irony was absurd.

If it wasn't so sad and stupid, he thought, I'd be laughing my ass off.

After finishing the first plate of food, Mark went back for seconds, and this time he was slightly more discerning, going for seconds on the prawn and chicken curry. There was so much he hadn't known or understood about his wife, or for that matter, about himself. Why hadn't they talked about it? He was afraid to lose her by exposing the darker side of himself, but what was her excuse? Elizabeth had secrets. Of course he had secrets, too, so he shouldn't feel betrayed. Yet he did.

Sitting on the comfortable lounge, Mark drank a bottle of Corona Extra. In fact, he had been drinking a number of beers, and had lost count somewhere around six. In a drunken haze, Mark listened to the audio of his wife and the expensive "sexual counselor" once more.

The second time he heard it made him feel even worse than it had before.

Chapter 2

Audio

André: "You are a treasure, Elizabeth, and Mark is a lucky man. Thank you for telling me this truth of yours. I am honored. You have not spoken of this to your husband, no?"

Elizabeth: "I..no, I haven't, Sir."

André: "Because you did not wish to hurt him, to make him question his manhood perhaps?"

Elizabeth: "Sir, I didn't want to hurt him."

André: "Because you love your husband Mark, very much, this is so?"

Elizabeth: "Yes, Sir."

André: "Again, I thank you for telling me, *ma chèrie*," he said. "You see? These little truths between us will not harm you. Tell me, have you ever masturbated in front of anyone?"

Elizabeth: "No, Sir."

André: "Not even your husband, Mark?" His tone was incredulous.

Elizabeth: "No, Sir."

André: "How often do you masturbate? And where do you do it?"

Elizabeth: "About once per day, I guess, and in the shower."

André: "Why do you not do it with your husband? He would enjoy watching, I am sure."

Elizabeth: "I don't know. I guess I'm a bit embarrassed and ashamed that I even do it. It is an impulse, a need that I just want to get over and done with. I never thought of telling Mark, or doing it with him. I don't even think I could climax with him watching - it would distract me. Besides, he might think I'm a slut or something."

André: "*Mon Dieu!* The truth from your lips is like the song of angels, *ma chèrie*. You do not shy around the difficult subjects, explain and make the justifications. I bow to you."

Elizabeth: "I've been worried about Mark. Is he alright? Is he…very angry?"

André: Laughing. "You know this man very well. He is very angry and not at all *convenable*, this large, tough husband of yours. *J'assure*, Mark does not suffer too much. The torment that comes to him he brings on himself. *Bon.* Do not fear, *ma chèrie.* As long as you are good, I will let you spend at least an hour each day together. If he does not obey me I shall punish him another way, not by robbing you of time spent with him."

Elizabeth: "If he finds out I've had sex with you…well, I don't know what would happen. Do you think he'll hate me for being a slut? I don't know what I'd do without him."

André: "I envy this husband of yours. You and I, together we have sex and respect. But with you and Mark there is love, no?"

Elizabeth: "Yes, we love each other, but he's also my best friend."

André: "You will not lose Mark, *ma chèrie*. I will manage this unmanageable husband of yours, this I swear. He is very *difficile*, no? But I have days to find the lever that will work on him. It is for me to tell him what we do together, and for me to resolve your concerns."

Elizabeth: "Thank you, Sir."

André: *"Ma chèrie.* You tell me that it is becoming difficult to climax with your husband, Mark? And that you have not told him this as you do not wish to hurt him. You are afraid he will feel less of a man, yes?"

Elizabeth: "Yes."

André: "And you masturbate to ease your need, but this is another secret, no?"

Elizabeth: "Yes."

André: "And you do not have the affair or go with another man?"

Elizabeth: "No! Of course not. Never."

André: "Then how often do you fake the orgasm, when you have sex?"

Elizabeth: "I..well," she stammered, "most of the time."

André: "Your husband, he is a sensitive and considerate lover?"

Elizabeth: "Oh yes, Sir. Mark is always very caring in bed."

André: Laughing. "And so, this is where he goes wrong. *Ma chèrie*, sex and love are two very different matters."

Chapter 3

Mark's Explosion

The video of André Chevalier fucking his wife, the audio version that confirmed that he was crap at satisfying her, the indignities he had suffered as a prisoner, all of these things culminated in an overwhelming surge of violence that couldn't be held inside.

With sudden uncontrollable wrath, Mark stood up and screamed out loud in a primal soul wrenching sound of pain. *It is too much!* he thought. *Everything! Everything I haven't said, everything I haven't done! So much time wasted!*

His body heated like a furnace and his vision blurred with rage. "Fuck this shit!" he yelled as he walked over to the large flat screen television and threw it across the room. It made an extraordinarily satisfying crash against the wall.

And I'm just getting started! he thought, exhilarated by the wanton destruction of the massive TV, the largest he had ever seen.

Like a bonfire made from thin, dry kindling soaked in gasoline, Mark's rage exploded as if lit with one well placed match. "Fuck this, too," he added, throwing the table the food was on, including the food, across the room. He picked up the expensive expresso machine and, going for distance, he heavily projected it, as if he were an Olympian making a shot put throw. It split into three pieces and Mark gave a bark of laughter as coffee grounds and beans flew like shrapnel across the room.

Still giggling like a madman, Mark tossed a chair, and when it didn't break he grabbed it and smashed it again and again until two legs came off. Then he flipped over the large leather couch, grabbing a table knife and hacking into it. Tossing each glass and plate hard against walls, as well as both side table lamps, and then ripping pictures off the wall and putting his foot through them, Mark reveled in the willful demolition of all things Chevalier. There wasn't much in that small room, but anything that could be broken, was.

Mark's rage burned bright and hot for a few extreme minutes, and then died down. After destroying the room and everything in it Mark felt better, but the thrill didn't last. The alcoholic buzz from a number of beers he had consumed began to ease into a mind-numbing low. With a deep sigh, he turned the couch back over from where he had thrown it. Then he sat down, his passion cooling to glowing embers of heat.

It was not long after that André Chevalier opened the door.

Mark watched André come in, the man's face composed, yet his eyes held a wary look to them. André gestured to the destruction that littered the room, "Did this make you feel better, *Monsieur?"* he asked.

Mark blinked and then stared at the bastard, the man who had been fucking his wife. What was with the clothes he was wearing? André Chevalier was usually dressed to the nines. *What?* Mark's mind whirled in befuddled confusion. *Was that a tracksuit? Had the man just come from the gym?*

Four inches shorter, and slimmer, André's darker hair was straight and cut short compared to his own longer brown wave. The man looked aesthetic and almost effeminate next to Mark's large muscular frame. André was always well dressed, with little chest hair compared to Mark's, "Hugh Jackman" Wolverine-ish pelt.

What does Elizabeth see in this little prick? he thought. André's arrival fanned the dying flames of his fury, and an ember of anger began once more to burn. Mark stood up as André shut the door, and approached him.

"Bastard!" Mark said, balling his big hands into fists.

"Monsieur," André said calmly. "We need to talk, I think."

Mark drew himself up into a skilled boxing stance, then came toward his enemy and started swinging. André ducked, dodging the blow by a narrow margin.

"Really?" Mark said derisively, drawing back another fist. "Because I think I need to beat the shit out of you."

Chapter 4

Andrè Chevalier

Merde! André mentally swore. The big man is fast!

André dodged the drunken man's blow without too much trouble, but he couldn't evade forever. It was too bad, because neither avoiding this fight, nor winning it would achieve his objective. In these circumstances, it was best to lose, or all would indeed be lost.

I have made many mistakes, André thought with a healthy chill of fear combined with calm inevitability. And it is for me to make it right. Yet I suspect this will hurt very much. C'est la vie.

"You rat bastard!" Mark shouted, cramming a furious fist into André's stomach, and then he caught him with another strike to the head as André jackknifed. André gasped. Ducking and turning, he escaped further blows.

That last hit had almost knocked the wind out of him. Putting a hand to his face, he wiped blood from his bleeding nose. Even drunk, the jealous warrior was utterly dangerous. André had been studying the big man for some time on the closed-circuit TV. He had watched and waited until after Mark had imbibed a large amount of alcohol, the effects of which he had hoped would make him less formidable. Then, after the man had taken his rage out on his furniture and possessions, expending his strength, André had come in. He had intended that the big man would be to some degree, worn down. Apparently the giant still had lots of energy left.

"I have fucked your wife Monsieur," André said, intentionally goading him, while holding a cloth against his nose to stop the flow of blood, "and your wife has fucked me. Elizabeth has had many orgasms under my hand, and under yours, perhaps not so many, eh? Tell me Monsieur, are you angry with her, or with me?"

André witnessed Marks face first turn white with rage, as he processed what he had said. Mark rose to his full height with his arms aggressively held at shoulder height. As the blood rushed back, making his face crimson, Mark screamed, "Fucking bastard! I swear I'll kill you!" With that he sprang toward André.

Another blow smashed André in the mouth, cutting his upper lip against his teeth, drawing more blood. Spinning on his heel, he moved to escape this punishment. This was a mistake, as Mark continued to rain physical blows in a steady stream, each strike punctuated with words that André hardly heard. "Fuck my wife, will you?" One pummeling blow gave him an agonizing jar to the kidneys. "I'm going to tear your arms off and jam them up your fucking ass, you piece of shit!"

André jumped away, and faced forward in a defensive crouch. With non-inebriated speed he was able to grab two fingers of Mark' hand, painfully twisting them, wrenching them back behind the man's torso. With the other hand he grasped the back of Mark's neck, propelling the man with considerable force, striking his forehead against a wall.

What followed was a ridiculous series of punches and falling blows pounding into male flesh. Mark, even drunk, and almost twice André's weight, had an extreme advantage. André's effectiveness was that he was fast, fit and fresh. But both men, he noticed, sweating and exhausted, were flagging under this exertion.

"Your wife loves you," André said, panting loudly and escaping behind the couch after getting a vicious thump in on

Mark's face. Unfortunately the strike, while cutting the big man's cheek, had little other effect. "It is not me she loves, Monsieur."

"This isn't what I wanted!" Mark shouted.

Je suis désolé, Monsieur," André said. "Excusez-moi, but do you love your wife?"

Mark paused, his eyes wild, looking as if he may explode. "Of course I love her!"

"Monsieur, if you love her then you will speak honestly to her. The way of silence is death to a relationship." Mark reached for André then and, with an evasive jump, André escaped, turning to face the bigger man once more, in a prepared stance. "Silence is the way of the coward. I do not know what you fear, Mark, but it is time to face this fear."

This last parting comment set Mark off, and André stood and took it, evading or minimizing any powerful strike as much as possible and landing a number of blows himself. "I swear I'll kill you!" Mark yelled and came at André with a charge of fury.

"Coward!" André shouted. "You do not deserve her! Elizabeth is too good for such as you."

Nimbly jumping over the couch, and leaping on top of the big man from behind, André landed a few punches before Mark spun in a circle and slammed André down onto the ground. This is like World Federation Wrestling, André thought in idle bemusement, lying in an agonized heap on his stomach on the floor.

Mark jumped on top of him, and wrapped an arm around his neck. André tried to butt him by throwing his head back, but he was caught. There was no escape. André gasped, his lungs heavily dragging air in despite the heavy weight pressing upon him. André could almost feel the big man's wrath lessening with the satisfaction at having beaten his adversary, and yet it was still at a dangerous level. André had received a rather savage beating, this was true. But it had been worth it. For even as he had endured the big man's onslaught, André could sense the cleansing effect of this violent battle.

Security burst through the door then, three huge burly men, with tasers drawn.

"Non!" screamed André.

Both Mark and André were panting, Mark laying on top of André, chest to back, with a strangle hold to his neck. Yet each had stopped fighting upon the entry of the security guards. André's nose was still dripping blood, but the flow had slowed.

André gave a rapid burst of French, and then in English he said, "We are having a personal dispute, my friends. This man will not seriously harm me, nor kill me."

"I won't?" Mark panted.

"No, Monsieur," André assured him. "For the most perfect Elizabeth would be made unhappy, and you would go to jail. Tell these men that you are in your right mind, mon ami, if you please. That you do not intend to maim or kill. Then they will go and then we will finish this, and resolve our differences."

Mark, whose eyes had been bright and wild, now seemed to have a more moderate tone about them. Relieved, André sighed, for the worst was finally over.

"Fine," Mark said. "I won't kill or maim him. I swear it."

The three guards didn't look happy, but they complied with their employer's demand to leave. Mark continued to lay on André, crushing him to the floor. L'homme was heavy, and massive, a powerful bear of a man. André thought of the small, slim body of Elizabeth then, and knew firsthand the constraint the woman experienced with Mark as a lover.

"Mon ami, I bow to your domination over me, j'assure," André said. "You win, I concede." He intentionally raised his eyebrows in query and said, "Do you plan to fuck me, Monsieur?"

Mark jumped off him, and began to laugh as André rose from the floor, and sat with his back resting against a wall.

"You are one sick fuck, you know that?" Mark said.

"Perhaps," André acknowledged. He held his hands out, palms up, in a gesture of submission. "You are a ferocious adversary, Monsieur. I retire, and as they say, the ball is now in your court."

André hoped that his plan would work. He had been comprehensive in his instructions with his security detail about when to come in. André's dissatisfied customer had given him a thorough beating. They had both released their passions and bonded in the most primitive of male traditions. After using their fists against each others' flesh, perhaps now the big man, Mark, could be made to see reason.

Then he could honorably conclude this case difficile. André sighed. Regrettably, after that he would have to say good bye to Elizabeth forever.

Mark's Dark Secret

What a mess, Mark thought. I honestly don't know where to go from here.

"May I get a beer, Monsieur? And perhaps for you, water? André asked. "Or shall I send for coffee as you have destroyed my expresso?"

Mark sighed and then shrugged. "Go ahead," he said with a gesture toward the fridge. "I'll have water." Mark sat leaning against a wall, and watched as André walked across the room, skirting broken debris. The small refrigerator was built into the room, or else he would have thrown that, too.

André returned with a bottle of water for Mark and a beer for himself, and slid down the wall, sitting beside Mark, carefully avoiding shards of glass. André pressed an ice pack against his bloody nose, and Mark's lips curled with satisfaction.

"Oui," André said ruefully, eyeing Mark's happy smirk. "Even drunk you are very dangerous mon ami. I am surprised that no bones are broken."

Mark gave an empty laugh. "I tried, but you're pretty quick. That finger twist thing of yours was a low blow. Pretty sneaky." He rubbed his forehead where it made contact with the wall. "Even drunk, I should have annihilated you. I've got a lot more height and weight. You did okay."

André, sitting on the floor and leaning against the wall, gave him a half bow. "Merci."

They compared battle wounds for a bit, remarking upon each other's better moves, and analyzing the best parts of the fight. After that, Mark went quiet. With nothing to say, a black depression fell in on him and all he could think of was the many ways he had failed himself and failed his wife.

"Monsieur," André said. "Do not despair, for all is well, truly."

"Is that right?" Mark said with a sardonic snort.

"Vraiment," André said. "You have marched yourself into this forest of tribulation, yes, but now take heart. Let me guide you out of these woods. If you are willing to face the hard truths, you can walk yourself out again."

Mark took a long swig of water, and wondered if he could discuss "hard truths" with anyone, much less the man who had fucked his wife. But who better to talk to than the man who had sex with his wife? They had that in common after all, didn't they? Mark also wondered if he could avoid breaking the law by telling his story. Perhaps, without giving details, he could.

He recalled André's question to Elizabeth, that he had heard on audio, "And if Mark wanted to dress himself in feminine erotic apparel during sex, would this disturb you?" and her answer, "It wouldn't bother me, because I love him, and if that is what got him hard that is probably what would get me hot, too."

Mark remained silent, brooding. She's too good for me, he thought.

"Elizabeth," André added, "is very much in love with you, Mark. If some things are perhaps difficult to face, it may be easier to confront them by thinking of her. Elizabeth would want you to face your fears." André stood up then and began to pace. "Does one get into trouble for keeping quiet? No! Only by communicating does one meet such trials. The passions do not come with silence," André said. "And without sincere communication there is death to love."

André began to gesticulate wildly with his hands while he paced and explained. Mark felt an internal laugh at the stereotype. André's energetic movements while talking was something he supposed that the excitable French were apt to do. "Mon Dieu, a lack of honesty is death to anything that lives. Oh, I do enjoy the passions, Monsieur! But I am French! And you are very lucky, for the beautiful Elizabeth is yours, Monsieur, only yours."

Mark stared at the bottle of water in his hands, not really seeing it, and said quietly. "I killed a man once. I beat him to death with a baseball bat. I was nine years old at the time."

In his peripheral vision Mark saw André become still.

Mark shook his head at the recollection. Who would have expected something like that in America? A Russian mob hit? Of course Mark's real father, from what he remembered of him, was the kind of guy that 'always did what was right.' His Dad had apparently gone to the police with sensitive, secret information. Mark had never been told what his father had known or how it had gotten him killed. But the idealistic idiot hadn't considered what the result of his actions would be to his family, had he?

Mark watched as André sat down at a comfortable distance from him and remained utterly quiet. Not too close, but close enough to hear. "I was big as a child," Mark continued to muse out-loud. "More like a twelve year old at nine, naturally taking control of my school mates, my friends and even much older boys." Mark frowned. "I don't think it was my size exactly, and I wasn't an asshole. Somehow things were always just done my way, is all."

Mark's mind went back and a shiver of memory went through him. He and his little brother Michael had hidden in the closet after witnessing the intruders shoot his mother, father and older sister in the head. Outside their hiding place, the two assassins had discussed who would finish Mark and his brother off. Then one man left and the other man stayed.

In the total darkness of the closet, Mark's fingers had felt the hard familiar touch of a baseball bat. As he had gripped it something animal inside had come out. It was black, tight and airless in the closet where they had hidden. Mark's little brother Michael was whimpering and had wet himself. The pungent smell of fear and urine filled the confining space, but it didn't matter to Mark. Nothing mattered, for Mark was no longer afraid. He didn't care if he died. It was as if some switch had been flipped and some dark personality, the animal hidden within him had taken over. All of Mark's will was focused, bent on beating his enemy to death.

"And so, after killing a man," André asked, "this instinctive reaction of yours felt like a sin?"

"I hammered him to a pulp," Mark said. "I must have spent thirty minutes just pounding his head into mush. Crying and screaming - all I felt was rage. I'd forgotten my little brother, Michael, I'd forgotten everything." He sighed and looked up, meeting André's gaze. What he saw surprised him. André's demeanor was composed, his eyes politely interested. Marked laughed and said, "You're taking this pretty well."

André said, "Mon ami, I have found that it is not what is, that is the difficulty. It is how the individual interprets what is. As a child you lost control. Bon. What did this mean to you? Particularly as it relates to your natural tendency toward sexual dominance?"

Mark frowned and spent a few moments seeking the answer. "I had plenty of psychological interviews and counseling. Our new parents in witness protection were very Catholic, more than we had ever been, and I confessed my sins many times. All I could get a handle on was the fact that there is something bad inside me, something I had to keep repressed. What would happen if I lost control and let that dark energy out? But I saw what you did with Elizabeth, how you dominated her. Fuck me, I've wanted to do similar things all my life."

"You listened to the audio," André asked, "when Elizabeth told of the fantasy she masturbates to, of you taking her hard and fast against her will? The time you were at the wedding?"

Mark snorted. "Oh yeah. I listened to the audio twice, and I saw the video twice." He sighed, "And I experienced the real thing in the first place. It was life changing wow holy shit sex alright."

André grinned, clearly amused. "It is her fantasy, mon ami, and very nice I think." His brows drew down. "What I wish to know is this, I believe that the wedding sex was a time you let the animal inside, out. Can you say why or how this occurred? When you have spent your life being careful?"

"Oh honestly, it was impossible to resist," he said with a chuckle. "I met Elizabeth the first week at my new school, not long after we started with witness protection. My brother, Michael has always been a bit thin-skinned, even before the er... "incident." Vulnerable, sensitive, he was an easy victim and a perfect target for bullies. I don't know what that is about, but it just seems to me that assholes always know who to attack. Anyway, I had to stay back, to talk to my teacher, and I didn't get out to him immediately after school ended for the day. Two bigger boys had him cornered and were frightening him, I could see that from far away. I started running but along came Elizabeth. I watched that little girl just jump right in, pushing those bigger boys around. Her indignant tongue lashing could be heard from afar. Man she gave those two what for."

Mark smiled remembering exactly what Elizabeth had been like, small and thin and fierce. "You know I think I fell in love with her right then. We three had so much fun together, and it went on for years."

"And at the wedding?" André asked.

"Oh, well. I hadn't seen her in such a long time. Elizabeth was so beautiful and I don't know. We lost our virginity to each other, did you know that? Anyway, seeing her again…well, I just had to have her right now, you know? I guess I was just in total agreement with the animal inside and let him off his chain. It was intense, unavoidable, and by God it was great sex."

André laughed. "I think I begin to understand. The brutish instinct that helped you kill a grown man when you were a child, this dark, powerful nature frightened you, yes?"

"You got that right," Mark said. "To pound a man to mush with a baseball bat? It was pretty overwhelming. I was amazed to have reacted that way."

"Bon," André said. "And then you aligned this threatening passion with your desire to dominate a woman in bed, yes?"

"Yes," Mark said. "Both are instinctive, both seemed dark and wrong. More like a vicious animal rather than a thinking, logical human being."

André gave him a small, knowing smile. "And now mon ami?" he asked. "What do you think now?"

Mark smiled back at him. "Elizabeth likes the beast, and I think it's time to let him out. I have a lot of catching up to do."

Chapter 6

Elizabeth

Elizabeth watched as the cappuccino maker spat its hot milky foam into her cup. Yum. Like everything André had, it was of the best quality and made a truly fine coffee. She looked at the clock on the bedside table. It was a golden sculpture of a graceful woman, dressed circa eighteen hundreds. Maybe the clock was an antique, it certainly could be, probably an expensive one, over a hundred years old.

It was after eight pm. Where was everyone?

"André Chevalier," she said out loud. Sir's name was André Chevalier. Sir had left her uncuffed, with a good bye kiss and instructions to do as she liked until Mark came to her, sometime after dinner. So she had had a luxurious bath, and had liberally rubbed in moisturizer. Sir had left clothes for her too, normal clothes, a simple yet elegant green silk embroidered skirt, classy underwear and a shear, almost see-through white blouse. She was so relieved to be dressed for her visit with Mark.

The last session with André confused and disturbed her. Why had her kidnapper left her uncuffed? And why had he told her his full name? Well, she knew the answer to that question. There was a bond there between them now, a tug of companionable affection that was so real it could even be called love. While André had turned her life upside-down it appeared that she had disturbed him just as much.

But what was she going to say to Mark? And would André set them both free now? Something important had changed, that was all she knew for certain.

After dressing and eating, Elizabeth had lounged around rereading the BDSM booklet. There didn't appear to be any set right or wrong way to do it, it was up to the couple involved. She learned about safe words, and various objects, and 24/7 slaves – something that would most definitely not appeal to her. But would Mark want to do any of this? Would he be appalled at the thought? Could she explain her desire for restraint? She shook her head. It was going to be hard to tell him that she had been faking orgasm, much less anything else.

Elizabeth took a generous sip of coffee, and sat down on the kitchen chair. The longer she waited the more nervous she became. André had told her that he would inform Mark that he had had sex with her. God she sure didn't want to be there for that, because he would be soooo angry. Would André be able to explain? Elizabeth snorted. Good Lord she couldn't explain it herself! Mark would probably hate her and think she was a slut. And truthfully she was a slut, so where would they go from there? Divorce?

But she wasn't really a slut, was she? Not with the negative implication society offered. The affirming words that Sir had said to her still rang in her ears: "*Ma chèrie*, you are so open, *oui!* Such a treasure. I love women. At their best they make the most generous, unselfish and giving lovers of all. You are such a woman, Elizabeth, I think. Your husband, as I have said before, is a very lucky man."

Oh God, she thought, *please let Mark think he's lucky. I don't know what I'll do if he wants to leave me.*

The door opened and Mark came inside, shutting the door behind him.

Chapter 7

Elizabeth's Confession

Mark's gaze met hers and his warm, devastating smile, as it often did, simply made her melt. Elizabeth knew instantly that there were no barriers. Mark's eyes shone with love, heartfelt relief, and joy.

Elizabeth gave a little unintentional squeal and found herself on her feet and in his arms before she was aware that she was moving.

"Lizzy," Mark said, a low voice against her ear, holding her tight against him. "God sweetheart, I've missed you so much."

"Jesus Mark," she said. "Are you okay?"

He took a deep breath, his big chest filling and his arms crushing her to him. "I am now." Stroking her hair, her neck, and back, he said, "How about you?"

"I'm fine. Really. But I've been so worried about you."

Mark reached down and swept her off her feet, picking her up and carrying her in his arms. Elizabeth laughed and wrapped her own arms around him as he walked over to the large lounge chair near the bed and sat down in it, with her on top of him. "You are not going anywhere, my love," Mark said. "Just stay right here on my lap. I need to look at you."

Elizabeth's heart swelled from the expression on Mark's face, the way he drank her in. His forehead rested upon hers, and he rubbed her nose with his own, then he kissed her a slow, generous kiss, a kiss of love rather than passion. Elizabeth felt so happy to be in his arms, but she was still nervous.

"Mark," she said. "Are we allowed to go? Or are we still prisoners? Has André finished with us?"

"Not yet," he said. "I'm not worried about that. André, that rat bastard, has done our relationship some good. We haven't been all together honest with each other have we? Right now I want to discuss us."

"Oh?" she said, wondering desperately, *Oh God, just what had André told him?*

Mark chuckled. "You poor thing," he said and cupped her face with his large hand, stroking her cheek with his thumb. "Okay, let me put you out of your misery. First, yes, I know all about how you and André have been having lots and lots of seriously hot sex."

An odd unintentional squeak of surprise left her lips, and she sat up straight and felt her cheeks begin to warm. With an expression that was dark and unreadable, Mark watched her intently, saying nothing.

"What...what did André tell you?" she managed to ask.

Mark blew out a breath. "I saw the video. I saw the whole thing - more than once I might add."

"Oh my God!" she exclaimed, putting her hands to her heated cheeks.

"It was the hottest damn porno flick I've seen to date," Mark said, his voice harsh with lust. "Gave me the hard on of all hard ons."

Mark has seen the video, she thought. *He knows! But I'm in his arms and on his lap and he isn't mad. Jesus God thank you!* Elizabeth giggled, almost hysterical with relief and laughed out loud.

"Really?" Elizabeth said. "Oh shit! Really? You saw it and you aren't mad at me?"

"I didn't say that," Mark said quietly.

"Oh," she gulped and took an anxious breath. "You are mad at me?"

"Yep, I guess I am," he said. "But I'm also mad at myself. I've been well aware that you haven't really been interested in sex lately, but I didn't have any idea that you were faking orgasms. I know you didn't want to hurt me, but I don't think our marriage can survive without honesty." Mark's intimidating brown eyes pinned her to his lap, which helped prevent her sudden, overwhelming impulse to run. "I want the truth from you," he said, with a pronounced crease between his brows. "You'll tell me everything. Right now."

Elizabeth stiffened at this demanding order, alert, and more than a little nervous. This was the dominant Mark she had glimpsed shadows of from time to time, the one that had turned her on so much. "Well," she said, swallowing hard in a dry throat. Then she began to tell him. Once the dam had burst, and Mark sat and listened without reacting badly, she felt more confident and resolved to make a clean breast of it and get every single secret off her chest.

Elizabeth unburdened her soul. The countless times she faked orgasms and why, and her fear of upsetting him. The fact that she masturbated daily, sometimes twice a day because she was horny, and she just found sex with him too difficult, because of faking it. Confronting him with the truth had seemed impossible. She told him how it almost turned her off when he went down on her, because he was so kind and considerate, when she realized that most of all she wanted him to take what he wanted from her, to use her body for his pleasure.

Elizabeth noticed that while she had been talking Mark's cock had been hardening, sitting solid against the outside of her thigh, but she ignored it. Mark had asked for her secrets and man oh man, it was such a relief! While Mark remained composed and listening she explained about how constraint or bondage had really done it for her, and how she had realized that she was submissive and that much of her pleasure came from pleasing her partner and being dominated. Mark let her run on and on, only occasionally asking a question or clarifying something.

Elizabeth finished by explaining how she masturbated to the fantasy of when he had taken her against the wall at the wedding. When she couldn't think of anything else she had hidden from him, she said, "So that's about it, honey. That's everything."

Mark shot her a broad grin. "Good," he said. "Thank you." He ran a hand over her head, cupping her face, and rubbing his thumb against her lower lip. "You did very well, Lizzy."

"But what about you? What happened to you today? Do I get to hear any of your secrets? You do have them, right?"

Mark pulled her against him and kissed her cheek, his rough bristles scratching her soft skin. While framing her face with his hands, he followed that up by brushing her eyelids, temple, and face with feather soft kisses. A long lazy kiss on the mouth was the finale – it was a kiss Elizabeth felt she could almost drown in. A warm liquid sensation pooled low in her belly, and she felt a surge of moisture between her legs.

"Tomorrow," he said, breaking off the kiss. "I'll tell you all about me tomorrow."

"But what now?" Elizabeth asked, licking her sensitive lips, and giving herself an internal admonishment for being such a slut. André had certainly awakened her sexuality. Uncountable orgasms already today and she still felt a stab of frustration because there wasn't enough time to get naked with Mark. "We only have an hour together," she said bitterly, finding herself inexplicably cross. "I don't want to waste it."

Mark gave her a crooked smile, one she couldn't quite interpret. "By all means, let's not waste it." He looked at his watch. "It's after eight and André said I'm staying here tonight."

He stood up and she was surprised when he brought her to her feet, a firm grasp on her arm. She was even more surprised by what he said next.

"I get to sleep here with you, sweetheart," he said in a low, seductive voice. Then his dark eyes flashed with dangerous intensity and he added, "But first I'm going to do all the things I've wanted to do to you for years."

"Oh!" Elizabeth said. She blinked with an inner vision of what Mark could possibly mean. In that split second, all irritation and frustration fled – leaving her with that sensuous liquid sensation low in her belly once more.

Chapter 8

Slave

For a moment Mark just stared at her, musing over his physical battle with André, the long conversation afterwards, including discussing his BDSM fantasies and how to best enact them. Elizabeth would be annoyed, and probably furious that he started this project by hiring André without her agreement. So it was best to hold off on telling her that, too.

His Lizzy was so small, so beautiful and yet so damn tough. It was a marvel even now that she was really his. And she wanted what he wanted. His big body was tense with growing arousal. There were so many scenarios going through Mark's head. He felt like an adolescent inundated with sexual fantasies, and now that he was going to give in to them, he wasn't sure where to begin.

I'm going to do everything I want to do anyway, he reassured himself. His dick throbbed and twitched with that thought.

Nerves warred with lust in Mark's mind, along with André's advice. He didn't want to screw this up, this first instance of knowingly dominating his wife, so he would take it slow, and keep control. Lizzy needed to get used to how it should be between them. Now was not the time to let the beast off its leash.

Mark spun her around and took both of her hands, twisting them behind her back in a firm pressure hold that was close to pain. Elizabeth gave a small shriek of surprise and bent slightly forward, lessening the pinch. With her back to his chest, he marched her toward the full length wall of mirror stopping about two feet away. He brought both her wrists up and slapped her hands in front of her against the mirror, a couple of feet above shoulder height, his big hands pressing them into the wall.

Elizabeth stared back at him in the mirror, her eyes wide with alarm, and perhaps a little lust. Mark wasn't sure, but it didn't matter. The lust would come. "Don't you dare move those hands," he warned her, and then ran his own hands down her body from her shoulders, to her flanks and hips, resting them upon her waist.

"Yes, Sir," she replied, her gaze trained on him.

"No," Mark snapped, his voice sharp and cutting as a whip. "You call *me*, Master."

If anything, Elizabeth's eyes got even rounder. "Yes Master," she said in a shaky voice.

Mark kicked her ankles apart, and one knee pressed hard, high up against her inner thighs forcing her legs open still further. "That's right. I want those legs spread," he said. He pressed his big body up against her, the rigid length of his erection pushed into her soft skin, her buttocks and back. Then he brushed his lips against her earlobe, and his rough bristles along her jaw. Mark hadn't shaved, and knew that her soft skin was feeling every scrape. Elizabeth trembled under him, and her excitement and fear drove him on.

With his face in close to her ear, he said in a deep, conversational tone. "I've wanted you to be my sex slave, Lizzy. That's always been my sexual fantasy." As he spoke his hands pulled her blouse out from where it was tucked into her skirt, then one arm wrapped around her, holding her firm against him, while the other hand began to move along her stomach, seductively tracing across the top of her skirt, and then across her hips.

Mark continued, "My slave to do what I want in bed, exactly the way I want it. Do you want to be my sex slave, sweetheart?"

Elizabeth moaned. "Oh God! Yes, Master!"

Mark laughed. "Good. I'm going to use that hot little body of yours for my pleasure. I'm going to fuck every single hole at least once tonight, maybe more than once. Would you like that, Slave?"

"Oh shit, Master," Elizabeth's voice trembled, and Mark felt the weight of her, heavy against his arm as her knees must have gone weak. "Yes! More than anything."

"I might want to hurt you, too," he warned her, breathing those dark menacing words into the warm hollow behind her ear. He tongued her earlobe, and then bit it hard.

"Oww!" Elizabeth yipped, but her hands stayed on the mirror.

"Do you mind if I hurt you, Slave? If I cause you pain while taking my pleasure?" Mark's lips moved along the tender skin of her neck and below the sensitive shell of her ear, kissing, nuzzling, and licking. From time to time he bit her lightly, possessively sucking, and nibbling her body exactly as he wanted, because she belonged to *him*. As expected, Elizabeth quivered and trembled under this sensual assault.

"Master," she said fervently, "You can do whatever you want with me, I swear it."

Mark chuckled and his dick throbbed in his track pants. "Excellent. I think for now we should use André's rules, they're good ones, but we need a safe word. How about the color red?" Mark's hand roamed higher, reaching her bra, tracing under it. He un-snapped it and began to stroke her breasts then, squeezing, and roughly exploring them. Lizzy had such fantastic tits, large, soft and round, perfect to suck, fuck or lay his head on. As Mark caressed them he felt them grow heavy in his hands, swollen and plump with desire. Grasping her nipples between his fingers, he rolled and teased, occasionally pinching hard, right on the edge of pain.

Elizabeth gasped. "Ah... red is good. I won't forget, Master."

"Okay." Mark kept one hand tugging at her nipples, and the other hand slid down her hip, to her round buttocks. The skirt hampered him slightly, but his fingers followed the crease of her bottom all the way around past her anus, caressing along the inside of her thighs, and advancing ruthlessly up between her legs to her pussy. Mark enjoyed cupping her mound and fondling her through her clothes. Elizabeth did too, as she made a soft "Ummm," sounds of pleasure. All the while his mouth and tongue continued nibbling her neck.

"Don't move," he reminded her, then he unzipped the skirt and it dropped to the carpet. Both of his hands slid under her silken panties, and Elizabeth gasped again as he forcefully gripped her butt-cheeks. "This is a great ass. I'm looking forward to fucking it. You have no idea how long I've wanted to push myself deep into your tight little butt. Do you want me to shove my dick right up your ass, Slave?"

Elizabeth moaned, "Oh, yes please, Master."

Mark put one hand on her breast and the other slipped into the front of her underwear, stroking along her slick folds. Mark heard himself growl with pleasure. It felt amazing! Lizzy had never shaved her pubic area before, and her soft, swollen, hairless flesh filled his hand. Teasingly, he parted her nether lips and stroked, not entering her pussy, just spreading her dripping juices back and forth, circling her clit but not touching it. Her slick moisture slipped easily over her smooth flesh.

Elizabeth squirmed under his hand and something inside just clicked. Mark's natural dominance took over, and he felt entirely comfortable with the task of controlling everything. Right now he had all the power, to make her orgasm, or to prevent her from reaching a peak. He could do anything with his willing slave, for she had surrendered herself to him completely. The beast inside him roared with joy. Mark continued to torment her until finally, breathless with need, Elizabeth gave a strangled moan and arched toward him.

"I told you to be still," he reproved, and bit her between her neck and shoulder, gripping her tender flesh hard, marking her with his teeth. With a whimper of protest, Elizabeth became motionless. Like a wolf with a rabbit in its jaw, he held her there for a long moment, making sure of her compliance, and then he released her. "That's right, don't move," he said. "Good slaves are rewarded by their master. If you're good, I'll fuck you with my fingers, and I may even let you come. Would you like that, Slave?"

"Oh God yes, Master," Elizabeth replied breathlessly. "Thank you."

Chapter 9

Climax

Mark began to slide his middle and index finger inside her pussy, just to the first knuckle. They both slipped in easily because she was so slick. Elizabeth made a sweet unconscious sound of pleasure and Mark's balls tightened. Moving his fingers in and out, he pushed them inside a little further each time, pulling and stretching her warm swollen flesh as he went. Finally Mark buried both fingers as deep as he could shove them inside her and she moaned.

Mark smiled. His Lizzy was flooded, he could feel her arousal dripping from his hand. Hyper-horny himself, his dick throbbed, demanding release but it was going to have to wait. André told Mark that he could do virtually anything he wanted with Elizabeth, as she was such a willing submissive, but advised him to fully arouse her first. Well, that plan was certainly working.

Mark nestled his aching shaft between the cheeks of her ass, driving himself against her backside in a firm pumping movement, just to give his dick some relief. Then he drew his fingers out of her pussy, and rammed inside once again, rhythmically out and in, while continuing to pump himself against her ass. Elizabeth shivered, and moaned, making wonderful noises of arousal and need.

With his own breath coming faster, Mark's tongue and teeth continued to kiss and lick, sensually tormenting her sensitive neck. Mark watched Lizzy in the mirror, noticing her every response. Her eyes were heavy lidded, her face a mask of sexual urgency, almost a grimace as she whispered, "Yes, oh yes, yes." All the while his big body erotically covered hers.

Horny, happy and in complete control, Mark laughed and pulled his fingers out. He met her gaze in the mirror as he put his slick digits near his nose and breathed in her potent essence. "I like the way you smell," he said, and then licked some of her juices off. "And I like the way you taste," he added. Something low in his belly twisted with desire. Mark put his fingers near her mouth and she took them in, like a fish snapping at bait.

"Um, um, um," she moaned, sucking both fingers hard.

Mark's chest swelled, knowing he could take her at any time, in any way and he chuckled. "You're very hot for it, aren't you, Slave? I guess you want your master to fuck you pretty badly, don't you?" Elizabeth just moaned her agreement. Mark could see the pulse beat rapidly in her neck, and her nostrils flared. Elizabeth was breathing hard with her mouth closed tight, while sucking his digits as eagerly as if they were his dick.

Taking his fingers away, Mark returned them between her legs, once more tormenting her. "I'm going to fuck you so hard that it's going to hurt. Would you like that, Slave?"

"Yes, Master," she agreed. Her blue eyes stared at him in the mirror, dilated, heavy lidded and dark with lust.

"That's good, because I'm not going to be careful or gentle." Mark was a big man all over and sex was a problem. When his long shaft bumped a woman's cervix it sometimes caused cramping in their uterus that really hurt. Early in their relationship Mark had accidently penetrated Lizzy too deeply. Consequently he had been extra careful ever since. It was inhibiting, and he had worried that the reason she had lost interest in sex was because of pain during intercourse.

André had laughed loudly at this and said, "*J'assure, mon ami,* when the vagina is fully engorged, it gets longer and wider in order to accommodate the man's penis. And if the woman is fully aroused, pain is not interpreted by the brain as pain, *comprenez vous?* Any pain caused will not truly hurt. *Non!* Such torment will heighten pleasure and intensify her orgasm."

Mark had snorted over that one, because it seemed a useful justification if one enjoyed whipping a woman, which the Frenchman most certainly did. André had highly recommended the use of a riding crop before vaginal penetration in Mark's case, keeping his partner on the cusp of orgasm and adding pain, so those two sensations became confused. Mark really loved the idea of whipping his Lizzy, he couldn't deny it, sick fuck that he was. But he hadn't made up his mind on that yet, either.

When he had mentioned his anxiety of somehow screwing this up, André had laughed and assured him that all would come easily to him. "You must rely on your instincts, *mon ami*, the innate desires that you have repressed. Of a certainty, to dominate a woman is natural to you, and this is not any woman. This is Elizabeth, your wife. You know her better than anyone. As long as she has a safe word, all will be well."

Finally André had assured him that he would be watching on the closed-circuit TV, and if he had any concerns whatsoever, he himself would come in well before there was a problem. "*Mon Ami*, I will sit watching, with my cock very hard, as you take your wife." Mark had laughed and told André he was a pervert, but inside he had been thankful for the backup.

Mark pushed his index and middle fingers back into Lizzy's pussy, slipping in easily because she was soaking. "Uh, ah, oh, God!" she sobbed breathlessly. He chuckled and then teased her clit with a thumb, noticing how thick and swollen it was. Damn she was hot for it. So fucking horny!

Elizabeth mewled in a plaintive whimper, indicating she needed more, and he gave a little snort at her craven demands. With two thick fingers deep in her pussy, he masturbated her clit with his thumb. Meanwhile his other hand was engaged in sensually pulling a nipple gently one moment, then tugging and pinching painfully the next, and all the time he pressed up hard against her, pumping his dick against her backside.

Elizabeth's arousal and need roared over him. Without thinking he suddenly picked her up, sliding her up. Thrusting his aching hardness against her, Mark roughly moved her up and down against his throbbing shaft, using her whole body to jack off with. Damn, even through his track pants it felt fantastic. Fuck he was going to come if he wasn't careful, so he set her down heavily and enveloped her small form like a stallion covering a mare.

Elizabeth was making a constant keening sound. Even though she had been ordered to be still, she seemed unable to prevent her hips from instinctively thrusting. The scent of her arousal filled the room, thick as incense.

Jesus Christ, Mark thought, *Lizzy is so desperate she would let him do anything to her.* A surge of erotic mental images flooded his mind from long term fantasies. More blood shot into his cock in response to this sexy imagery as well as Lizzy's craven hunger and he swelled bigger. Mark loved every minute of this arousing sensual foreplay. Should he let her climax? Or make her wait? It was his decision and knowing that made it all the sweeter.

Breathless and writhing, Elizabeth began to sob and chant, "Oh Master, please, please!" as he stroked her clit with his thumb, flicking his fingers in and out of her dripping channel. Her skin was flushed and shining with sweat and Mark felt her body tighten and her pussy ripple with a pre-orgasmic pulse. He made up his mind.

"Now," he said harshly, his voice thick with lust. Elizabeth's dark eyes flew to the mirror to meet his intent gaze. "Come for your Master, Slave. I want to feel it." Mark thrust three fingers up hard onto her G- spot and curled them against her, scissoring inside her, his thumb pressed firmly, working furiously upon her clitoris.

"Ah, ah, ah, ah, ahhhh!" Elizabeth screamed.

Her instant reaction both mesmerized and astonished him. It was like being in an earthquake! Elizabeth bucked wildly and her cunt clamped down on his fingers *hard*. Mark tightened his arm around her waist, just to keep her on her feet as her knees had buckled. Still trembling with aftershocks, Elizabeth's eyes, glazed and blank, opened for a moment. They shut once, more making Mark wonder, had his wife actually passed out?

Wow, he thought. *That sure as hell wasn't faked.*

Chapter 10

The Slave Teases

My God, Mark thought in awe. Such an explosive reaction. How could I have been fooled by those lukewarm fake orgasms of hers all this time?

Mark continued stroking her lightly, soothing her through her aftershocks, his entire hand covered with her liquid spendings. When it seemed as if it would take some time for her to regain any sort of equilibrium, he swept her into his arms and sat her on his lap once more.

When she finally seemed to come out of her mindless state and blinked up at him, he asked, "Are you alright?"

Elizabeth smiled. "I'm just great. Oh my God, Mark, I'm so happy. When you take over like that." She sighed, and there was both bliss and awe in her expression. "Jesus. This commanding sex, this Master and Slave sex... it's just amazing."

Mark smiled. "I think so too, Slave," he said. "But you've had enough of a break, especially when there is work to do. My dick is really hard. Stand up now, and take your bra and panties off, and do it in a hot, slutty way."

Mark decided to remain perfectly still and watch the show. Elizabeth jumped up, and lowered her breasts out of her loosened bra, then held each of them up toward him for inspection. When she brought one close enough to lick, he obliged her.

"Oh yeah, that's good. Stroke them and pinch your nipples for me," he ordered.

"Oh yes, Master," she cooed provocatively. Elizabeth licked her fingers and circled her dusky pink areolas, making her hard little nipples wet, while undulating her hips in a manner highly suggestive of the sexual act. Mark chuckled at her antics, and the impish look on her face that proved that she was enjoying teasing him.

Facing him, Elizabeth slowly shimmied her underwear down to her thighs, and Mark felt his eyes widen, captivated at the sight of her shaved mound. Fuck it looked so incredibly hot. It was the first time he had seen her hairless pussy up close, and he liked what he saw. Nothing of her would be hidden from him now - by God he would have it all. Mark swallowed, imagining the taste of her. Tonight he was going to spread her legs, lick every inch of that soft skin, and eat her right out.

Mark's eyes had been fixed upon her naked sex, and Elizabeth seemed to be aware of it, remaining motionless and letting him look his fill. When he gazed up to meet her eyes, she gave him a knowing smile. Then in one quick movement she pulled her panties right off and stepped out of them.

Elizabeth surprised him then, by turning around, placing her naked buttocks only two feet from his face. Then she spread her legs. Mark's slave rose on to her toes, putting her feminine parts at the exact height of his mouth. Hot damn, he thought. The woman is trying to provoke me, and it's certainly working. He wondered just how far she would go.

Shooting him a mischievous grin, she looked over her shoulder at her ass, as if checking that it was still there or perhaps she had been making sure that her position was just right. Nodding, Elizabeth bent right over with her hands holding her knees, her legs wide spread. This beguiling posture fully displayed both her ass and her pussy, making them both fully open to him. The dominant beast within raged, demanding release.

Mark took a deep steadying breath, smelling the heavy scent of sex. Shit! Both irresistible and enticing female holes were at Mark's eye level and so close to his face. Her pussy glistened with her spendings, arousal dripping down her thighs. While he made himself remain still, staring in hypnotic awe, his Lizzy began lifting and gyrating her round white buttocks invitingly. Mark's blood surged as he enjoyed the view.

"How's this, Master?" she purred.

"God damn it! You teasing little slut!" Mark said with a laugh. He jumped up, ripping his clothes off. Mark's cock was hard as a thick iron bar, and it swung and bobbed as he leaned forward, and pulled her into his arms. He held her there for a moment, just staring at his Lizzy. No, he thought. Not Lizzy. My Slave. Mine, to do with as I like. His jaw tightened with that thought. He wanted to fuck her hard in her ass, or her cunt, but he held back. Before he came into this room he had a plan. First she would suck him off, and make him less urgent. Then he would take her pussy, then her ass. It was safer that way - there was less chance of losing control. He needed to stick to the plan.

The Plan

Mark kissed her. It was an open mouth kiss that first caressed her lips, and then became more bruising as he slipped his tongue inside her mouth. He heard himself moan as his dick pressed against her while her questing tongue found his. Mark licked and sucked her tongue, and then her mouth. Pulling back from her he thoroughly licked her lips.

"I want those lips of yours nice and wet, Slave," Mark growled. "That way they'll slide better up and down my shaft. Get on your knees," he ordered her. "I want you to service my dick with your hands and that wet mouth."

Eager and enthusiastic, Elizabeth was quick to obey. Mark threw a pillow down for her to kneel upon, and made sure to position himself as André had, so he could watch her swallow him while looking in the mirror. Elizabeth didn't know how to deep throat, but André assured him that she could learn to take a cock - even one of his size - with training.

"Yes, that's right," Mark said when he saw his willing slave kneeling before him, ready to receive his jutting shaft. With one hand he cupped the back of her neck and directed her mouth toward the engorged head. André's words from the video echoed in Mark's ear, and he felt the truth in them: "You were made to please a man, *ma chèrie*, this is your most basic desire." Mark shook his head. Was he the luckiest guy in the world, or what?

Fuck yes, he thought, as his slave curled one small hand over his shaft and the other on his balls, and then sucked him in with her warm, wet lips. Shit. After all this foreplay he wasn't going to last long. "Do you want me to shoot my cum right down your throat?" he growled, thrilled by the idea of spurting in pulsing waves as she swallowed.

Elizabeth, devotedly servicing him, moaned and nodded her affirmative.

Mark couldn't take his eyes from her. His slutty slave seemed transported just to be allowed to suck his cock. He felt his dick swell further at the erotic sight of her naked and on her knees before him. Elizabeth was worshiping him, skillfully working his rigid length, coaxing him to climax and ejaculate inside her.

"You want to take it all, Slave?" he grated, smoothing a hand from her chin down along her neck, showing her exactly where his seed would go.

Elizabeth, while still skillfully masturbating him with her hands, popped his cock out of her mouth. Then she said in a tone of fervent need and desire, "Oh yes, please, Master. I want to drink it, it tastes so good! I love it when you allow me to swallow all of your salty, hot seed."

Mark chuckled, amused by how completely Lizzy was taking on and acting out her role of sex slave. It was a good game for both of them, the absolute best, in fact. André, that rat bastard, was worth every penny. Mark's jaw tightened then, because for him, it really wasn't a game. Mark wanted to use her, to own her completely, and make her do anything, everything he wanted her to do - sick fuck and beast that he was. He leaned down and took her breasts, one in each hand, squeezing and rubbing her hard nipples with his thumbs.

"You are a very good slave," he said, "and I shall reward you. Keep using your hands, your tongue, lips and mouth exactly as your doing and I'll let you swallow every drop of my cum."

Elizabeth gave an "mmmhumm" as acknowledgement, but didn't falter as she industriously licked and sucked his dick, clearly enjoying her work.

"There you go, fuck that's good. Yes, like that," he said after a few more minutes of this exquisite torment. Mark was contriving with great difficulty to hold back his orgasm because he was enjoying the sensations so much. However, one could only take so much and he was reaching his breaking point.

"Oh shit," he said and drew in a deep breath at the intense spike of pleasure that seemed to radiate along his spine, buttocks and balls. "I'm going to come!" Mark shouted. He gripped Elizabeth's head then, wrapping his hands in her hair, and began to powerfully pound into her mouth, with a short fast rhythm, still careful not to thrust too deep.

"Oh fuck, I'm going give it to you," Mark said and he felt his muscles bunch and flex. An animal sound tore from his throat as his balls shot their load and his sperm erupted, pulsing out from his cock. Elizabeth, her mouth tight around his shaft, ravenously continued sucking and swallowing Mark's semen as he climaxed. One last grunt caused a second wave of pleasure, as the last of his jizz blasted from his swollen dick.

Mark looked down at his slave and cupped her chin. Broken from the mesmerizing spell, Lizzy looked directly up at him with adoration in her eyes, and her mouth still tight around his cock. There was drool all over her face, her lips were swollen and red, and her eyes were watering, tears streaming down her cheeks from the strain of taking him as deeply as she had. Mark's devoted slave kept licking and sucking his dick, as if his pleasure was the most important thing in the world to her. Right then he thought that it probably was.

Mark saw her there, on her knees before him, and the emotional response that swelled inside him felt both profound and divine. He thought with wonder that his Lizzy had never looked more beautiful.

# Chapter 12

The Flogger

Mark could never remember feeling so happy, except perhaps when he was first married, and he knew Elizabeth would be his forever. The two cuddled on the bed together, laughing and giggling like errant school children.

"Well, I think we should be kidnapped more often," Elizabeth said, after being tickled, and getting her own back through a rather underhanded trick. Mark had, he thought, rather magnanimously allowed the deception. His little terrier had to have something on her side as she was so hopelessly outclassed by his strength and weight. "Seriously, look at us," she said. "We're acting like we don't have a care in the world. I wonder what André plans to do with us now?"

Mark rolled on top of her, and grabbed her wrists, holding her arms over her head. Then he gave her a bruising, lust-filled kiss. He had intended to distract her, to make sure she changed the subject, but his dick was already hard. What was going through his mind was what he really wanted. Yes, he wanted to try anal sex with her, that much was true, but even more than that he wanted to fuck her deep and hard without holding back. Using André's advice, he should be able to do it, despite the size of his cock.

"Oh," Elizabeth cooed mischievously, clearly turned on. "Master, there is something very hard pressing up against poor defenseless little ol' me. Can your slave serve you?"

"You most certainly can," he growled, and then jumped up, his erection waving in front of him. "Go to the toilet if you need to, because I'm going to keep you here on this bed forever," he said. "I've wanted to tie you up for a long time, sweetheart. My God, I can't believe how much hot sex we've both missed out on, but I swear I intend to catch up every minute."

Elizabeth's eyebrows rose over that. "Really? Well, how terribly providential for us both. You like to tie me up, and I like to be tied up." She gave him a brilliant smile, full of love and trust. "I'll be right back."

Mark, having rummaged through the armoire, was ready for her when she returned, but his dick had gone half mast. Truthfully, while inflamed with the idea of finally doing as he liked with her, he was also nervous. What if he screwed this up? The beast had overwhelmed him once as a child, but he was a man now. What was there to worry about?

Smiling, Mark fastened soft handcuffs to her legs and wrists, and then he positioned his slave on her back, down the middle of the bed. Mark secured Elizabeth's wrists over her head, noticing how she licked her lips with nervous arousal as he did so. He stroked her face. "Scared?" he asked.

She gave a slightly panicked laugh. "Yes!"

He sat beside her then and kissed her forehead. "We don't have to do this sweetheart. Honestly," he said. "I don't need to tie you up to have my way with you." Mark raised his eyebrows up and down meaningfully at that. "I can overpower you at any time Lizzy, with my hands and body. But tying you up gets me really, really hot."

"No, honey," she said, pulling a little at her chains. "It's okay, really. This is fun. I just get this strange combination of excitement, fear and lust when tied up. Such and adrenaline rush! The fear is a little overwhelming at first, is all. But the lust makes up for it in the long run."

"Good," Mark said. "And you remember your safe word, right? Use it at any time. I won't be mad if you do. We are both new to this. I'd rather stop too many times at first, than not enough."

Elizabeth agreed and Mark continued his work, intently arranging the mechanisms, confining her exactly as he had imagined. When he had finished he was once more fully erect. Elizabeth had her arms cuffed over the golden fan of hair on her head, stretched out to the bed head, while her legs were spread, cuffed and up high in the air about even with her shoulders. Her ass was lifted, just slightly off the bed. Mark thought she looked fantastic, all bound for his pleasure, open and fully exposed for whatever he wanted. And he wanted so much. He may not be an experienced Dom, but in his mind he had done everything already, many times before.

Sitting on the bed beside her, Mark stroked her breasts and said, "Okay?"

Elizabeth seemed a little shaky, but she nodded.

"I'm not going to ask for your permission for anything, Lizzy," Mark said. "Because I intend to use your body for my own pleasure and I'm going to do exactly as I like. Do you understand, Slave?

"Yes, Master."

"You have your safe word to use at any time," he continued. "I'm going to employ André's trick of pain and pleasure." Mark reached under the bed and pulled out a sophisticated gold and black flogger, showing it to her. He had wanted to smile, or make some sort of joke, but nothing would come. Solemn and straight faced, Mark cleared his throat. *Focus,* he thought, *focus!* But it was difficult to do so as his mind was filled with depraved, erotic pictures of flogging Elizabeth's soft skin, of seeing her thrashing and quivering, and hearing her cry out from the attentions of his whip.

Elizabeth looked at him, with wide, fearful eyes.

André had explained to Mark the ins and outs of flogging, particularly concerning "sting" and "thud." Sting was caused by the type of hide used, where "thud" was decided by how thick the hide was and how many tails. The number of tails increased the thud, which was good, as it gave the sub the solid slamming feel. Mark had settled on a suede, mop-like flogger with lots of tails, for a hard thud. It had a two or three extra deer hide tails which created a fairly low level sting, unless vigorously applied.

Mark swallowed, forced a smile, and put the flogger down next to her on the bed. Anticipation was going to send him mad. There was a subtle tremor running through Elizabeth's body, and her transparent fear and alarm only made his dick harder. "There will be pain," he said in a rough voice that didn't sound like his own. "But first there will be pleasure."

Chapter 13

The Beast

Mark ran his hands up and down her calves and thighs as he moved around to the end of the bed. Fuck she looked good. Never had he so clearly seen her feminine form, and not once had she been spread and ready for him. "I could simply eat you right up," he murmured. Instinctively he grabbed both thighs and dove right in, licking her wet slit, and sucking on her clitoris. Elizabeth called out loud in surprise, but Mark didn't slow. If anything he pushed his face against her further, nibbling, licking and ravaging her open sex.

Elizabeth began to shake and moan, raising her hips to him by bending her knees, causing the chain to shorten. Mark chuckled at her response and decided not to chastise her enthusiasm by demanding that she remain still. Was she excited by her own needs, or his? Or simply by what he was doing? But her shaved cunt was delicious, and he spread her nether lips with his fingers and tongued every single part of it. No doubt André would have used more finesse, but Mark figured his dick was just too hard to consider that.

When Elizabeth was panting, stiffening and moaning in a pre-orgasmic haze, he stopped. Then he picked up the flogger and without a word of warning, brought it down lightly on her breasts. Lizzy gave a little cry, but it wasn't of pain, her eyes were dilated and her expression mindless. Mark began to work her over in earnest, enjoying the color of her skin as it turned a rosy pink. By God, whipping her sweet flesh was as amazing as he had hoped. Hips, ass, pussy, stomach, and nipples – nothing evaded his careful blows. He wondered how much pain Elizabeth would take for him. Would it be even more exciting if he used real force? His throbbing dick seemed to think so.

When she was moaning and writhing in front of him, Mark said, "Do you like it, Slave?" There was a long pause, while she apparently processed these words.

"Oh God, yes. It feels amazing, Master."

"Good," Mark replied. "Then, my sweet Slave, you should say, 'Thank you for whipping me, Master."

"Oh God, yes. Thank you for whipping me, Master."

He stroked her golden hair. "You are such an excellent slave," her murmured. "But remember," he warned. "You are not allowed to come without my permission."

"Oh no, Master. Can I tell you if I really need to come?"

"You may beg me to let you come, yes. I'd like to hear you beg. But if you climax without your master's permission you'll be sorry."

Mark put the flogger down and found the nipple clamps. Squeezing each breast, he sucked each nipple to a tight little point and then he put the clamps on. This throbbing ache would distract her even more. The main thing was that when he drove in deep and hit her cervix, he wanted his slave so hot and confused sexually between pleasure and pain that she loved it.

"Do you like it?" he whispered after applying the clamps.

"Yes," she said.

"What do you say?" he asked.

"Oh. Thank you, Master, for clamping my nipples."

Mark kissed her in reply, anchoring her face with his big hands in a brutal, passionate kiss. "Fuck, seeing you like this…" Mark couldn't finish his sentence. She was so open and willing to accept his dominance. He loved that she surrendered to him, to whatever he wanted. How far could he go? She had a safe word, but would she use it? Would his slave really do anything for him? André had assured him that Elizabeth was a natural sexual submissive. With training, she would gladly endure anything in her desire to please her master and obey his will.

Mark stood up then and her eyes went to his swollen shaft. It was dripping with pre-cum. He got to his knees on the bed, put his hand on his dick and guided toward her luscious swollen lips. "Such a good slave," he said. "You may lick up my cum."

"Oh thank you Master," she murmured, and greedily lapped at his broad head, licking him clean, tonguing him with a mummm of pleasure.

Mark returned to work between her legs, using his fingers to penetrate her, and admiring the way her cunt gaped, opening wide, enticing him to fuck her. Using his teeth, he bit her numerous times, and while she squealed and shrieked, Mark could tell she was still enjoying everything he did as her slit was flooding. André had spoken to him about sub-space, how endorphins released from inflicted pain could cause euphoria. It was an art form, apparently, to know how to constantly bring a sub to this state. Mark knew he had much to learn. Once he had his slave close to orgasm again, he returned to the flogger, but this time he applied it with even more force.

For some reason a sense of betrayal and anger was building within Mark. Why was it Lizzy could get wet and climax now, when she couldn't before? Elizabeth had been selfishly denying him sex. How could she have been masturbating - sometimes twice daily - when he had been forced to go without? And lying to him. Well, she would never, ever do any of this shit in the future.

"Does it hurt, Slave?" he asked, after a particularly brutal strike across her breasts.

"Oh, yes, Master," Elizabeth said, "It really hurts!" Her tone was one of surprise, panic and unspoken accusation.

"But you deserve it, don't you? This is punishment now," he added in explanation. Moving toward her pussy, Mark applied the flogger with effort directly upon her clit. "You will never fake an orgasm again, will you?"

"Oh no, Master," she shrieked as he continued to flog her.

"If you want to masturbate, you will first obtain my consent and will only do so at my direction."

"Yes! I swear, Master," she screamed her agreement.

"This is my cunt. My clit! Mine! You may never, ever have an orgasm without my permission, do you understand?" he growled. The beating was merciless, and his anger was all directed toward her clitoris and pussy, the sexual parts of her that she had withheld from him.

Elizabeth was crying, large tears were streaming down her face, her chest heaving, her face splotchy. "I won't Master," she sobbed with a pitiful hitch in her voice. "I'll be good."

"This is my cunt, and my clit," he repeated, hitting them harder. "And your ass is mine," he flogged it too, "Your breasts are mine, your body is mine to do with as I please. You will always remember who your master is."

"Yes! Yes! Yes!" she shrieked, "I swear it! I'm yours, Master, your slave. All yours. Please don't hurt me anymore. I promise to be good!" Her beseeching pleas and heartrending tears pierced Mark's mind, shocking him into sensibility. For a moment he realized that this was not what he had so carefully planned. He wanted her to associate pain with pleasure, not to think of it as a penalty. Stunned he saw the brutal red welts of his flogging, and froze. What was he doing? Jesus! What had he done?

Chapter 14

Punishment

Mark stared at his wife and the burning red stripes he had given her. This was against everything he believed in, or was it? What had he been thinking? And yet Mark knew. He had been angry and possessive and furious that Elizabeth had betrayed him. She had been enjoying her body without him. Without him! But he shouldn't have flogged her so hard. Had the beast taken over? Or had he? Was there any difference anymore? Such confusion made him ineffective and he remained perfectly motionless while he tried to decide what to do next.

André's voice carried over the sound of Elizabeth sobs, "*Mon ami*, this is very good work, I think." A firm hand gripped his shoulder and Mark turned to look into André's composed gaze. The Frenchman was wearing a silk bathrobe with green velvet trim, but on André it looked better than an expensive three piece suit.

"André," Mark said, and looked at his mentor with heartfelt relief.

André gave him a serene smile. "As I have said, this is good work. A disobedient slave must always face discipline. You have taught this one a lesson she will not soon forget."

Mark's confusion vanished. André was so calm - he radiated a sense that "all is well." The man was solid as the foundations of a high-rise building, and his certainty and confidence boosted Mark's own.

"*Voila, mon ami*," André said. "I have come as you requested. I believe you wished me to help you pleasure your slave. As we discussed, this little cum slut desires to serve us both at once. It is time for her to get her wish, no?"

Mark cleared his throat. "I believe so," he said. Walking over to the bedside table, Mark put the flogger down. Then he sat beside his Lizzy on the bed, and looked into her eyes. There was pain, confusion and uncertainty there – she was completely off balance. It was up to him to steady her. Leaning down into her he licked a tear away, and gently stroked her face. "All harsh discipline is over," he said, voice as impassive as possible. "You'll remember who you belong to next time, won't you?"

Elizabeth sniffed. "I'm so sorry, Master. I should have talked to you sooner." Her breath hitched. "I'll never do anything like that again."

"Your Master has whipped you, what do you say?"

There was a long pause. "Oh," Elizabeth said. "Thank you, Master," she whispered, a little hesitantly. "Thank you for disciplining me."

"You are welcome, and you are forgiven my sweet, sweet slave," Mark said. "You were so very brave the way you took your punishment. The debt has been paid. I couldn't be more proud of you."

Mark saw that she had brightened at his praise, pathetically grateful for his kind words. "Really, Master?" she sniffed again.

"Yes, really," he said, smiling down at her and wiping her face with a tissue. Her transparent desire to please him stabbed him with pleasure. This was the real Elizabeth, a woman with all social masks ripped away. He felt as if he was gazing at her soul. "You were amazing," Mark said, making no attempt to hide how he felt. He wanted her to see his avid admiration in his face. "I whipped you very hard, sweetheart, for I was mad that you had kept yourself from me. I'm afraid I took most of that punishment out on your cunt and clit." He looked up at the mirrored ceiling. "Can you see from here? How red and swollen and welted your pussy is?"

"Yes, Master."

"It looks incredible. Seeing you cuffed in this exposed position and knowing you have taken your punishment makes me extraordinarily hard," Mark said. "Does it hurt very much?"

"Yes!"

"Good," he replied, aware that he was strangely unperturbed by her discomfort. "But it won't hurt for long. Say hello to André."

Elizabeth looked up at André, standing nearby. She gave him a faint smile and said, "Hello, Sir."

"André is here because we are both going to reward you. I understand that you enjoyed the thought of André and me making love to you at the same time. I've lots of ideas of how we will take you, the two of us, using your body for our pleasure."

"Oh God," she whispered.

"Precisely, sweetheart. You are my lovely Sex Slave," he said and gave her a slow, thorough kiss and added, "Mine. You belong only to me." Mark gave her a boyish grin. "But it just so happens that tonight I want to share."

Chapter 15

Ménage à Trois

Mark looked up at André. "I'm thinking that you should use her pussy, while I take her mouth. How does that work for you?"

"Very well, *mon ami*," André said, tossing his dressing gown over a chair, exposing the long clean lines of his trim, muscular body as well as a bobbing erection. "All shall be as you command, for Elizabeth is your slave, and I am honored to be allowed to share her with you."

"Yeah, right," Mark said with a laugh. The irony killed him. Earlier today his wife was André's sex toy, but he couldn't fault the man really. André's methods were extreme, but he couldn't argue with the results. "Just tell me when you feel her getting close so I can give her permission to come. I'd like to reward my slave with multiple orgasms tonight."

"*Bon*," André said. "I do enjoy how you have restrained your submissive, so her beautiful pussy and ass can be clearly admired. This was a well considered piece of art, *n'est-ce pas?*"

The two men each moved to different positions. Mark began by removing her nipple clamps, and gently soothing each abused peaked nub, while André used his tongue on Elizabeth's sore, ill-treated clit and pussy. The two Dom's worked in a strange unplanned concert, driving their slave to soaring heights. André, ever skilled, tormented Elizabeth by bringing her close again and again, while Mark gave her the added oral pleasure of being able to suck him while she was being fucked.

"*Mon ami*," André finally said, when Elizabeth moaned and thrashed with Mark's cock in her mouth. André's own cock was deep inside her pussy, right up to the balls. "I think she is close and will come at your command, if you are ready."

Mark had his right hand holding tight to Elizabeth's hair, and his left tugging on a nipple. He said in a husky voice, "Thank you. I'd like you to climax with her, or just after André."

"As you wish," André said. "*Merci beaucoup.*" Holding her open thighs for leverage, he began to forcefully pound inside Elizabeth, in shorter and shorter strokes, his face in a grimace of exquisite lust and desire.

Mark pulled his dick out of his slave's mouth, and looked into her sex-glazed eyes. "Come for me, Slave. Your cunt and your clit are both mine. I want to see you come, I want to hear it."

Elizabeth was moaning loudly. Mark could see her pleasure building, she was at the top of the pinnacle, but she hadn't yet started to fall over. Meanwhile André grunted with each forceful thrust, pounding himself into Elizabeth, and calling out something in French as he began to climax. Watching André orgasm while he was fucking his wife almost made Mark shoot his own load, and he sought to understand why. There was pleasure in seeing his mentor come, and even more pleasure in knowing that his slave had served him.

"Come for me you little slut," Mark said, using a stern, authoritarian voice, "Can't you feel it? André is shooting his seed right up your cunt, and I want your tight pussy to squeeze him hard." He twisted and pulled on both of her nipples. "Come, Slave. Right now."

These erotic words pushed her over the edge. Elizabeth began to climax then, thrashing, writhing and wailing, with crazed keening shrieks. Mark could barely understand her, but somewhere in there she shouted one word quite coherently. Mark's chest and cock both swelled larger at the sweet sound of her screaming "Master" as she came.

Mark had not climaxed, and he moved to release Elizabeth's legs from her cuffs. André looked at Mark's massive erection and raised his eyebrows, a question in his eyes. Mark's lips curled, and he gave André a mocking smile.

"André my friend, I don't know why I found the sight of you fucking my wife, and climaxing inside her so damn hot, but I did. We can discuss it later. Right now do you mind uncuffing my slave and constraining her arms above her head with your own hands? I don't want her in cuffs for this."

"*Mais oui*," André said, and obediently moved into position. He sat at the head of the bed, his back to the bed board, and after uncuffing Elizabeth's wrists, he held them firmly, a form of human bondage.

Mark looked at Elizabeth and smiled. "It's my turn to mount you now, Lizzy, my beautiful wife, and willing slave. I want to drive deep inside your slippery cunt. It's dripping I see, not only from your flooding pussy, but from André's semen. It's going to be a wet slick ride for my big dick, and I'm looking forward to it. Do you want your Master to fuck you, Slave?" he asked.

"Oh God yes, Master."

"Do you want my semen to shoot into your tight little cunt, right up there where André has already left his hot jizz?"

"Yes! Yes! Please, Master."

"Then that's what I'm going to do," Mark said. "You're such a horny little slut. You'll come for me again while I'm deep inside of you, won't you?"

"Oh yes, Master, if you allow me to."

"You got that right." Chuckling, Mark fondled her for a long while, rubbing slickness all over her, circling and tracing her labia, pulling the hood back on her clit, teasing the nub and occasionally licking or sucking it. Mark felt hypnotized by her response to him, the helpless little noises she made - he could never get enough of her. She was his opposite, so small, so soft, and so feminine. While he still felt a little guilty at the red welts between her legs, he also got harder, for Lizzy belonged to him. She was his to protect, to love, to fuck and to punish. Raw need coiled tightly in his gut. Mark wanted to be inside her, *right now*. Yet he also wanted to wait, to drag these moments out and to send her crazy with sexual desire. As he carefully masturbated her, she began to loudly respond, begging him desperately, wanting more.

"Please, Master, please!"

"Please what?"

"Please!" she begged. "Oh God, fuck me! I think I'm going to come."

"No," Mark said sternly, and instantly stopped playing with her. "Not yet. Don't you dare come, Slave. You'll wait until I give you permission."

Mark rose up the bed on to his knees. Then he threw her legs over him, so they rested, hooked just under his shoulders. Bracing himself with her knees draped over his arms, he lifted her ass and spread her to allow for deep penetration. It was a position he often fantasized about, but always avoided. With his right hand he guided himself into her entrance, enflamed by a wet cascade that drenched the swollen head of his cock. Was it Lizzy's arousal or André's seed that dripped from her feminine depths? Goddamn it, he was so close. Almost anything could set him off. A muscle twitched in his cheek as he leaned forward, forcing her even wider as he slowly pressed into her. Elizabeth moaned.

'You're going to take me deep, Slave," he said, his voice husky with passion. "Your Master is going to push himself all the way into you and fuck you rough and hard. And when I pound into your cervix it's going to hurt, but you're going to love it, and only want more. Do you understand me, my sweet Slave? Do you want your Master's big dick as much as your Master wants to give it to you?"

Elizabeth moaned and thrashed, clearly right on the edge of orgasm. "Oh! Oh! Oh, please, please, Master. Yes!"

Mark shut his eyes for a moment, fighting for control. *Jesus*, he thought, clenching his jaw and shuddering with desire. *So open, so trusting, so vulnerable, so horny. Submitting completely to me. Mine. All mine.*

Mark's large shoulders hunched then, and he let the beast go, with no thought of harming her. If his slave could take that brutal flogging without using her safe word, she could certainly take all of him. A powerful need clawed at him, and he gave into it. With his full force and strength he jack hammered into her, fast and furious, like a rutting stallion.

It felt amazing to just let loose, to not worry about hurting her, fearing that she wouldn't want him if he did. André had assured him that Elizabeth was the kind of submissive that could learn to love anything her Master wanted, even the most merciless pain, and by God right now he wanted to pound her to pieces with his massive dick. With her arousal and André's full load inside her, Lizzy's tight little channel was as slick and smooth a ride as could be imagined.

"Yes! Yes!" he shouted as he rode her hard. "Take me, take all of me, my sweet, sweet Slave!"

The sound of flesh hitting moist oozing flesh could be heard, as well as moaning and incoherent "Ah! Ah! Ah!" feminine sounds, the pitch reaching higher and higher as she climbed toward orgasm.

"Oh God, oh God, Master, please!"

Sliding in and out in a rapid rhythm, Mark felt her body beginning to tighten. "Come for me, Lizzy," he said urgently. "Come now! I want to feel you milk my dick."

Elizabeth screamed then as her entire body stiffened, the prelude to an orgasmic explosion. Mark said, "Let her go, André. Let her go." André released his grip on her wrists, and Lizzy's arms flew around Mark, hugging him to her. Elizabeth embraced him as if he was the only other person alive, as if she had been totally lost and alone until that exact moment.

Mark felt her urgent tightening hold, the smell of her, and the feel of her soft damp skin as she crushed herself against him. Elizabeth's pussy clenched and tightened, again and again and again as she climaxed. Mark's need was savage, and his own orgasm took him without warning, unexpectedly slamming into him. With a guttural incoherent shout, Mark cried out in surprise. Then he lost all control. Hips jerking ruthlessly forward as he convulsed, Mark's head flew backwards as he arched and thrust, spurting inside her in fierce waves of pleasure. His violent spasms seemed to go on and on, longer than ever before.

They lay together afterwards, he on top of her as if felled by an axe, too exhausted to pull away. Chest heaving, heart thudding, covered in sweat and other body fluids, Mark utterly sated, smiled. They had both been well satisfied. And he noticed that his Lizzy even then, while barely sensible and shivering with aftershocks, continued to clasp him firmly in a loving embrace.

Chapter 16

Brothers

They all washed up. Then Elizabeth lay on her stomach, while both men massaged her, particularly her legs and back, loosening any muscles that had been held in an unnatural position for too long. Elizabeth lay on the bed between André and Mark, her eyes shut. Mark thought she may have fallen asleep. The emotional, mental and physical stress they had put her under certainly could have caused this reaction, and he let his hard working slave rest. When she began to softly snore, making little sounds almost like a chipmunk, Mark and André both quietly snickered.

"You have worn her out, *mon ami*," André said.

Mark snorted. "You started it," he accused. "But yes, it really has been a big day for her."

Mark and André lay on their sides facing each other, propping their heads up with one arm. The other arm of each man rested lightly on Elizabeth's back, in a sharing, comfortable manner, each man idly caressing her, and chatting in companionable whispers. When both men stroked her soft round buttocks at the same time, they exchanged a look, and grinned at each other.

"I like the stripes," Mark said.

"They are from my little cane. So pretty. It is a most perfect ass," André said.

Mark gave him a proprietary, self-satisfied smile. "And it's all mine. I'm so going to fuck it. I'm going to fuck it so hard that Elizabeth won't be able to walk properly for a week."

André laughed, and shook his head. "*Mon ami*, I believe you," André said. "I would like to offer my compliments. You arranged a masterful scene, and played it out quite skillfully. I told you to trust your innate gift. I tell you again, you are one of the most natural Dom's I have ever had the privilege to watch. It is in your nature to dominate, as it is in Elizabeth's nature to submit."

"Ah, thank you, my friend," Mark said. "But I would've failed without your support, as you well know. I faltered right from the start."

"*Non*," André said. "You acted correctly and you had stopped flogging your slave without the safe word, by the time I arrived. It was a small mistake that you were, even then, setting right. The punishment was appropriate, your sub has, as they say, learned an important lesson."

"I worried about the beast."

"*Eh bien.*" André arched an eyebrow. "And yet, *mon ami*, I find the beast oh so charming, and not at all troublesome."

Mark laughed. "If you say so, but I don't know if I will feel comfortable dominating Lizzy without back up for a while. I find it curious, my interest in watching you, my pleasure in seeing you climax. Part of it was because you were fucking my wife. Do you have any idea what that is about?"

André gave him an impish grin and clenched his fist, bringing it to his chest with a thump. "We are brothers now, my friend. Bonded."

Mark laughed. "You mean because I beat the crap out of you?'

"*Oui*," André said. "I am no danger to you *mon ami*. For all your problems you are not threatened by me. You have dominated me in the most primitive manner of all. More importantly you know that the *inestimable*, most perfect Elizabeth loves you, and only you."

"But why should I enjoy seeing you climax?"

"You are gay perhaps?"

They both laughed. André said softly, "You do not fear a man's touch, *mon ami*, but no, I think it is the pleasure of having your slave serve me so well. She is yours, and thus you are serving me, via her. You appreciate my small efforts on behalf of your marriage, I think?"

Mark's response was heartfelt. "That much is true. I owe you big time. But it was also weird how I enjoyed the fact that you had climaxed inside Lizzy, before I entered her. She was slick with your cum and I loved that. It was kind of like sharing blood, only in this case semen."

André gave a wry smile, clenched his fist, and once more brought it to his chest with a thump. "Warrior brothers, sharing the same woman – sleeping in the same cave."

They both chuckled, again quietly, as they didn't want to disturb Elizabeth. Mark explained how he was going to tell Elizabeth everything in the morning, and asked that André particularly make sure all recording was turned off, as his childhood events were sensitive. They discussed the beast for a while, and once more André explained that if Mark humored his animal needs from time to time, it need not be so unmanageable.

André said. "And now I will, perhaps foolishly, tell you *mon ami*, that I have fallen in love with your wife."

"What?"

"It is true," André said. "But do not be jealous, for I am the one that is jealous. You have love together and respect. Now you have love, respect and excellent sex. For the first time in my life I feel incomplete and bereft. It is your wife that has opened my eyes. *Oui,* and seeing you together. Now nothing can be the same."

"Why did you tell me?"

"Ah, *mon ami,*" André said. "Why not? Perhaps so you can even more appreciate what you have? But you have many more days of vacation, and you have paid for my time. I will teach you all I know of BDSM, and you may teach me of love, for it pleases me to see it between you. I have given Elizabeth many orgasms this day, as I am skilled in bed. Yet nothing I did compared to what you shared together tonight. I saw Elizabeth's arms surround you the moment I released them. Poetry should be written about such an embrace. I feel honored and privileged to see it, *oui.* Such devotion and passion brought tears to my eyes."

André gave Mark a boyish, irresistible and utterly appealing smile. Just then Mark could completely understand how anyone – male or female - could fall in love with André Chevalier. The man was charming, honest, and he seemed to perfectly understand *everything.*

André shrugged his shoulders in a depreciating manner. "But I am French, you understand, and the French are not ashamed to appreciate such beauty."

Chapter 17

Explanations

André bid Mark good night, and left. Mark fell into bed. He cuddled into Elizabeth, and she unconsciously snuggled into his arms. After that he fell almost instantly asleep.

Mark woke sometime in the middle of the night, achingly aroused, and reached for her. In the darkness with only a digital clock for light, he stroked her awake, erotically caressing her sensitive skin. His chest was against her back, the hard length of his erection pressing against her buttocks. Mark's probing fingers found she was already wet and ready for him. He lifted her leg to give himself access, and when he pushed inside her, she made a cute mewling sound of pleasure. Sex was slow, sweet and easy, graced with soft whispers of love and tenderness. They surged together in the darkness, the sound of their ragged breaths loud in the empty room. When Mark felt her close, he told her to come for him, and she did. Their near mutual completion satisfied them both, and they went instantly back to sleep.

Breakfast arrived in the morning, the silver serving cart brought in by a stranger while Elizabeth was in the shower. Mark, dressed only in a bathrobe, thanked the waiter and then frowned in consternation when he realized he didn't have his wallet. The attendant, a tall, stocky man, had an understanding smile in his eyes. "No need to tip, Sir. I'm an employee of Mr. Chevalier."

Mark and Elizabeth sat down to strong coffee; "baguettes;" French cheeses including Gruyere, and Brie; ham omelet's, and hot milk to dilute their coffee with. Honey, strawberry and apricot jam was available as well as a kind of slightly sweet light bread, rather than toast. Mark burst out laughing. There wasn't even any orange juice. Clearly André had not yet acclimatized to American breakfast food.

As they ate, Elizabeth, also in a bathrobe said, "So, it's your turn, Mark. Can you let me know what happened to you? What has André told you? You said you would tell me your secrets. You were no paragon this year either, you know. You avoided the whole sex issue, too. Do I get to flog you for things you shouldn't have done?"

Mark gave her an intent, heated look. "You can try, sweetheart," he said in a deceptively mild voice.

Elizabeth, who had brought her coffee mug to her lips, almost spilled it when she choked on a surprised giggle. "Forget it. Anyway, I'm all ears."

Mark decided to start from the beginning. For some time he had noticed that she was subtly avoiding sex, and when they did end up in bed together he knew that something was missing. He spoke to her of how he worried about hurting her during intercourse. Elizabeth burst out laughing at that, murmuring that he seemed to have gotten over that problem - as seen by the way he had mercilessly flogged her the night before.

"Yeah, well," he said. "I didn't know that you could like pain."

"I don't know if 'like' is the right word," she said. After he stared her down she lowered her eyes and blushed with embarrassment. Mark chuckled, and stroked her face, deciding to leave it for now, and not to trace *that* thought. This was about his confession right now. "I'm glad you do like it, Lizzy," he said. "It turns you on, and it turns me on too."

"That is probably why it does turn me on," she said, her blue eyes flashing with exasperation. "It's not my fault that your pleasure is my pleasure. Apparently I'm built that way."

He brought his chair closer, and pulled her into his big body, kissing her neck and collarbone. "We are a very good fit, sweetheart, and I can't tell you how glad I am about that."

"A perfect fit would be about an inch or two shorter," she observed with asperity.

"Yeah, well, that's not going to happen," he said. "Come here," he added, dragging her into his lap.

"Oh no you don't," she said. "Don't try to distract me."

Mark simply picked her up and carried her over to the big couch. "I just want to hold you a bit, particularly while I talk."

Elizabeth's brows drew down in a frown, and her eyes glinted with suspicion. "Just keep talking big guy. I'm thinking you want to divert me with sex, to get out of 'true confession' time, but it isn't going to work."

Mark grinned, staring at her lips, wanting to kiss her. "I bet I could make it work."

She snorted. "Yeah, you probably could. But c'mon honey. Give."

Mark started to tell her about his childhood, witness protection and his real father and mother. The strange overwhelming response he had with the baseball bat, his fear of the darker side of himself, the fact that all his life he was drawn to BDSM but he had intentionally kept away from it, associating it with sin and the dreaded beast. The early "other" childhood fascinated her, and Mark spent some time talking about his older sister, and how he had once lived. He didn't tell her which city he came from, or details from the case.

Lizzy was attentive throughout his story, moving through the full gamut of emotions including concern, sympathy, shock, anger and horror. Under that tough, feisty trial lawyer exterior, Mark knew his wife was incredibly kind. As for the beast and BDSM, he explained that he had a sadistic side. He confessed that he wanted to explore it with her, and discussed some of his more comprehensive, recurring fantasies. Mark said that from now on, if they were both honest with each other, he hoped they could work everything out. He admitted that, like her, he also had been jerking off daily, because he had felt like he was imposing on her with his constant need for sex.

With his arms tight around her waist, Mark added, "I'll never show you so much consideration in the future, Lizzy, because now you're my willing sex slave. From this moment on you'll serve me whenever, and wherever I want."

"Oh," Elizabeth said in a small voice, and Mark saw her face heat with arousal. They both got a little frisky then, kissing and nuzzling after this demanding erotic proclamation, but Elizabeth refused to be diverted.

"Is that all?" she asked.

"Well," he said. "Not quite." He told her about how he had woken up spread eagle on a bed, except in his case he was on his stomach. And he told her how André, the rat bastard, had put a vibrator up his ass and punished him with whipping and forced ejaculations. Mark told her how André had soon discovered Mark would never yield, and how he had subsequently released him. Elizabeth said she sympathized with André.

"No one is more stubborn and wants his own way than you do, Mark," she laughed. "Not even me."

Elizabeth also laughed over the big fight and how André and Mark, beating on each other had resulted in a form of male bonding. "So typical of a man," she said, "to only feel better after hitting something. But I don't understand. Are we free? And why did André do all this? It makes no sense. Did you come to an understanding?"

Mark heaved an inward sigh. This was the part that he had been dreading. "Do you recall meeting Ronald Billingsworth? That red-haired guy? You would have met him at a work function. Anyway, remember when I worked with him on that difficult account? Never mind," he said, realizing that he was beating around the bush. "I told Billingsworth I was worried about our marriage."

"You did what?" Elizabeth sat up outraged. "You talked to *him* about our sex problems and not me?"

"It wasn't like that," Mark said, shifting uncomfortably. "Billingsworth had marriage troubles of his own, and he said that he had solved them with the help of a sexual counselor. The man he heartily recommended was kind of expensive, but really got results. His name was André Chevalier."

Mark saw that it took a moment for the significance of that remark to sink in, but when it did Elizabeth jumped up off his lap. Her blue eyes blazed with fury, pinning Mark to his chair. "What?" She stormed back and forth for a bit, and then pointed a finger at him. "Does that mean what I think it means? That *you* hired André Chevalier?"

Mark nodded and said, "I'm afraid so."

Enraged, Elizabeth threw up her hands and screamed. "Oh! That's right," she said. "I forgot. We should just be honest with each other, right? You think?" She stood directly in front of him, red-faced and wild-eyed. "What a good idea! You bastard!" she said, and slapped him across the face *hard*.

Chapter 18

Elizabeth's Anger

Elizabeth's eyes flew to Marks' face, gauging his reaction to her slapping him, but Mark hadn't moved and she couldn't read his unfathomable expression.

How could he? Elizabeth thought. *André scared the shit out of me yesterday morning, tying me up and strangling me, and I worried about Mark all day, too. And what do I find out? Mark set the whole thing up.*

Elizabeth began pacing in earnest, needing to expend the energy from her overwhelming rage. Her pink bathrobe flew out behind her with the speed of her long strides. "Mark, are you telling me that you talked to some stranger rather than me? And you got André to kidnap us?" She spun on her heels, turning to face him. "I thought I was going to die!"

"I didn't know what he was going to do, Elizabeth, I swear," Mark said, standing up in an attempt to make his case. "Do you think I sat down with André and said, 'Oh, here's a good idea, why don't you drug us and abduct us?' Besides," he added with a sarcastic ringing tone to his voice, "while you spent the first day screwing your brains out, I spent it getting butt fucked with a vibrator and starving to death. You think that was the result I was going for?"

Elizabeth intentionally disregarded the sex comment. It was true, of course. Mark had apparently suffered all day, while she had been having the most intense orgasms of her life. But she was going to ignore those circumstances right now, because she was angry. Instead she said, "You flogged me for keeping my secrets! And look at yours! I didn't even know who your parents were!"

"Oh, perfect," Mark replied, his dark eyes becoming stormy. "Just perfect. You're going to hold that against me too, are you? Right, that seems fair. It was fucking witness protection, Elizabeth! I broke the law just telling you about it! I'm not supposed to tell anyone!"

"Not even your wife?"

"No! Not even my wife," he said, blowing out a deep breath. Mark stood with sagging shoulders, looking kind of defeated. For a moment Elizabeth could clearly read his expression and unexpectedly she saw a world of hurt there.

"I've never even been to their grave, Lizzy," Mark said softly. "Not my mom, my dad, or my big sister. Nor do I have pictures. Everything is locked away in evidence. I've been told that someday I'll have access to it, but not for many more years."

As quickly as her rage exploded, it evaporated. "Oh God, Mark," she said, putting her arms around him. "I'm sorry, honey. I'm so sorry. You went through so much when you were only a child. I'd no idea. You were nine years old when you killed a man, but I'm really glad you did. You suffered so much. Oh baby, forgive me. You married an unfeeling shrew."

Mark put his arms around her, pulling her closer. "I should have talked to you about the sex thing, but I don't know how much it would have helped. I'm pretty sure we needed a professional. I was afraid, sweetheart. I was such a coward, so afraid that I'd lose you."

"You'll never lose me!"

He laughed and firmly gripped the nape of her neck with his long fingers. "You're right about that, because I'm never going to let you go," he said. The feel of his strong hand implacably holding her, combined with such possessive words, made her instantly wet. She mentally shook herself, returning her attention back to the subject.

Mark was staring at her. "Do you know how important you were to Michael and me, when we first started school and you became our friend? New parents, new home, new school and new life - it was difficult to adjust. We were both so traumatized and scared. You were such a feisty, determined little thing, and you took care of us. I don't know what would have happened if we hadn't met you, Lizzy."

"Really?" she said, totally charmed to think that Mark had needed her back then. "I was pretty little and only a child, but I do remember being so angry when those two bullies went after Michael. He looked so terrified. I swear, small as I was - I could have taken them, Mark. I was that mad."

Mark gave a joyous bark of laughter, grabbed behind her knees and back and swung her up into his arms. She curled herself trustingly around his neck. "I'm sure you could have taken them both, sweetheart," Mark said, "you tiny, tough, big-hearted woman." Mark kissed her soundly, until Elizabeth felt her toes curl.

When they came up for air, Elizabeth smiled. "I think maybe we ought to do something nice for your Mr. Billingsworth," she said. "Perhaps we'll bring him a little thank you gift from Las Vegas."

Epilogue

André Chevalier sat in his penthouse apartment, looking through his case files, his eyes browsing over "Active," "In Progress" and "Pending." He flipped through the pages of Elizabeth's section of the Nelson's active file, amused over the details he had gathered, fondly recalling the pleasure he had in helping her discover her sexuality. There was less information on Mark, and the data he did have was classified so he hadn't written it down. André couldn't help but like and admire the big man. If he didn't he would have seriously considered finding a way to steal *une femme fantastique* from him.

André sighed. Elizabeth and Mark. Finalized? *Mon Dieu, no,* he decided, *a thousand times no. Pending, I think.* He didn't want to retire their file. The last seven days of their vacation had been a light-hearted holiday for him. All three had spent every day together, touring the city, seeing some shows, but mostly having sex *extraordinaire.* Sometimes he worked with Mark alone, discussing his fantasies and how best to incorporate them in to his wife's desires. Mark and Elizabeth had both studied advanced BDSM materials with him, and seen the photo's depicting numerous toys and positions.

André's cock twitched as he recalled some of those positions – the three of them had tried quite a few. Of a certainty, Mark had made up for any inexperience as a Dom through his inbuilt confidence and natural animal instincts.

André shifted restlessly, making room for the growing constriction in his trousers. He remembered a night they had all three slept together. Elizabeth, upon waking in the morning had opened her eyes, and smiled widely. "My two most favorite men in the entire world," she had said. "How did I get so lucky? Hey André, can we stay here with you? I don't ever want to go home."

For one mad moment André had considered somehow employing them, and keeping them both with him always, but ultimately he didn't think it would work.

André recalled the saying: *'Life's most obvious truths are the hardest to see but once you've burned everything to the ground they are the only things left standing.'* Such hubris! André had imagined that by the time he finished with Mark, there would be little left standing. Perhaps only the man himself - and the love he had for his wife.

Instead André had been the one caught in the fire. And with everything burned away, what was left for him?

Merde. André consoled himself, thankful for the experience of such impossible love, and the chance of knowing them both. He really did enjoy his work. He flicked on the hard drive, and the DVD of Elizabeth came on the big screen. It was of the first day he had taken her. Watching was a punishment more painful and cutting than a bull whip. Yet it was also an exquisite pleasure, to have access to these memories of her.

Checking his Platinum Cartier wrist watch, André realized that he had a prospective client to interview in a few hours. He switched the recording off and left the room, headed for the basement where he kept his Bugatti Veyron *tres rapide*. A fast drive through Red Rock Canyon would end this mood *mélancolique*, and sharpen his wits.

André was glad he had left the Mark and Elizabeth case pending. They had already booked a two week holiday next year. The three of them were going to France together, where André was looking forward to introducing them to some French clubs.

I can afford the luxury of being in love, he thought, *for I will see her again. And such pangs of the heart make life more poignant and vital.*

Perhaps he would find a woman like her someday. One he could keep for himself. As he descended in the penthouse elevator, André realized happily, that he didn't regret a thing.

The End

Want more?

Connect with me for free promotions and new releases!

Facebook: www.facebook.com/onlysexystories

Website: www.NikkiSexStories.com

Twitter: @NikkiSexAuthor

Printed in Dunstable, United Kingdom

63943766R00191